THE
MADONNA
OF THE
MOUNTAINS

The MADONNA

of the MOUNTAINS

A   N O V E L

ELISE VALMORBIDA

SPIEGEL & GRAU / NEW YORK

Copyright © 2017 by Elise Valmorbida

All rights reserved.

Published in the United States by Spiegel & Grau,
an imprint of Random House, a division of
Penguin Random House LLC, New York.

Spiegel & Grau and Design is a registered trademark
of Penguin Random House LLC.

Originally published in the United Kingdom by
Faber and Faber Limited.

Grateful acknowledgment is mader to Bixio Music Group Ltd. for
permission to reprint an excerpt from "Faccetta Nera," music by
Mario Ruccione/SIAE and lyrics by Renato Micheli/SIAE, copyright ©
1935. Reprinted courtesy of Bixio Music Group (ASCAP).

Library of Congress Cataloging-in-Publication Data

Names: Valmorbida, Elise, author.
Title: The madonna of the mountains : a novel / Elise Valmorbida.
Description: First edition. | New York : Spiegel & Grau, 2018.
Identifiers: LCCN 2017034435 | ISBN 9780399592430 (hardcover) |
ISBN 9780399592454 (ebook)
Subjects: LCSH: Domestic fiction. | BISAC: FICTION / Historical. |
FICTION / Sagas. | FICTION / Family Life.
Classification: LCC PR9619.3.V32 M36 2018 | DDC 823/.914—
dc23 LC record available at https://lccn.loc.gov/2017034435

Printed in the United States of America on acid-free paper

randomhousebooks.com

spiegelandgrau.com

9 8 7 6 5 4 3 2 1

First Edition

Book design by Barbara M. Bachman

For my mother
and my sister

CONTENTS

THE
MADONNA
OF THE
MOUNTAINS

1923

Snow-melt

HER FATHER HAS GONE TO FIND HER A HUSBAND. HE'S TAKEN his mule, a photograph and a pack of food: homemade sopressa sausage, cold polenta, a little flask of wine—no need to take water—the world is full of water. It's Springtime, when a betrothal might happen, as sudden as a wild cyclamen from a wet rock, as sweet as a tiny violet fed by melting mountain snow.

Maria Vittoria is embroidering a sheet for her dowry trunk.

Everyone is working hard, making use of the light. Twelve huddled households chopping, fixing, hammering, cooking, washing, hoeing, setting traps, pruning vines, stripping and weaving white willow, planting the tough seeds, oats, tobacco, cabbage, onions, peas, and the animals are making their usual racket—but the whole *contrà* feels wanting without her father. A body without a head.

In his breast pocket he has the only photograph there is of her, made when she was seventeen, together with her sisters, brothers, parents, grandparents. She's almost unmarriageable now, at twenty-five years old, but she's strong and healthy and her little sister Egidia says she's pretty. It's just bad luck, or God's will, or destiny, that there are no eligible men in this valley or the next one, just sickly inbreds and hunchbacks and men mutilated by the Austrians.

It doesn't help that the *contrà* is so hard to get to, so far from the towns. And her father won't accept the hand of just anyone—he has his name and standing to consider. He owns some property. He is a man of business. He even has notepaper with his name printed on it.

Before the photograph, before the evacuation, Maria had a proposal. The fellow had come all the way from Villafranca, he had documents saying he didn't have to fight anymore, that he'd have a proper pension and special privileges. But he'd lost a finger and an eye.

Who knows what else he's missing? her father said when he turned down the offer. *We can do better than that.*

And Mama said what everyone says, all the cousins, all the women: *no se rifiuta nessun, gnanca se l'è gobo e storto.* Refuse nobody, even if he's hunchbacked and crooked. And Papà told her to shut up with her stupid sayings.

Maria whispers to herself, imagining a field daisy, pulling off one petal after another.

El me ama	He loves me
El me abrama	He covets me
El me abracia	He hugs me
El me vol ben	He cares for me
El me mantien	He supports me
El me ama	He loves me
El me abrama	He covets me
Nol me vole	He doesn't want me
El me dise su.	He tells me off.

She repeats prayers from *The Christian Bride*. This book, her only book, is dear to her. Small, bound in blue leather, with tiny gold lines around each page, it has more prayers than she can say and more sermons than she can remember, but the guidance at the beginning—*for my dear young girl*—lifts her spirit and shows her the way. *While you pray, you do well to add light mortifications of the flesh. This is a way of offering sacrifice and also releasing your spirit from life's petty irritations.*

She pricks herself with the needle, in her fingertips. She watches as the blood appears. Her sewing must wait. She wipes the dots with her handkerchief.

"Please Lord, grant me the piety to accept the Holy Sacrament of Marriage," she whispers aloud, even though there is no one to hear her. "Holy Mary, Mother of God, ask Him to grant me a man who will protect me and give me a devoted Christian family . . ."

But secretly she is thinking of how handsome her beloved will be, as kind in the face as Jesus, as straight-backed as the priest, as tall as her father, and sweet-smelling like a woman. Will he have a mustache like her Papà, thick and bushy? Will he have a beard like her grandfather, a swath of old tobacco masking his face and neck? Or will he have a mustache like her brother, two thin lines ending in points? She imagines the hair on his handsome face tickling her cheek. Her heart beats like a bird's wings. She banishes these thoughts and pricks herself. Once in each fingertip, neat as a rosary. At the Cana wedding feast, where Jesus turned water into wine, the bride and groom had no appetite for blind passions—they knew that God would hold them strictly accountable on Judgment Day.

Maria pricks herself at each wrist now that she has done her ten fingertips. She wipes the blood with her handkerchief again. She must keep the wedding sheet clean and white, like her soul, like her body, immaculate and new. But she is old. Twenty-five years old and untouched by a husband. Her fingers are without thimbles. She has hands that can wring an animal's neck. Arms to stir a pot of boiling polenta. She's a good investment for any man, if only he can overlook her age.

She gazes out of the window. The eaves and sills are dripping; the world beyond is dripping as it thaws. Some of the trees are still under snow, stooped and blanketed. She hears a mule complaining. And then the church bells, clear and bold despite the distance. One continuous minute of tolling. Single notes. They are melancholy, not happy-sounding like a baptism. Then there is a pause. Someone is dead. Then another minute of bells. If it stops now, it is a woman who has died, perhaps the old witch who lives like a lunatic in her nightdress. There is a pause. Then another minute of ringing. It's a man who has died. Another dead man in the world. A man gets three minutes, and a woman gets two minutes, because a man is more important, because Adam was the first man, and Jesus was a man, and God is the Lord, and the disciples were men, and priests are men, and the Pope is a man.

Her father is making his journey up and down the valleys, picking his path against steep slopes of softening snow, risking avalanches, and wolves perhaps, who knows what dangers he will have to brave?

People wander but mountains stay put. And yet mountains are fickle—a chasm can appear suddenly with a slip of the foot, a sunny sky lulls a hunter like a child to venture too far, a freezing fog blinds the world in moments, a sly air creeps into the lungs and becomes pneumonia.

Maria sews and sews. White blossoms in a wavy line. The linen is not the most expensive, but it's good enough in quality, and tough—it will be years before she has to darn or patch it. Her betrothed will admire her handiwork. He will stroke her embroidered flowers and then he will stroke her cheek like a flower. And they will hold each other as close as two walnut halves and children will eventually appear, with God's help, because children and flowers make a house a home.

Fioi e fiori i fà la casa.

The border of her bedsheet is almost complete. It must be a sign. Just three more blossoms with curling stems and sprays of tiny buds in between. Satin stitch and chain stitch and stem stitch. All white. She feels sure that when she reaches the hem at last, her father will appear with her beloved. He's been gone more than two days. She will hide behind the door, and she will catch a glimpse of her sweet-faced, sweet-smelling betrothed and he will recognize her from the old photograph.

She puts down her sewing and pinches her cheeks, runs her fingertips along her jaw, touches her full lips. What is it like to kiss a man? She almost let her cousin Duilio kiss her once, before he went to the seminary, before he became a soldier. She kisses her fingers and remembers her mortifications.

On Sundays and for sacraments, she still wears her dark brown dress, high-collared and tight-waisted—she has taken good care of it. Her husband will recognize it as soon as he sees her, even though her dress was new in the photograph, crisp and undarned. Will he think well of the darning because it shows her thrift and skill? No, he'll think her father isn't rich enough to buy her a new dress in eight long years. She hates being poor. Hates it. But she won't be married in November like a really poor girl, when the hard work of Summer and Autumn is done, and a girl is just one more mouth to feed through Winter. *Na boca in più.* If she marries near Easter, people will look up to her. How much can her father pay a man to marry her? It's not enough that she is pretty and strong. She hates the war and the Spanish flu and the evacuation and her isolation for making her unmarried and past her prime.

The traveling photographer had lined them up in the schoolroom at Albarela, twelve bodies in front of a big curtain painted with misty columns and a floral frame. That was a sorry day. The first photograph of Maria's life, and perhaps the last time they would all be alive together. The entire family dressed up as if for a wedding, but with fear in their bellies. The girls were ready to be sent to Piedmont—if they'd stayed at home, they'd have been taken by the foreign soldiers to do with as they pleased.

For every Italian man or gun: four Austrian men and four Austrian guns. Everyone said that, doom in their voices.

For the photograph, a potted plant was placed between her father's feet. And there was another plant, tall and strange—*a palm,* the photographer said, *from the Bible Lands.* The emblem of martyrs. Did the photographer think they were martyrs? Did he pity them? Maria stared hard at his camera, silently vowing never to be pitied again.

Palm or no palm, her beloved will be able to see her upright modesty in the picture, her tiny bright medallion of the Virgin proud on the yoke of her dress, her regular features and steady gaze. No squint, no crossed eye, no blindness. He will surely see that.

And now, despite her years, she is still healthy, she has nice firm fat on her hips and bosom, her bones are straight and her hands are strong. He will see all that, because he'll be looking for a long life with her, and thinking of his children with her. He'll be looking for a woman who can do the work.

Maria can do the work. Everyone in the *contrà* says that.

How long did she live as a servant with the *signori* in Piedmont? She gave those rich people her best years. She learned to cook, and clean, and grow food. She already knew how to sew. She learned to protect her virtue, the *signori* taught her that. She learned to crave wealth, they taught her that too. When she and her sisters returned home after the War in Snow and Ice, there were no animals, no glass in the windows, not a sound. Just devastation. They thanked God for the American soldiers who gave them livestock to start all over again. And they thanked God for the lucky men in their family—they'd survived.

But where is he, this man for her, who has survived the battles with the Austrians? The valleys have been officially declared a monument to war, and an ossuary like a lighthouse is being built on one of the peaks, but half of all men are dead, or else there wouldn't be enough bones and teeth and skulls to fill it.

She must have a wedding this year or it will never happen.

You've got to get married or you'll end up like that witch in a night-dress, Mama says whenever Maria is excitable or ungrateful.

La Delfina wanders from *contrà* to *contrà*, she belongs to nobody, she sings to the moon like a wild dog, when the light is so bright at night it's like a cold blue day, and the shadows are sharp as granite, and the rocks glitter. Sometimes she hangs about the *cesso* in the daytime, muttering obscenities and blasphemies. Little Egidia

won't use the privy when la Delfina is around, but Maria is determined not to show any fear of her. Sometimes she gives her food.
It's charitable to do so. She leaves it at a safe distance, or she throws
it. Secretly she is terrified of the madwoman's curses. What if she
has the power of a gypsy? It's less dangerous if she sings, so Maria
calls out through the wooden walls and asks for a song while her
cacca drops down into the mountain earth.

And sometimes la Delfina cooperates.

L'uselin de la comare	The godmother's little bird
L'è volà su le tete.	Flew onto her breasts.
L'uselin sbatea le alete,	The little bird beat its
E un po' più giù volea volare!	little wings,
	It's a bit further down he
	wanted to fly!

Maria sews and sews. She must be married this year or she will
be like the matrons in church whose childlessness marks their faces
with hollow sorrow, whose breasts hang empty, women who spray
spit when they talk, and talk too much, and fuss, and complain, and
find fault with everything. *La dona senza fioi come 'na vegna morta.*
A woman without children is as useless as a dead vine.

Her father will save her. He will find her a war hero without
wounds—perhaps just the one dashing scar on his cheek or shoulder. She pictures his shoulder.

Now she has to stop sewing and prick her thumbs extra hard.
The new blood is a ruby, two rubies, three rubies, four.

When she is married there will be rubies on the sheet that she
has embroidered, because a virgin must bleed, but she doesn't know
how or why. She must ask the Madonna of the Mountains. She will
find her some flowers and place them before her statue in its glass
dome, and pray for answers.

Maria Vittoria knows that blood comes with pain, like the blood
of Jesus all over His crucified flesh, tender and soft and pale as a

woman's. Maybe wedding blood is as terrible as the pain of child-birth, which is God's punishment for Eve. There is nothing about a bloody bed in *The Christian Bride*.

She has only one blossom to go.

The mule outside is still complaining but there's another animal braying further down the valley, on the track from Albarela. It's her father's mule, she knows the sound, and the chickens are hysterical, and the last heap of snow falls with a dead thud off the roof, and the air through the window is full of sparkles as she looks out and sees no one.

"Maria!" her mother calls from below, loud and jittery. "He's coming!"

~

THERE'S A STORM IN Maria's body. Her knees tremble. When did she last wash? Yesterday. No—the day before. No time to wash now. No time to fetch water. Besides, he might be near the well. There's a bucket in the kitchen and another by the fireplace. No time. She washes her face and neck with water from the dressing-table bowl and the mottled brown soap that she made after butchering last year's pig, its fat rendered into tallow, mixed with olive oil and caustic soda from the shop in Monastero. She holds a cloth to her skin. Wipes it clean. She dabs her pricked wrists with her mother's perfume, saved for sacraments and special days. She has not asked permission. She crosses herself. She inhales the scent. How many violets had they picked? Hundreds. She strips off her pinafore and day-dress. The cold hits her. She takes her dark brown dress out of the wardrobe, and steps into it, but her legs are useless, like a foal trying to stand. She trips. She tries again, careful not to rip it. Attaches a clean, new collar. Buttons it up. Straightens her petticoat and undergarments. Smooths the skirts. Arranges her tiny gold Madonna medallion in the center of her chest, the same as the photograph. *The godmother's little bird flew onto her breasts.* Maria banishes la Delfina's song from her mind. It's bound to be unlucky. She looks in the mirror, even though it is the Devil's work. She tidies her hair. She pinches her cheeks to bring out the pink. A mouse, loud as a pig, scrabbles in the granary above. No matter. The mouse can eat all the corn it likes. She crosses herself and goes downstairs to meet the stranger who will be her husband, God willing.

There is nobody on the ground floor. Her younger sisters are away at work, doing domestic service, earning money. But little Egidia, where is she? Her older sisters are with their husbands and families, many kilometers away—valleys and plains away. Her brother Severo is with his wife in Padua. Her brother Vito is working in the fields. But where is her mother?

Mama's voice calls again from outside.

Maria grabs her shawl. In the bright light of day, she sees the straight back of her mother past the walnut tree, standing rigid at the top of the track.

She gathers up her skirts and runs to join her, boots firm on stony patches where last week there was snow.

"He's got you a husband," her mother says, all the while looking down the track. Her voice is calm, relieved. She almost smiles, but her thin mouth is down-turned as usual. "Three more to go!" She stamps her boots, three times for three daughter-burdens.

But Maria doesn't care about her younger sisters. She gazes down the valley. And there he is, her father and his mule, walking up the slope, with a figure beside him. A man.

What if he is bad or ugly? What will she do?

Don't trust anybody, her parents say, her grandparents say.

He looks strange, like some fantastical apparition, with a man's body and a giant head. He's wearing what looks like a huge hat, deeper than a millstone, wide as a cart wheel. Her father walks under its shelter. It's a *gavegnà*. The woven wicker is packed high with some harvest load—she can't tell what. Has the stranger brought a gift?

Her heart is trapped. Her mouth is dry. Words spill out before she knows it. "Please, dear God, make him good and handsome."

"Stupid girl," her mother says. "When the children are hungry, they won't cry *Papà, belo*, they'll cry *Papà, pan!*"

Yes, it's bread they'll want, not looks, but Maria can't help herself. She has waited so long.

He is tall, taller than her father. He is lean. He doesn't limp. From this distance he could be handsome. His head is wedged into that huge *gavegnà*, so his forehead is hidden. The basket is easily a meter wide and loaded with leaves. It must weigh more than thirty kilos. And yet he doesn't stoop. He walks straight and easy, as if he's taking an idle stroll.

The men come closer, slowly climbing the track. Her father looks happy—she thinks she can see that, even from here. Thank God there is no mist, and the air is clear.

His cheeks are smooth. He's not an old man. He is not mutilated by war. He is close enough now that he can look her up and down, still twenty meters away. Perhaps he smiles a little. Does he approve? Her father says something to him, but she can't hear. What if he disapproves?

She wants to faint, but she won't.

She hides behind her mother.

"You've seen him now," Mama says, shooing her away. "Get back in the house."

And Maria obeys. She flies past the walnut tree, past the firewood stacks, past the rabbits, the fowl cages, past the pig in its stall, past the cow. Past the neighbors, her cousins, half the *contrà*. Past the well. She has gone too far. Back to the house. She runs like a storm-wind into the kitchen. Stands panting by the fire. Her lungs heaving. He is not mutilated. And he is handsome. And. He has brought a gift. Dried tobacco leaves. Masses of them. Her father will love that. Something for nothing. Something he can smoke or sell or barter. She will be. Married.

Two wooded fields

"SHOW HIM YOUR TEETH," PAPÀ SAYS.

Maria is not sure what to do. She is standing by the doorway to the kitchen.

Mama is standing near the fireplace, watching like a crow. Papà is seated at the table with the stranger.

The stranger is handsome. His thick black hair has been flattened by his hat and the *gavegnà*. His eyes are chestnut. His complexion is smooth. His mouth is straight. He has a mustache—not like her brother's or her father's or her grandfather's—his is a neat black square under his perfect nose. She can smell him in the room. His manly sweat. How can she show him her teeth?

"Smile—show him your teeth!" Mama repeats.

Maria smiles, still standing by the doorway. It is not a joyous smile. She doesn't know how long to smile for.

Mama's mouth is down-turned. "She's had no illnesses. No weaknesses of the blood."

Maria can't remember the last time she saw her mother smile.

"You see what good teeth she has?" Papà says. He stands up and approaches her. He squeezes her arm the way he'd test a farm animal. "Good strong arms."

He goes back to his seat and pours his best homemade wine into the stranger's glass. Then he drinks from his own. The glass looks worn and cloudy. He pushes the plate of cheese and sopressa toward the man.

The stranger eats and drinks.

"Despite her age, she's fitter and stronger than most. There's not a crooked bone or weakness in this family, we're from good stock, wait until you see the others, you can believe me when you see them with your own eyes. She can cook and clean, not like those useless girls who are brought up like princesses. She did service for a family of *signori* in Piedmont during the war, so she knows how to run a household, and she's no crybaby. What's more, she's had three years of schooling, so she can write."

"Can she speak?" the stranger asks.

"Of course I can speak!" Maria says before she can help herself.

"Keep quiet, idiot!" Mama says. "Or God won't give you a single child." *Tasi ti o el Signore nol te dà gnanca on fiolo.*

"And you keep your mouth shut, stupid woman. This is serious business. Achille here has come a long way."

His name is Achille. His voice is deep and soft, not gruff like a coarse *contadino*. How could her mother call her names in front of him?

"He has his own field which he's going to sell so he can move down to the plains and set up a shop. He's accepted your dowry trunk and my gift of two wooded fields. I'll keep the land but the takings are his when he logs the lot." Papà looks Achille straight in the eye. "You can get a good price for the timber—they need it for the railways and the ships. But let's see where we go with all this moving about."

"To America, perhaps," Achille says.

"I'm staying put, and I'm keeping my trade mixed," Papà says. "With land I've got minerals and produce. And any livestock I want."

Achille eats more cheese. He takes his time. The room is still and listening to each of his words. "I've been thinking the real money is to be made in America. It's something I might try one day."

"La Mèrica?" Mama gasps.

But Papà looks pleased. "You can make a fortune there."

Maria feels her heart leap with the adventure, and the pain of it. Will he be her husband? Will she go to la Mèrica one day? She will be rich. He is too good to be true. What is wrong with him? *Don't trust anybody*—everybody says that. *Don't trust anybody, not even your own kind.*

"It will take you two weeks to clear the fields, depending on the weather. We can help you. In that time you can meet with Maria and get to know her a little, under supervision at all times, of course, by her brothers, or by me. Her reputation is intact, and we're going to keep it that way. You still want to go ahead with the arrangement? Shall I write up the dowry account?"

Achille drinks his wine, drains his glass and puts it down.

Everything—the world—is silent. Even the animals outside.

"She is perfect. We can get married near Easter."

Easter. Like a rich girl.

Maria wants to smile and laugh now. Poor girls are married by Saint Martin's Day. Easter. Everyone will know. *Che bela figura.*

"While we're clearing the fields," Achille continues, "you can get the nuptials organized—"

"She knows her catechism," Mama says proudly, almost boastful.

"Good." Achille smiles. "And the gold and the veil. Then after the wedding she can come and live with me at my parents' house." He turns toward Maria now. "Will you have enough time to make a new dress?" he asks. "You know they're wearing them shorter now."

Maria burns with shame. She has seen shorter dresses in Monastero. She has seen fashion cards with the new exposed look. It's not thrift or modesty this man is seeing in her old brown dress, but backwardness, ugliness.

Mama fidgets with her own plain, long dress. Her boots are clumsy and scuffed and old. "We've taught her thrift. It'll be your blessing. Of course we'll make a beautiful new dress for the wedding. I have the cloth ready. You can picture what a lovely, properly Christian bride she'll be. And her wedding trunk is full of good bed linen and tablecloths and stockings and shirts. And nuptial clothes. She's embroidered everything. It's another skill. She's even better at needlework than me . . ."

Maria fingers her Virgin medallion.

Her mother is babbling.

But Achille speaks. He grins. "We'll have a fine wedding. And a fine Christian family."

The two men do not shake hands. The deal is done in words.

Maria is ecstatic as a saint.

~

AT DUSK, MARIA GOES to the place where she knows Winter's flowers grow. Rivulets of ice-cold water trickle through green creepers and stones, seeping down the embankment along the track. She picks tiny cyclamens from their rocky perches, careful not to loosen their delicate roots. She bunches them together and heads home.

In her parents' bedroom, she places the posy carefully before the Madonna of the Mountains. Set on the chest of drawers by her mother's bed, the golden statue is like a beautiful doll on a plinth, forever safe inside her glass bell jar, gazing heavenward, round-faced and sublime. The little peasants, barefooted and humble, huddle inside her blue and gold cloak, their necks twisted upward to gaze at her. They look like children.

Maria stands before the shrine, bows her head and prays until the Madonna speaks.

You are named after me. Your mother is named after me. Your daughter will be named after me. If every girl in the world could be called Maria, they would be.

My little lamb Maria, my baby goose, my child, you love to gaze at my crown of gold. Imagine how much it must be worth—you do imagine that.

You admire the pearl earrings that hang from my hidden lobes—you count the pearls.

You're good at counting, Maria.

You've never seen anything like the gold of my dress—except on the Pope or a bishop. But you don't get too close to popes and bishops, not where you're from. Your dress, even your best dress for a wedding, is plain blue wool. But you will rise above the plain wool days, and the scuffed boot days, and the darned days, if you work hard enough, and pray morning and night, and first Masses and rosaries, and confess to the priest as often as work will let you.

You are ripe for Christian children—but conception is immaculate only for me. You will know man, and man will know you. Do not ask your mother what this means. Your questions will only lead to curses. Leave everything to time and God and me.

Achille will know what to do, because men do. They have been out in the world, they've traveled and traded and built cities. You must show him what a prospect you are. He has ambition. Show him how hard you work. Let him glimpse you with perspiration on your brow. Let him admire you.

Yes, you are betrothed, but what he thinks of you now will stay in his heart forever.

Polenta e bacalà

Today is the day of the first Spring wash. It makes no difference that Maria is newly betrothed. The river has unfrozen, and its waters are flowing fast and full.

Today she'll set aside the usual weekly laundry—the dirty collars and handkerchiefs, the sweaty vests and shirts, the petticoats and pinafores, the working clothes, the delicate underclothes, the flock of socks and stockings. Today is for big things. Bedsheets, towels, tablecloths, house cloths. Stained and soiled, they've been piling up in the laundry chest since last Summer.

First, she starts a fire in the hearth, gets it going with a wax match and tinder twigs, blowing and shielding the precious flame with her hands, building a nest of wood from the stack, stoking and choking off, adding wood until she knows the fire has a life of its own.

Then, shouldering her carrying-pole and pails, she walks to the well, step by stony step. It's early in the day, still dark as night, but she knows the path. The animals are noisy in their stalls. Mama is milking the cow.

Maria carries the hard mountain water back, pail after pail. She goes and she returns, to and from the well. She pours each cold liter into the huge washing pot that hangs on the fire. It starts to heat, slowly, surely.

Soon the kitchen is busy. Mama heats fresh milk at the fire's edge. Papà and Vito pack their tools. They'll meet with Achille and head up to the fields. Little Egidia wraps cheese and bread and sopressa into waxed cloth parcels for the three men to eat before noon. Claudia and Edda are dressed for work, ready to walk the tracks down the valleys to the villa in Monastero. Everyone huddles over polenta and hot milk, warming hands on bowls, not talking.

Maria makes quick work of eating.

"This year Egidia can help you with the rinsing," Mama says. She picks up the waste pail—peelings, skins, crumbs, husks, rinds, guts, claws, bones—and Egidia returns from the granary with a basket of dried corncobs. The two go outside to tend to the animals.

With water pails hanging from the pole across her shoulders, Maria treads to and from the well.

At the door of the house, Claudia grasps her by the arm and whispers into her ear. "Mama says you'll be married, dear sister! Is it true? When will we meet him?"

Edda listens. Curious. Envious.

Maria looks into the pails and shrugs. "It's not true until it happens." But she can't stop herself from grinning.

Claudia hugs and kisses her. "The nice ripe fruits are harder to reach. Congratulations, dear sister! You deserve the best of all of us."

"Congratulations!" Edda hugs and kisses Maria. "My turn next!"

"I'll never get married," Claudia says. "I can feel it in my bones."

"Don't say it, or it'll come true," says Edda. "Come on, we'll be late."

The house empties, and Maria is alone again.

In the yard, she settles the wooden tub on its stand. She checks the pipe at its base, to make sure it's not blocked. She sets the scrubbing board on top, and the draining tray below.

She takes her boots off to go upstairs. She opens the laundry chest. It smells rancid, despite Mama's little posies of lavender and quince. She lifts out as much as she can, a hefty pile. And then another. Even dry, the laundry is a heavy weight.

Outside in the fresh cool air, in the half-blind gloom between night and day, she scrubs the filthiest things with the soft soap cream kept specially for this wash. The smells of rendered animal fat and stale human sap and faded lavender fill her nose. This is the scent of Spring for her. The marking of time. She is twenty-five but this year she will be a married woman. The scrubbing brush feels good in her hands. She is mucky up to her elbows. She is full of grateful joy.

She removes the scrubbing board and places the dirty linen, starting with the small pieces, layer upon layer, in the empty tub. It's pungent and packed high—she must make space at the top. So she stands on it and presses it with all her weight, as if she is crushing grapes for wine. Then she gets the ashing cloth from the storeroom and drapes it over the pile, careful to sink it in, just so. She fetches the ash cask and, gently, avoiding clouds and coughing, pours a thick layer of ash onto the cloth and lets it settle. She made the ashes herself, burning wood in the hottest fire to yield the whitest powder.

She uses the grooved pole to unhook the pot from the hearth. She pours the boiling water onto the ash, careful not to spill or splash. Through the cloud of steam she can see the water soak right in. It leaves a dark slurry on top. Later, she will dig the ash slops into the vegetable garden, feed the soil that feeds the plants that feed the family.

Time for more water. The sky is a shade lighter now, but the sun is still hiding. Everything—the tub, the scrubbing board, the house, the ground, the path—has sharper edges, easier to see.

She returns to the well. Draws up water. Remembers the time a mouse died in there and everyone got poisoned and sick, and there was no fresh water in the *contrà*—thank God for the river down in the valley. She gazes into the well. Sees nothing. It is like life, she thinks, a black-bottomed mystery, and only God knows what comes next.

Two cousins make their way up the path. Their pails are empty. They nod in greeting. It's too early to linger or chat, but they must know about the stranger, her betrothed.

Maria refills the pot on the fire, pail by pail. The spilled drops sizzle. The kitchen is steamy, and she feels hot, despite the season.

She heaves more boiling water onto the stewing laundry and watches it soak in. The tub creaks on its three-legged stand.

To and from the well she goes, filling pail after pail. She counts the steps. She knows the stones. Tiny new shoots of grass are growing bright between them. She knows the rocks. She knows the trees. A cuckoo sounds in the distance. She will never again hear another cuckoo's call with spinster ears. The air smells sweet and green.

"Greetings," Duilio's wife says, passing her on the path. "All good?"

"Yes, all good," Maria says. She can hardly contain her excitement. "I'll have news soon. An announcement."

"Me too, God willing."

As she continues up the path to the well, Maria wonders what Duilio has told his new bride about her. He sulked for years after Maria rejected his kiss. She hadn't known what to do, turned her face away, shoved at him, for fear and virtue both. And there had been another fear: a shifting shadow in the pines behind him. Someone watching.

"COUSIN!" a voice shrieks from the slope below.

It's as if the madwoman has been summoned forth just by thinking of her.

Duilio's wife has gone.

Here is la Delfina before Maria, on the path, in the weak light. She stinks. She has never been this close. She's panting. Half-dressed. Filthy.

Maria feels trapped. She can't speak.

The madwoman grins. "I've got an announcement. Me too."

Maria shudders at the words, her own words, heard and repeated, hollow and changed like an echo.

"Greetings, cousin."

"I'm not your cousin," Maria says, trying to sound firm.

La Delfina laughs at her. "The one who goes with the wolves learns to howl. We're all family. We are bastard cousins. Embrace!" She throws her arms wide.

Maria recoils. She is ready to run, or hit the woman if she has to. She loses her footing. "I'm not your cousin," she repeats stupidly.

The madwoman quietly howls like the wind in a roof, taunting. Then she stands up tall, braces herself. She is tall, too tall. She is blocking the path. She kicks at a big pale rock. "I'm all-seeing, all-knowing, like God in Heaven—that's blasphemy and I know it. You have no secrets."

"I have work to do," Maria says, failing to keep her voice steady. "I need to fetch the water."

"I am your face in the water," Delfina says. And then she spits on the earth. She stares at Maria hard. "If you marry you'll die. I say that to all the girls. But what would a madwoman know?"

What does she know? What has she seen?

Delfina hops from foot to foot. She sings, *"Kill the old women but not the young."* And then she disappears, faster than an escaped pig, down the slope and into the gloom.

Heart thumping, Maria stamps her boots, adjusts the pole across her shoulders and continues to the well. She feels relief—the witch has not cursed her, although she nearly cursed her marriage.

As Maria draws up water, she decides to fill her heart with pity. Starving, ranting, wandering Delfina is lucky to be alive. She is one of God's mistakes. She may not even have a soul.

"I AM THE WASP!" The wild voice rises from the valley, quite far away now.

Wasps do not have souls, Maria thinks.

She whispers a prayer of thanks for her own life—and for her healthy, handsome husband—before making her way back to the house.

She pours more boiling water into the tub. Now the sheet-sauce oozes out from the pipe. It's thick and coffee-colored. It's her job to get it clear and pure.

She starts over again. More water, more boiling.

She hears the thuds and echoes of distant chopping. She must not dare to dream of her wedding day. Achille is clearing the two wooded fields further up the mountain, where the snow still holds. He is claiming his reward for marrying her, he doesn't care about the extra work. The fields will be logged and she will be married.

If you marry you'll die. The madwoman has it all upside down. If you *don't* marry, you'll die.

To and from the well she goes. It's light, and the animals are quieter now. No sign of la Delfina. Mama and Egidia are feeding the fat young pig, tending to the cow, the rabbits, the pigeons, the quail and the chickens, having gathered up their rich droppings for the dung heap to make manure. Everything is food and feeding. Nothing goes to waste.

Eventually the flow from the washtub is cloudy, sudsy, fatty. Maria thinks of soup. A bad broth for thieves and gypsies—or a witch. She will leave the washing to stand and soak now, until the afternoon, when Egidia instead of Mama will help her carry the wet load all the way to the river, ready for thrashing and rinsing. They will wring each cloth into a twist between them, like a twirling girl dance, and spread the damp linen over bushes, as clean and almost as white as new snow.

Now Maria fills the black polenta pot with fresh cold water. She hauls it to the hearth, and the water inside swings around, as it does every day, but today she thinks of the way a snail feels, just picked up, muscles moving inside its shell. She hates snails. *Look at this*, her brother Severo teased her one time. He was holding two snails, stuck together like twins. *This is what mating looks like. Try taking them apart.* And she took the snails from him, one heavy with the other, and forced them apart with her fingers, horrified by the strength she had to use, and the slow release of a slimy worm, one creature deep inside the other.

Is that what mating looks like? She shivers. She knows that every animal is different. She knows that humans are set apart and above the entire animal kingdom, that humans have souls and clothes and God and marriage. But what is la Delfina?

She's no better than an animal, Maria thinks.

She'd flung the snails at the wall. A tiny gob of slime had hit her in the forehead, and she'd felt dirty there, on that spot, all day. And Severo had laughed. He loves to mock her for her innocence.

While the polenta water warms up, Maria fills the basin on the bench, and the barrel below it. There's spare water for the enamel washbowl upstairs.

But what of her shoes? If her ankles are to be exposed on her wedding day, she will need shoes with heels, not these boots for marching on stony paths back from a well. And stockings. Nice new stockings, not these thick old darned ones. And a dainty purse. And a dress coat with fur or satin trim. And a hat, a smart hat, perhaps with a bow or a feather. And a proper engraved ring, solid gold, a weight in the hand, one for her, and maybe one for him. Her father will hate the expense, all these expenses, but that is the curse of a girl; he has known it his entire life, and she has known it too.

She is hot. There is perspiration on her brow. She wishes that Achille could see her now. He will see her, soon enough. The men will come here for lunch. They will eat freshly made polenta and the baccalà from yesterday, even tastier today.

Achille will like her cooking.

~

"IT'S GOOD," HE SAYS, oil on his chin. There are flakes of fish caught in his teeth. He has good teeth. He eats with appetite. He mops up the sauce with slabs of polenta, careful not to waste any.

His fingers are callused and his fingernails are black, like her father's, like her brother's. All three men hunch over the table in the same way, guarding their plates, smelling of tree resin, tobacco smoke and hard work.

Maria stands with Egidia and Mama by the hearth. She tries to isolate Achille's smell, but the fire behind her seems to melt everything together into the air.

"Maria knows how to cook," Papà says, oil in his mustache. "Not like that milksop you're after," he says to Vito. "She's not getting you until she knows how to cook—right now she's a liability." He sucks shreds of stockfish off a bone, and turns to Egidia. "You already know more than his fancy girl does."

Vito says nothing.

Mama shakes her head. Mama hates Severo's wife and criticizes any girl that Vito likes. No girl is good enough for her sons.

Papà licks his teeth and faces Achille again. "You won't go hungry."

Vito looks up from his plate. "Not like during the war."

"We ate dogs and toads," Papà says.

Achille shakes his head. "Damned Austrians!"

"We give thanks to God for the Americans." Mama crosses herself.

"The girls did better with the *signori* in Piedmont, didn't you," Papà says. It is a fact.

Maria dabs her brow, but there is no perspiration now, even though her back is to the fire. She has cleaned her face and private parts with the leftover warm water. She stares at Achille with silent wide eyes. She wants to talk, but she can't.

"Two of her sisters are in Monastero, you know the villa there?" Papà says. "The money's not bad. The oldest girls live with their husbands, of course. You'll meet them soon enough. God gave me six girls. Six. Severo should be here, but his wife is sick again, so he's taken her to the sanatorium near Padua."

Maria is worried thinking about her unmarried sisters. Achille will meet them before the two weeks are over. They are young. What if he falls in love with them instead of her?

Claudia is twenty and very pretty—but she is prone to melancholy, how long will it take for him to see that? In any case, she's stupid. Two years of school and she can barely write.

Egidia is thirteen, too young for him, but not too young to be betrothed. No, she is just a child. Look at her: she's daydreaming and humming some baby song to herself.

But Edda is sixteen, nearly seventeen, money-wise, ambitious, well-formed and in her prime. Is she too young? Three years of schooling—no, almost four. *You must study so people don't cheat you,* she always says. She put off working until she was twelve. Clever sister.

Edda would love to fall in love. Maria has heard her praying at night.

Will Edda come home and dazzle him? Steal her beloved? No, their father would not stand for that. He has made a deal, man to man. And older sisters must be married first, or else . . . Or else, what? There is no rule. And if Claudia marries no one, would that make the little ones spinsters forever?

Maria feels the heat of the hearth behind her, and she is reminded of the Hellfire that is envy's punishment, but it is envy she feels, and fear. She must remember this for Confession.

What will happen when Edda returns this evening?

In Winter, everyone sits in the big stable with the animals for some heat, darning in the light of the lantern, fixing tools and basketware, sorting twine, singing songs, telling stories. Men and women together. But the daylight hours for work are longer and warmer now. The girls will go to bed with their mother, all at the same time. The men will stay up and smoke and talk and drink grappa. Achille won't get a chance to be alone with Edda, or any woman. Not with Maria, not even with Mama. For two weeks he'll sleep at the other end of the *contrà*, with the animals at Zio's house. He has a bed of straw in the warmest place.

Maria thanks God that her marriageable sisters work away from home all day, every day, except for Sunday—

"Are you not hungry?" Achille says to her, his eyes tender.

"In this house, the men eat first," Papà says.

"We'll eat what's left," Mama says.

"I was saying Grace," Maria answers. Her voice sounds foreign even to herself. She must confess to the priest for lying. Envy and lying. "I was thanking God for sparing us all. I was thinking about you poor men, all that fighting, all that danger. And nothing to eat unless you were fighting. And I was thanking God that you saved us all. Where would we be now without your fighting?" She feels herself blush.

"You see, she's grateful too." Papà nods. He will keep saying good things about her while there's still a chance that Achille can pull out, or run off. Papà is a business negotiator.

"She knows her luck," Mama says.

"Shall I tell you a story?" Achille says.

Maria nods. He is courting her. Her stomach flutters. She can't eat now.

"It's about a donkey. It's about the war." He wipes his mouth with his hand, then pushes his plate away.

Maria takes it to the bench where Egidia will wash it.

"I was called to arms seven years ago, it was Springtime, like now. On the paperwork my profession was *contadino:* a peasant, no more, no less. But then I became a soldier. I was in the mountain artillery. You know about all those tunnels and caves?"

Maria shakes her head. How would a girl know about war?

"All the way up, from twelve hundred meters to nearly two thousand, there are tunnels and caves—dug out, or blown out, built by Italian men. We're a nation of engineers. One of those tunnels goes up like a corkscrew into a cone of granite—like a spiral staircase in a steeple. We're not stupid. We outwitted the Austrians, even though we had less money and less equipment. Thanks to those tunnels, we could travel without being seen. We could transport arms and men and supplies for kilometers without the Austrians seeing a thing. All they could see was rock. And rock doesn't move."

Papà snorts. "There's nothing worse than an Austrian." He pushes his plate away.

Egidia clears the table as quietly as she can, each plate, each fork and knife.

Maria helps her.

Achille continues telling his story to everyone. To her.

"But every now and then there's a valley where you can't hide. No tunnel. You can't build a tunnel. It's just a path, open to the sky, and exposed to the Austrians. When there's a full moon at night, it's lit up like daytime. The sky is big over your head. The path is cut into the rock and the slope going down is steep and dangerous."

The women sit and listen, but still they don't eat.

Achille looks like he's the head of the family. Papà is letting him.

"My captain told me to go across the worst valley with a donkey. To take water to the men on the front line. The entire journey was dangerous, but I knew that when I got to this valley, I'd be shot to pieces in a second. Past one big rock—it sticks up like a monument—the sky opens up and you're just a little animal waiting to be shot. I would be killed for sure. So I protested. But the captain put a pistol to my head. He said he'd shoot me if I didn't obey orders. So what choice did I have? Die now, or die later. So I obeyed. I took the donkey and the water. Big barrels strapped to its sides. A donkey's worth more than a man."

"More than a man?" Maria is shocked.

"Because a donkey can carry more than a man."

Maria wonders how much the washing weighs.

"Except me," Achille says. "I can carry a mortar on my back."

Vito gasps.

"Eighty kilos or more."

Papà addresses the family, "At Sassone, I heard about this lean young fellow who'd knocked a man to the ground with one blow. I wanted to meet that young man. He must be strong as an ox." Papà looks pleased. "*This* young man."

"Don't tell me you carried the donkey on your back?" Vito laughs to show Achille that he's being funny.

Papà laughs like bellows, puffing in and out.

Maria is amazed. Her father never laughs.

Egidia's mouth hangs open.

Achille smiles and waits for quiet again. "So I took the donkey, I can't tell you how many tunnels and paths we did. We ducked and made a run for it. Until we got to that big rock. I could see it from the safety of the last tunnel before it. We hugged the mountain, that poor donkey and me, the barrels were scraping against stone, but we were still out of view. When we got to the rock, my heart was beating faster than a pig's on slaughter day. I won't pretend: I was terrified. And then I remembered my brains. I made the donkey go first, round the bend, past the rock. Sure enough, it was shot the moment it cleared the rock. The barrels were shooting water. The body was shooting blood. The poor beast fell off the side of the path, like a bundle of rags, down the slope, which was this steep, *this* steep, I could see its body almost bouncing. Then it stopped dead at a tree. It was stuck there. The valley was full of firing. I don't know who was shooting who then, or what was an echo, or what was my heart, boom, boom."

Maria gazes at her beloved's frown. She is so glad it was the donkey that died.

"Could have started a landslide," says Vito.

"I didn't know what to do. If I went back, the captain would shoot me on the spot for not getting the job done. And what about the animal? I couldn't go back with nothing. I hid in some bushes. I waited until night. It was freezing. I thank God it wasn't a full moon. It was cloudy and dark. My body was frozen but I climbed and fell down a crack in the mountainside—so steep and dangerous you wouldn't believe it—until I got to that tree. The donkey was hard as a rock. In the dark I found the hoof with the registration number on it. I took out my knife and cut off the hoof. Sounds easy, but it wasn't. It took me maybe an hour, maybe longer. I didn't want to make any noise, but I had to break it and hack it—quietly—in this valley that makes echoes, without catching a sniper's attention. So I kept stopping to listen and be quiet. I put the hoof inside my jacket, under my vest, and drank water from one of the barrels. I could taste blood. Maybe from my hands, maybe from the water. I climbed back up the mountainside, groping like a blind animal, putting my fingers and feet into cracks and anything jutting like steps. The hoof, inside my uniform, got in the way. I was injured all over, cut to pieces."

Maria studies Achille for scars. Here is a man who has served in the war and is not mutilated or limping, just scarred. Her whole body is alive and racing inside.

Papà gives her a look that promises a beating.

She tries hard to think of something sad, like a funeral. She imagines her sister Edda lying ill in bed, disfigured with pox.

Maria knows her own face is more virtuous now. She can enjoy the end of her beloved's story. But inside, she is madly in love—madly, madly, madly in love with this handsome, adventuring, square-browed fighting man.

"By morning I made it back to camp, cut and bleeding all over, my uniform like rags, and right away I presented the captain with his donkey's hoof. I'd been gone for a day and a night. I told him I was shot at, and lucky to be alive. Captain was in a generous mood. He didn't shoot me. He cursed the donkey. The men on the front line didn't get their water. And I didn't have to do that job ever again."

Achille pauses, but he has more to say. He slips his fingers into his pocket and takes out a leather pouch. He opens it and holds up a brass shotgun cartridge to show everyone.

"Look."

He twists the cartridge shell to reveal a window with a secret inner scene: a miniature golden statue of the Madonna—no, it is Saint Anthony of Padua, with his tonsure, his cowl, his robes—holding the baby Jesus in the crook of an arm.

"When the war was over, and everyone was dead," Achille says, "the captain sent me this, the saint for lost things." He grins. "So I never lose a donkey again."

Vito thumps the table with his fist. "What a story!"

Egidia giggles. "What a story!"

Papà looks pleased again. "We welcome a hero to the family, not a fool."

Mama's mouth is down-turned in the usual way, and she stares at her hands, held in prayer.

And Maria knows not to say a word.

Sugared almonds

IT IS A PROPER BED, WITH A HEADBOARD AND WOOLEN MATTRESS. Maria stands near it. There's a thin tallow candle on the bedside table, and the light is flickering yellow and shadowy on the rough wall.

Achille stands by the door.

This is the first time they have been together, alone.

His father, his mother, his brothers and sisters-in-law, his un-married sisters and all the warm animals, an ox, maybe two, a pig and a mule, are in the next rooms. They have given the newlyweds a bedroom. It is strange and sparse, more run-down than Maria imagined. The walls are cracked. She can smell mildew. His mother and his sisters looked poorer than her family in the church. Their dresses and hats were shabby. Why did he say that her own brown day-dress was out of fashion? His entire family is rougher than she imagined. Sassone is a miserable *contrà*, almost a tumble of ruins, almost no place at all.

But she has a new husband, handsome and strong. They were married today. In Springtime, like a woman of means. They were blessed by the priest. Farewelled by her family. So many tears. She stands by the bed because she knows that a good Christian bride must lie with her husband. She has made the bed with new matrimonial sheets stitched by her own capable hands, blossom by blossom.

On the bedside table, she has placed the Madonna of the Mountains—her mother's parting gift. *She'll keep an eye on you,* Mama said. *Remember to honor her every day.* In front of the statue, Maria has placed a jar of fresh cyclamens in water, their tiny heads bowed, as in prayer.

Achille leans against the door. He looks at her.

Maria wants to show him the embroidery. He will admire her handiwork. But she doesn't know what to say. She is terrified, and her voice is trapped in her throat, below her throat, a place where it can't get out. She can't speak, not a word, even though they have spoken today, vows and introductions, and before—conversation, a little—with chaperones—with Mama, with Papà, with Severo. No, she cannot say a word. She can only gulp.

He is smiling, but he looks very serious at the same time.

She is heady with the day—wine and quail, and perfumed flowers in the church, and cake and sugar-coated almonds and solid gold rings and dancing and ankles on show and high heels that make her taller and put the pressure into her toes. Her feet hurt now, but she doesn't mind the pain. She is taller for him, upright and elegant, almost on tiptoe. Her blue wool dress is beginning to feel hot and scratchy. She touches the ring on her finger, she loves the weight of it, the gold of it. She has a new nightdress made of softest white lawn—when and how will she put it on? She must ask him to turn away. But she wants to show him the embroidery. The little birds in satin stitch.

She hiccups. She blushes.

Achille holds a finger to his lips and points next door. His entire family is there, Maria can feel them pressing against the walls, breathing, listening. The night is strangely quiet. It sounds different here in Sassone. Muffled, as if this lonely spot on the stony slopes is silenced by a cloud or a blanket, and even the animals have no voice. She hears a low grumbling drone and recognizes it at last: a snore. Of course his family is not listening. His father is snoring.

Achille makes his way toward her, slow as a hunter, but a little unsteady on his feet and smiling without showing his teeth.

Still, she cannot speak. What is the matter with her? Her heart is sitting on her chest, like the Sacred Heart, exposed and beating. What must she do? What will he do? He will know what to do, because he is a man, he is a *contadino* and a soldier, and he never wanted to be a priest, she knows that much. She has tried to imagine this moment so often, but her imagination has always failed her. She has clutched at fragments—overheard stories, jokes, knowing hints. The madwoman's song. She yearns to kiss him. She has never kissed a man before, not even her cousin Duilio all that time ago. It would have been a sin. She feels tickled all over. She wants Achille to soothe her, stroke her.

He glances at the Madonna and frowns and smiles again. He reaches out and turns the statue on its plinth to face the wall.

Maria is taken aback. What can the Mother of God not see?

"Sit on the bed," Achille says, close now. He knows what to do. His voice is a whisper. He smells of cologne and tobacco and grappa.

She obeys. There is a song in her head.

The little bird beat its little wings—

He is undoing his shirt. His eyes are gentle. "Are you ready?"

She nods as if she knows what she is ready for. She can't help looking for his scars. Still, her voice is trapped and swallowed. She gulps again. And then another hiccup. A laugh explodes from deep inside her. It sounds mad, like la Delfina. Shocking.

Achille clamps his hand over her noise. His face is fierce. He pushes her back onto the coverlet, his hand still on her mouth and against her nose.

She can hardly breathe. He feels heavy on top of her, despite his leanness.

He's staring into her eyes. He holds her there and stares and stares, crushing her with his weight.

At last she can see a scar, like an ant tunnel in his hair, pale and raised.

Suddenly he puts his hand up her skirts, and she hits at his guts hard with her fist.

"No!" she cries out—her voice at last—it's what she did in Piedmont when the *signore* tried to touch her.

Achille raises his hand as if to strike her and then he stops. He is angry. But then his face softens. "There, there," he whispers. "You're a flower. And I will love you, God knows I will." He strokes her cheek now, and it tingles under his callused fingertips. He strokes her hair, and keeps stroking, strokes her neck and strokes her arms, caresses her hands, kisses her neck.

"Close your eyes," he says. "Don't resist." And he unbuttons her. Pulls at her petticoat and drawers and stockings. Her clothes are caught and twisted. She's in a tangle. One of her shoes falls to the floor. He parts her legs with his, just like that. Clamps his hand on her mouth as he pierces her, smothering her cries, thrusting at her until he stops, shudders, heaves a sigh, pulls away and rolls off.

She opens her eyes now. Stares at the ceiling. There is perspiration on her brow. She is half off the bed, half-dressed, cold and damp where she is exposed.

She can't look at him yet. She stands and takes her shoe off, moves toward the gloom beyond the candle's reach, removes her undergarments and overgarments, folding them neatly in a pile. She feels a trickle down her legs and sees a run of red and white along her thigh. A dash of blood on the floor. She puts on her bridal nightdress, perfectly pressed. It stains. More washing for her to do. Her body feels mad all over, pent up and hurt and fluttering.

She hears a cough next door. She listens for more sounds.

Still standing, she turns to look at him.

He is gazing at her, leaning back on his elbows like a man catching the sun. But it's cold. And their breaths make steam.

She's not sure whether to be modest with him, now or ever.

The candlelight flickers on the edge of his face. He looks exhausted. Expressionless. His clothes are undone and his private parts are wet and exposed and monstrous in their nest of black hair.

Maria has never seen such things before. She has never seen her father naked, or her brothers. But she remembers the mating snails. A drake flattening a duck, its barbed spike. The rabbits she has gutted. Donkeys, sows, boars. And yet man was created superior to the beasts, different from them. Animals don't wear clothes, animals don't cook, or pray.

Maria's body is hot and cold and full of commotion.

Achille's pizzle dwindles and she watches it.

So this is making love. And this is what it means to lie with a husband. How often does it happen? Do her married sisters do this? Did her mother do this? Does Severo do this with his sickly weak wife? Has Achille done this before? With what kind of girl?

He sits up, strips and gets under the covers. "Come on." He yawns, patting the pillow. "Time to sleep. Wife."

Maria gets into bed. She reaches over and turns the Madonna statue to face the room again. The little table wobbles. Maria snuffs out the candle. In the darkness Achille holds her, his arms wrapped around her waist, and she feels safe and protected, wet and seeping, wild and confused all over.

> The little bird beat its little wings,
> It's a bit further down he wanted to fly!

The night is quiet, it seems to breathe with her husband's breaths, this stranger, this man who is going to sleep with her, body next to body, every night, for all her life, forever and ever.

~

MARIA WAKES IN THE MORNING after dawn. It's later than usual, she can tell, even though the shutters are closed. Achille is not in the bed. The sheet is cool where he slept. There is blood on her nightdress, on the sheets. She will have to wash everything. A cockerel crows. The air is cold.

She glances at the Madonna's serene face.

She gets out of bed and shivers, kneels before her, hands clasped, silently imploring her for guidance.

The Madonna takes her time.

So, my little Spring flower, my hazelnut-husker, my child, you prayed to me for guidance on your wedding night. You set my shrine right by the bed, within reach of your matrimonial pillow. I take my crown off to your embroidery, though he didn't even look at it. Men don't appreciate the finer things like sewing, or the way you made your hair soft as corn silk with your best olive oil. Perhaps he noticed the nape of your neck. You try to see the nape of your neck but mirrors are the Devil's work—how many times do you have to be told?

I can give you comfort for your trapped feelings, moist and yearning. You can pray them away.

I can give you comfort for the pain. I have endured pain. I escaped like a lowly gypsy into Egypt, and sobbed at the Cross, and held my bleeding son's body, and . . . Seven swords of sorrow have pierced me, Maria—but I do not seek pity.

Girls are born unknowing, and die unknowing, which is a kind of purity, but if we're lucky, we die cunning too. Be cunning, my dear girl, you know you can be. You've got yourself a good husband—mind you, I thought he was better heeled—now together you must make money and Christian children. This is the future you can give to the Fatherland and to the Holy Roman Catholic Church.

Whatever you do, you must be like me, Maria, a mountain, solid and enduring. And yet floating, light as a cloud. Vanishing if you need to, like a vapor. Blanketing and comforting. Emanating the glow of God's light from within. All this you must do, my darling pierced wife, all this you must do.

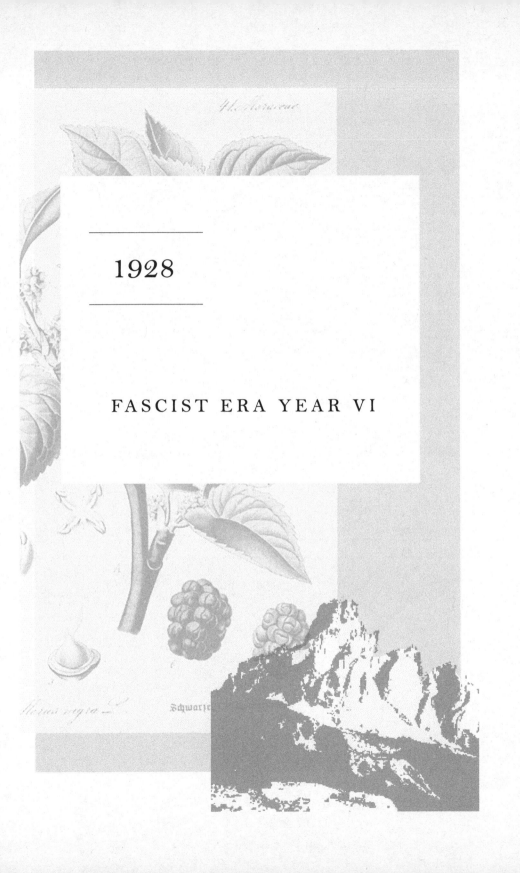

1928

FASCIST ERA YEAR VI

The plains

MARIA IS USED TO THE PLAINS NOW, THE SUN THAT RISES from Venice and sets beyond Verona, the nearby hills that are not mountains, the water ditches that edge the roads and fields, the mosquitoes and long muggy heat of Summer, the orchards and vineyards, the early ripening of fruit.

Fosso is not la Mèrica, but it is a new start. It's more of a village than a town, small and humble compared with Monastero, but ten times bigger than the *contrà*. The main street runs in a near straight line of shops and workshops and homes all joined together like a jumbled wall along the pavement, without space for trees or colonnades. Past the little *comune* where the office-men work, and around the main crossroads, there's the *osteria* for wine or lodging, then the church and bell tower on the piazza, and the school.

It was a stroke of luck that the old man who owned the grocery store was ready to die at last, and that he had no children, no siblings. Or it was part of God's plan.

GENERI ALIMENTARI reads the sign on the façade in big faded capital letters. The property has living quarters above, reached by steps outside at the back of the shop. It has a cool cellar below. A granary in the terracotta-roofed attic. A neglected garden with a few vegetables in the *orto*. Coop and cages and hutches sit empty, waiting for new life.

Achille owns it all. Without debts. He has earned it with his labor, different jobs in fields and ditches and shops—Maria is proud of her resourceful husband who works so hard and can turn his hand to almost anything. But his savings would not have been enough to buy the property outright, and there are two hungry children to feed. She thanks God for that field of his, which he sold at a good price. More than anything, she is thankful for her father's generous dowry settlement. She sighs sometimes when she thinks of Papà with his notepaper and his fields, so far away.

It is quiet here, without sisters and brothers or cousins. If only they could see her new home, her real home after all that time in rented rooms. If only they could see the work she and her tireless husband have done already. Her children need company. She must arrange to get some animals.

It is Lent. Springtime. The time when the rivers back home are rushing, ready for the big-wash rinsing. Egidia and Claudia do that work with Mama now.

Maria and Achille spend their hours cleaning and sorting the old stock in the shop. There is sweat on her brow, sweat on his brow. They have scrubbed the walls and floors, got rid of the dust and spiderwebs. He has replaced and fixed the woodwork. Together they have done the stocktaking. They are both deft with numbers, both of them quick. They make a good team. She feels a settled satisfaction.

She's wearing a nursing corset to contain her aching breasts, heavy with milk. Her swollen belly has been subsiding day by day; it's nearly back to normal. All this work is good for her. She wants to be shapely for her sister Edda's wedding. She wants Achille to desire her again. She wants more children.

In the middle of the shop floor, little Primo is playing with walnuts and keeping an eye on the baby. Darling Primo. He is her bold, clever boy. The baby is a girl—but she was longed-for after years of miscarriages and nothing, and she's strong, conceived as she was in a dying moon, growing in the womb during the Battle for Births, born quiet and happy like a gift on the Epiphany. She's easier to feed than Primo was. She's no trouble at all.

Calvinetto the bachelor butcher appears at the shop door. "Welcome to your new home!"

Achille and Maria put their scrubbing brushes down. They drop their wet rags into their pails. They wipe their hands on their aprons.

They shake his hand.

He smells of fat and blood. "It's a blessing to us," he says. "You're young. The old fellow here gave up years ago. He was always running out of things. And he was getting a bit . . ." Calvinetto taps his temple.

"The notary mentioned it," Achille says.

"You mean the bureaucrat, the swindler Nevoso?"

Maria wonders if the notary cheated him.

Achille nods uncertainly. "And Beppe from the *osteria* said as much. We'll make it good. Onward and up."

"And look at your fine young children!" Calvinetto says.

"This is our boy, Primo," Maria says.

"And this is Maria Amelia." Achille smiles as he leans down to give the baby's hand a squeeze.

"My husband chose the names," says Maria.

Primo stands up, straight and proud.

"Are you helping your Mama and Papà make the shop nice?" Calvinetto asks him.

Primo puts his fists on his hips and stamps his feet apart. "We own it."

"Good boy, good boy." Calvinetto laughs. "Will you be the one who looks after the rabbits and birds?"

Primo frowns. "But we don't have any . . ."

"It'll be my gift," Calvinetto says. "To help you get things going. I have some newborn rabbits for you. Their ears aren't long yet.

And some downy chicks, and what do you think of some nice fat wood pigeons? Will you feed them and muck them out? Make them grow up big and strong like you?"

Primo looks to Achille for the answer.

In the *contrà* everyone helped one another, but Maria didn't expect this kind of generosity in a village full of strangers. It augurs well. "Are you sure?" she asks.

"Of course I'm sure. It's the season," he replies. "It's easier for me. And you're just getting started."

Maria knows it's not that easy for him—he's an unmarried man, so his taxes must be very heavy. Mussolini wants children. Fecundity.

Achille looks along the shelves and gathers goods to give in return. "Here," he says, handing them over. "Brandy. And tea. Imported."

Maria fills a cone of straw-paper with balls of sugar. "And this," she says boldly, checking that Achille approves. "Also imported."

"Well, then, I'll get you some guinea pigs too." Calvinetto smiles. "Anyway, you know I'm next door if you need me. The local farmers will bring you eggs to sell, as well as honey, grappa, sweet young cheese, cured cheese, cows' milk, goat, ewe . . . You won't need bank money. Just barter."

~

MARIA IS PUTTING THE REMNANT stock back on the shelves. Arranging goods in rows, the nicest things at the front, the daily things within easy reach, the fancy things at the top where she has to use a ladder.

The shop is not open yet. But everything is immaculate, the windows gleam—who'd have thought the old glass would be so clear? Achille has placed orders for new imports and local goods: hundred-kilo jute sacks of wheat flour, two types, and three kinds of sugar; fifty-kilo boxes of pasta; tea, coffee, pepper, spices; big tins of olive oil; wheels of hard cheese; barley, oats; caustic soda, soap; a barrel of scopeton pilchards in salt. They are all on their way, no-tions in the air, soon to appear. Maria thinks of the Holy Ghost.

Achille worried about the tariffs making food prices too high. He worried about the cuts in people's wages with the Battle for the Lira.

But everyone has to eat, Maria told him, keeps telling him. Even in the *contrà* they had to go to the shops in Monastero sometimes. And people here are less self-sufficient, almost like city folk. They buy soap instead of making it. They like to get their meat from a butcher. And who can grow coffee? Or cocoa? They have a taste for foreign things.

People have to eat.

Achille listens to her, even though he's the boss. He likes that she's so strong and practical. She has given him a boy. And there will be more. *Thank you, dear God,* she prays silently as she works, *thank you, for we have married well.* She wasn't so sure at the start. Two years with his family, living tight under his drunken father's roof, packed in with his brothers and sisters and the animals . . . her husband's run-down *contrà* was not the step up in the world she had imagined.

She is organizing the lowest shelf behind the counter when an office-man enters the shop.

He's well turned out. A good-quality suit. Cologne.

She straightens up and fixes her hair. This feels important, talk-ing to a man of social standing.

"Good morning, and welcome to Fosso." He makes the Roman salute, arm stretched out flat in front of him. A clean, pale hand without calluses.

Maria wonders whether she should return the gesture. No, she doesn't support the Fascists, even if they're good for peasants and workers. She wants no part in politics. That's for men.

"We're not open yet, but we're getting there." She feels a little thrill as she says it. The shop will be ready just after Easter, the Tuesday before Edda's wedding. So many things are happening at once, everything is exciting.

"Yes, I can see that. Thank you. I'm looking for Montanari, Achille . . ."

"He's outside," she says. Digging and hoeing, preparing the yard for planting. He has pruned the fruit trees. He's repaired the coop and hutches. The new animals from Calvinetto are settled in with straw and feed. "I'll get him for you."

Maria wants to ask the office-man's name, but she thinks better of it. It's not her place. Achille probably met him when he was settling the transfer of ownership. There was so much paperwork.

The man greets her husband with a Roman salute. "I've come here to welcome you officially to Fosso."

Achille pulls an apologetic face and looks at his own hands, black with dirt. His work clothes are filthy. He smiles politely, without showing his teeth.

"You've invested in commercial and domestic property," the office-man says, "here on our main street. You are one of us now. Part of this flourishing little community."

"We're looking forward to a long life here, and a big happy family." Achille grins, too confidently. "We have two children. We want four or five, or more." He glances warmly at Maria.

She blushes.

"More than six, and you won't have to pay any taxes," the office-man says. "And you know about the loan rebates? The Battle for Births?"

"Yes," says Achille. "But we paid for this place without loans."

"Of course. And you know you need to be on the local register here?"

"We've just moved from Dueponti," says Achille. "I'm registered there."

"Yes, we know."

"We're catching up."

"You have time . . ." the office-man says. He looks about him, as if checking that nobody is listening. "You have a good military record. You're decent hardworking people. I've never seen this place so clean and ready for business. And, as you say, you have no debts . . ."

Maria can't imagine what he will say next.

Achille looks confounded.

"If you like, I'll keep an eye out for good investments. Situations arise . . . Opportunities. Sometimes on the quiet. Think you might be interested? With children, you'd qualify for the rebates . . ."

Don't trust anybody, Maria thinks. She looks to her husband.

"It's early days," Achille says at last. "We're just at the beginning of things. We need to get the new stock in and make a profit. But yes, I am interested. And I thank you."

"Not at all." The office-man smiles. He salutes again before he leaves.

Alone with Achille in the shop, Maria wants to get back to her work, and she wants him to get back to the yard, but she's feeling flustered. "I couldn't tell what he meant about opportunities."

"He has power," Achille says. "He's a customer too. If people ask you about politics, just tell them you don't know, you're a woman. We're not politicians. We're in business. We want as many customers as we can get. We can't afford to cross anyone."

"Do you think the notary cheated you?" she says without thinking.

Achille's face whitens.

She has seen this look before. It panics her.

The shop door opens.

"So you've had the municipal welcome! I'm Benedetta, the station-master's wife."

Achille greets the new visitor. "I'll leave you two women to your talk."

"Did I disturb you?" the station-master's wife asks once he's gone.

Maria shakes her head. "Nothing important."

"That official's a Fascist, that makes him important." Benedetta shudders. "At least we don't have any militiamen around here." She crosses herself. "Not yet anyway. Have you met the student priest?"

Maria shakes her head.

"He's a Communist. He has nightmares that the Blackshirts

come and take him away. I tell him they'd stop short of a priest, but I wonder."

Maria searches for something to say. "I asked the main priest to bless the shop when we open."

"Don Goffredo knows everyone here at Fosso. And Campolongo."

Maria feels sure that Benedetta does too.

"He knows about births, deaths, marriages," Benedetta adds. "And everything that happens in between!"

"He's giving us a set of brass scales—"

"People give him things all the time, money, of course, and things he doesn't need. He says Masses for them, and so on, and then he *redistributes wealth*, as the student priest would put it."

"Everyone has been so kind already—"

"Have you met Attilio the baker? He's not so kind. I think he doesn't like the human race. He's a loner, never mind his wife and children. Proposed to Maria Rosa when she was up a fig tree and he was on his way to the war, running, actually running, to the piazza to enlist with the other boys. I don't think he expected to come back. Most of them didn't. He called her down from the tree. They barely knew each other. And now Maria Rosa wonders what would have happened with her entire life if she hadn't come down from the top of that tree . . ." Benedetta snorts. "Life is a staircase. People go up. People go down. Or life is a fig tree! I hear your sister's getting married, not far from here?"

So news moves in a town just as it does in a *contrà*. Maria doesn't like to chatter. People say all kinds of things, and gossip is the Devil's work, although this woman seems harmless. "It's about fifteen kilometers away," Maria says. "In Altavilla."

"I hear your brother-in-law has a big estate. You can get the train, with a walk at both ends."

"They're sending a motor vehicle with a driver."

"Fancy! Do you have your outfit?"

Maria looks down at her plain old skirt, her cotton twill shirt, and the scarf knotted under her collar like a big necktie. Before this recent pregnancy, she'd make herself one new outfit for each season. No more than that. She has nothing for a special occasion. And her clever young sister Edda is marrying up in the world. Apparently Rodolfo has a farmhouse like a villa. "Of course I'll have something new to wear. We've been so busy with the work here—"

"The dressmaker's really good. Her husband's the tailor. Isn't that funny? It's a monopoly! I wonder what they talk about in bed at night." Benedetta snorts again. "Here, I'll draw you a map."

~

WITH BABY AMELIA IN the basket and Primo at her side, Maria walks down the garden path to the back gate.

His boots deep in dirt, Achille stops digging for a minute. "Don't get carried away," he says gruffly, but he smiles. He has agreed to this expense, a proper dressmaker's dress for her sister's rich wedding. *Bela figura.*

She plants a kiss on his grimy forehead.

He smells of sweat, that bitter manly scent of his, her handsome husband with his strong shoulders and his war-scar like an ant tunnel on his scalp. He has no need for the tailor. He's not going to the wedding. It will save them money. Besides, the shop will be open by then and in its first days.

The back-road houses have front and side gardens, fruit trees and nut trees in young leaf—peaches, almonds, walnuts, cherries—little plots of vines and vegetables, sprawling artichokes, wildflowers, chickens wandering at the edges. The sun is delicate but warm. The songbirds sing. The day is like a holiday.

Following Benedetta's map, drawn in shop-pencil on yellow straw-paper, Maria walks past the schoolteacher's house, the watchmaker's, the herbalist's, and other places she doesn't know about yet.

Primo chases a chicken and can't stop laughing.

The little one sleeps in her basket like the baby Moses.

A scowling man walks toward Maria and surprises her with a

greeting. He has big hooded eyes and a wart on his lower cheek. His head is like a friar's, bald on top.

"Attilio," he says, with a fast-vanishing smile. "The baker."

She introduces herself.

"Yes, you got the grocery store," he says. "I guessed. Are these your children?"

Maria nods.

"How old is the boy?"

Maria pats Primo's head. "He'll be three in August."

"You've ordered flour?"

"Yes," she says.

"Which types?"

"Red and white—"

"Very well, good day." And he continues walking, just like that.

Maria tries to imagine the boy who called a girl down from the top of a fig tree. He must have been more charming then.

As she reaches the house of the tailor and dressmaker, a soldier is leaving.

He looks into the basket and tickles the baby's cheek. His fingers are fat, dappled and tight as pork-meat sausages. But his name is Scopeton. "Like the fish," he says with a laugh. "I'm a small fish in a big world."

"You defend our country. Nothing small about that," says the tailor, and his eyes look moist, almost tearful, behind glasses thick as bottle bottoms.

"Let's pray for no more wars," the dressmaker says as she ushers Maria inside. She touches the dainty cloth-covered buttons that make a continuous line down the front of her jacket, one by one, like rosary beads. "Let's pray for weddings and baptisms."

The workroom is cool-floored and white-walled. Between cut-out paper sewing patterns curling on hooks, there's a picture of Saint Veronica holding out her veil with the face of Jesus on it. Tacked clothes, half-finished, hang on a metal rail. The sewing machine is set up with a giant spool of ivory-colored thread.

"My sister's marrying just after Easter," Maria says, twisting her gold wedding ring round and round. She loves the feel of it, smooth and comforting. She's never paid a dressmaker to make her a dress. "I want to look special for her, even though I'm still nursing. And Primo, my boy here, he needs something nice."

Her own wedding was five years ago. Before Easter. *A Carnevaleto se sposa 'l fioreto, a Pasqua roba ca vanza.* Before Lent, the well-off girl is wed, at Easter the one who'd be high-bred.

Her homemade wedding dress of plain blue wool was dark and practical—she's had plenty of use out of it—and for Mass and feast days she still wears her black wedding shoes too.

Her white veil, though, is in a drawer, wrapped with tissue paper and herbs. She will give it to her girl for her wedding day, one day. Her daughter will be married all in white like a *contessa*.

For now, baby Amelia is asleep and dreaming, a cozy half-smile on her rosebud mouth.

Blessings

ON THE TUESDAY AFTER EASTER, DON GOFFREDO ENTERS the shop with his altar boy. All the shutters are open and morning sunlight sifts through the window bars, lighting up the priest's lacy surplice to dazzling white against his long black skirt. His face is round and his neck is fat.

He eats well, Maria thinks.

"Greetings," he says, nodding to Achille, Maria, Primo, even to baby Amelia, cradled in Maria's arms. Everyone is clean and dressed in their modest best, standing in a straight line, as if for an inspection. There's still work to do, but the shop is full of new stock and everything is spotless.

Don Goffredo looks about. He touches Maria's arm gently. "I see you have the holy water ready."

The little altar boy is silent at his side.

Maria nods. She genuflects, uncertain. On Easter Saturday last week, she joined the procession to the barrel of blessed water positioned in front of the church altar. She filled a little bottle for herself.

This morning she poured a finger's depth into her best drinking glass and set it on the wooden serving counter, which is polished to a mirror-shine. Next to the glass she placed an olive twig preserved from Palm Sunday. Now she wonders if she should have moved the big brass scales out of the way, because they are for commerce, and Jesus got angry when there was trading in the temple, but the priest doesn't seem to mind; the scales were his gift after all, and perhaps to him they look golden and symbolic, like the virtue of Justice.

He dons his gold-glittering stole.

He walks slowly to the counter with his head bowed and his hands in prayer. He makes the sign of the cross, and everyone does likewise. He kneels before the counter as if it is an altar. Then he stands.

Softly he utters benedictions in Latin as he takes up the olive twig and dips it into the water. Praying all the while, he waves it at the counter, the scales, the shelves high and low, the slicing machine, the produce in boxes, tins, bottles, sacks on the floor, the door to the storeroom, the back door, the street-front door, the windows, and finally he sprinkles holy water on Achille, Primo, Maria and baby Amelia.

When the prayers are over, he replaces the twig beside the empty glass, turns and makes a blessing sign of the cross. He bows his head and closes his eyes.

Then the altar boy walks over to Achille and Maria, holding out a basket.

Primo is thrilled. He's been waiting for this moment. He unpockets the coin Achille has given him for the collection and puts it in the basket, grinning and looking up at Maria to make sure she's watching.

She ruffles his hair.

Achille places a bundle of money in the basket and bows his head.

With the baby still asleep on her arm, Maria goes behind the counter and picks up the basket she has prepared for the priest, full of the best fresh Spring eggs.

The altar boy holds both baskets and bows his head to show the priest's gratitude.

Primo starts clapping. He can't help himself.

The priest laughs.

Everyone laughs.

Achille grins and kisses Maria.

Primo hugs her leg.

The baby wakes up and is clutching to feed.

Maria can feel her breasts leak.

As Don Goffredo bids them farewell, with his altar boy and the whole world in high spirits, she thinks of the faded old picture she saw inside the Fosso church, painted on the wall. It is of blind Fortuna and her wheel. The man at the bottom is falling off the wheel and into a monster's jaws, but the man at the top is sitting on a throne, upright and smiling, like a man who is blessed with good health and good family, ready to open a good shop.

Sugared almonds

T HE WAY HOME FROM HER SISTER'S WEDDING SEEMS WILD
and wandering. *Where the pig ran, they made the road.*

Maria sits on the straw mattress at the back of the motorized
harvest-truck. Primo lies next to her, exhausted by the long days,
the relatives who doted on him, the other children, so much attention and playtime and excitement and food. Now he's asleep, thanks
to the lullaby of engine noise and motion. She wants to remind him
to look after his suit. It has to last, for feast days and special occasions. But she will not disturb him now. Her bold, beautiful boy is
dreaming.

The baby is lying on her back, cooing and gurgling, legs kicking, fists flexing, eyes open wide and reflecting the sky.

Maria doesn't properly know the places between Altavilla and
Fosso. She recognizes a bell tower here, a farmhouse there, but the
vineyards and cornfields merge in her mind. She knows the names
of towns and villages. Places like Cantinon, and Bierara. And Santa
Croce where all the thieves live.

The driver knows which way to go. He has strict instructions
from Edda.

Maria's younger sister was a bride in white, beaming on the

Altavilla church steps, standing still for a photographer on a strip of felt laid out as a procession carpet. She wore a pearly crown, fixed to a bonnet with a chin strap, and a long train. So much fabric, so much lace. She looked like a princess. Even her shoes were white. Her sleeves were all handmade lace, with cuffs that draped over her basket of Spring flowers arranged in trails. Her bridegroom had the airs and graces of a man who owned all of Altavilla, if not the church.

She doesn't really have to work, said Rodolfo later, cold and proud. *But she's my wife, she can do whatever she wants*. And then he winked at Maria. *Lucky Achille's not here to hear me say that*.

Maria is glad Achille was not at the wedding, looking like some poor brother-in-law, a *contadino* shopkeeper with his make-do suit and boots. There was work to be done, finishing the shop. Her strong handsome husband doesn't like parties or weddings anyway.

She presses her hat to her head as she gazes up at the wide Sunday sky. She is tired, but she is upright, alert, taking care not to stretch or strain the fabric of her new dress and dress coat, dovegray crepe, machine-stitched and hand-stitched and decorated carefully with lace and satin ribbon.

She's beaten Claudia to it, said Mama, dear hard Mama smiling at her second-youngest daughter's marriage. Mama worries that Claudia will never marry. *Have you seen the house? It's like a Palladian villa*. Maria doesn't know what that means. Nor does her mother. The words are someone else's. *But my sons, my sons! They've chosen badly. I pray for them both, I pray to all the saints, but those girls need a miracle, one each, to turn them into good wives*.

And, close by Mama's side, there was Zia Luigia. No sign of her son.

Our cousin Duilio's grown strange, Egidia whispered into Maria's ear. *Ever since his wife and baby died, God rest their souls. Her hips were too narrow. He's like a hermit. When I do see him, he talks about saving Italy. He says he has to get away from the mountains*.

Maria says a silent prayer for Duilio's dead wife and child. How can a man recover from such misfortune? She says a prayer for her cousin to be strong. It's no wonder that he has withdrawn from the pitying gaze of the *contrà*. She remembers the boy who tried to kiss her when she was just a girl and knew nothing of the world. Everyone, everything, has changed.

With the squinting sun on her face, and the harvest-truck motor louder than bells or birdsong, Maria rests her hand on Primo's head. She strokes his forehead, gently sweeping the hair from his sleeping eyes.

She lifts her wrist, and the violet oil is still there, lingering sweet and precious. It is the scent of home for her: gathering flowers and Mama's handiwork.

Papà was at the wedding, of course he was, dressed in his morning suit and looking scrubbed but somehow old. *My regards to Achille*, he said, as if he'd seen Maria just recently. *You married well enough*. He was keen to hear about the shop. Maria told him everything. About the accounting, her new skill. The stocktaking, the official's visit, the repairs, the animals from Calvinetto, the gifts, the blessing, the opening, the appreciative customers and profits from the very first day. *Your sister's done even better than you*, her father said with pride.

And Maria's older brother Severo, who used to tease her, was full of the newspaper news. *You open your shop, so you're happy, but then someone tries to kill the king with a bomb, and everyone else is dead or wounded. Nothing is safe. Not even your shop. Not even the king.*

And her brother Vito, with Valeria sweet-faced and silent at his side—all he could talk about was cycling and the Giro d'Italia due to start in May.

Dearest sister, said Edda, hugging Maria, enveloping her in lace and perfume, giving her a chiffon purse of sugared almonds, the wedding memento. *I'm here with you in the plains! I'm not so far from you now. We can be close, and visit, and look after each other. I'm so happy.*

~

WHEN MARIA ARRIVES HOME, she's surprised that Achille is not in the shop. The work is not quite done, there are finishing touches to do: the storeroom door that catches on the floor, the broken light . . . Perhaps he is upstairs. It is Sunday after all, the day of rest. Perhaps he is waiting for his family to return. Why is he not at the door, arms open, the father who has looked out of the window and run downstairs because he has missed his son? Or perhaps he is in the granary, clearing out the old corncobs and dirt.

She takes the little ones upstairs. There are no signs of his smoking or his lunch. He has been gone all day. She doesn't need to call his name. Where is he? It's too late for Mass. He doesn't go to church, apart from holy days. The *osteria*? He could be playing cards there, smoking and gambling with matchsticks, sipping coffee and grappa served by Beppe or Teresa. Men need to be in the company of other men.

Maria puts the baby's basket on the kitchen table. She changes Primo's clothes. She gives him a glass of water, then sends him down to the garden, to let out the chickens and play with the rabbits. In the bedroom, she hangs up her dress and dress coat. She puts on her day clothes and clogs. She is plain again, but the violet oil lingers on her wrists.

She sits on the bed and undoes her nursing corset. The baby takes to her breast, sucking healthily, her plump hands squeezing, her chubby face drunk with pleasure once she's done.

Achille is still not home.

Maria settles the baby and wonders what to do.

Is he with a woman? She has had the thought before. But Fosso is a small town, a village really—he wouldn't be able to go here or there without somebody noticing. People talk.

Perhaps there is a woman elsewhere. Back in Dueponti, where they rented rooms before the move here. That quiet silk-working woman, maybe, or that coquettish girl at the blacksmith's. Is this why Achille didn't want to go to the wedding? There could be a dishonest woman in Santa Croce—the town is full to its walls with robbers.

Maria goes to the wardrobe and tries to see what's missing. She looks in the chest of drawers. She knows all his things, it is she who washes and presses his undergarments, darns his socks, sews his buttons when they come loose. He must be wearing his Sunday suit.

Downstairs she notices his wooden work box, which he has left in the middle of the shop floor. Underneath the tools, she finds a small brown leather ammunition case. She undoes the buckle. Rust stains her fingers.

The contents are not so old.

Here is that cartridge shell of his with the miniature saint inside. She remembers him holding it up when he told that story about the donkey. Her father and brother were wide-eyed and impressed. The brass is tarnished.

Here is something she has not seen before: a PNF membership card. With his name on it, and a note of his military service from the War in Snow and Ice. A stamp with a picture of Mussolini. Montanari, Achille—Il Fascista. It seems he joined the Fascist Party during the Battle for Grain, two years after their wedding, almost on their anniversary date. Did he do it for her? For the family? *We're in business, we don't take sides,* he always says.

Her guts are knotted. Why didn't he tell her?

Here is his certificate of unlimited leave. No wonder he was free to marry, alive, and handsome, with only that one big scar. All the men in those days were mutilated or killed. His military hospital card shows the dates of his malaria treatment. It's been nearly ten years since he was taken ill. She says a prayer of thanks that he is well now.

But her fingers are trembling. Here is a photograph of him with a woman. A beautiful young woman. And he is a handsome young man, just a little younger than he was when he first appeared in the *contrà*, striding up the mountainside with the loaded *gavegnà* on his head.

He holds the woman's hand. They gaze at each other like lovers. Tenderly. They look like they're betrothed.

Achille never looks that way at Maria.

The woman wears a fox stole and holds a lady's net purse;

Achille wears a button-hole rosette and carries a gentleman's walking stick—things that must belong to the photographic studio. The shiny striped cravat too. But his boots are his. And the woman's high-heeled shoes show off her dainty ankles.

Maria was wearing her old brown dress when she met Achille. Plain. Darned. Long to her shoes. He said something about the fashion for skirts being shorter. Now she understands why he said it.

On the back of the photograph, she reads someone's handwriting, not his: *Maria Amelia.*

The name he chose for his firstborn girl.

Maria looks for a date, a year, another clue, but there is none. Even so, she knows that this woman found Achille before she did.

And he loved her.

Maria puts the documents back and buckles the leather holder, then buries it underneath his work tools. Her hands are still shaky. Her heart is full of jealousy, stabbing like a sword of sorrow. She closes the lid on the wooden box.

Where is her husband now?

After dark

ACHILLE COMES HOME IN THE DARK. MARIA CAN HEAR HIM before she sees him. He stumbles up the steps outside, swearing under his breath.

She is seated at the kitchen table, relieved that the children are asleep in the bedroom. What can she say? She has prepared words of happy greeting, as if nothing is wrong.

He is here. He smells of wine and tobacco smoke. Sweat. He stands at the door looking stupid. His eyes are tired and watery. He freezes like an animal pretending not to be there.

"What are you doing here?" he says.

She has no answer.

"I thought you were coming back tomorrow."

"You were wrong," she says quietly.

He straightens his jacket, tugs at a cuff. "How was the wedding? How long have you been sitting there?"

She can't answer.

"Maria, what's the matter with you?" There is spittle on his mouth.

She can't look at him now. "Nothing."

"Good. Then I'll go to bed." He begins to move toward the bedroom door and his heavy boots make too much noise on the floor.

"No," she says. "You'll wake the children."

He stops obediently in the middle of the room. He waits.

But she doesn't know what to say. She wants him to love her. "What have you been up to while I was away?"

"Nothing."

"Who were you with?" She tries to ask the question lightly.

"Nobody." That one lying word is sour. His face is irritable now. "I'm going to bed. We can talk in the morning."

"Why did you join the Fascist Party? Why didn't you tell me?"

His mouth hangs open.

"Why didn't you tell me?" She gets up and walks toward him, arms crossed. "And why did you choose that name for our girl?"

"It's a beautiful name." He stinks. "For a beautiful girl."

"Which beautiful girl?" she asks.

"You are my life, Maria." He looks shifty now.

"Which beautiful girl?" she repeats, trying to keep her voice calm and even. Has she lost him? She stares at him, looks for signs in his face, his shifty speechless angry face. She waits, dreading his answer.

"The one I wanted to marry," he says at last.

She gasps.

"Don't push me, Maria."

"Push you?" Maria jabs at his chest. There's a storm inside her. "Why didn't you marry her? Is that where you were today? With her and her high heels and her stupid face?" She wants to hit him.

But he hits her. His hand catches her jaw. "Shut up," he says. "Shut up."

She stares at his hand. The gold wedding ring on his finger. She panics. She can't hit him back. She doesn't want to make him angrier. He is stronger than she is.

Then he strikes her head with the back of his hand, heavy and loud, that wedding ring hard against her skull, and she almost loses balance, but she rights herself. She puts her hands out to stop him, but he hits again, first her arm, then her shoulder.

Shaking, hurting, she backs away. Toward the bedroom door. She doesn't want to wake the children, but she has nowhere else to go. She can't run for the back door to the steps outside. It is night. He is in her way. He seems to fill the kitchen. She can't leave the children. She has no choice. She braces herself.

He hits out again, this time knocking her shoulder.

She totters and steadies and lets herself sink to the floor.

He stands above her, fist raised, face tight, eyes red and streaming.

She gives in, she gives up—if she lets him hit her, he will stop soon enough and then it will be over.

Suddenly he lets his arm drop.

Their boy is at the bedroom door.

"Primo!"

How long has he been there?

"And you: go back to bed," Achille says. "Or there'll be trouble."

Then the baby wails, and Maria feels milk escape from her breasts. She lets the baby cry until she knows it's safe to get up and walk into the darkness of the bedroom. Feeding will make her baby quiet.

~

IT'S NOT UNTIL THE MIDDLE of the night that Maria remembers to pray. Her body hurts when she gets out of bed.

The children are sleeping.

Downstairs in the shop, Achille is sleeping.

She can hear his snores through the floor, muffled and rumbling.

The Madonna of the Mountains is invisible in the darkness, but Maria does not light a candle. She touches the glass and gazes blindly, waiting and waiting until the Madonna speaks.

Oh, Maria, my startled bird, my bruised violet, you've never been hit like that.

Your loving father took his belt to you. Children, like animals, need discipline.

You've seen the Madonna of the Manganello holding cudgel high in one hand, baby Jesus in the other. Sometimes even the Mother of God needs to use force.

Il Duce says a good beating never hurt anyone.

Strive to be like me, Maria: solid and enduring as a mountain, pure and hard. Pura e dura. *And yet floating, light as a cloud. Vanishing when you need to, like a vapor.*

Count your blessings.

Your earthly milk flows freely. Your little ones are growing up strong. Your husband is good and resourceful and hardworking. And he's yours. Not anyone else's. You are his life, he said so.

Men will do what men do. Their needs are different from yours. They have the stresses of the world on their shoulders. They need the comforts of your cooking. They need your admiration—see how your husband's eyes light up when you praise him.

It is the horsefly wife who loses her husband. Don't ask him any more of your pointless questions, Maria. Not knowing is a kind of happiness.

Make yourself sweet as a chestnut, happy as a lamb. When you work in the shop, work for him. When you make gnocchi, make them for him. Make his bed warm and welcoming. You have promised to live and pray and stay together, forever and ever. Together you can make more children, and so you should.

1936

FASCIST ERA YEAR XIV

Martedì grasso

It's Shrove Tuesday, the last day before Lent. Maria can take time off from the shop to attend her sister-in-law's funeral, and Achille can manage without her for a week. He hit her yesterday—arguing about Edda's husband, Rodolfo, some business deal that went wrong. He hit her hard, but not on the face. She thanks God that there are no marks on her face. Does he miss her face on purpose? No, she's sure he doesn't think at all when he gets angry. It doesn't happen often. She can forget her aches and bruises. She has made herself look beautiful. She wants to make a good impression. *Bela figura.* She wants the people of Monastero, and the people of the *contrà*, to see how well she's done. She has ambition. One day she and her husband might go to la Mèrica.

But today she is going to the mountains where she was born thirty-eight years ago.

First, to the big church in Monastero for Confession and Mass.

Then to the *contrà* for the viewing of the body and, later, the funeral.

She is bringing her children, like ducklings in a line behind her. Primo, Maria Amelia, Arsenio, Cecilio—the living ones. She imagines her lost ones in the air, like dust rising from the track: infant

Tito, who died in the crib while she was heavy with Cecilio, and stillborn Ignazio, who would be a yearling now if he'd lived. God rest their innocent souls.

She's wearing black, her best wool coat. And her new stockings are made of real silk, despite Autarchy—Mussolini would have her wear make-do-and-mend stockings, or those damp synthetic ones that ball and bag at the knees. She is dressed in her finest, as are her children. They carry gifts and flowers. She wants the people of Monastero to see her like this, and she wants the people in the *con-trà* to see her like this. She is a woman of means.

They catch a train, smart and new, leatherette and chrome and sliding windows. They glide through stations, smart and new, past long platforms and ticket offices, marble and concrete and changing signs, and guards in handsome uniforms, everything new, from Fosso to Vicenza, and then Vicenza to Monastero at the end of the line. It's the modern era. The War against Backwardness.

They have to walk from the station. The town nestles in the place where two valleys meet, but the mountains seem to wall it in and jut against the clouds. The roads are steep. Maria feels the thrill of the altitude and the quality of the air, its coldness, its purity, the huge and close-up sky. She settles Cecilio on one hip and walks with a stride, despite the pain where her bruises are. Her boots stamp the ground as if she's crushing vipers underfoot. Her stamping boots are new, made of the best leather, lined with rabbit fur. Her ducklings have to trot to match her pace.

Vito's wife is waiting to greet them by the fountain in the piazza. She huddles in her shapeless coat. She has no fat on her, no muscles. Her skin looks gray. She barely glances at the children.

Arsenio is openmouthed. He's never seen anyone so thin.

"Welcome, sister," Valeria says without a smile.

"Nobody else?" Maria says, forgetting herself.

Valeria holds her tight and whispers in her ear. "Everyone has to work. What can I say? Your mother hates me. I can't lift the washing or the weight of the water. Vito has given up on me. And Severo's wife, I don't have to tell you, your mother hated her too.

She hates us for our weakness. She hates us for marrying her sons. She's killing me too."

Maria is appalled at her sister-in-law's indiscretion. She lets go of her. She wants to push her away. "Onora died of consumption."

Valeria looks at Maria's children. "Hello, remember me?" she says. "I'm your aunt. After Mass we'll walk home, back up the mountain, for some nice food."

Valeria doesn't eat, she doesn't even cook, but the children know to say nothing. And nobody mentions the laid-out corpse that waits for them at the *contrà*.

During Mass, Maria senses the envious gaze of the congregation. She knows that she is feeling pride, and pride is a sin, and fighting with Achille is a sin, and she should tame his temper, not stir it up, and she has just been absolved by the priest for all her sins in Confession. She should be feeling grief for her dead sister-in-law—but she can't help herself: she is feeling pride, she is warding off pity. She remembers the palm tree, the emblem of martyrs, stuck in her family's photograph like a sign. She is determined never to be pitied again.

She barely hears a word of the sermon. How do her brothers cope? The wife of one is dead. And this wife, Valeria, is consumed by melancholy, wizened, stooped, old before her time. Can a person just fade away? Who does the washing for the men now? Thank God for them that Claudia never married. Maria is proud of her children seated beside her. Primo, wearing his new eyeglasses, her perfect, clever boy. Eight-year-old Amelia, dark-eyed and pretty with her glossy chestnut hair. Arsenio, already tall for his age. And little Cecilio, good-natured and plump, his feet dangling off the pew.

When Mass is over, people linger outside the church doors on the high terrace overlooking the piazza. Others stand on the marble steps that spill down in a steep cascade. They can see Maria's coat up close now, admire its quality. They greet her, offer condolences, pat her children's heads, admire their good straight bodies and nice clothes.

"Signora Montanari," some say.

"Maria Vittoria," others say with more familiarity. "Are these your little ones? Look how grown-up they are!"

"How is life in the plains?"

"How have the sanctions affected you?"

"Is your husband well? Give him my regards. Condolences."

"CREDETE! OBBEDITE!" a voice shouts from the piazza below. It's almost Mussolini's motto. *You believe, you obey.*

Maria looks down to the very first step.

There is a ragged creature with a blackened face and two tall horns. The word *obey* is like a howl. The head tips back, and the mouth opens wide to shout at the church above. "I hate church— but I must love it! Because it's the priest who feeds me, feeds me the best scraps, because it's the priest who gets the best food. I obey. I fight—no, I don't!—fighting is a sign of madness."

A nervous laugh ripples through the congregation.

"A Carnevale ogni scherzo vale," says a fellow beside Maria. At Carnival time, any jest is fine.

La Delfina is not playing tricks or making carnival jokes. She probably doesn't know what day it is. Still, she has an audience and they are disturbed, or amused, unable to move. Perhaps they are afraid of her. She is blocking their way.

"It's a day for costumes," someone mutters. "But look at the wretched woman: she has no idea what she's doing, she's a dis-grace."

La Delfina shouts up at the crowd. "I would sew the priest's vestments if I could hold a needle still enough. Or if I didn't smell!"

"How do you know you smell?" someone calls out, mocking.

"The priest says so, and the squinting children in any *contrà* say so. But *they* smell. They smell of the animals they sleep with." She stops and the silence is hers. "The shit-hut smells the same for all of us. We all spill the same, we ooze the same, we all boil down to the same stinking sludge."

"Are you a devil with those horns?" someone shouts out, laugh-ing.

"Or a chimney sweep?" another asks. "Look at her black face."

But Delfina doesn't answer. She starts singing "Little Black-Face," the marching song from Abyssinia about the pretty slave among the slaves. Her voice is cracked and out of tune. *"Faccetta nera . . . moretta che sei schiava fra gli schiavi . . ."*

Some people sing along. They know the words. One fellow starts to move his arms about as if he's conducting an invisible military band. But Delfina gets the words mixed up, and some people lose their places. Soon they are laughing, and telling her off. Others are grumbling and cursing. One man calls out that tomorrow's the start of Lent and it's the time for charity, not Fascism.

The crowd starts to break up and move down the steps.

The madwoman plucks out her horns—they are just sticks stuck in her matted hair. She throws them high into the air. She hops from one foot to the other in a dance.

The people stand back. Their laughter puffs into steam like a cloud. The sticks clatter to the ground.

Delfina starts making her way up to the church. She climbs three steps at a time. She's used to mountains. Her legs are rangy like an alpine goat's. The crowd backs away.

Maria can smell her now. She remembers it in her nose. It is the stench of Hell.

And here is Delfina, standing in front of them, too near.

Arsenio looks scared enough to cry, but instead he kicks at the hag and misses. Cecilio tries to copy him and falls over. The children titter.

Delfina spits. She points at each child. "Boy, girl, boy, boy. One, two, three, four. Laugh, laugh, laugh, laugh. Dark, dark, dark, dark." She sucks in a breath. *"Live dangerously!"* she shouts, even though they are close enough to hear.

The words are familiar, more words from Mussolini.

Maria shepherds her children back behind her. Cecilio clutches at her leg.

La Delfina pauses. Her wild round eyes in her blackened face stare at Maria.

"You—you used to tease me from inside the shit-hut—in those days—before they married you off and sent you away. *People move, but mountains stay put.*"

She turns to the crowd. It is like a political speech from a palace balcony. Her voice is big. She spreads her arms wide. "She made the soap. She did the washing. The little wash every week. The big wash every year. As natural as the moon's cycles."

Maria shudders. How often was the madwoman watching, listening? She haunted the *contrà* like an unlucky shadow, worse than the worst gypsy.

Turning back to Maria, la Delfina says, "It gave you purpose. My purpose is mysterious, like the wasp, no use to anybody, but part of a plan. You are good for cooking and washing and breeding—"

"Enough, enough. Where's the priest?" An older woman speaks out.

"No, let her be," a fellow replies. "She's harmless."

La Delfina locks eyes with Amelia. "I tell all the girls, as they empty their girl bladders and girl bowels, *If you marry you'll die*—but what does a madwoman know?"

Amelia shrugs and blushes. She takes Maria's arm, clutches it.

La Delfina points a filthy finger at Maria. "You—you craved your ring of gold."

Maria touches her wedding ring, wishing she'd worn gloves. She smiles at the onlookers, but it's a smile like her own mother's, with the corners of her mouth turned down. She feels paralyzed. Should she curse, or laugh, or dismiss, or take charge—what can she do?

Delfina crouches and draws breath. The noise is ghastly, one breath after another. Her shoulders rise and fall. She springs up like an insect and grasps Maria's wrist and holds it high and shouts, "She isn't one of those wives who hand in their wedding rings for the Fatherland. She's. Not. Stupid! She knows that gold in the hand is worth more than steel from the State, even if the Leader of the

Blackshirts, son of a blacksmith, engraved it himself." She lets go of Maria's trembling hand. "Which he didn't."

The madwoman stares at Valeria. Looks her up and down. Her voice softens. "You—you have the will to die. I could have told you: *If you marry you'll die!* But you would never have listened. All any girl wants is to marry. Not Delfina. No, no, no, no. You've lost the fight. His parents say to him: *Who will mother the children when she goes? Poor disgraced orphans. Who will do the work?* There's talk of taking you to the madhouse."

Valeria gasps.

Others mutter and look away, walk away.

"I've heard them," Delfina screeches. "Better you than me! Better you than a madwoman!"

"This is too much," Maria says. She wants to curse. She picks up Cecilio and holds him in her arms. She nods at the other children and Valeria to come away.

"Everywhere in Nature there is fighting!" Delfina bellows to the people. She elbows the air. "I know the words. *The Italian character has to be formed by fighting.* And the washing! We must fight rot with soap and boiling water. The Lamb of God washes away the sins of this world. Even in the highest *contrà* where the snow is pure, they're close to Heaven, but they live like animals in their stalls, just a whisker between them and the all-seeing, all-stinking witch."

Primo hisses at Arsenio. "What are you grinning for?"

Arsenio goes red in the face. He clings to Maria's elbow.

Maria and her family proceed down the steps like royalty, holding their gifts and flowers. But she doesn't feel regal, not at all. She is full of shame and fury all at once. She wants to run away from here. She must get to the *contrà*. To the funeral. To her family. There are too many steps. And now there are more steps.

When they reach the piazza, la Delfina is still ranting up there on the terrace in front of the church doors. The priest has appeared and is trying to calm her. Maria wonders if this is the one who feeds her.

Maria strides to the fountain. She doesn't know where to go or what to do. She must rise above her disappointment. The sound of dashing water soothes her.

"Mama, is that a witch?" Primo tugs at her sleeve.

"Don't be silly," Maria says.

"Do you know her?"

"I saw her sometimes in the *contrà*. When I was little. The woman's mad."

"Poor thing," says Amelia.

"She doesn't want your pity." Maria looks around the piazza. There's the blacksmith's shop. The butcher's. The herbalist's pharmacy. The dairy. The *osteria*. And windows shuttered shut. One or two people stand on little balconies here and there, watching the wild display at the top of the church steps. The madwoman's voice echoes.

"I tried to kick her," says Arsenio, grinning.

"Me too!" says Cecilio.

"I'll kick you both," says Primo.

"Valeria, wait here," Maria says. "Mind the children."

Inside the butcher's, she can hear the ranting continue outside, God knows what filth and nonsense now. The crowd is clapping. Someone jeers. There is laughter, in a chorus. Another voice calls out for more.

Maria pays for a neat sopressa wrapped in straw-paper. It's the last meat-eating day before forty days of abstinence. When she was little, she used to leave the woman a piece of cheese sometimes, or sausage. God will be happy if she gives food to a beggar.

But it's not so easy to do.

La Delfina is on top of the fountain now, perched like a bird of prey in the marble basin, her dirty shift soggy, gray and brown. The crowd has gathered around, idle and uncertain.

"Here," Maria calls out. She tries very hard to smile. People are watching. Her own children are watching. Her sister-in-law is watching. "Something to eat. Some meat. Nice and fatty. Before Lent." She approaches the fountain.

Someone applauds.

Delfina points at Maria, or at the proffered gift. "You—cousin—"

"Don't be silly. I'm not your cousin," Maria says firmly, but her voice catches. She has heard the words before.

"COUSIN!" Delfina roars. She's ungrateful. Completely mad. "My cousin!" she shouts. Then her eyes narrow on something further away. Her mouth hangs open. She is silent.

Someone is standing in the shadows of the arcade, near the dairy, behind the wide low arches. The figure is darker than the shadows.

La Delfina draws herself up as the man emerges into the light of the square. He carries a cudgel.

"And you!" she screeches at the Blackshirt. "*Squadrista!* Volunteer! Illegitimate! You are half my brother! No more, no less. Your father is my bastard father."

Maria is all commotion inside.

Duilio walks, he doesn't march. He is in MVSN uniform, tight black necktie against black shirt, black shiny boots. He wears a black-tasseled fez with a gold *fascio* badge. A Sam Browne shoulder belt. A holster. A dagger. He swings his cudgel as if it is some kind of sport. Like lazily hitting a ball.

How long has it been since she's seen him, the dark-eyed handsome boy who tried to kiss her? The malcontent, the sensitive one who was going to be a priest, or a soldier. The unlucky one. She can't think. Here is the menacing militiaman who is her cousin. He's wearing black gloves, but she knows he has two steel bands on his ring finger. *ORO ALLA PATRIA*. His wife died in childbirth years ago, so he gave away her gold wedding ring, as well as his own. His grief is deep in his face.

He hasn't seen Maria—has he?

The people stand back.

Delfina addresses him. "Brother!" She's not afraid. "BROTHER!" she repeats, louder, as if he hasn't heard her.

Maria can see the shadow of truth in his eyes. She feels panicky. She heard a rumor once that her uncle had excessive appetites, that he may have sired other children. Poor Zia Luigia. But people say all kinds of things, and gossip is the Devil's work.

"Brother! Cousin! You two, together!" Delfina points at Duilio and Maria. "Once upon a time, long ago, before the War against Whatever, I saw you!" Delfina makes a show of kissing the air, stroking herself. She wiggles her hips.

Maria's children are watching. Her silent sister-in-law is watching. Amelia looks upset. Arsenio's mouth hangs open. The people don't know what to do now. Some huff. Some mutter. A few loners edge away, making their excuses to the Blackshirt.

Delfina still has him in her sights. "But now you have the hat, you have the pace, you have the face, face, face, you go around every *contrà*, and Albarela, and here in the lap of Monastero, and further down the valley, and to other valleys, and as far as the cities, I'd bet on it. You call yourself an apostle of violence. I never saw you slaughter a pig."

Duilio salutes the crowd, his arm stretched out straight before him. His face is impassive. He looks at Maria but there's no sign of recognition in his eyes. He looks at her children. He looks at every last bystander.

"Some of you must have work to do." He swings the cudgel onto his shoulder.

A few people salute or half-salute. Some stay. Others mutter to themselves as they drift away.

"Come down off that fountain before you break it." Duilio's voice is hard and quiet. "It's public property, and you are putrid."

"*Liberty is a putrid goddess,*" Delfina says. Mussolini's words again. "I am Liberty." She laughs and splashes herself all over, as if she's washing.

"And I am the police. I arrest you."

"You want to cleanse me."

"I will climb up and get you if I must."

"And sully your precious uniform?" She howls. She hoots. But now there is fear in her eyes. "*CREDERE. OBBEDIRE. COMBAT-TERE,*" she chants. "I know the words."

Maria knows those words too. *To believe, to obey, to fight.* The motto is everywhere.

Teetering on the fountain's edge, Delfina roars, *"The Fascist despises suicide!"*

Then she climbs down, splashing, arms and legs slipping, her grubby shift slopping with fountain water. She is shivering now. Her eyes are wide and round as she locks her gaze with Duilio's. "The priest washes out my mouth when I blaspheme. His soap is made of olive oil and lavender. It smells like angels but it's a devil in the mouth." There's a puddle of water at her feet. "I don't want to be *cleansed.*"

Maria is still clutching the sopressa—her charitable gift—and Amelia is leaning against her as Duilio leads the madwoman away.

The stragglers are sheepish now. Their entertainment is over, and they have nothing to look at but one another. The square is quiet, and the fountain seems very loud.

"CHARITY!" Delfina screams, suddenly back in the piazza. She has escaped. "We are all the same blood. Look: my brother loves me now." She rushes up to Maria, paws at her sleeve, grabs the butcher's parcel and runs away again, back to Duilio. "Putrid Liberty!" she shouts at his face.

And the two of them disappear into the shadows of the arcade.

Maria's heart is drumming.

Valeria has a face like a rain cloud. "Is it true?"

Maria shakes her head. "That beggar's no relation of mine."

"Our family is first-class," Primo says. "Our nonno has notepaper with his name on it. Printed."

"No," Valeria says. "I mean about the madhouse?"

"I don't know about that," Maria says. "I live in the plains."

"But they write to you. They tell you things."

"Vito doesn't write to me."

Valeria pulls her coat tight around her. "So it's true."

"That woman sits half-naked in a fountain. She's possessed. I don't know why you believe a word she says. It's like listening to the Serpent." Maria stamps her boots. Her feet are cold. Everyone will talk. Could that disgraceful creature be her blood? *Bruta canaja.* Ugly lowlife. And Duilio, what has Duilio become? He doesn't even recognize her. His face is a mask. Tight, haunted, changed. And that cudgel he carries. She's heard about his fanatical politics. He's as crazy as the hag.

"Don't be sad, Mama." Primo strokes her hand.

The children are waiting patiently, still holding gifts and flowers.

"You must be hungry." Maria leans over and picks up Cecilio, ignoring the pain in her arm where Achille hit her. "*Porco can.* Damn. My feet are cold. Yours must be too. We have a mountain to climb and a funeral to go to."

Delfina

*No desmentegar che al mese de zenaro, vive ben chi ga
el frumento nel granaro.*

Don't forget that in the month of January, he lives well
who has grain in the granary.

At the end of the old year, Delfina's people slaughter
the pig.

She can smell it in the air, as natural as snow or the Epiphany.
The conditions are ideal: the Winter world is an icehouse.

She sits on her rock to watch.

They have fed the pig on chestnuts and acorns, but mostly on
scraps. All year long, the pig mops up the slops that would otherwise turn into piles of rotting rubbish.

The pig grows fat.

It grows up.

It never quite grows old.

The people work by daylight.

They lead the pig out from its cozy stone-walled stall by the kitchen and onto the snow. This is a novelty for the animal, almost exciting.

But the pig's not stupid. It knows something is amiss. Its nose is in a rope, and its jaw can still open wide enough to shriek. There's fight in it.

The pig is canny, but this is its first time, whereas *they* have done this every year, every generation, every century. They have the upper hand. They are superior, a better class of animal. They have tradition and they have strength.

They—Delfina's people—surround the pig and slit its throat and the blood pours out, in heaving breaths, resistance and surrender. The animal takes a while to die. Even when the blood stops, the body still moves. They gather its blood, trying not to waste a drop, sickly sweet for blood pudding and blood sausage.

The snow is spattered.

Inside the house, they have boiled water in a blackened cauldron on the fire. The woodsmoke curls into the sky, rich as church incense, clouding the clear air.

The people of the *contrà* heave the cauldron outdoors.

They are Maria's family. Anyone's family. Everyone is related, back up the family tree.

Delfina is a bastard.

Delfina's father is Duilio's father.

The family won't own her, they can't keep her, but they can't let go of her either.

They pour boiling water over the dead pig—it is a thing now, with more uses than Delfina can count. One thing, two things, three things, more things, more things, more things.

They scrape off the bristles, the soft ones, the hard spiky ones. *Porca miseria*, they curse—it is a hairy beast. The knife and water and hair make a hundred little fountains inside a fog of steam. They clean its dead face and ears.

They string up the body, and it hangs from its feet off a tree like Saint Peter—that's blasphemy and the priest would wash out her mouth with soap and water if he heard her. His soap smells like angels but it's a devil in the mouth.

They slit the pig straight down its middle, the unsuckled teats like rows of buttons on either side of the seam. They slice the vitals into a bucket. They knife out the lungs, the liver, the kidneys. They behead and they quarter.

Delfina is sure the same happened to this or that martyr. This or that lonely soul who railed against the Leader of the Blackshirts. This or that mad person who shot at Mussolini's nose, or gave voice to heresy. Who would dare to question the draining of the marshes or the building of the bridges or the Roman Empire? *Il Duce ha sempre ragione.* He's always, but always, right.

Delfina has seen his photo.

He's like God, he's everywhere, even here in the mountains, so far away from everything. He sent them sea salt, brought an end to a long line of mountain cretins—all brains need salt. It took him a while to get here. He was stabbed by shrapnel, maybe a hundred times, and he carries the weight of it in his body. But he is alive. Stronger than poor dead Saint Sebastian.

Soap and water, soap and water.

Live dangerously, il Duce says. He exists to mate, he is a man, but she's heard he plays a violin afterward. He says Liberty is a putrid goddess.

"I am Liberty," Delfina says out loud, as if to him. "I am a goddess." In need of soap and water.

Her cousins cut away the finest, purest fat—the suet—it's like a solid cloud around the kidney. A smelly job, tallow.

They take good care of all the fat, not just the suet. They cut and cleave and saw in the short Winter light. They throw the carcass about on their wooden table. Turn it this way, slump it there. The dreaming pig is in Heaven now, its dear soul risen.

Delfina knew its voice. She knows all the animals' voices as if they are her own children.

Her people slice off hunks to make lardo, white with thin pink stripes, to be salted and peppered and herbed and sealed for two weeks under smooth stone.

Oh, how she loves slipping through their kitchens and into their storerooms—the beams hung with salami, plaits of onions and garlic, slabs of baccalà, their shelves loaded with jars of fat, preserved vegetables, bottles of wine, cheese, drying grapes and herbs, baskets of nuts.

So. Much. Food.

It looks like they'd never go hungry, but they do, or they will, or they have, and they'll never forget it. They remember the Spanish flu. *La Spagnola*. They remember the War in Snow and Ice. They remember the Crash of '29.

She goes hungry sometimes, but she never steals. She sleeps in a stable, or she sleeps in a hut. She has nothing. She wants nothing. She could not steal from the family that is everyone. *CREDERE. OBBEDIRE. COMBATTERE*. That's the new prayer. *Believe, obey, fight*.

But Delfina likes to touch, to smell, to savor. Bury her hands in a bag of rice. Stroke the prosciutto like a man's salty thigh, a soldier in Abyssinia, a war without tears, a war of modern things and new roads. They have a new road here too, further down the valley, beyond the track of stones.

And further down, Delfina has seen trains. And factories.

In the stony light of the mountains, they cut the pig into meat. So red against the snow. This cut, that cut, the other cut, it's a fine art, and Delfina wouldn't want to miss it.

The pig is just a jumble of shapes now, a cathedral of ribs, loin of her loin, chops, ossocollo, coppa, pancetta, piles of fat and skin to make cotechino, the best flesh for mincing into sausages, intestines for the casings, and the well-washed, well-soaked gullet pipe ready to make a big thick salame.

Delfina likes to sit here, on this rock. Her haunches will wear it smooth if she sits here for centuries.

But she won't.

SPRING

Delfina has lasted this long.

A marzo, ogni mato va descalzo.

When March is afoot, every lunatic
goes barefoot.

Here at her bare feet are cyclamens, tiny, tiny, and wild straw-
berries, tiny, tiny, babies that stay babies. Newborn sweet grass.
Wild asparagus pierces through earth in the woods.

The locals, her cousins, the extended family of Italy, are out
looking and picking, vipers or no vipers. They—she—all—love
foraging. Nature gives! In the mountains, they're closer to the sky
than most, though not closer to God. Sometimes Delfina thinks
God is not the Father or the Son but just a spirit, like the Holy
Ghost, in everything. That's blasphemy and the priest would wash
out her mouth with soap and water if he heard her. His soap smells
like flowers, but it tastes like factories.

There are factories in the valleys. Factories in the plains.

War is good for factories.

Her people used to hate war, they always hated it, but now they
can see the point. Fight the Abyssinians. *Faccetta Nera*, they sing as
they march as they sing, as they ban slavery. Little Black Face will
wear a Black Shirt.

Fight Communism.

Did they win the Battle for Grain?

Her cousins have manured their plots, planted vegetables,
checked that the wheat sowed last year before the frosts is sprout-

ing as it should. Nature obeys. *CREDERE. OBBEDIRE. COM-BATTERE*.

What is the Fascist emblem—what is the *fascio*—but a bundle of sticks tied together?

The people are all tied together, blood is thicker than water. That's why, like Nature, they believe, they obey, they fight.

Everywhere Delfina looks in Nature there is fighting. Songbirds fight for territory. Sucklings fight for milk. *The Italian character has to be formed by fighting*.

Beyond the valley, there's a granite peak—is it black or is it blue? Is it even there? Delfina forgets its name, and yet every piece of rock has a name.

Delfina is a mountain girl, and she is forty, or maybe fifty, none of the people know which day she was born, or where—above a shop, or on a pile of straw, one of a litter maybe—nobody's alive who cares or remembers.

Her mother died.

Her father denies her.

They evacuated girls during the war, but they didn't evacuate Delfina. She has no dowry, no assets. She is mad. She slept with soldiers. Who would feed her if they knew? Italian soldiers—she was choosy. She gave them her meat. She is a silkworm feeding and growing, preparing to weave, to be boiled, to die before she can fly.

Delfina feeds off the priest. He never goes hungry. He never touches her because he is filled with the Holy Ghost. She sleeps in his stable, but sometimes she sleeps in a mountain hut, close to the stars and smelling the earth. She likes to wander.

People wander but mountains stay put.

Delfina runs to the woods, to find the wild asparagus before they do, before the shoots get spindly and prickly and impossible to eat. She hits the ground with her stick to ward off vipers, but in truth she's never been bitten by one. Here's a shoot, here's a shoot, shooting up straight, and shooting up curly. Dinner for one. Here's a clump. She gathers them in her dress.

She takes a bundle—a *fascio*—of wild asparagus. She would fry them but she doesn't have a kitchen. Or a frying pan. She doesn't have a father. He's not in the ossuary, not there, in the monumental zone, where the visitors go, where Delfina goes to be appalled at the dead, all the men she didn't meet, all the men she didn't marry, five or six thousand of them, countless bones and teeth and skulls and cranking jaws and holes where eyeballs used to be. Delfina has been there, she put her fingers through the cage and wobbled a tooth, more than one tooth, struggled with this one and that one, twisted and rocked it, tried to pull it out, but a skull holds on tight to its assets, grips like a living man.

Not her, not Delfina. She's losing teeth like a dying man.

Come May, her cousins, the people with land, will plant the corn, one bean plant per six corn plants, the strong upright stalks to hold up the wiry ones, just like people. The beans are grateful. Delfina is grateful.

Delfina is fifty or maybe forty. She doesn't know. She doesn't count. It doesn't matter. The country is rich enough for beans and witches. It is Spring. Nearly Summer. The valleys are green. The valleys are soft. The valleys are hers. And everyone—her people— they all hate war, they always hated war, but now they say that war is right.

SUMMER

Se piove tra lujo e agosto, piove miel, ojo e mosto.

If it rains between July and August, it rains honey,
oil and wine-must.

Summer roses nod under the weight of bees. Irises lean and fall if they're not staked, awkward as antlers. Songbirds, the ones that haven't been eaten, sing with their tiny hearts full and beating. The frogs are fried, a delicacy. And little fish are lifted out from the river's clean and shallow waters. In valleys, the wheat has grown, the people have harvested the wheat, reaped what they have sown, bunched it and piled it up to resist rain in case it falls before threshing time. Straw is itchy. Men and women work in rows, headscarves and buttocks in rows, hot scythes in their hands in rows, hard at it from long before dawn, bellies full of milk and polenta.

The weak wife dies before the days of itchy straw. Delfina's people don't put her in the monumental ossuary with all the heroes. They bury the unfighting one in a white drawer in a white wall in a white cemetery. Delfina's cousins are too busy to mourn, busy with the work, they must make more money, they never want to eat dogs again, they're all too busy to stop still and fall apart like a woman. Delfina is a woman. All things fall apart. She has seen it. She is mad.

They have harvested the corn, straight after the wheat. And the beans, the weak beanstalks grown among the strong cornstalks, now picked and laid out in their pods, on yard stones and hard floors, in huge numbers, like crowds, to dry before Winter. Her people work so hard.

Delfina loves the beans.

She loves the corn.

She loves the cheering crowds.

Her people won the gold medal for soccer, *ORO ALLA PATRIA!* They hate all wars, they've lost their appetite, they hate the Germans but, in the month of August, her people love all the Olympiads in Berlin. *GOLD FOR THE FATHERLAND!*

Delfina hates soccer.

Delfina hates men.

Now it's the hunt for mushrooms. That's what they—her people—do in Summer, as predictable as the trains. They hunt for the one they call *granulato*. They seek out the long-legged brown *ganbarolo*. They stain their hands with the blood of the *sanguinelo*: its orange leg goes yellow when it's cut, then green. They stain their hands black with the slimy *gonfidio*, whose rafters are white. They hunt for the *farinela*, the *munaro*, the bright white one that smells so strongly of flour. Each miller mushroom may be a sign there's a *porcino* nearby. They're like informers—maybe there's a traitor lurking, growing fat. Delfina's people love *porcini*, they go mad for them. When they are in hiding, they're creamy white and lying down, pretending to sleep, sometimes nibbled at by little snails.

Duilio the Blackshirt is coming after Delfina. Her half-not-brother wants her locked up. Sent away. She is the wrong kind of mushroom. He thinks she is poisonous. But she is the *vescia:* a lamp. Bright white and bubbled. And when she gets old—she *is* old—the old *vescia* is a brown balloon. Step on her and she'll explode, sending out a brown cloud of spore-dust everywhere.

Duilio will hunt Delfina down.

She dares him to find her.

She must constantly be on the move. Hide. Stay in the dark. Cover her tracks. Scatter leaves. Walk light-footed, wash in the river so she doesn't smell. She knows she is a disgrace. *Putrid Liberty.* Unwashed and blasphemous.

Here are the tiny frogs, moist and brown among the grasses. Innocent of everything.

Here is a nest of ants in an old stump.

Here rainwater makes a mirror pool in a huge cow pat.

Here is a nest of ants in a huge cow pat.

Here are blue gentians and tiny buttercups. The carpet blooms with stars, it is Delfina's Heaven underfoot.

Before her, the valley rises up like a wall, planted with fruit trees and nut trees, trees for wood and food and fuel and fodder.

But her people remember the time when they had to eat dogs and they curse it, *porca miseria*, they hate themselves for it, *porca, porca, magnagati*—did they eat cats too? She hates war. She hates men. She is mad.

At night the rain on each terracotta pantile makes a song, a tripping up and down of notes on the roof, and in the daytime there are pointing fingers of shadow from the tiles that jut along the eaves— blessed are those who have a roof. But Delfina must escape the places of people. She must return home to the woods with the shyest mushrooms and the silent snakes. The brown striped vipers that love streams and forest clearings and mountain meadows. The nose-horned vipers a meter long. She cradles a fallen pantile like a baby, lichen-scabbed. She drops it.

She abandons her watching rock.

She runs.

AUTUMN

It is Autumn, and Delfina is still alive, so she sings.

> *Per i morti e per i santi, se se veste pì pesanti. Gh'è che porta,*
> *anzi, de sera le mudande de lana vera.*

> For saints and the dead expired, we are more heavily
> attired. Some folk, in evening's cool, wear underpants
> of real wool.

They—Delfina's cousins—they have taken the melancholic wife to the madhouse where she belongs, where she came to belong, though she started off quite differently. The shame of it. The woman is thirty or forty, Delfina doesn't know which, she loses count, something in between. It doesn't matter, she never knew the number. That's two grown men without a wife in one year.

The Fascist despises suicide.

Delfina could have told the girls, *If you marry those boys from our family, this hard-bitten, money-grubbing, runt-hating, cunt-hating family, you'll die*—but they would never have listened.

Here, mothers give their sons more food than their daughters—so their sons will grow up strong and provide for them in old age. Here, fathers side with their sons because they will work for them and earn their keep—

but daughters are just fickle things with wings that fly away to other families. Delfina is a girl without a family.

Now the people from each and every *contrà* are harvesting grapes in the hills and on the plains. Delfina's people make wine. If Delfina had a white ox, she'd yoke it to a cart piled high with barrels of grapes. If she had a cellar or a storeroom, she would keep oak barrels filled with rotting juice pressed by her scaly peeling feet.

Now her cousins and half-cousins lay manure, thick and stinking, on the cleared ground. The dung from the donkeys, the pats from the cows, the droppings harvested from stalls and cages.

Soon her extended family can plant the wheat again, before the frost spins icing across the fields and hardens the earth underfoot. Delfina cannot survive another Winter, not with the blackness of the shirt, not with the skull on the hat, not with the stride, the face, the men, the face. She hates men. She hates war.

Her people pick the plums and cherries, pick the apples and peaches—sweet soft giving Nature! So generous, yet blushing, so yellow and red and purple and pink. Some of her people sail away to the farthest lands, America, Argentina, Australia: all the countries of la Mèrica.

Her people have signed a treaty paper with Germany. Her people hate them for everything from before, a German accent makes them all feel sick, but the Germans can save them from their sins and enemies. The Germans can give them fruits and friendship.

Se son rose, fioriranno. Delfina's priest says so. If they're roses, they will bloom.

But she has run away from the world of people and priests, taken her blackened feet into the darkest corners where the vipers hide, and the slimiest mushrooms.

She sits on rocks. New rocks. She moves every day. No time to stain them with her filth. Mountains stay put, but la Delfina moves like a bat.

Her cousins are eating stewed tripe with polenta, cooked greens while there are tender green things to cook: beans, radicchio, peas ... And mushroom risotto. Gnocchi with meaty sauce that shines on the plate. She has taken fruits from their trees, and somewhere else she found a sausage, the dry sort, the sort that keeps, that's the whole point of that kind of sausage, it doesn't need cooking, the hard meat minced with fat and salt, feeds an army, can travel to warring Africa or warring Spain, fits in a pocket, lasts forever.

Porca, porca. As she chews on the pig's intestine, she apologizes to its soul in Heaven.

Her cousins, the people of the *contrà*, will have oranges at Christmas. She runs out of food. She forages. There are things to eat, raw things and moving things. God's spirit is in all things. Nature gives.

But Delfina hears the armies coming, the trail of men in black shirts marching behind Duilio, and behind, another Duilio, the face, the *fascio*, the skull, another Duilio, too many to count. One Duilio, two, three, four, more, more boots, more emblems, more, more— she always loses the numbers.

Delfina never had money, so she doesn't know how to count.

Here, on this rock, she can see the valleys rising up below her. It is cold, it is always cold, even in Summer it is cold, but this is almost Winter now.

Dighe de sì, dighe de no,	Say yes, say no,
Copa le vecie, le giovani no!	Kill the old women, not
A le giovani on bel grembiale,	the young!
A le vecie el diaolo a spale	To the young, a nice apron,
	To the old, the devil on
	the shoulder

Here, on this rock, today's rock, Delfina sits and sings with the devil upon her shoulder.

He takes her hand in his black hands and turns the knife, shiny as a mirror, this way, and that. This is a novelty—almost exciting. Nobody has led her here with a rope on her muzzle. She wouldn't let that happen. She's mad, but she's not foolish—she's seen them slaughter the pig year after year. They are a superior class of animal, they have power, they have uniforms and gold, they are used to squeals and blood. They are hunting her like mushrooms, like the witch that she is, the black-mouthed whore, the fruit of a straying father.

She weeps for all of Italy, weeps for the things that nearly were, the unripe plums, the fallen peaches, all the eaten songbird songs, the silkworms that spin and die before being able to fly.

The Devil takes her hand, with the butchering knife, into his hand, black as her own hands, and slides it across her throat, neat as cheese, cleaner than water.

1942

FASCIST ERA YEAR XX

Wartime grain

Five children. Maria has five living children and two dead in Heaven. She crosses herself. The shop is quiet enough to pray out loud.

Maria Bruna is playing on the cement floor next to the sacks and barrels. The child is restless but knows not to touch or get into things. She knows the back of Maria's hand. She's two years old, born just when Italy declared war and invaded France, almost to the day, and nobody with a memory wanted a war, nobody, not even soldiers.

Maria thinks of those bones and skulls heaped up in the ossuary. The devastation and the silence. She thinks of the new wars in places far away, so many, one after another—hungry Italians, greedy Germans—and she feels tired.

It's good to have a shop. People always need to eat.

Everyone seems to be thinking about food these days. People need to feed their children, rations or no rations. But another child, another girl . . . Maria feels frayed just thinking about this one. Little Bruna is always under her feet. Whimpering or tugging at Maria's ankles, wanting attention. And she is prone to rashes and

ailments—unlike Amelia, who at fourteen has never had a fever or
a cough.

There are no customers for now, so it's a good time to clean the
shop, despite the heat. Maria likes things clean. She likes working
hard. She has always worked hard. She is forty-four years old and
strong enough to give birth to more children, that's what Mussolini wants, births, many births, that's what he said to all the women
in a speech when he came to Padua, but Maria has had enough
children. She has learned to distract her husband in ways he doesn't
seem to notice: she gets him worried about money, asks him what
happened to his dream of la Mèrica, his ambition to make a fortune
after the First War, before the Second War. She tells him about a
neighbor who's been asking suspicious questions: *Why hasn't Achille
been sent away to fight in France or Africa? Why doesn't he join the Fascist Party?* Or she brings the baby to bed.

She trips over Bruna. *"Bruta canaja!"* she curses. All girls are
trouble. Wherever there is trouble in the world, even when it's
men, there's a female somewhere.

Bruna starts to cry.

Maria picks her up and smudges at the tears, her fingers red and
lined against Bruna's smooth white skin.

"There, there," she says softly, guiltily, but she's feeling impatient. "You've got to be strong." She gives her a piece of sweet
pecorino cheese. "Don't eat it all at once. Make it last. As long as
you can."

It works. Bruna is distracted.

Maria settles her on the floor again and sets about cleaning with
a hemp cloth and water. They have a bore pump here, out back—
it's so much less effort than the well. She uses a dash of vinegar, but
not too much. Everything is dear. She cleans the large wooden
counter where every day she weighs produce in the big brass scales,
takes money, takes coupons, hands over goods—dried beans, prosciutto, precious fat, pasta—her hands wrapping powders and
grains in rough blue sugar-paper, aviator blue, her fingers a flutter
of precise movements guaranteed to prevent even the tiniest spill

of flour or sugar or soda. One spilled granule and the customers would complain.

Maria knows she has to keep the customers happy, but she hates their questions. *Why don't you join the Fascist Party? You'll get special privileges, even good tobacco, not this crap, like smoking potato leaves.* They don't know that Achille is a card-carrying Fascist, has been since the days when Fascism was good, long before the mass subscriptions. But he's no Blackshirt. And he keeps his politics to himself.

Achille and Maria don't take sides. They'll serve anybody—peasants, priests, aristocrats, Fascists, Socialists, Catholics, Anarchists—as long as the customers pay. Money is money, no matter who pays it. To sell is to be like water. Business does not take sides.

Why didn't they send Achille to Greece or Egypt? It's usually a loud-mouth's wife who asks. A Monarchist. Or a teacher.

Maria has to keep them all happy. The Communists are never happy.

Because of his malaria, she answers. *He spent all that time in a military hospital. Months and months in Godforsaken Apulia. Then all the way to Piedmont. They moved him from hospital to hospital. There was more quinine in him than blood.*

Officials are easy. She knows they find all the answers in documents. *He has the documents,* she says. Despite their different loyalties, *carabinieri*, militiamen, prefects, bureaucrats and soldiers are constant in their love of stamps and seals and certificates. They like praise. *It's thanks to all you brave men we got Monfalcone back from the Austrians. Long live Italy!*

She distracts the gossips with feelings and stories. They forget their prying questions with her answers. *He might have died serving his country. He fought the War in Snow and Ice. Thank God that was before we met—I would have died worrying. You should see his scars.*

She wishes he had more scars. She loves that raised white one, like an ant tunnel in his hair. Why doesn't he have more scars? That story with the water and the donkey should have given him more scars.

Someone saw your cousin here in the shop. Did he move down this way to be near you? Maria answers that it's just a coincidence. Duilio lives in Campolongo, but she hardly ever sees him. He buys his groceries elsewhere. *He's a fanatic.*

He came into the shop one day, showing off his fancy new uniform, his holster, his long black boots, his black cap stuck with a silver skull gripping a dagger in its teeth. He spent money like a rich man, keen to impress the other customers. No doubt he did choose the plains to be near Maria, and Edda—he has no other family, except back home.

The serving counter is clean now, and the dark wood almost shines. She has sweat on her brow. She wants Achille to see it. She works hard for him. He is her husband. She must love him until the day she meets God—she prays that it will be Heaven, but she knows it might be Purgatory or Hell.

War is like Hell, she thinks, endless as Hell, and everywhere. And Italy's enemies are everywhere: Abyssinia, Somaliland, Egypt, Albania, Greece, France, Britain, Russia, Mexico, America—even la Mèrica! Never mind Achille's dreams of the New World. In December, when the radio announced the war against America, the village crowd was quiet. It was just a couple of weeks before Christmas. There were no cheers. Everyone has a relative in America, or they dream of emigrating there. Nobody wants to fight Americans. Maria remembers all the goods and animals the Americans gave her family after the Austrians destroyed everything. It was a new start. Nobody likes the Germans. How could Italy get caught up with Germany? Last year Germany saved face for Italy in Greece, and Africa, and Sicily, so everything is tangled together now.

Maria wipes the perspiration off her face. It's hot. She's been thinking and scrubbing hard. Her arms are still strong. She may be middle-aged, but she can lift a man's weight of washing without straining her back, and she can still heave a giant polenta pot onto a fire. Summer is always hot here in the plains, not like in the mountains. The air is breathless, heavy. She wonders if she'll ever get used to it. Mosquitoes from the canals and ditches haunt the evenings. But the crops and fruits ripen without a struggle. She could never grow a fig to sweetness at home.

Bruna has fallen asleep on the floor. She's delicate, poor child. And yet it would be wrong to cosset or coddle a weakling in a war. She needs to be tough to survive.

What if she ends up like Severo's wife? Achille says sometimes, when Bruna coughs or looks too pale.

Maria remembers her sister-in-law Onora, always sickly and taking medicine, going to the sanatorium, shirking the work, eating nothing but bland food—she was so particular—then dead of consumption, just like that, and leaving unmothered children in the world.

Or Vito's wife, Achille says. *You mustn't let her get like that.*

Valeria was so weak she gave herself up to melancholy and went to a madhouse.

More unmothered children in the world. *O, che bela figura!*

Maria pauses to say a prayer for her poor, unlucky, wifeless brothers.

The shop door opens. It is Achille. He looks guilty. Or angry. Like a married man who has been with a woman. She twists the gold band around her ring finger. No. He wouldn't do that. She must trust him. He sowed his wild oats before settling down. He's a good Christian. He even comes to Mass sometimes, which is better than most men. The only men at church are old or crippled, or close to death—

"Where are the children?" He checks the empty shop. "No customers?"

"Primo is out with his friends. And Amelia . . ." Maria pauses at the name. "Maria Amelia, Arsenio and Cecilio are with their cousins, helping with the harvest." She does them in order, starting with the oldest. "In Altavilla. They're there all week. Out from under my feet. But you know that."

He looks distracted, as if he hasn't heard her.

Maria feels the fear start to rise in her. She doesn't want to show it. *War is a word that does not frighten us*, Mussolini said. *Guerra, una parola che non ci fa paura*. But the war makes everyone fearful. She has learned to be stony-faced and composed. "We'll get something back for it. And Rodolfo is our brother-in-law, after all." Maria nudges Bruna with her shoe. "Our baby's here behind the counter, asleep."

Achille stands at the counter like a waiting customer. His face is white and tight.

He's my age, Maria thinks, *and still handsome. How many other women find him handsome? Is that why he can be put off in bed? Or have I lost my looks?* There is war all around, and people get angry, and she just wants to be safe and sound, with God's mercy. She crosses herself. But his frown is deep, he's all bottled up, she can see it, has seen it before. It's what he looks like when he has to hit her.

She searches her heart for something she has done wrong. Women, like children and animals, need to be kept in order, that's how it is, she understands that. He whips a donkey, he belts the children, he hits his wife. That's what some men do. But this time she's done nothing wrong. What on God's Earth has she done wrong? She shouldn't have mentioned Rodolfo. He hates Rodolfo, they argued about business, he even put a curse on Rodolfo, meaner than a gypsy's—but he knew the children were going there for the harvest, and Edda is her sister, her blood.

Achille thumps the counter hard with his fist. The brass scales shudder and tinkle like strange music. The pile of sugar-paper jumps a little. Bottles rattle. Then everything is still. Not Bruna. She bawls.

Maria picks her up and holds her to her chest. Army lorries are rumbling past outside the shop. She doesn't look. She keeps her gaze fixed on the countertop. The world is full of machines and rumbling. The trucks go on forever. The shop windows shake. She's glad she's not pregnant. Will he climb over the counter or walk around behind it? He has never hit her in the shop before. A customer might come in at any moment. He has never hit her in front of anyone, just the children.

"I've been denounced," he says at last.

Maria knows not to say a word. But she wants to ask who has denounced him, and why. She wants to curse. She waits.

"Your cousin warned me," Achille says. "They're going to arrest me, unless I escape."

Maria feels rage rise inside her. Achille's news is worse than a beating. She can cope with a beating. She can't cope without a husband. Five children and a shop and war everywhere and a husband in jail—she can't cope without her brave, strong, resourceful husband.

Bruna's whimpering distracts him. Every child has its uses.

Maria holds her tighter, kisses her forehead, rocks her, jiggles her. But she is looking at Achille. "Quick," she says, moving out from behind the counter.

Will he let me pass?

She rests Bruna on one hip and goes to close the shutters on the shop windows, locks the door. The rumble of army engines tails off. How many this time? It feels like hundreds.

"We're closed—we had an inspection—we were taking inventory—the girl had a fever. Something. Come out the back." Maria doesn't dare look at him. This is the moment. Will he obey her? She's taking charge. With Bruna on her hip, she walks into the storeroom, her shoulders stiffened in case he hits out.

He follows.

She pulls on the light and sits on an unopened sack of rice, rough against her legs. She sets her feet firmly on the floor. "Did anyone see you and Duilio talking?" she asks. Her voice is quieter now, softened by the narrow space, the crates and boxes, the hanging curtains of baccalà.

Achille remains standing. "We hid behind the corn. Left the field two different ways. Why are you worrying about stupid things like that?"

"You can't be too careful. Everything matters." Her heart is beating fast, her heart is strong, but she hates this feeling. "Where could you escape to?" She remembers where mad Delfina lived in the mountains and valleys, everywhere and nowhere, hiding in stalls and stables, hiding in huts, in woods. Mama could leave food for him. A body could live like that for years. Maybe until the war ends. Will the war *ever* end? But mad wandering Delfina, who knew how to hide, who was tough and wild, was found dead as meat on a rock, shameless and homeless, a lesson to anybody.

Achille stamps the floor, again and again. *"Porco can, porca miseria, porca Madona . . ."* He punches at the thirty-kilo wheel of cheese.

Bruna wails.

"Shut up, you stupid girl," he says.

"Or I'll put you outside with the chickens," Maria says.

It works. The child is learning.

"If I escape, and if they catch me, it'll be worse," Achille says. "Hanging, shooting, I don't know—"

"What for?"

"For wasting their time. For running away like a coward. Bad Fascist, bad Fascist. Worse than a bit of black-market grain. Better just to let them arrest me."

"And then what?"

"Porco Dio, I don't know, Maria! All these stupid questions!" He's angry again, but he's not going to hit her. His face is white like a dead man's face.

"So it's about the black market," she says.

Achille nods.

"But you've been a good Fascist for so long—how long?" She knows exactly how many years.

"Nearly half my life."

A Fascist of the first hour, and still it's a secret, almost a lie. "That must count in your favor. And Duilio—"

"Your damned lunatic *squadrista* cousin—"

"He's already warned you. Maybe he can help us, put in a good word or something—"

"What, and say I didn't do it?"

"Find a good reason for you doing it . . . Everyone does what they can to get by—"

"I've been denounced, Maria. Some bastard jealous village spy has—"

There's a clattering at the shop door.

Maria and Achille stop and listen. The door rattles. It sounds like thunder. Bruna doesn't move. The world holds its breath.

Are they here already? Will they take him away?

From outside, beyond the shop, beyond the road, church bells ring the hour.

Maria feels her eyes prickle. She misses the campanile at home. The bells were sweeter. She misses Egidia, her baby sister. But Maria doesn't cry. She is strong. She's no milksop, no weakling, no princess.

There is nobody at the door now, she is sure. Whoever it was has gone away. Maybe it was just a customer.

"Duilio has connections," she says quietly at last. "I know you can't bear him—"

"He's a thug. There's nothing worse."

"He's family."

Summer salvage

MARIA KNOWS THE MILITIAMEN MIGHT COME AT ANY TIME. But she wants everyone to eat together, as they normally do. She wants to gather her family as her father did in the First War, knowing that it might be the last time. She wants a photograph, and at least one last supper, perhaps another last supper the next day, and again the day after. Perhaps many days after. She can't guess when the men will come. She wonders if it's better to know danger in advance, and worry, and prepare for it, or know nothing, and be happy right until the final breath.

She prepares a pack of food: a piece of aged Asiago cheese, today's ration of bread, some plums from the tree, and—for her sister—salt and real coffee. She fills a bottle with water and twists the stopper tight. She checks the anti-shatter paper on the window glass and closes the shutters. The lights are switched off. With her food parcel under her arm, and Bruna on one hip, she locks up the shop from outside, and pockets the keys.

"You closed?" Calvinetto calls out from next door. He's holding a sheaf of polenta-yellow paper. His butcher's apron is bloody enough to make a tasty broth.

Maria nods. "I have to collect the children from Altavilla.

Achille's away." She wonders whether her husband is peering down at her from the bedroom window, through a tiny gap. She restrains herself from looking up. Perhaps he's already moved into the safety of the cellar. But if the men want him, they can find him in no time. They can crowbar the bolt on the shop door. The whole world would see. The back door is easy—if they can make their way through the rabbits and chickens without spoiling their fancy boots. Would they look in the cellar? They might not know it's there.

"Sickness in the family," Maria says.

Calvinetto shakes his head. "Harsh times. I heard workers are fainting in the factories, they're so hungry."

"We'll be back in business tomorrow," she says, willing it to be true.

"You're not taking the bike?"

"It's too hard with the little one. And I'll have three more coming back." *Besides,* she doesn't say, *Achille might need to get away fast.*

It's a long walk to her sister's but, if there's no trouble, Maria can be there and home before dark. She might even get a lift from somebody—a *contadino* with space on his cart, or a soldiers' truck.

She straps Bruna into a bundle on her back. It's too easy, her baby girl weighs almost nothing. But now is not the time to fret. She stuffs the food parcel in with Bruna. She knows the rubber soles on her shoes will be hot, but old tire treads are probably better than crumbly cork, and certainly better than cardboard. She ties on her wide corn-straw hat and starts walking.

The road out of town is mercifully free of busybodies. She passes the bakery. RISPETTATE IL PANE—MUSSOLINI. The old posters are still there, yellowed, but the words are big and black. RESPECT BREAD—MUSSOLINI.

It was last Autumn when they started rationing bread. Only 200 grams per person a day. Cut to 150 grams in early Springtime. It's not enough. *Give us this day our daily bread,* Maria thinks, she prays. She has left her coupons with Achille. Just in case something happens to her on the road.

There's a new poster on the baker's window. It wasn't there this morning. It's a picture of a sly, short man with a black eye mask and a gangster's hat. IL LADRO NERO! LO CONOSCERETE TUTTI. He holds a bulging bag in one hand, money in the other. He casts a big shadow. THE BLACK THIEF! ALL OF YOU WILL KNOW HIM. On the way to Alta-villa, she'll pass the little town of Santa Croce, where it's quiet all day every day, not a sound, not a baby crying, not a kitchen pot clanging, because everyone from Santa Croce is a thief, and they've all been so busy robbing by night, all night, every night, that they must sleep during the day, war or no war. Maria wonders if the people from Santa Croce look like the man in the poster. She won-ders if it was Attilio the baker who denounced Achille. He always smiles in his strange cold way and greets her like an ally.

She passes the last houses of the village. Another poster, stuck to a wall. LA CARTA È ORO. NON SPRECATE. A woman holding on to paper, reusing it, not burning it. PAPER IS GOLD. DON'T WASTE. How much paper is wasted making posters?

Bruna sleeps with the rhythm of walking. The sun is fierce. The heat of cement and stone gives way to a faint breeze off the corn-fields and the damp warmth of roadside ditches. The irrigation water is low. Frogs sing like unsuspecting fools, waiting to be caught and eaten. Insects hover in clouds, unaware of their hunters. The sky is free from enemy planes. After dusk, there will be the special sound of the blackout plane, checking on everyone. At night maybe there will be bombings. Some of the big cities have been bombed. The city people are escaping to the countryside, where the food is, where the bombs have not yet been dropped, where a per-son can keep rabbits. The country feeds the cities. But many people are hungry. Workers are fainting in the factories. So the black mar-ket is necessary. Everyone gets by, the best way they can.

Maria keeps walking. The road is flat. It twists and bends. *Where the pig ran, they made the road.* It's true, Maria thinks. An escaping pig runs this way and that in blind panic. Not she. Not Achille. Is this where Duilio warned her husband? She is walled in by corn-stalks, straight and tall on either side, two meters high and ready to harvest. The corn has been counted, and it will soon be part of the community stockpile, pearl-white maize for the white polenta they like to eat here in the plains, and yellow *granturco*, the corn she knows from the mountains. Human feed. Do they count animal feed too? The officials have calculated everything. It's hard to work around them, though Achille managed it for a while. But at this moment, on this road, there might not be a war on. This might be just another Summer's day in the countryside, and she is walking to visit her dear sister Edda who has done so well for herself with her villa and her farmhands and her stables. Clever Edda. *You've got to study so people don't cheat you.* Rodolfo hardly even works, and he cheated Achille in business. What will Maria tell Edda? The truth—that Achille has been denounced and is hiding like a gypsy in the cellar? Or something else, a better story? *Bela figura.* Her younger sister will look down at her, with pity. The shame of it. Maria keeps walking.

The roadside is edged with grass, and poppies red as blood, and other small flowers, blue and white and yellow. When a wildflower here is picked, it withers in minutes—not like mountain flowers that dry and last forever. Such a difference between the mountains and the plains! The *stella alpina* tucked inside her *Christian Bride* book stayed intact, and the gentian flowers kept their blue for years. Perhaps she will have a long life too, because she's from the mountains and made of strong stuff. That's why Achille married her, and not the delicate, high-heeled Amelia. His parents forbade it. That girl was from weak stock, from a family burdened with sickness and frailty. Like the wives of Severo and Vito—her own brothers didn't listen to Papà. Achille is smarter, he obeyed his parents, it's a good sign, he's honorable. And healthy children are good for all of Italy. How would children have enough to eat with no black market? Without slowing her pace, Maria checks the roadside for edible plants—*pissacan* dandelions, nettles, fennel, herbs—although it's too late in the year, and she knows it. Nearly everything was picked in Springtime.

She hears a train and tries to work out the distance. It's not one of the State trains, but the Vaca Mora, the slow, soot-blackened,

local steam train. Perhaps Achille could escape that way. She imagines him jumping on and hiding with the freight. How far does it
go? Venice isn't far enough, it's not America, but it is on the sea.
Achille can't swim. She imagines him being captured and executed
by men in uniform. Nobody knows how to swim. The entire family
could be drowned in a ditch without too much effort. Duilio spends
his nights around ditches guarding crops and crossroads. He must
oil his smart boots to resist the water.

The uniforms are smart. Il Duce would have employed someone
fine to design such costumes. *A dressmaker or a tailor?* Maria wonders. Every time a uniformed Fascist appears in the shop, ordering
goods or demanding the coupon sheets, she can't help but notice
the cut and the rank and the fabrics. *Orbace*, felted wool, in Winter.
Or Lanital wool, made magically from milk. Fancy braid trims. She
likes sewing, likes the feel of cloth in her hands. The officers let her
examine the stitching, touch their cuffs and hems. And now, with
the heat, they wear Cafioc, made from broom and hemp, and ordinary, real cotton. With Bakelite buttons and wooden ones. They're
dressed for Summer—just like the poor soldiers they sent to snow-
bound Russia.

Bruna is still asleep, and Maria thanks God. What did the Virgin Mary do with her baby Jesus when they were escaping the
armies of Herod? Did Jesus cry? No, He was God even if He was
human, and God knew not to cry, even when He was a baby. And
spiders knew to weave webs. And stars knew to shine. There's hope
for Primo. He's quick to learn, cunning and bold. And he's
handsome—the girls are all after him. He's almost seventeen—too
young to fight—but in just a year he could be called up and killed.
Or mutilated. The thought is unbearable. Perhaps his poor eyesight
will make him exempt. He is the light of her life. They said the war
would be short, and that the banquet would be great, thanks to the
Germans, but it isn't. The banquet! What banquet? Maria crosses
herself and prays for Primo, the rhythm of the words in time with
her footsteps.

She looks up to the big blueness of the sky. There are two swallows high above. If only the family had emigrated to la Mèrica. She thinks of the people who went far away, all the way to Australia: Dal Molin, Rossi, Moro, Marangon, Volpato . . . Calvinetto's cousins, and the tailor's brothers, half of Albarela by all accounts, half of Bierara, every last one of the Visentin family . . . and God knows how many others. Primo could take over the business and make it grow in the New World. Achille has taught him all the important things: money, customers, inventory, risks, deals. *Don't trust anybody.* They could sell Achille's fields, each one edged with mulberry trees for extra income. There's money in silk. And the shop. They have the stash of savings from Achille's unofficial trade without coupons. Primo isn't strong and tall like his father. Achille can carry thirty-kilo bags of sugar hidden beneath his *tabarro* cloak, and his walk is just the same, just as casual as a man with empty hands. Nobody else could pull that off so well. What will she do without him? They could be arresting him right now. She has warned Primo, so he can watch out for his father. What will she tell Edda? And the little ones? So many secrets. Appearances, appearances. *La figura.*

She must speak to Duilio. As soon as she gets back. It's only because of him that Achille has had a warning. Duilio thinks he can do anything because of that death badge on his beret—he's beaten up Anarchists and strikers, left-wing soldiers, people who say unpatriotic things in public, even if they're card-carrying Fascists, anyone who gets in his way, people he doesn't like. She hates the thought of going to him and begging, but he's sure to have some answers. And he's family. He can put in a good word, or alter a document. Or make a deal. She has saved up money of her own, there's no need to tell Achille—but no, Duilio's a fanatic. He hates corruption as much as he hates Communism. He wouldn't take a bribe.

What is the penalty for black-marketing? The poster didn't say. Why hasn't she thought about this before? It could be a month in prison. Achille has the license to run the business. She can cope without him, the shop can be closed—for a month. But it might be more. Two months. What if it's a year? Or a work camp in Germany? They will lose the business. Starve.

Maria is impatient to get to Duilio. She wants to turn around right now. But she must collect the children. She must gather them for one last supper before the family gets broken up. They may never be all together again. Her father gathered everyone for that photograph—Maria is being the father now.

The road is long, too long. The crooked, leaning campanile of Santa Croce is close now. It is silent. The bell-ringer is probably a robber too. Maria is at the four-field crossroads, halfway to Altavilla. A thresher rumbles nearby. She stops to rest. Her feet are hot and sore. She releases Bruna and sits at the edge of the ditch. The water is green with algae, thick as paint. She adjusts Bruna's bonnet and cleans her pale, sticky face. She's a good-natured girl in this heat.

Maria kisses her forehead. *"Carissima,"* she says softly, gratefully, and squeezes her daughter's skinny little arm.

They both drink. And eat. Cheese, bread, plum. They drink more water. And do *pipì* into the ditch, infant first, held hovering, then mother squatting, both scattering the green surface below. Insects hop and skate. A lizard darts across the ditch bank into the stubble.

Wheatfields are precious. Grain is rationed, taken to the stockpile, divided up according to the community's numbers and needs. More of this for old people, more of that for children. How do the officials keep track of each and every gram of food from a field? What passerby is not tempted to pluck something ripe and tasty growing close to the edge? What more than that has Achille done? This is what she must say to Duilio. She must find him.

The threshing machine thuds rhythmically in the eastern field by a farmhouse, separating grain and stalk. Stalks for straw, grain for the stockpile, grain for millers and bakers—perhaps it was Attilio the baker who denounced Achille. Or it could have been Benedetta the station-master's wife. *Don't trust anybody.*

Despite the heat and the time of day, three *contadini* are forking wheatsheaves off a huge haystack into the mouth of the thresher. It's backbreaking work, but not as hard as cutting or bundling or gleaning. There are others on the ground, stacking bales of straw and heaving sacks of grain to the portico. Maria wonders at the hour. They should be indoors, eating lunch or sleeping. She thanks God she works in a shop. At the field's edge, there's a military truck and armed men standing by, on guard. The truck's engine is turned off. The soldiers are smoking.

The farmers will be planting the *cinquantini* next. People will eat anything these days, they'd suck the juice out of a dwarf corn-cob meant for chickens. They'll eat cats and dogs. Not like those SS men in Germany, eating like kings, being cooked for by Teresa from the *osteria*. They took her away, and her eldest daughter who helps her, both to a prison camp. To cook and—God forbid—what else? The children they left behind are in an institutional home, might as well be orphans. And Beppe has let the *osteria* fail. He's becoming a drunkard. Maria is lucky, so far her family is still together, and no-body's a drunk. But there's a stone in her gut as she tells herself silently, over and over, *Achille has been denounced.*

Maria is walking fast now, Bruna is babbling to herself, and the soundless campanile of Santa Croce is behind them. Ahead, there's the long row of poplars that she recognizes as the road to Bierara. Between the trees, there's a convoy of army vehicles, dark and thundering. And after Bierara, the vineyards of Cantinon, a haze of brightest green, with cypresses in faraway lines marking distance, marking time, and blue beyond, the foothills to the mountains. Maria touches her pendant, the tiny Madonna medallion hanging at her neck. It won't be too long before she reaches Altavilla, where her rich younger sister lives.

~

A SHIMMER OF HEAT hangs low in the sky. At the end of a dusty white driveway lined with oleander shrubs in flower, and fenced fields on either side being worked by *contadini*, Edda's house looks like a villa. *In the Palladian style*, she said after moving in. And Maria found out that Palladio made palazzi for aristocrats and her sister was boasting.

The noisy thresher is set up in the courtyard, tall as a house and shuddering, its spinning wheels and pulleys in constant motion. Ragged workers are unloading baskets full of corn off the harvest cart. There are children all around. The young ones are squatting in the sun, peeling off husk leaves and silk beards. The older ones are throwing the stripped cobs into the conveyor running up into the machine. A shuttle rains kernels into boxes. The *scataroni* are shooting out into boxes on the other side.

Edda is nowhere to be seen.

A militiaman in tight-belted khaki leans against the portico walls.

"Mama!" Maria's two boys run out to greet her. Arsenio is the fastest. He's tall for eleven, and long-legged. Cecilio is next, her placid baby boy, just eight. They've both turned black as Arabs since she left them here a week ago.

"We've picked two kinds of beans, and corn, and I poured a pot of *pipì* on an ants' nest!" Arsenio says, jumping up and down.

Maria unbundles Bruna and sets her free, but her little one clasps her by the leg and won't let go. It's too hot for this. She feels caught in her skirts. Maria wants to kick like a cow at milking. Arsenio grins and toes the white dust with his shoe, waiting for her attention. She pats his head. She stoops to kiss Cecilio. He needs her more than the others do. He was born during the Battle for Grain.

Where is Amelia? Inside with Edda, perhaps, working in the kitchen, or spreading out bean pods to dry in the paved yard.

Edda appears at the main door, drying her hands with a towel.

Maria thinks, not for the first time, that she is looking at herself, but prettier than she ever was, and nine years younger.

"Dear sister!" Edda says. "You're days early. We haven't finished."

"You're like a *contessa*," Maria says, embracing her. "All these workers. And in the afternoon heat."

"We can't afford to get caught by rain. And we've only got the thresher for so long before they take it to another farm. Besides, the State runs on its own time." She nods toward the guard. "All *he* has to do is smoke."

"And count."

"Yes, and count. Most of this is going to the stockpile."

L'ammasso. Maria shivers at the word.

"But we do what we have to. We get by."

"You still make a profit," Maria says.

"Rodolfo makes everything work." Edda smiles.

Maria has never told her sister how much Achille hates Rodolfo, how he has put a curse on him. But perhaps she knows anyway. People talk.

"How is Achille?" Edda asks.

"I have news—not here," Maria says. "Children, stay outside, and keep helping. Zia Edda and I have to talk, and then we're going home. Your little sister needs water. Put her in the shade. Find Amelia to look after her."

"She's picking beans," Edda says, as they go into the dark cool of the entrance hall. "So much energy! I wish I was fourteen again."

"She's patient too. I've been thinking she can learn to work silk."

"Don't you want her in the shop?"

"Too many soldiers about. She'd be safer out of sight. And Achille has those mulberry trees past Fraoleto. There's money in silk."

Edda nods. "A trade is as good as a dowry."

They sit at the long wooden table and drink water from fancy decorated glasses.

"Have you got beans at home?" Edda asks. "I'll give you a bag. Shelled."

"And I've got something for you." Maria opens her pack. "Coffee."

"*Surrogato?*"

"No, *caffè-caffè.*"

Edda opens two folds of the paper, closes her eyes and breathes in the perfume. "Where did you get this?"

Maria hasn't told Achille that she helped herself to his secret supplies. She wants to impress her sister. "And here's some salt—but only if you need it."

"Everyone needs salt." Edda strokes the sugar-paper. "And you call *me* the countess. This is better than money. I can give you cream, some veal—all nice and fresh from the ice-chest. We'll have to wrap it up well against the heat outside. And as much corn as you can carry. Those guards won't find out. Now tell me about Achille. Is the malaria back?"

"No, it's worse than that."

~

EDDA'S OX-DRAWN CART, with its special wicker barriers for the corn harvest, takes Maria and her four children home. On the way, they pick up an elderly widow from Bierara and drop her off at the Santa Croce bridge. The driver turns around at the crossroads just outside Fosso, lets them off and waves goodbye.

"It's like being a high-up *gerarca*," Arsenio says, looking proud. "With our own driver."

"Don't be silly," says Amelia. "It's an ox and cart."

"It's better than walking," Maria says. "And *there's* your *gerarca.*"

An expensive car approaches from behind them, its black enamel shining, its white trim spotless in the evening light. It slows as it passes. Inside, there's a glimpse of officer uniforms. Italian and German too. Outside, the smell of proper gasoline, not the fumes of *gas povero* or *alcool.*

Maria wonders if inside this car is the person who denounced her husband. Some of their best customers are high-up officials—they have the money to pay for special goods. She doesn't know what she will say if anyone asks her about the cream she's carrying, or the meat. And the uncounted grain strapped to her children's backs.

She smiles at the car's windows. "Cecilio, wave like a good boy."

He obeys.

All is well. The car purrs past the bakery and continues straight ahead.

Maria holds her breath and keeps walking.

The car slows outside the shop, or at the butcher's next door, no further, she's sure. But then it moves on and round the corner toward the *comune*.

Maria exhales and her dreadful rubber-soled shoes hurt, and she wants to rip them off but nobody goes about barefoot like a gypsy, except a gypsy, and Achille is hiding like a gypsy, or they might have arrested him already, and she hasn't told her children anything about anything, and she hasn't told her own sister half the truth, and Edda doesn't even know that Achille is a Fascist, it's bad for business if people know, and the blackout plane drones above, and it's twilight, another day almost gone, but here is Primo striding up the road to meet them, and his pants and jacket are flapping like sails, and with a son like him everything will be taken care of, she knows it in her bones, and she says a prayer to the Madonna of the Mountains, just to let Her see the gratitude that overflows from her own motherly heart.

~

THE PHOTOGRAPHER ARRANGES THEM at the back of the shop. They pose against the whitewashed wall between the barred windows. Maria and Achille sit on chairs brought down from the kitchen, placed on the dirt path, facing the *orto*. Achille doesn't gaze devotedly at Maria; he doesn't touch her. Not like his first love a long time ago. He sets his face for the camera. He is the head of the family.

The photographer stands between two lines of radicchio. "Eyes this way!" he calls from behind his big folding camera.

Maria crosses her ankles modestly. She looks straight at the camera's eye. Her family is together. Upright. Serious. United.

The photographer's equipment flashes and makes a noise like a trap catching a big bird. Then it is over. Maria lets go of Bruna and Cecilio. The job is done. Her father will be proud. Her family has been gathered, all together, as they might never be again. They are undivided and undamaged, despite this Second World War.

Rabbit stew

WHEN ARE THEY GOING TO COME AND ARREST ACHILLE? Maybe they won't come at all. It could be enough that he's had a warning—if she could only ask Duilio. He's the one person in the world Maria can ask. But his house is locked and shuttered, and at the Casa del Fascio they say he's gone on a mission to the Dolomites. Perhaps he chose his mission on purpose, to be out of the way.

Every conversation, every moment, is sharp and loud and slow. Business is good, but whenever the shop door opens, Maria is terrified.

Primo and Amelia help her at work. Arsenio too.

Achille doesn't know what to do—keep out of public sight, leave town, skulk in the cellar like a criminal, or carry on with his work as usual to show that he has nothing to hide . . . So he stays upstairs and fixes things, he does the accounts, he smokes, he grumbles, he tinkers.

At lunchtime each day, when Maria shuts up shop, Achille comes to the table and the whole family sits together. They say Grace, thanking the Lord for His Providence. Since her return from Altavilla, Maria makes sure they eat better than those SS officers in Germany.

The veal from Altavilla one day.

Bigoli co l'arna.

Bacalà in tocio.

It's a matter of days. Not quite a week. The militiamen arrive before lunch is finished. Today she has cooked meat and greens from her own backyard. Not even the toughest bureaucrat would monitor that. Stewed rabbit with roast potatoes. Braised peas. Bitter greens steamed and dressed with olive oil and wine vinegar. She's used more salt than most people can afford. Achille has seen to that. How will she cope without a husband? The sauce pools on the plate, because she hasn't held back on the oil, but the rabbit must have been hungry—its limbs are rangy and lean.

Achille is still chewing when he stands. He opens the kitchen door and lets them in. They have picked their way through the coops and cages, the *orto*, the droppings, the chickens on the path. They have crept up the stone steps. Three Blackshirts. Badges glinting gold and red. The *fascio* ax. Submachine guns. Two ordinary foot soldiers and an officer. Their uniforms are smart. Their fancy boots are mucky—good. Achille is strong enough to take out all three of them—more—an entire *squadra* by himself.

Maria stands, but she knows not to say a word.

Everyone is quiet, even Primo. Even the little one.

"Montanari, Achille?"

Her husband nods.

Two of them take him by the arms. Now she recognizes them from the shop. She forgets their names—normally she remembers everyone's names.

The other man, with a taller hat, with more emblems, more red and gold on black, reads from a document. He has pocked skin, eyelashes thick and long like a pony's. His accent is from another province. Perhaps they have chosen this one specially because he is a stranger. Even the way he stands is different. He's German. No, from Bolzano, they're as good as German there. No, she can't work it out. He's foreign. What is he saying?

"As the Fascist Montanari Achille, son of Olmo, was denounced to the Judiciary Authority for the acquisition of grain taken from the common store, and suspended from the Party, and investigated for the above, and found guilty of this breach of moral behavior, and violation of true Fascist conduct, according to Article 31 of the Statute of the PNF, I hereby enforce the following disciplinary measures: one, withdrawal of Party Membership, and two, arrest for incarceration in attendance of further justice, with the maximum penalty of death by execution."

Death by execution? Maria slumps into her chair before her legs fail her. She clatters a bowl or a glass on the table and something feels wet on her hand.

The children, none of them move.

"I'll see you soon," Achille says quietly. He looks at Maria, at each and every child. "Or in Heaven."

The men blindfold him and take him away—this time they go through the shop to the front.

Maria suddenly remembers the local men's names. Scopeton. Fratasso. They both have wives.

There's a document on the table. *Partito Nazionale Fascista. Federazione dei Fasci di Combattimento.* A letter, signed by someone, stamped and typed and numbered. *VINCERE* in big capital letters printed across the paper.

L'ammasso. He has stolen from the stockpile, the community store. And the punishment for that is death by execution.

Maria can hear her heart beating loud and fast as a thresher.

Amelia bursts into tears, sobbing into the silence, howling like an animal. "They've taken Papà!" She goes to the front window and presses her face against it. "Papà! Papà! Mama, do something!"

Maria is at the window now, looking down onto the street. The children crowd alongside her. Sniveling and whimpering. Putting oily finger-marks on the glass and the anti-shatter paper. They watch as Achille is shoved into the back of a truck. He doesn't resist. His head is bowed. He's easier than a lamb.

Scopeton always makes jokes about his name and how he'll forever be a little fish in a big world. Fratasso gets extra rations because he has six children. Will they still be her customers at the shop tomorrow? Will she have to close the shop? Who has seen the shameful arrest of her husband? They left by the front, under the façade painted with the shop words GENERI ALIMENTARI, the public way, so anyone could see. For a moment, Maria wonders if Calvinetto is next door, and if he's seen it all.

The vehicle disappears around the corner.

"Where are they taking him?" Amelia cries.

"I don't know," Maria answers.

"I'm the boss now," Primo says at last, adjusting his eyeglasses.

"You're the man of the house," Maria says as she makes herself tall. Her voice is croaking. There's blood on her wrist, she doesn't know where it's from, and it's all mixed up with sauce and squashed peas. She has cut herself. She wipes her hand on her apron. She clears her throat. "You're the man of the house, my dearest boy, but I'm the boss, God knows I am. Now eat your food and shut up. Everyone." *Magnè e tasì.*

They obey.

Graspa co asperula

MARIA SENDS AMELIA WITH A MESSAGE FOR DUILIO. SHE gives her a bundle of used woolen garments for the soldiers overseas. It's good citizenship. It may be noted at the Fascio. Amelia wears a floral blouse made from an old silk scarf. Surely the militiamen won't ask a pretty fourteen-year-old questions about her father.

When Amelia returns, Primo is running the shop, and Maria is on her knees in the *orto*, clearing the last vegetables of weeds, slugs and snails. She gathers them in a pail for the chickens. She wonders when the real food will run out, and people will be driven to eat pests again. To become edible, snails have to be starved for a week, de-slimed with cornmeal, gutted. She hates them. Her fingernails are black and her hands are earth-raw. With no outward show or gesture, she prays to the Madonna of the Mountains: for Amelia's success, for Achille's release, for the war to be over, for emigration.

"He wants you to visit him at his house tonight, after the shop is closed. He says to watch your back. Don't take the bike. Look nice. And don't tell anyone." Amelia's eyes brim with tears. "Will we get Papà back?"

"We'll do our best," Maria says. "Change your blouse and help me here. Then take care of dinner. The boys will need feeding."

Look nice. Will officers be there?

Maria continues with the weeding, but her hands feel clumsy. It was Duilio who warned Achille. It is Duilio who can help her now. Never mind that he's a fanatic. He has influence. He likes to impress people. And he's family. No matter that she never visits him. He will have to understand. She can beg. She can kneel before him, weep if need be. She will promise to hang flags in the shop. She must be woman and man too.

When she closes the back door, she's wearing her Sunday-best dress, even though it's Tuesday and she's not going to Mass. The evening is still warm. She has a basket of food, a gift for her cousin, as cousins do. Nothing in it is unlawful. Her dress is hardly new, but it's made of real Italian silk crepe, olive-colored, and it has quilted shoulder pads. On her lapel is a brooch of flowers she made with recycled felt and wire. Her long hair is brushed back in a plaited bun, a *cocon*, the gray showing in patches at her temples. She's wearing perfume—a touch of violet oil behind each ear, a touch at each wrist. She has scrubbed the *orto* dirt from her fingernails.

The chickens make a racket as she picks her way past them. Calvinetto next door will think there's a fox or a thief about. She looks up at his windows. There's no light, no sign of him. Of course not. It's blackout.

She closes the back gate and checks the road in both directions. There is no one that she can see, and no light but sickly moonlight. She doesn't want to be spotted. What officer will be with Duilio? A *comandante*, or a *centurione*, perhaps. What is her cousin's rank? She should know. He must have got somewhere after all these years. He can't still be a lowly private. She walks carefully around the corner, along the main road. She's not used to heels. Last time was a funeral; before that, a Christening. The road is dark and silent as a nunnery. It's hard to believe that there are people behind these façades—electric light, oil lamps, acetylene lamps, fires, candles.

A couple approaches from the other direction like shadows.

They nod in greeting as they pass. She recognizes them from the shop. They get extra rations for an elderly invalid.

Boys in a straggle, not yet old enough for military service, head toward the darkened *osteria* at the corner.

Don Goffredo emerges from a house—maybe there's been a death. "Bless you, Maria," he says. "Pray for peace."

"Greetings," she replies without slowing her pace.

She passes the church and the school. She passes the cemetery where her dead babies rest. She passes cornfields and vineyards.

There's no *gerarca* car outside Duilio's place, no special vehicle. The *fascio* emblem above his front door catches a glint of moon. He'd have paid good money for that. Anyway, what does he care about money? The Militia Volunteers get all kinds of luxuries.

She raps with her knuckles.

A fox howls somewhere nearby, or it could be a baby.

The door opens. Duilio is holding a candle. He doesn't switch on the electric light. He looks casual without his tunic-jacket. Just his black shirt untucked, loose over his pants. Boots. No tie. No holster. No shoulder belt. But he's wearing a beret with a badge, a hideous silver skull with a dagger clenched in its teeth.

Does he sleep in that? she can't help but wonder, despite her nerves. *He's a madman.*

"Who knows you're here?" he asks, checking the street outside both ways.

"It's quiet as a church," she says. "I've brought you some food."

He softens. "Welcome, cousin."

They kiss. Right cheek, left, right. He's wearing cologne, or he uses fancy soap. He smells of verbena and pine.

"Come in. You're looking nice."

Maria blushes in the gloom. He can't see it. Does he remember that day by the well when he tried to kiss her? Of course he does. And another day, in the forest. Who was watching then? She rejected him twice. She'd wanted to kiss him too, but she was terrified and knew nothing about the world. All she knew was that her virtue was her greatest gift, and she was compelled by God to protect it, for fear of becoming a fallen woman like Eve cast out of Heaven, or one of those girls they send to a house of correction. Duilio sulked for years afterward, never forgave her.

And here he is now, this same cousin, her own blood, gaunt but handsome despite his years of fighting and wars, despite his grief for a wife who died in childbirth, and his years alone since.

"Are the officers here?" Maria asks as he closes the door behind her. The moment she says it, she knows it's a stupid question. She blushes again. This time he can see it.

"There's nobody here," he answers. "Come in. Sit down. You never visit."

She obeys.

His home is a bachelor's place, with none of the warmth of a family. *Fioi e fiori i fà la casa.* Children and flowers make a house a home. His pale face is hollowed by candlelight. There are deep shadows under his lined eyes. He turns on the electric light and the shadows vanish.

"Thank you for warning Achille." She hands him the basket across the table. "Polenta. Quail. Plums from the tree."

"Family is family. But I couldn't stop them from arresting him."

"It gave us time to prepare."

"I thought he might do something stupid and run away. You married beneath you. His father's a drunk. People like that ought to get cleansed."

She remembers Achille's father, stinking of grappa, cursing, lashing out at his wife and children, with the belt, with his fists. The family cowered like kittens around him. But even if Achille hits her sometimes, he is nothing like his father, and he is not a drunk. Maria thanks God that the *contrà* of Sassone is far away now. She writes them letters sometimes, and that is enough.

"Remember that crazy woman who thought she was my sister?"

Maria nods. "La Delfina."

"She did herself in, did you know that?"

Maria shakes her head. "I just heard she was dead."

"She slit her own throat. We were spared the trouble. Mind you, cleansing is glorious and patriotic."

Suicide is a mortal sin, Maria thinks. But perhaps it's not a mortal sin for a madwoman. *If you marry you'll die*, Delfina used to say. But she didn't marry, and she died alone. Why is Duilio talking about her at all?

He stops to peer into the food basket, as if he's looking for something. "And Achille's mother is a simpleton. His entire family— well, you saw them all at close range. No discipline. No brains. A bad example. I don't know how you lived with them."

"Life is hard, cousin," Maria says. It's almost a whisper.

Duilio is lifting out plums now, one by one. "Almighty God, we thank you for all the blessings you have granted us."

Perhaps he's expecting to find money hidden in the basket. There is none.

"What will they do to him?" Maria asks. "What can you do for us?"

Duilio shrugs.

"Everyone's in the black market. Everyone does what they can to get by—"

"I didn't hear you say that, cousin. He's committed one of the worst crimes. A bit of extra flour in the shop here and there, a bit of backstreet bartering, that's one thing. But stealing grain from the common store . . . You think the authorities don't notice a man with all those fields of grain?"

"They're tenanted, he just gets the rent for now."

"Not all of them are tenanted, and you know that. Besides, this is a matter of many, many kilos. It's theft, plain and simple. It's an offense against the whole community. Depriving veterans and poor children. No wonder supplies run out, even though the rations are calculated so carefully! It's an offense against the State, my dear cousin. Your husband has committed a political crime against all of Italy. It's anti-national. Shameful."

Maria nods. Has he asked her here just to humiliate her?

"But I haven't even offered you a drink. A drop of grappa?" He pours two little glasses full. There are herbs floating inside the bottle. "This one is special. With asperula. A taste of home."

It's slightly bitter in her mouth, familiar and warm. She drains her glass.

"It's good, isn't it?" Duilio says. "Makes me feel homesick."

She nods.

"You know the penalty is death?"

She nods.

He pours another two glasses. "I've never seen it happen, execution just for theft. Not yet. He's hardly a Bolshevik. And he did do his bit in the Great War. His record is good. But things are getting tough. The sanctions, the enemy bombings . . . And nobody sees your children in any of the youth organizations. Or at political parades. Our leaders might want to make an example of a thieving father. They could confiscate his property. Or they could send him to a camp, like those barbarian Slavs. There's not a lot you can do for him if that happens."

So it's not too late. She can save her husband.

Duilio drains his glass and wipes his lips. He pulls his cap down at the front, showing more of that silver skull clenching that silver dagger in its silver grin.

"Tell me what I can do," Maria says at last.

"What's that perfume you're wearing?"

She tries to hide her confusion. "Mama made it. Violet."

"Another thing that makes me homesick." Duilio gazes at her. "You know, my mother made the same one. Come closer so I can smell it."

Maria leans forward, holding out her hands, wrists upward. Her heart is kicking like a rabbit. She knows what he wants. He is a man, and he has power. But what can he do to save Achille?

Duilio takes Maria's hands into his, her wrists held together like a prisoner. He inhales her perfume.

"So sweet, my sweet cousin. You've not lost your looks."

Can he feel her pulse? The skin is so fine there, transparent, she can see her veins in blue bundles, one untidy *fascio* just below the surface at each wrist. Her heart beats in her outstretched hands. She tries to keep them still and steady. "I'll do whatever you want," she says, looking him straight in the eye. "But what can you do for my family?"

"I think a few months in prison, that's the least he can do. Then we get him out. Banished from the Party forever. He's a bad Fascist."

Maria can feel her hands trembling.

"You, meanwhile, must sign up. They won't let you run the shop now without a PNF card. It would be radical to assume that your finances, and your morality, are separate from his. To do that would be a special kind of trust. A favor, because of your connection with me. But the conduct of your business would have to be without blemish. Immaculate. Like Maria-Maria!" Duilio looks at her for a response. "Maria Vittoria." Nobody uses her full name anymore. He's still holding her wrists. Lightly. But not letting go. "Whoever denounced you could do it again."

Her arms are getting tired.

"There's a story I like," he continues. "The priest tells this man he has to climb the steps of Monte Berico for penance. That's seven hundred meters going up. He tells him to put five dried beans in each shoe, like little pebbles under the soles of both feet, to cause pain. Later, the priest asks the man, did he do his penance? The man says yes, all seven hundred meters . . ." Duilio chuckles. And waits. "But he cooked the beans first!" The laugh turns into a cough. He doesn't let go of Maria's hands; he turns his head away to cough. "I spend too much time around those damned ditches. Too much dampness. Anyway, I'm sure we can arrange for Achille's beans to be cooked and soft. You know what I'm saying."

Maria nods. He has stopped saying *they*—now it's *we* who can arrange things.

"Can you manage just a few months without a man?"

Maria nods.

Yes.

And then she shakes her head.

No.

She is hating this man, her brute of a cousin, for holding her like this, with her hands outstretched, with her breasts falling forward, for treating her like some fallen woman, but she is gazing at his dark eyes and he is still handsome, his eyes are black, and his black beret has slipped, and the silver skull is grinning, it's too happy, and his skin is smooth and shaven, and he would never hit her, and he has always loved her, and he smells of pine and verbena, and he is clean, and he is favored, and he has the power of the State on his side, and her head is light with grappa, and she hates him, and the way he holds her hands hurts, but the little bird that is her heart beats its wings.

Duilio pulls her toward him and kisses her on the mouth. This time, this time, she knows what to do.

Blessings

Oh, Maria, you are a hen without your fighting cockerel, a mateless bird in a cage. You would pay any price to get a black-market husband out of prison. He is your vine post in this wicked world. You are the weak and wandering vine, saving the strong husband you love and need—

That's what you tell yourself.

You told yourself you'd weep and you'd beg, you'd kneel before your mortal cousin as you kneel before me.

Now you tell yourself you had to do it, there was no choice, there's a war on.

But you lie, even to yourself.

I quake at your deception.

Really you were hot as a goat, as disgraceful as that self-pleasuring witch who used to wander through the contrà with the stains of her hands on her filthy shift.

I am blanched white with disgust.

La Delfina was penniless. Homeless. Shameless.

Everything you don't want to be.

Everything you fear to be.

~

AT THE END OF OCTOBER, the whole of Fosso and the other villages of Campolongo celebrate the twentieth anniversary of the March on Rome. Nobody speaks out or makes a mockery of anything. Nobody discusses the latest bombardment that devastated Milan in naked daylight. The recent photos of Mussolini's pouchy face and worry-white hair are not mentioned. Achille's absence is not mentioned. Not one person complains of hunger, not even Nevoso, the loudmouthed notary. Everyone turns out dressed in their best—*bela figura*—even if that means patched coats. The schoolteachers' sleeves are frayed. Calvinetto has lost his paunch. Beppe from the *osteria* looks like a sorry ghost of himself. Some people wear *zoccoli*, nothing but a clumsy block of wood strapped to their bare feet with leather. Even the soldiers look shabby.

Not the Fascist officers, though. They wear warm black *orbace*, smart coats and tunics, real leather boots. Their wives are dressed in tailored black suits, and silk scarves printed with *fascio* emblems, the word *DUCE* in a scatter-pattern. They are strangers, many of them, some German strangers too. Scopeton is there, and Fratasso, the militiamen who arrested her husband, alongside other customers Maria knows from the shop.

And the Campolongo schoolchildren parade like an army, first the little Sons and Daughters of the She-Wolf, younger than Cecilio, excited and distracted. Then the Balilla—Arsenio at eleven could be right among them—and then the taller, older Avanguardisti boys, flanked by MVSN men who call out the old question: *"A chi la vittoria?"* To whom is victory?

There is only one correct response. A Roman salute and a shout, all the children together. *"A noi!"* To us!

And there is Duilio, Maria's first cousin, the man whose skin she knows, wearing his parade uniform, and calling out that same word, her name, claiming her in public. *"A chi la Vittoria?"*

Only one side can be victorious. Duilio is winning for now.

At Mass, Don Goffredo blesses the flags and banners. He doesn't complain about the men wearing hats in church: tassled fez hats, Alpini caps with their single feathers, death-skull berets. He doesn't seem to mind the daggers and guns and cudgels.

Duilio takes a mysterious object up to the priest, and places it before him, kneeling as he awaits a blessing. The thing is round and ridged, like a big lead weight from bulk-grain scales, painted shiny black. The priest delivers his benediction. Duilio bows and prays.

When he walks past Maria at the end of the pew, he turns to show it to her, proud as a boy who's made his first kill.

"Admire," he whispers. "He sees everything."

She realizes that the thing he's carrying has a profile: Mussolini's forehead and nose and mouth and chin, spun into 360 degrees. It's distasteful, almost profane. Only God sees everything, only God knows everything.

The rosary beads slip out of Amelia's hands and onto the floor with a clatter. She kneels beside Maria to pick them up, blushing at the commotion. She crosses herself.

Duilio has lingered too long. It's not enough that he's a cousin. People will talk. They'll start thinking Maria's a Fascist. They'll know—

She closes her eyes. As he moves on, she pretends to pray. She can't pray. She can't think. She feels the heat of shame rise in her face.

Who in the gathered crowds of young and old knows? Attilio the baker? Lonely Beppe without his Teresa? Benedetta the stationmaster's wife? *Don't trust anybody.* Who has seen Maria go to Duilio, week after week, every week since Achille's arrest? One of her own children? Amelia? Who has spied her in the darkest blackout nights, under the glare of starlight, entering or leaving his *fascio*-adorned door, or slinking home? Who smells the sex on her skin?

Violet oil

WHEN NOVEMBER COMES, IT IS COLD, AS IT OUGHT TO BE.
But after the harsh Winter last year, the coldest time anyone can
remember, this cold is actually frightening.

Everything is frightening now. Noises, laws, news, health,
weather, today, tomorrow . . . Maria feels fear all the time, like a
stone hidden in her belly, or a shadow that won't leave her body, no
matter how hard she tries to leap away from it.

People are hungry. And hunger feeds fear. A thin dog shakes
because the cold goes straight to its bones. A thin dog shakes when
its master gets out the thrashing stick. Same thing. A thin dog
shakes.

It's been three months since Achille's arrest, and three months
make a season, a passing from fruit to rot, or flesh and leaf to bare
bone. Three months without word of her husband's fate, not even
through her cousin.

Duilio says he knows nothing, it's not up to him. He makes
boasts and promises, he tells her to be patient, he shows off his uniforms, but he has less power than he likes to think. Achille's fate is
in the hands of the secret political police.

At home, the bed is cold. There's only one *monega*, so the children take it in turns to heat their beds. When Maria tries to sleep, she shivers. If she could see in the dark, she'd see steam where her breath goes. When she was little, before the wars, the whole family would sit in the stable with the big animals to keep warm at night, the men playing cards, *briscola* and *scopa*, the women crocheting and sewing, everyone singing. Nobody sings now. If she could see herself from Heaven's view, she'd see a solitary middle-aged woman with not enough fat on her, huddled and pressed under the weight of coats and blankets. At least she has coats and blankets. And sometimes little Bruna, soft and innocent, clinging to her for warmth, giving her comfort. She has precious firewood for the next few months—she thanks God for her family in the mountains who sent it to her, crosses herself, touching her forehead, touching the valley between her breasts, each shoulder, with her cold fingers. She thanks God for her children. She has good food for them, because she has a shop. But the shop supplies are low. The rations are never a match for the customers with their endless coupons. *Why's there no butter? What have you done with my share?* She has started to scrape out and sell the fishy salt from the scopeton barrel. *But the children are sick and fainting.* She falls asleep at night, waking and dreaming at the same time. The cold makes her brain swim and drown, and anxieties rise up like ghosts.

She hates herself for thinking selfish thoughts. Her husband is in prison, in Padua or Vicenza, maybe Venice. Duilio doesn't know where they took him after the local police station. Her husband's cell must be stony-cold and full of vermin, he must be shaking like a thin dog. He was always lean, despite his strength. How long is it before muscles waste away? She has heard that there are prison camps in the Veneto. Are the Fascists feeding him properly, the strong man she has fed every day since their wedding? Perhaps they are not feeding him at all.

He should be eating gnocchi with meat sauce. She knows how to make the gnocchi so that they are firm but tender, so that they hold their shape, but give way in the mouth. No cheating with too much flour. The right potatoes: fluffy white inside, yellowish outside.

Skins on for the boiling. Tough hands for the peeling. She has tough hands. She could be cooking him mushroom risotto, one of his favorites. Stirred gently, patiently, no scraping, no mashing, no bruising the rice. Or pasta with beans. It's Winter now, and a man needs food that is filling and warm and made by his faithful wife.

What *are* they feeding him? Kitchen salt to induce agonizing stomach pains? Castor oil to empty out his bowels, reduce him to an empty sack? She's heard about their punishments. She's heard of men staggering home in their own excrement, after a force-feeding of castor oil in the piazza. Foolish men who speak out against the PNF in the middle of a card game, or declare the wrong allegiance in a public place, or make a mockery of Mussolini.

L'APPETITO È IL MIGLIOR CONDIMENTO, his posters say, as if people needed more appetite. GLI OBESI SONO INFELICI—but where are the overweight people who can prove the point about unhappiness? What do the well-fed politicians know about hunger? Are they the unhappy ones? What do they know about cold?

Tonight, Maria is not cold. She is with Duilio. She has come to crave the warmth of his bed and his body. The grappa makes her warm too.

She lies on his bed like a child.

"You know that today is the Feast of the Immaculate Conception?" he says, undressing her, not expecting an answer.

She nods.

He takes off his black beret with its death badge and puts it on her head. "So you've joined the Party at last—what took you so long?" He likes to tease. "You're an independent woman with your own business permit—and where would you be without the shop?"

"With hungrier children," she says. She's thinking he looks thin and hungry too.

Maria is a proper Fascist now, but her children and her customers don't need to know. Her new card says that she belongs to the Fascio Female, which belongs to the Battle Fascio of Campolongo, which belongs to the Federation of Fasci of the Province, which belongs to the National Fascist Party. They are all one big complicated family, tied together by duty and love and fear. *VINCERE*.

Duilio slips off her shoes, peels away her darned stockings, as easy as corn leaves. He unbuttons her dress. His movements are graceful—it's difficult to think of him as a militiaman, despite the uniform that he seems to wear all the time like a fanatic. He's not even a high-up officer—they haven't rewarded him for his loyalty. There's a worm in his heart. He deserves to be shunned. But he smells so good she wants to inhale him, all of him. She wants to consume him. And he can play her now—he knows how to work her body, admire it as a revelation. He breathes in the violet oil at her wrists, caresses her skin like a martyr in ecstasy, eats at her neck, licks at her nipples, at the soft inner sides of her arms like blessed rice-paper, at her waist, at her belly like a plate, at her thighs. He laps her up like ripe fruit, eats and drinks from her, peels her apart, enters her, equals her, makes her forget everything and know only this. Their bodies swim in sweat, slippery as newborn babies, muscular and resilient, then soft as pillows, wet and hot. He shivers. He coughs. His voice is cracked. He tries to hold her close, but he coughs. And then she remembers herself and God and Achille. And she sees this man at her side, the cousin who loves her, the handsome arrogant cousin she reviles, who smells so good she cannot breathe in enough of him, who is sick with some affliction caught in the long damp nights hiding like a savage in the canals and ditches, guarding things and blocking things and shouting things and beating people with his cudgel—and she wonders at how much a woman can loathe a man after sex, and if it was always like this, since Adam and Eve. And she feels the fear again, the constant stone in her gut. Fear of retribution, of getting found out, fear for her family, the curse of hungry poverty, the terrors of Hell.

"When will Achille come out of prison?" she asks. "It's nearly three months now. You said three months."

Duilio doesn't answer. He just coughs and coughs.

Before bombs

TWO DAYS LATER, SCOPETON WALKS INTO THE SHOP LIKE A regular customer, as if he's never arrested anybody. He wears civilian clothes—it's almost impossible to recognize him.

"I'll have some butter," he says, holding out his coupon sheet like any other citizen. "And sugar, lentils, pasta."

Maria stares at his hands. These are the hands that arrested her husband, took him by the arm, pushed him blindfolded down the steps and into a truck. The fingers are stubby and mottled like miniature salami. Smaller hands than her own. She has noticed this before, but she can't remember when. Where has he been since the arrest? He has a wife. There's a steel band on his ring finger. His wife must be the one who usually buys the food. Of course she is. Women get the food. Not too many men do the shopping. Maria wonders which customer is his wife. She should know. It doesn't matter.

"It's a good thing you joined the Party at last," he says. "It was beginning to look bad."

"Please don't tell anyone, I beg you. I've got a business to run," she says.

He makes no sign that he'll comply.

"I can give you the lentils," she says. "And I have some honey. Will that do?"

"Whatever you've got," Scopeton replies. "Actually, I have a message for you from your cousin."

Maria's heart beats so hard it must show through her thick pinafore. She weighs the lentils and pours them into a fold of paper, crimping the edges, swift work, until her pinching fingers meet in the middle, and the contents are sealed in with the last tuck.

"You know they've promoted him?" Scopeton says.

"I didn't know," Maria says.

"He's an *aiutante* now."

The rank is lower than Duilio would like, she knows. But he'll be showing off his new green and gold insignia.

"It's an honor for him, although he can't do much with it," Scopeton continues. "He asked me to tell you he's in the hospital. He has tuberculosis. He can be visited, but you must know that the disease is extremely contagious." Scopeton passes her a note with the address.

Her thoughts are stuck in her mouth. Her hand is shaking as she passes a sticky jar of honey toward this salami-fingered man whose family name is a salted fish. The honey is unfiltered: there are bits of dead bees and honeycomb caught inside. Sugar has crystallized around the lid. Thank God for the bees and their sugar. Thank God for the farmer who sold her the honey. She adds up the prices in her head. She charges the militiaman extra. He pays without seeming to notice.

"It's in your interest to visit him. He has more to tell you— information." Scopeton drums his fingers on the counter, as if he's thinking. But he has said what he came here to say. Now he's just standing there, waiting.

"Thank you," Maria says, because it's what he wants her to say, but she wants to throw curses at him, just like an angry gypsy. "Thank you."

Scopeton takes his goods and salutes before leaving the shop.

~

OH, MARIA, MY CORNERED chicken, you must gird your loins. You must go to your cousin, beg for information, for help, for clemency—he's been promoted.

But he is ill. You fear contagion.

Are you sick?

He caught his punishment in those ditches. He deserved to be punished, just as you do. You've been lying with poison. Licking it up like a dirty dog. I weep to think of your children—they'll be defenseless orphans if you get sick and die.

Are you pregnant?

You can't survive the war, let alone prosper, if you keep having babies. Forty-four years of age, and you're still fertile as a floodplain, rich as compost. And yet you would not commit the mortal sin of murder, the political crime of abortion in the Battle for Births.

You didn't think, my ripe one.

I didn't hear you pray.

You don't even confess properly, you cunning forager of weeds, you slinking she-wolf in lambskin. You keep too many secrets. There's so much deceit in you the priest would die to hear it. You recycle wool, like a good war-girl. You salvage anything you can. But you can't salvage your reputation, not without extreme punishment and repentance, not after these three months of sin.

~

THE COCKERELS HAVE CROWED, the church bells have rung, and Fosso is awake. Maria and Primo open up the shop for the day. She checks the floors and corners for traces of mice. He unfolds the window shutters. He starts sweeping the floor. It's still dark outside.

Maria has been to the baker's and collected the family's pitiful ration of bread for today. Now she stands behind the counter, getting the paperwork in order.

"I'm going to Vicenza this morning," she says without looking up.

"Vicenza?"

Her identity documents are already in her bag, and plenty of cash, just in case. "To see about your father."

Primo stops sweeping. "Is there news? We don't even know where he is."

"Amelia called out in her sleep the other night. She was dreaming about Saint Anthony." Maria crosses herself, for the saint and for the lie. "Your father is not lost. We can find out where he is."

Before Primo can ask more questions, she says: "I won't have time to mop the floor or the steps. You can do it today. Or you can ask Amelia. Use just enough bleach, not too much."

"Do you have an appointment with someone?"

Maria nods. "An official."

"I'll come with you." He's being the man of the house. Her blessed boy.

She doesn't want him to go with her. She doesn't want to tell him that she's going to the hospital, where Duilio is, not to a government office or a prison. "Your brothers and sisters need you. I'm asking you to look after them."

"I should go instead of you. It's dangerous."

"No," she says, firmly enough that he won't argue. "Anyone could come into the shop, any man, anytime. Think of Amelia. We need a man here."

Primo doesn't know what to say, she can see it in his face.

"All this," she adds, waving her hand and looking about her, "we need to keep it safe."

The back door opens and Arsenio edges in, then Cecilio. They're carrying something weighty. It's Bruna hidden in a bedsheet strung between the two boys like a hammock. Cecilio's end of the load is dragging.

Arsenio grins at Maria. "This is our infantryman, wounded in Africa."

"We're stretcher-bearers!" says Cecilio proudly.

Little Bruna laughs and wriggles inside the sheet.

"The soldier is dying," Arsenio says, shaking the load as if it's wet washing.

Cecilio loses his grip.

"Get out of here," Primo says. "I'm talking to Mama."

Arsenio lets little Bruna drop to the floor. She sits in the middle of the cloth, startled, blinking.

Maria stamps her foot. "Why isn't Amelia looking after you?"

Arsenio shrugs. Cecilio shrugs.

"Go outside and see to the animals," Primo says. "I don't want to see your faces again until you've done the water and the food." He shoos them both away with the broom. "*And* the mucking out."

The boys frown and fidget for a moment before running off.

Bruna struggles to free herself but gets caught in folds of linen. She's about to cry.

Maria gathers her up, bedsheet and all. Her baby girl feels tiny in her arms. "Don't cry," she says. "He wasn't cross at you."

She takes the bundle upstairs to Amelia.

~

MARIA GOES TO THE hospital in Vicenza. Getting to the city is an expedition—it feels as far away as Rome, it might as well be Austria, or Africa—but it's only a matter of kilometers.

She walks. Past bedraggled Winter *orti*, cut cabbage clumps, ragged chard, red radicchio under cover.

She catches a train. She sees ditches and canals in every direction. Leafless lines of white willow, hazelnut, mulberry, poplar. The silver-green of olive leaves, bare black vines and more vines, cypresses and yews, ivy, the glossy leaves of magnolia—all inedible. She sees rotten black almond pods clinging to the top of one tree, then a solitary pomegranate fruit, fiery red, extravagantly unpicked—it must be for luck. She remembers places. She sees the distant gray-brown wall of mountain against the sky. Beyond that, the invisible peaks where she grew up in granite and woodsmoke. She and her cousin.

Maria and Duilio.

She walks. She has no child on her back. She carries her PNF card. It gives her privileges. Checkpoints are easy. The soldiers and the militiamen love her card. They think that she *is* her card. She looks for Duilio in their faces. She's distracted by their uniforms. Their uniforms make them all look like brothers, cousins, lovers.

Vicenza hasn't been bombed to dust, but it could happen any day. They're bombing all the cities. It's just a matter of time. Those air-raid sirens and refuges aren't for nothing. There are warning posters everywhere telling people what to do.

When at last she sees Duilio, it is through a mask and a screen. He wears a white shirt. He stares at her with wild black eyes. He looks frightened.

Not like her Achille.

And yet he looks less broken than she'd imagined, less deathly. Apart from the bloodstained bandage on his head, he almost looks well. She's disappointed. She wants him dead. The thought shocks her. Then it's guilt she feels, and shame. Why does he have a wound on his head? Did he fall or faint? She thinks she wants to weep. But she never was one to cry. She barely wept when her babies died. There was no time. There was too much work to do.

"I knew you'd come," Duilio says. His voice is cracked.

"I had to."

He smiles, almost boyish. "We'll be together when I get out."

He coughs and grabs for his handkerchief. His black eyes are panicky. His white shirt is spattered red.

She doesn't know why she wants to weep now. She doesn't know what she wants, or wanted, with this shadowed man she obeys. She couldn't have married him without a special permit from the vicariate in Venice. He is her first cousin. He has gone up in the world, so he has power, and yet he's mortally ill—are the two things connected? She's thinking so hard these days it gives her headaches. She's not getting enough salt. That makes headaches.

Duilio whispers, "I've seen Achille."

She can't speak. It's as if she has been hit in her gut.

"I've been promoted. I think I can save him." Duilio's gaze is searching. "Is that what you want?"

It's why she has come here. She nods slowly. She begs him with her eyes.

"It would be my gift," he says. He coughs. "If you promise yourself to me."

Maria's heart tightens, stops beating, turns to stone. She holds her hands in prayer as she looks at him. She remembers to breathe, summons up her voice. "I promise."

"They will execute him if you disappoint me."

"I won't disappoint you."

He grins. "When I get out . . ."

"When you get out." She strains to smile. She stares at Duilio with love and hate in her face. She can see the bones beneath his skin. She tries to pray that he will save Achille. But her head is a confusion of words.

She leaves, not knowing what he will do, wanting him to die.

Winter salvage

"I SAW YOU AT THE CHECKPOINT YESTERDAY," THE NOTARY'S wife says. She's standing at the counter in the shop, hand out-stretched, armed with coupons.

Maria still doesn't have the goods her customer was entitled to buy last week, or last month. This kind of shortage happens regularly now. It's all very well having rations, but the coupons don't match the supplies. *That's why the black market is necessary*, Achille would say. *That's why the black market is an evil*, Duilio would say.

Which checkpoint? And why is Nevoso's wife talking about checkpoints anyway? Perhaps she has pieced two and two together—she suspects Maria of adultery. Or she saw her PNF card—depending on her loyalties, this woman could be after Maria's blood. Or perhaps she is simply a sower of discord.

Maria gazes hard at her. The woman's mouth is pinched like a badly darned hole, her eyes are narrow, she's the sort of person who is envious in her bones, who covets her neighbor's goods. But Maria knows to be friendly to all customers—everyone, no matter which side they're on. And only God in Heaven can know which side will win.

"Which checkpoint was that?" Maria says, light as a butterfly.

"Between here and the city. Ventana. By the bridge. You know where I mean. You have business in the city?"

"Times are tough," Maria says. It's her all-purpose response to any difficult talk. "We have to travel—but we're still out of flour, I'm sorry. I have some unrationed goods, if you're interested."

"They let you through fast."

Maria wonders whether to answer. "You know what men are like with not enough to do, and a woman on her own—"

"And your husband, where has he gone? I haven't seen him since . . . since . . ."

Everyone knows that Achille was arrested. Calvinetto next door must have seen the militiamen. Others must have seen too. The men went out the front way, through the shop, to the main street, on purpose. Achille has been away for three months. It's been a quarter of a year with an impassive face, without a husband. From Summer through Autumn, a season's worth of hours and days, breaking God's Commandment in the dark of blackout.

"Times are tough," Maria says again, at last. "You know what happens, you say the wrong thing to the wrong person, and you have to go to Confession, even if you're a law-abiding person—as *you* are. It was a mistake, and they'll see that soon enough. My husband is like an oak. He's strong and good. Everyone in Fosso knows it. And beyond. Further than Campolongo. He'll be coming home soon. The children will be . . ." Maria doesn't finish what she's saying. Amelia will be overjoyed.

The woman's thin mouth is working, as if she's chewing gristle.

Maria must keep her happy. "I'll give you some firewood from the mountains. Half price for your loyalty—but don't tell everyone. My brother only had so much. You know, I've heard people are stealing vine posts to burn. We all have to forage, but it's shocking, isn't it?"

The notary's wife doesn't know what to say. She has forgotten about checkpoints. She's tempted by the special deal.

Winter is here. The fruit is well and truly finished. The grapes and chestnuts have been harvested. The wheat has already been sown by those who have wheat and fields to sow. The frosts have started. Any time now, snow and ice will grip Fosso more thoroughly than a few checkpoints here and there. The people who are already hungry will fall prey to the cold.

"How much for the firewood?" the notary's wife asks.

"Let me fetch some for you." Maria knows that she has won this little battle. She is the one with the shop.

~

IT IS NOT CHANCE that the notary's meddling wife should see the shopkeeper's wife just at the moment she clears the Ventana checkpoint. Maria has listened to parables. God is Destiny. God knows. He holds the secrets and the purpose of war, sorrow, everything, even when mortals are confounded by mystery and unknowing.

It is not chance that Duilio should fall mortally ill, and now. This too must be the work of God. So the spies and gossips of Fosso will come to know that good Maria was tending to an ailing cousin, a man with no other family here in the plains. That's why she has visited him so often these last few months. Even though he is known to be a thug. She was doing her Christian duty, that's all. Familial responsibility. This is her exoneration, her way out in Confession, her defense with Achille.

Will the Blackshirt set the black marketer free? She convinces herself that she saw clemency in his eyes. She prays for it to be so. Duilio loves her in his way. But she knows that it will be like a game for him, yes or no, a flip of a coin, because he has the power. He has the power and he likes to show it. It makes no difference that he's facing death.

She wonders how her husband will be if he returns—when he returns. Like a lizard without a tail. Or fierce as a bull. People have been talking, of course they have—he's a man who got arrested for cheating the common store. *Che figura!* And yet if he avoids execution . . . nothing can be more important than that.

But the shop looks empty. The customers are complaining, not getting their rations. There can be no black-market trade to make money flow now. Still, there are small distracting signs of luxury at home—*caffè-caffè*, a new coat—thanks to Duilio.

Maria imagines her husband walking home all the way from a prison in a city—she doesn't know which city, she doesn't know which road, or how long, and she doesn't want to know. She is afraid.

~

AFTER SHUTTING UP SHOP in the evening, Maria heads off to Duilio's place. It's dark outside, but it's earlier than her usual visit. There are people about. It will be Christmas soon—a year since war was declared against America. Tonight she is not wearing her good shoes or her Sunday-best dress. No violet oil. She doesn't care. And she doesn't care who sees her. She walks fast. She strides.

When she reaches his house, she can't help but look up at the *fascio*. She always does. To check that it's there. Like a sign. Like a plague-cross painted in blood, or the altar-light showing that God is home. She's had a key for more than two months now. She unlocks the door and goes in. The place is bitterly cold, even though it's only been four days since he left.

When she reaches his kitchen, she turns on the light. There's that hideous black head of Mussolini with its endless profile facing all directions. She can't even turn it to look away. *He sees everything.* She finds a slab of speck prosciutto, half a kilo of grana cheese, two lemons, a bottle of grappa with sprigs of mountain herbs floating inside, precious *etti* of salt, real coffee, butter. He has his comforts, but he's not rich. A *comandante* would have more, and better. She piles everything onto the kitchen table.

In his bedroom, there are uniforms—they can stay. There are toiletries—shaving soap, cologne. She opens the bottle. It smells like him but sharper, untempered by his skin. She sinks onto his bed and steadies herself. She could take the cologne with her as a memento, but what if Achille should find it—use it? She stoppers the bottle and puts it on the floor. She lies down, presses her face into Duilio's pillow, smells him, and smells herself there, stale traces of their perfumes mixed together, verbena and violet, their sweat and sex, comforting, warm. And then she sees stains of blood on his bed linen, the balled-up handkerchiefs under his pillow. Is this her moment of damnation? Has she just breathed in the greedy spores of TB? Only God can know.

She must act fast. She gathers his socks, his vests and undergarments. A pair of shoes—they'll be too big for Primo, too small for Achille, but Arsenio will grow into them someday, he's already tall. Decent leather. Soles as good as new. She can barter them if need be. Did they take her cousin to the hospital in his fancy boots? No, here they are, waxed hard as wood. And his death-cap. For the first time, she sees the grinning skull as the image of Duilio's own death. And here's his rucksack.

She shakes it out and fills it with his shoes and underclothes, then the food from the kitchen, his half-used hand soap, ration cards, coins. She runs back to his bedroom and opens every drawer until she finds his box of documents.

Here is his marriage certificate. Here, the newlyweds' photo. So young, but he was frowning even then. And here, a photo of his dead wife and baby, both in bonnets and lace-edged dresses, laid out in a single coffin, with hands composed in prayer, smiling stretched wax smiles. And here, a picture of his father—could Zio have sired that witch Delfina? It's an unbearable thought. And here, a picture of Zia Luigia, scowling as much as Maria's own mother ever did. Mama is still alive. Maria crosses herself. At the bottom of the box she finds the two engraved steel rings that symbolize Duilio's marriage and his faithfulness to the Fascist Party. *ORO ALLA PATRIA*. He used to wear both rings. He hasn't been wearing them. Since when? Stupid fool. His two gold wedding rings were worth so much more.

At last, something worth taking: some proper money. She packs the bills into the bag without counting.

There is a war on. She is a scavenger, a forager, so be it. *The Ital-*

ian character has to be formed through fighting. She is not a thief. She's not chopping down big old mulberry trees for corn, or thinning flour with sawdust, or stealing posts from vineyards to burn. And she's not taking supplies from the stockpile. The angels in Heaven understand. Family is family. And Duilio, Maria feels it in her bones, is never coming back to Fosso, or to anyone.

Meat extract

THE SHOP IS CLOSED. MARIA IS DOING THE RATION-BOOK WORK by candlelight, gluing the coupons she has collected from customers onto large sheets of paper for the authorities. Primo is out, but the other children are upstairs.

It is Tuesday, a week to the day since the Feast of the Immaculate Conception. So much has changed in this one week. The world is like that. Fortuna's Wheel painted on the church wall has the man at the top sitting smug on his throne like a king, but the same man at the bottom is falling off toward the jaws of an infernal monster. It might be a picture of war. First one side, and talk of conquest, then another side. Mussolini might win, the others might win. *A chi la vittoria? A noi.* This is a politician's prayer, not a certainty. It's as real as emigration to la Mèrica, or getting rich, or finding a perfect husband.

She senses Achille before she properly sees him. He's at the edge of her vision beyond the bars on the shop window. He's in the cold darkness outside. Her stomach knots. She can't look. She pretends to be deep in her work, to give herself time, just a few more moments. She wants him back, she begged Duilio to save him, she has hoped for this happy event, prepared herself for it, but now it feels as if her husband has returned to catch her out. She stares into the shop, to make sure everything is in order, but the candlelight doesn't reach into the shadows.

Achille is peering in through a gap in the blackout paper. She thinks she can see his eyes. Her husband raps on the window glass. The noise is shocking in her head. She crosses herself. She searches for the keys and drops them.

She goes to the shop door. She fumbles with the keys. She knows what to say about Duilio. She has been visiting him because he is sick. He's a bad man, but he's dying.

She has trouble with the bolt. She lets Achille in.

He's wearing a scarf on his head like an old woman. He pulls it off. His head has been shaved to stubble.

Maria bolts the door and folds out the shutters.

"They should have been closed," he says.

"Yes, yes, I'm sorry." She clasps her hands in prayer. "You're here!"

He's thinner, wearing *zoccoli*, someone else's coat, dirty as a tramp's. There are bruises on his face and scalp, scabbed cuts, swollen bumps. Deep shadows under his eyes. The old ant-tunnel scar is exposed.

She embraces him, but he flinches and pushes her away.

"Did they torture you?" she says. Her voice is a shriek. "How did you get here?"

He studies her. "Is that how you greet me?"

"I thought I would die without you—"

"But you didn't. In fact, you're looking well. Fatter. Happier."

"What's the matter? Is your malaria back? Did they torture you? What can I get for you? Some broth? Grappa? Polenta? They hurt you—your nice thick hair." She goes to touch his head, but he recoils.

"You're hysterical."

"You're here! The children—"

"What about the children?"

She takes her time to draw breath. She has provoked him. Too many words in a hurry, too many questions. He doesn't want her to touch him. "The children will be overjoyed to see you—"

"What did you do to get me out of prison?"

They're standing in the middle of the shop. He smells smoky and sour, like someone else, a foreigner, a stranger. She can't imagine embracing him at all now. She doesn't know what to say. Did she get him out of prison? No. She is powerless. Duilio has that power. She asked Duilio. But she doesn't want to say her cousin's name.

"I did what I could," she says slowly, quietly.

"Tell me what you did."

"Nothing—I worked hard—I didn't know what to do."

"You did nothing?"

"I did what I could," she repeats. It sounds like an apology or an excuse.

"I saw Nevoso's wife just outside Fosso."

Maria stiffens. "She's a troublemaker. You know not to give the time of day to people like her. You're smarter than that."

"She said she saw you . . ." Achille is almost unable to get the words out of his mouth. What did they do to him in prison? He's red in the face, teeth gritted, eyes watering. "Where were you going alone, dressed up and—"

"I've kept the shop going. We still have a business—"

"On its last legs—"

"Others are worse off. You should see—"

"And they took away my permit. But you won't answer me, and that says everything. What were you doing with that lunatic—that bastard—when I was—"

"You mean my cousin?"

Achille flexes his fist. "I should have killed him."

"I visited him because he's sick, he could be dying, he's family, I was doing my duty."

"He said that you—"

"When did you see him?" She can't work it out. Duilio was too ill to go anywhere. Unless he went to the prison before. The prison must be in Vicenza. "Did he come to save you?"

"No, Maria. He came to jeer at me." Achille's rage is working up into his muscles.

She can hardly breathe. She was in bed with Duilio last Tuesday. He was in the hospital on Friday. Earlier. What did he say? Enough for Achille to feel murderous.

"He wasn't unwell, Maria. He—"

"Whatever he said, it's not true."

Achille stares at his hand. "But I haven't told you what came out of his filthy mouth." He looks up. His face is white now, his breathing is heavy. He raises his hand to hit her.

"Don't you dare." Primo is at the back door. He's taking off his glasses. "I'll kill you first, I swear I will."

Achille swings around to face his son. His arm is still raised.

Maria edges away.

Primo lifts his fists like a boxer. "I mean it. I mean it." He's shorter, and he's not a fighting man, but he's puffed up with a rage big enough to match his father's. "You touch her now, you touch her one more time—ever—and I'll kill you. God knows I will."

Achille roars and runs at his son.

They set upon each other, limbs thrashing, a dreadful quiet in between the hitting as they clutch and thrust at each other's arms and chins, and grunt, and fall, and roll, and hit out again, heavy as hams.

"Stop it!" Maria cries out. She deserves to be beaten. She is guilty. "Stop!" She can't bear the thought of Primo's beautiful face being broken or scarred. He's been safe until now. God forbid that his own father should wound him. *"Basta!"*

But the men are caught in a wrestle, and Primo suddenly punches his father hard in the face, and there is a shocking spray of red from his nose, and now Primo is quiet, and Achille's eyes are squinty and leaking, and both men are motionless, although their chests move up and down with deep breaths, and they stare at each other with panicky eyes.

Achille clutches at his bloody face and almost stands, stumbles, then manages to stand upright. Without speaking or looking at anyone, he makes his way to the storeroom and disappears into the gloom. There are drops of blood on the floor, thick and shiny.

Primo gets up, carefully wipes his knuckles, checks for rips in his shirt and pants. He is unscathed. Even his glasses are unbroken.

Maria and Primo gaze at each other. Stunned.

Dear, dear Primo! There are tears in his eyes, angry and remorseful. Her boldest and best. He has stepped in like a guardian angel to protect her.

But what now? She hears groans, horrifying and strange; she's never heard such sounds before, and it's all her fault, and the groaning doesn't stop, and Achille is sobbing in the darkness of the cellar.

Maria wants to protect him, and hold him, and feed him, and make him whole again, her man, her lizard without a tail. But she doesn't move. She can't move.

Nobody moves, until at last Achille's cries die down. It is minutes or hours.

Maria stoops with a rag in her hand and rubs at the drops of blood, spitting at the floor to clean each spot. The color clings. Blood is stubborn. She follows the trail, bending over like a gleaner gathering grain. It would be easier to kneel, but she must be careful of her clothes.

At the storeroom entrance, she stands up straight. She spits and wipes her hands clean, but they feel sticky. She walks into the gloom, past the hanging baccalà, and stares past the open trapdoor into the cellar where she can just make out Achille, the man of the house, a shivering shadow halfway down the steps, a foul-smelling body in someone else's coat. He is nothing more than a raw baby boy curled up below her feet.

Primo is at her side now, holding a lamp. The baccalà throws strange shadows on the storeroom walls, like tattered ghosts. "Come on, Papà," he says. "Time to come home."

Maria and Primo take Achille by the arms and help him upstairs. They both know they'll say nothing to the children about the fight. And Maria knows that she'll say nothing about Duilio to anyone, not even the priest.

She knows, too, that as long as Primo is nearby, her husband will not hit her again. Achille won't—can't—be in charge of the shop, he has no *tessera*. She decides, as they stumble up the outside steps, gasping at the ice-hard cold of the Winter night, exhausted now, that she will not sleep in the same bed with him again.

~

AMELIA DOES NOT RUN across the room to embrace her father. She remains seated by the woodstove, darning. She has put Bruna and the other children to bed. The kitchen is spotless. No doubt she has heard the noise from the shop. She may have tiptoed down the steps to see what was happening.

"Look what they did to him," Primo says. "Get up, will you, give us a hand. Is there hot water? Something to clean him up."

"Papà," Amelia says, as if her father is dead, not a saved man. "We missed you." There are the beginnings of tears in her eyes. Slowly, she puts down her sewing and fills a big bowl with hot water from the stove. She picks up the soap, Duilio's half-used olive-oil soap. She dips a cloth into the water. "Let me wash your face."

Achille is like Lazarus, stinking, hollowed, returned from the dead after three long months. Maria watches as her daughter does her duty, patiently swabbing his blood, wiping his swollen nose, cleaning his bloodshot eyes, scrubbing the grime off his neck. Amelia doesn't seem to mind the blood. She doesn't seem to notice when her father winces. She might be embroidering, or plucking a bird.

The bedroom door opens, and little Bruna, drowsy and shivering, toddles into the kitchen. "Papà!"

"Get back to bed so you stay warm," Maria says.

"I'm exhausted," Primo says as he leaves. "Mama, you get some rest. Papà, we'll talk business tomorrow."

Maria mixes a teaspoon of meat extract with hot water in a cup and offers it to Achille. "Here," she says. "You need to build your strength."

Amelia moves out of the way and packs up her sewing work.

Achille drinks his broth, holding the cup with dirty, bruised hands.

"Amelia, you come and sleep with me now," Maria says. "I'm up with the chickens tomorrow."

"I moved the *monega* to your bed when I put the boys to sleep. I added more coals, but it might have gone cold by now."

"It'll be warm enough. Your father needs to wash and rest. He can sleep here by the stove and heat his bones."

Achille says nothing.

~

OH, MARIA, HUSBANDS DON'T grow on trees, and they don't grow in incestuous beds.

Your husband is free.

Your cousin is in the hospital.

The two things are connected. You know it's no coincidence, you receptacle of men.

You love both men, you poor, unfortunate, stained child.

You hate them both.

Your husband has escaped death, but he is like a lizard that has lost its tail. You've seen the bloody stump on a lizard where its tail used to be. That's how they get away. They're never the same afterward.

Your cousin has honored his promise to you. He has given you a husband—for now. You have promised something in return. Duilio will not forget. He's not the kind that forgets.

I can see your frightened beseeching face, even here in the deepest dark of night where you struggle to see me. But I have no answers.

Cossack boot

BENEDETTA THE STATION-MASTER'S WIFE COMES INTO THE shop with a basket on one arm. She walks slowly. Her legs are bloated. Her hands are swollen too, and reddened. But her eyes shine. She always has news.

"We'll be getting the refugees soon," she says, as if she and Maria have already started a conversation. "The cities are no place for children now. They're sending the little ones everywhere, from Genoa, Turin, Milan, away from the bomb-sites, south and east, everywhere."

"Even here to Fosso?" Maria asks.

"Just you wait," says Benedetta. "And I'll be the first to see them coming off the train. They're looking for anyone with space. The factory owners, the *signori* with a villa or two, the bosses, they've all got plenty to spare, haven't they? And Beppe at the *osteria* with half his family gone. And the refuge in town. Come to think of it, even me, I've got a room and a stable. Better children than soldiers or spies. They're smaller. They eat less. Speaking of eating . . ." She gazes blankly around the shop. "Every time I come in here, I wonder how long before we'll be eating cats and dogs. Mind you, the posters say not to eat cats."

"We need them to eat the mice." Maria is reminded of the other war. Cats and dogs. Spanish flu. "Times are tough," she says, sick of hearing herself say it.

"Calvinetto was talking about turning his hand to lizards and squirrels. But he's a butcher, not a hunter. There's always the frogs, if you can catch them." Benedetta snorts.

"Not much meat on them." Maria pinches her own thumb. "But a delicacy. You just need the butter to fry them. Or a nice sauce. You can ask one of those city children to do the catching. They'll think it's a game."

Maria surveys her shop. She sees the gaps where once there were fat sacks and full barrels, and bags stuffed with real things, not substitutes. But even if stocks are low there's still homegrown and bartered produce from Autumn: nuts, dried mushrooms, preserved fruit, dried beans hard enough for a penitent to put in his shoes. There's wine in the cellar. Bottled tomato passata. And some manufactured goods: local cheese, baccalà, chicory powder, artificial sugar. There are no imports—it's been years since the luxury of imports, except for goods from the lost colonies. There's Abyssinian red tea, which isn't tea at all. And there's Caffeol, which isn't coffee. If there's a siege, and no customers, she has enough to feed her family and survive the Winter. If there are bombs, the family can hide with the food in the cellar.

"I brought this for you," Benedetta says. "I found it on the tracks just by the crossing. I don't know if some child threw it out of a train window, or what."

Maria wonders how long Benedetta has been standing there like that, holding a doll out at her.

"Do you want to barter it?" Maria asks. She will say no to this particular offer. It's not useful or edible.

"No, I mean, for your dear girl," Benedetta says. "It's so sweet— look at his eyes."

The doll has big brown side-glancing eyes that look moist, as if they've just been painted.

"Amelia's too old for that kind of thing, she's fourteen and work-ing now—"

"I meant the little one."

"Bruna?"

"All she's known is war. I thought—it's nearly Christmas, it came as a gift to me, it might have fallen out of the sky . . ." Bene-detta is still holding the doll out toward Maria. "It's made of felt and soft stuff, so there was nothing to break. I think it's a Russian costume, what are they called—Cossacks? And real leather boots, not like us! Well, one real leather boot . . ."

The doll looks expensive. It has an embroidered appliqué felt coat in pretty, bright colors. Its face is sweeter than the face of baby Jesus, and its bright red hair makes a jagged fringe beneath a black felt hat with fur trim. It's missing one boot. On its bare foot is a stamp: LENCI. An Italian name.

"While I'm here I'll buy some provisions." Benedetta is still holding the doll. "Here, it's a present, take it. For Bruna. What are you waiting for?"

Maria holds out her hand and takes the doll from the station-master's wife, who is a customer. The station-master's wife expects nothing in return. She pays for her groceries and goes.

As the shop door closes, Maria stares at the body lying on the counter next to the pile of blue sugar-paper. Its lips are cherry-red. Its sad, innocent eyes are painted to look forever sideways, but Maria half-expects the gaze to shift, there's something so lively about its face. She stares and stares at the doll's eyes, willing them to look back at her. The doll keeps looking away. Why this gift? Any gift?

Bruna has never had a doll.

Amelia never had a doll.

Maria never had a doll. She looks sideways, like the doll, toward the shop door. Why this kindness? Now she is crying, leaning over the counter, weeping, for the violence and the kindness, for the station-master's wife, and soft little Bruna, and frogs' legs, and lost leather boots, and hard work, and being afraid, and being innocent.

The crying doesn't end, it seems to come from deep inside her, in wrenching breaths, and it's as if she is crying for all the years she didn't cry, because she was never a milksop or a princess and she never cried—never—and all her tears have been building up in her belly, like water in the deepest well, and she sobs for Duilio, and for Primo's bold and beautiful face, and for Achille, and for her father, for all the men, the strong protective men, and for her very own sinning hateful selfish soul.

~

YOU ADORE MY SERENE face, Maria, but I am not meek and mild when I think of you. Do you think of me when you go to Mass, and Holy Communion, and Confession—or do you think of skin touching skin?

You've lost your Christian Bride *book—where did you see it last? Did you leave it behind in the mountains? Do you remember reading it in Fosso? Remind yourself of your Christian duties.*

You have been neglecting your prayers, your rosaries, your mortifications.

And on my day, the Feast of the Immaculate Conception, you were bedded down with the Serpent.

War is no excuse. There is no excuse.

You've been neglecting your children—the very reason you were put on God's Earth. Children need more than food and boots. And don't forget the little ones here in Heaven with me, looking down upon their mother with horror in their innocent eyes.

Maria, Maria, misnamed after me, you are so close to Hell's torments, I can almost feel the heat of the flames licking at your feet. Your boots will not protect you from the fires of eternal punishment. Do penance. Pray while you still have breath.

~

THE BOYS ARE AT SCHOOL. Maria leaves Primo to run the shop while Amelia takes care of Achille and little Bruna.

Maria walks along the road to the railway crossing.

Ragged white veils of mist clothe the ground. Buildings hover without foundations. Bare trees and evergreens float rootless.

Soon the entire world is fog. Impenetrable. Solid blue-white in all directions. A sudden ghost of a nearby tree. A golden point of light from someone's house. No knowing if there is ditch or road or vineyard or lake or field. The fog has become the world.

Maria walks blindly through it. She knows her way. She strides as if she can see but she braces herself, at every step, for the crash of a stranger, an animal, a sudden vehicle. There is nothing. Just fog and thick ice.

At the crossing, there's no sign of a *carabiniere* or a Fascist, not even the station master. Good. She'd have trouble explaining her purpose. She has trouble explaining it to herself. Only a madwoman would go looking for something in a fog. It feels like a task she must do for penance. The Madonna gave her a sign from Heaven. A test. Now Heaven is out of sight.

The cold is extreme. Ice crunches under her footsteps. She doesn't know when the doll fell out of the sky. If the snow fell after, her search is utterly futile. It's Christmas in a week or so. Why on God's Earth must she find the missing boot? The chances are not good. She should be on her knees, like a real penitent, in snow and ice, but she must protect her woolen coat. It has to last. Her stockings must last too. So she stoops.

Perhaps it's in another country by now. God's Mother in Heaven can see everything, even a doll's little boot in a fog. God's Mother in Heaven can see a woman's earthly guilt, her sullied soul—a mortal is as transparent as glass.

Bent over, Maria walks along the train tracks, examining the edges, and the railroad ties, and the spaces between them, one by one. Will she see it? She focuses on each rotten brown leaf, each loose stone. Brown against white or gray, brown against brown. She walks in slow, tiny steps one way, then back, meter after meter the other way. There is nothing. Just old snow and ice and stones. Not even twigs or bits of wood or paper—they've been gleaned for kindling. She finds Italian cigarette butts—Milit, Giuba, Macedonia, Africa—how many soldiers have passed through here? And how many good Italian boys and men, military and civilian, have been deported to work camps in Germany? She thanks God in Heaven that Primo is safe. He's too young for conscription. But the war is insatiable.

And then she sees it. At first, it looks like a cardboard cartridge from a shotgun. It's frosted with crystals.

Ecstatic now, she dislodges it gently, careful not to tear the iced leather.

She holds the boot like a treasure.

It's a sign. God's Mother in Heaven hasn't given up on her. Stroking the cold, worn, unlucky boot, so precious now, she stands up straight and tries to pray. For the second time in two days, in twenty years, Maria cries.

Promised Banquet

"THEY'VE TAKEN YOUR COUSIN UP NORTH," SAYS SCOPE-ton. "Back to Monastero, near where he's from. Near where you're from."

His face is forgettable, he looks like nobody in particular, but Maria recognizes the fellow this time. His uniform helps. And his fingers, stubby and mottled like miniature salami resting on the counter.

"There's a military hospital there," he says.

"You mean he's not going to die?" Maria says it before she can think.

"He's got fighting spirit. I've seen it in others. Their love of the Fatherland keeps them going. And he has his promotion. When he gets well, he can start recruiting up there. Weed out trouble."

It's not nationalism, Maria thinks. *His anger keeps him alive.*

"The mountain air will be good for him," she says out loud. She remembers Duilio in that piazza long ago, tight-lipped with his sense of duty, taking the madwoman away. Now he's close to home again. People from the *contrà* will see him. They will ask him about her. Whatever he said to Achille, or says now to anyone, it's her word against her cousin's. People believe what they hear. If only he would die.

"You won't be able to visit him, if that's what you're thinking," says Scopeton. "I know he's dear to you."

"He's blood," she says quietly. She still doesn't know if she's pregnant. Or contaminated. Or both.

"He says your husband saved him. Perhaps that's why he returned the favor, despite being assaulted by him—"

"I don't understand," Maria says. Scopeton is playing games with her.

"The doctor who tended your cousin's injury diagnosed the TB. Just in time, I suspect."

Injury. The bandaged wound on Duilio's head.

"Now your cousin has the best possible medical treatment and a second chance at life."

Maria forces herself to speak. "I'll say my prayers of thanks to God."

Scopeton tilts his head, just so. "His place here was robbed, did you know that?"

"*Dio mio.* Times are tough," she says. She's always saying it. "Nothing shocks me anymore. Anything valuable?"

"I don't know. Some personal effects. He didn't have much to steal. We've cleared his place. He lived a frugal life. Exemplary. Anyway, he asked us to give you these." Scopeton slips his sausage-fingers into his coat pocket. He pushes something small, like coins, across the counter. Those two steel wedding rings.

The madman. People will talk. "*Oro alla patria,*" Maria says. Gold to the Fatherland.

"Oh, and this."

A tiny envelope. Printed with a *fascio* ax and sealed.

"You've been very lucky. Your boy too." Scopeton salutes and leaves the shop without buying a thing.

When she knows he's safely gone, Maria opens the envelope. Her fingers are trembling.

My dearest cousin, his words begin, his frail handwriting a scrawl across the paper. *I was meant to live. He saved me for you. Your heart is my heart. When I summon you, when I am well, you must come. A chi la Vittoria? D.*

~

THERE IS NOT ENOUGH food to go around. APPETITE IS THE BEST CONDIMENT, the posters say. As if anyone needed encouragement to eat. The choicest food went in the days before Achille's arrest. The worst of Winter is still to come.

The chickens produce eggs. They're as good as money. Maria will not kill the chickens. The rabbits are fur and meat. She must take good care of them and make sure they multiply. Some *signora* from the city bought a ham from Calvinetto's cousin with a set of twelve solid silver spoons—but a man cannot eat silver. Apart from cabbage and a few root vegetables, everything from the *orto* has been gathered, or eaten. Maria has bottled what she could, and dried what she could, more carefully than usual, not a bit wasted. She sold and bartered half of the Autumn harvest when it was fresh. She knows how to salvage rancid oil, cook rotten meat, make coffee out of spent grounds and chicory.

There is always the shop—she can raid what's left in it—and yet without goods to sell . . . No, they must have money. Maria thinks of a snake eating its own tail. When does it reach the stomach? Whatever happens, they need money. Even if bread is rough and heavy as cement, it costs money. Doctors and medicine cost money. Electricity costs money, no matter what she can save with wood and tallow. She remembers her mother paying for the things she couldn't make—cloth, caustic soda, pots and pans—with eggs instead of money.

There is always the Ente Opere Assistenziali for handouts—but the EOA is Party-run—and they might ask about her sons. There is always Edda. She must have secret supplies in her granary, enough to spare. And yet Maria cannot go begging to her sister.

Achille would not stand for it. There is always polenta. They can all live on polenta. She has firewood from her brothers. But no more until Spring: they are walled off from the plains by snow.

Perhaps Mussolini with his white hair and overfed face will die soon, or surrender. Perhaps Germany will take Italy under its wing and the promised Banquet will begin. The Banquet! Not plunder, not spoils, but the Banquet. Perhaps the war will end before the end of Winter, and the sanctions will end, and Spring will bring with it a harvest of peace and plenty.

At last her monthly blood comes. Maria welcomes the pain. She doesn't send Amelia out to forage for dandelion leaves. She says a rosary decade in thanks, every morning that she bleeds and every night. The fruit of her womb would have been cursed, and the Mother of God could not smile upon a bastard born to a dead man—but Duilio is not dead. He is waiting.

——————

1944

——————

FASCIST ERA YEAR
XXII

Fasoi, formajo, graspa

THE WORLD IS FULL OF NAZIS. THEY HAVE OCCUPIED ALL of Northern Italy. They have used captive Italians to build the Gothic Line across the girth of the country: trenches and forts and bunkers and barbed wire from coast to coast. They have installed their colonels in cities, taken over trains and stations, bridges and crossroads, invaded every palazzo and *comune*. The Veneto is full of them. Verona, Vicenza, Padua. Campolongo. Even Fosso. On the streets. In every spare room.

Now, suddenly, the shop is full of Nazis.

The cellar is a secret. The trapdoor is hidden.

Maria tries to count the men, but she's distracted and panicky. They all look the same, with their rosettes, their eagles and epaulets. Their weapons.

"Good evening," they say, as if in pleasant greeting. *"Buona sera. Heil Hitler."*

It's the curfew hour, sunset.

They know they'll be the only customers. *"Heil Mussolini."*

That must be a joke. The Italian leader has no power, no country. Italy declared war on Germany a year ago.

They are fastidious in their greetings, each and every one of them. As if they are welcome here. As if this is some kind of special family gathering. She hates the German accent. Every time she hears it, she thinks of the First War, and the old fear returns. A sickness in her belly. She can't get used to it.

They take their time. They are prolonging whatever violence they are planning to unleash.

"What is this?" they say in German, and in proud Italian too, picking up a bottle without a label, or a repurposed box.

"Funghi," says Primo from behind the counter. When he can, he uses dialect. It's harder for them to understand. *"Fasoi. Formajo. Graspa."* Beans. Cheese. Grappa.

"What is this? *O, bello, bello!"* they say.

They start helping themselves to groceries, farmers' goods, rationed goods, substitutes, pasta, homemade bottled fruit, October's harvest, November's stores. Sometimes they pick up a jar, look quizzically, mutter to one another in German and laugh. They call Italians pigs.

Achille uses the ladder to get things down from the higher shelves. He is the invaders' mute assistant.

Little Bruna hides underneath the counter which is being loaded up with food. She's clutching her doll as if it is her child. She soothes it, strokes its felt face, rocks it like a baby.

"We love Italian food," the Nazis say. *"Bello, bello."*

When at last they have cleared the shelves and accumulated what they want, making a big pile in the middle of the shop floor, the supervising captain gestures to Maria to total up the goods.

Is this another joke? More humiliation? She tries to brush the idea away with a gesture of the hand. She tries to make it friendly— as if she's offering them a gift today, a special deal for loyal customers.

"No, no," the captain says. He is insistently, ridiculously polite. As he nods, the eagle on his peaked hat ascends, descends. "We are paying you. Good business!" His expression is one of sincere propriety. It's as if he's doing the Italian pig shopkeepers a favor. Is this how they took over Edda's place? Maria's sister is living in the stable with her family and her workers while Germans roam around her house. It's like a Nazi hotel. There's even a grand piano.

The captain pulls out a leather wallet and opens it for Maria. He smiles kindly. He's almost proud. "Look: Reichsmarks. We pay you. A very good sale for you today."

It's an insult. The exchange rate stinks. They have all but emptied the shop. Most of Fosso is starving. This is robbery disguised as proper trade. But she feels relieved to get . . . something. Even this shameful money. She is overcome with gratitude. The twisted decency of it all makes her want to vomit. She does not dare look at Achille—who would knock down ten Nazis with one blow—or at Primo. She can feel her son's fury. But he helps her weigh the goods and add up the bill. He is being closely watched. There will be no mistakes. The numbers matter. The Germans want to do things right. They are so very principled.

100 marks equals 1,000 lire.

One German equals ten Italians.

Two months ago, in Bassano, they showed their arithmetic to the people. The avenue trees became gallows, one by one, and the bodies were left hanging, heads bowed, hands tied behind backs, cards at their necks reading BANDITO. In the news photographs stuck on the *comune* walls it looked as if those dead feet might touch the ground, close enough to walk. One was a woman, just like herself.

Item after item, column after column, Maria and Primo do the sums.

The invaders haven't guessed about the storeroom or the cellar. Can they tell from her face that she is hiding something? She thanks God that they let the house and *orto* be. It's months since she buried hard cheese and butter in a jar under the squash patch. She's got preserved fruit and nuts in the linen chest. Duilio's money is inside an old tobacco tin.

She has hidden her middle children too. They're in the granary attic. Amelia is sixteen and pretty. She was safer at the convent, out of sight, learning to work silk, and a trade is as good as a dowry, but she couldn't stay in a convent forever. Arsenio is tall for his age, and not too young for a labor camp. Cecilio is in their care.

Achille is carrying the provisions to their vehicles on the street, to and fro.

The Nazis make a show of being impressed at his strength. "Why are you not invited to Germany?"

Primo helps him now.

"And you also?" the captain asks. "No matter about your eyeglasses."

When Primo is with Achille outside, Maria pulls her PNF card from deep inside her pockets. "Here is my Party membership," she says to the captain. Her throat is so tight, she can barely speak. The card should make a good impression. Most people were compulsorily subscribed. Most people have got rid of their cards. Anyone who still has a card must have faith in the Fascist cause. Perhaps his men will be more careful, hold back, destroy less, take less . . . "And I have this." She shows the captain her travel permit, typed on one side in Italian, German on the other. She checks that Achille is still out of earshot. "And my first cousin is a Fascist officer. MVSN. CCN Blackshirt Corps. Now Black Brigades—"

"Yes, yes," the captain says. The eagle on his hat goes up and down approvingly. "It gives me a fine feeling."

Maria is eager, hopeful.

"But we are working very hard. And we need to eat," the captain says. He points with his handgun. "Receipt please."

At that moment, one of the others whistles and beckons him to the storeroom.

Maria's hope sinks heavier than a rock in a well.

"A moment," the captain says in his heavy Italian. "What is that door?"

"The storeroom," she replies. There's no point in lying.

"What is hiding in there?"

"Nobody." Achille walks across the shop floor and opens the door. He switches on the light. "Just food."

"Our livelihood," says Maria.

"You do well from us today," the captain says.

You do well out of us, she wants to say. But she is too frightened. In the storeroom are the last remnants of the family business. Saleable goods. Unbroken cheese. The Germans love cheese.

"I will have a look there," says the captain.

"Here!" Maria Bruna leaps out of her hiding place beneath the counter. She holds her doll up high and waves it at him. "You need this."

He is stunned for a moment and bursts into laughter as if he's heard the most amusing joke and there's no war.

Maria sees that his pistol is cocked and ready to shoot. Other men are pointing their weapons at her dear child. Maria must hold herself back. Bruna must not cry, Maria wills it. Nazis shoot children, she knows it. They shoot anyone. She wants the pistol to backfire and blow a hole into his gut.

Bruna is staring up at him, like a fool or a politician. Her big brown eyes are moist, but she doesn't cry, she coughs. "He's lucky," she says, shaking the doll. "He fell out of the sky."

Maria remembers crawling along the railway tracks looking for that little leather boot.

The captain pats Bruna's head. *"Bella bambina."* His expression is kindly. "We have big work to do."

The Nazis get Achille and Primo to clear out the storeroom, leaving only the baccalà.

They don't see the trapdoor. They don't go down into the cellar. Perhaps they're stupid. Maybe Bruna distracted them enough. They go through the perverse ritual of weights and sums again. They pay their Reichsmarks, paper money with eagles and buildings, zinc coins with holes in the middle. More eagles. And swastikas. They request their receipt.

"I thank you, dear child, but you keep your doll. The Cossack is our friend and yours. *Heil Hitler.*"

Bruna doesn't make a sound.

As they go, one of them whistles a tune. Someone says *buon appetito*. Someone says he needs a Jew-shoot.

Achille walks over to the window and peers through gaps in the paper. "They're clearing out Calvinetto, whatever he's got left. Hedgehog if they're lucky. Criminals."

Maria feels relief.

There was no murder. No arrest. No rape. No vandalism.

Just robbery. And Reichsmarks.

She feels relief. And yet she has no livelihood.

Maria and Primo and little Bruna stand motionless in the near-empty shop. There are spilled grains on the floor. Broken bits of pasta. Dried beans.

Primo's eyes are watering with rage. His teeth are gritted. "Scum," he says. "Scum."

"Help me," says Maria. "We mustn't let anything go to waste."

At her side, Bruna gets down on her knees to pick up every edible morsel with her precise fingers.

"Clever girl," Maria whispers. "You distracted them."

Eventually the engines outside stutter and rumble. The shop windows rattle, even with paper on the glass, as the Nazi customers drive away.

Food is power

"YOU DON'T HAVE TO GO," MARIA SAYS TO PRIMO AT THE back door.

"We can't survive with an empty shop." He has a tough cardboard suitcase tied to the family bicycle. And a knapsack on his back.

"We can get produce from farmers here," she says. "We'll have corn in the Spring. Maybe with our fields—"

"They're confiscated, Mama. Two years on, and you think—"

"I've got some food hidden. And dried corn in the granary—"

"That's animal feed."

"It'll do for polenta. Besides, there are no animals to feed, apart from the guinea pigs, and they're happy with grass."

Primo gazes at the miserable *orto*. "It's November, Mama."

"Onions and greens will grow."

"There's nothing to forage. They knew it. Those criminals took the last of the Autumn harvest. I'll head for Vicenza. I'll see what farmers in the back fields will sell me. Or around Padua. Rice, cheese, who knows what else. I'll go to Altavilla. Zia Edda must have something to spare."

"Her place is full of Nazis. You think she'll have food to spare?"

"I'll come back with something. From someone."

Maria has given him most of the cash she kept aside from the sale of unrationed goods. And the money she took from Duilio's place—but it's not worth very much, inflation has been so steep. And most of the Reichsmarks.

Primo has hidden the big bills in the bicycle bars. There's money in his socks and underwear.

She frets. "You've got your documents?"

To reassure her, he takes out his new identity card. Since the Summer, everyone has to carry one anywhere and everywhere—except Jews, who have no card at all. It's clearly marked with his Aryan race. STIRPE ARIANA. He shows Maria his permit card too, just like hers. It will get him past queues and checkpoints and deportation gangs, as far as Verona. He's the man of the family now. Achille can't go anywhere.

"You know I won't sleep until you return. You are my blessed, my only . . ."

"Mama, I'm nineteen now," Primo says quietly.

"Yes, just the right age for them. To fight, or work. Or die."

"I'm the only one who can do this. You know it as well as I do. I can't stay at home doing nothing. We've got to eat. We've got to sell. Food is power."

"Yes, food is power," she repeats. It's like a motto. She wonders if she's seen it on a poster. "Respect bread," she says, she doesn't know why.

"I'll be back tomorrow, or the day after, no later." Primo embraces her, then walks the bicycle down the garden path.

Maria watches him all the way to the gate, watches the gate open and close, listens for the sound of him on the road, and keeps standing there, as if he will return. Her beautiful, bright, beloved son.

~

PRIMO HAS BEEN GONE two days when the Partisans come. There are seven of them. Their breaths make white steam in the darkness.

Maria knows who they are before she sees the grubby hand-drawn CLN badge. It's held before her like some kind of holy relic.

Their leader wears a heavy coat, which he opens at the collar to show his knotted red neckerchief. He says nothing. His other gloved hand grips a rifle. They all have weapons. They all have coats—the *tabarro* cloak is banned.

Maria is holding a candle, it's after curfew, after blackout. She's wearing every woolen garment she can, to keep warm. Still, she shivers. The backyard is frosty under starlight. The sky is alive with fireworks fields away, thuds and crackles, flickering spans of light. Maria knows that they are not fireworks. Sometimes the ground shudders. All of Fosso is cowering.

"Sister, we need food," the leader says. He speaks Italian, not dialect. He's not local.

"So do we." Maria wonders if she can turn them away.

"You have a shop."

"It's almost empty—"

"Almost. That's better than nothing. Sister, let us in. We're liberating Italy."

"My husband is a veteran," she says. "He fought for us and nearly died. The Fascists put him in prison. He came back a broken man—"

"Then you'll be sympathetic to our cause," the leader says.

The air-raid siren starts its howl.

"Let us in," a fellow behind the leader says. She can't see his face. Yes, she can. It's blackened like a madwoman's. His eyes are white gleams.

The Partisans with their blackened faces and wide eyes enter the shop and scour the place by candlelight, shelf after shelf. A packet of something here, a box there, a bunch of beets. They put what they can into rucksacks, bags, coat pockets. It's a meager yield.

They don't need to ask about the storeroom. They go straight in.

Achille is here now, by Maria's side.

"Look frail," she whispers.

"Baccalà!" A Partisan comes out of the storeroom, arms full.

He's grinning. He nods at Achille and then he stops to look Maria in the eye. "Isn't your cousin a Blackshirt?"

"He's a madman," Achille answers before she can. "We hate him."

"Even if he's blood," Maria says. "He is our enemy."

"And ours. We have him in our sights."

"He's in Monastero," says Achille.

"Yes, we know. Recruiting. And torturing."

No, thinks Maria. *Convalescing. He's sick.* "We don't know anything," she says.

Achille glares at Maria. "He's lucky he's not dead."

The Partisans don't need to be told about the trapdoor to the cellar. They just know. But they need Achille to help them move the shelving unit out of the way. Nobody in the world is as strong as her man.

Maria does inventory in her head. She tries to calculate how much wine they can carry. And how much grain. She wonders how they will render the baccalà if they're on the move and hiding out. Her mind starts swimming with the practicalities.

The men gather more than they can possibly manage. There must be others waiting outside.

They work quietly, and fast. They divide everything into seven piles. Wine, cheese, nuts, onions, dried beans. Fruit in syrup. The baccalà.

They tie double bundles and swing them over their shoulders like mountain peasants. They carry more in their arms. They don't go upstairs to the kitchen, where the guinea pigs are hidden in a cloth-covered cage. They don't bother with the granary. They leave as swiftly as they came. No sums, no receipts, no money. Not like those twisted Germans.

Now the shop, and the storeroom, and the cellar are empty.

She hears the noise of the chickens outside. The Partisans are not stupid. They're taking them too, greedy and fast as foxes. They're liberating Italy.

And here is Amelia, wrapped in coats and a blanket. "Mama, Papà, what's happened?"

"Get back upstairs to the fire, or to Bruna," Maria says. "We have nothing now."

Outside the firework noises continue in sputters and whines, and hammering, and boxes being wrenched open, and shivering, and trapdoors being slammed shut, and vine posts being burnt, and flickering sheets of light, and madwomen howling, and shooting stars, and church bells plummeting, and bicycles crashing, and money crackling, and the Madonna of the Mountains toppling over and over again, and Primo shouting calling screaming, all night long.

Polenta e osei

"LOOK AT THIS," SAYS ACHILLE.

There's not one bird stuck on the nets, not even a robin or a finch. The *orto* shrubs look like skeletons in fine lace.

"It'd be easier with a calling bird." He starts detaching a net. "And that's the last of the *ves-cio*."

"We can make some more," Maria says. "We just need more mistletoe."

"Do we have the oil? Or turpentine? A bit of humidity, and the birds get away. If it's not waterproof, they don't stick, and we end up with this. Nothing."

"We've got some oil buried in a jar. But I want to save that," she says.

Her strongman husband helps Nazi raiders load their trucks. He owes his life to Duilio. He doesn't get around Partisans. The chickens are gone, and he can't even catch a songbird. She remembers the handsome hero who strode up the mountain with a weighty *gavegnà* on his head, the survivor of the First War, with just one scar—the clever soldier who outwitted his commanders and was rewarded for a dead donkey's hoof. His record was good, even Duilio said so. But ever since the imprisonment, Achille has been hopeless. She has chosen not to share his bed. He hasn't even tried to touch her.

And dear Primo, who stands up to him, dear Primo has still not returned. He said he'd be gone a day, two days at the most. It's three days now, and there's no sign of her boy. He could be on one of those trains, heading for a work camp. Or in Padua being tortured by the Banda Carità with their "Special Services"—cigarette ash in raw wounds, electric shocks, salt feedings. They dump their victims on the streets like rubbish. Primo said he might go as far as Padua. Don Goffredo caught a glimpse of him in Vicenza.

"Do you think Primo is safe?" she says.

Achille sits in a slump on the damp ground. "As long as he doesn't show off."

"He's not stupid."

"He loves Americans."

"They're liberating us," she says.

"But he's an open book. And he's hotheaded."

"Primo is the future," Maria says under her breath. She wishes she'd given her son something as protection. Her PNF card. Or those steel wedding rings of Duilio's. Anything. Her Blackshirt cousin still hasn't left the sanatorium—he's too ill to help her, he can't help Primo.

"We can find someone with oil to spare," she says. "It'll be cheap if it's rancid. But first, we need the mistletoe berries. Amelia and I can go foraging after Mass. We'll try the slopes past Campolongo." She is thinking her daughter can climb a tree if need be. The low bushes will already have been picked. "You wait and see: when Primo comes back, we'll have polenta with stewed birds."

Achille looks at her doubtfully.

She wishes for her words to be true. But these days, her mouth and her heart are not as one. She says the things she must say. Her gut knots up with half-truths, and they are half-lies.

She gazes at her husband with the net in his big strong hands, and she wants to kick or curse—no, she is filled with pity. She pities him. It looks like the net is for him. She should respect him. But he is stuck at home. He can't go anywhere. He has a criminal record and no Party card. If he got caught black-marketing now, he'd be shot in the church square.

The posters are everywhere. It's as if the German *comandante* of the zone is shouting all the way from Verona, or from some palazzo in Vicenza, threatening death as punishment: POSSESSING PIGEONS AND RADIOS PROHIBITED, CONSORTING WITH AN ENEMY PROHIBITED, WITHHOLDING GOODS FROM GERMAN ARMED FORCES PROHIBITED, WEARING A TABARRO CAPE PROHIBITED, PHOTOGRAPHY PROHIBITED . . .

Maria did not withhold goods from German armed forces when they came into her shop. Her husband and her son even helped them load their trucks. If only she possessed a pigeon. She wouldn't use it to send messages, she would eat it greedily. A nice fat pigeon would be delicious. She pictures the Partisans finishing off her chickens. Roasted. Grilled. The dark thigh meat, so tasty. Her mouth waters. She is hungry. Everyone is hungry. But they're not starving yet. The children need meat, especially the boys, to grow and be strong, they need more blood in their cheeks. She must keep the guinea pigs alive—they eat grass, which is easy, and they might breed again. There's a butcher next door, but no meat. Calvinetto's secret bartering supplies have dwindled to nothing, not even off-cuts or trimmings. The Nazis eat everything—they ate a cow they found hidden in an empty grave. There are posters that say not to eat cats, because cats are needed to catch mice and rats. *Magnagati.* That's the nickname for the people of Vicenza. *Cat-eaters.* Why is it right to eat bird, or horse, but not cat?

"Perhaps all the birds have been eaten," says Achille, pathetic.

"We'll catch plenty, you watch," Maria says. "We'll suck the meat off their bones, and we'll eat the bones too."

~

BEYOND CAMPOLONGO, UP THE pale stony paths and still-green slopes, Maria and Amelia walk very slowly, very carefully, on the lookout for any plant or creature that is edible. They search for mushrooms that may have sprung up. Or nettles. Or blackberries— even though the Devil spits on them after September. The sun is shining softly. It is warm for November.

They both have their identity cards. They are full of the grace of Holy Communion. The Bible reading this morning was about civil war in the Holy Lands long ago. The sermon was about the civil war in Italy now. The final prayer was a prayer of thanks that the Campolongo church has not been damaged. Fosso has not been so lucky.

Amelia is carrying two sackcloth bags. Maria has Duilio's rucksack on her back, and one of those unlucky nets draped over her shoulder, ready to grab and cast onto a bird, squirrel, frog, hedgehog . . . anything that has meat.

In the Winter weeds and rough stone walls, they find snails.

"There are more here," says Maria. "Fosso has been picked clean."

"They're beautiful," says Amelia.

I hate them, Maria thinks. *Thank God these ones are hibernating, not mating.* "They have to be starved for a week. We have to get rid of the slime and the gut. It's a lot of work. And these are small ones . . ."

"Bruna has small fingers," Amelia says. "She's patient and careful. She can do the work."

"At least it's meat."

Where is Primo now? He's been gone too long. Three days already. Is he in Padua, being starved in a cell? She imagines feeding him stewed snails, teaspoon by teaspoon, her first baby boy, emaciated, wounded.

With gloved hands they cut at mistletoe, poisonous white berries in balls of bright green leaves infesting bare-branched trees. Enough to make more *vischio*. They hack at deadwood too, to burn in the stove.

The big sack is heavy and awkward to carry, but Maria is not going home. She's hunting. She has yet to throw her net. The birdcatcher back in the *contrà*, camouflaged in moss green and nut brown, would surely fill the intricate wooden cage strapped on his back. Maria is not so well-equipped. And there's not a bird in sight.

"Listen," she whispers. A twitching in the bushes.

Amelia is motionless.

But there is nothing.

The world is quiet, Winter-quiet, though not as quiet as snow. And not as quiet as peacetime. There is always the sound of engines.

"Mama, let's go home. The animals have all gone," Amelia says. "And maybe Primo is back."

"One more possibility while we're here," Maria says, leading her daughter uphill. "There are caves higher up. But we don't have to go that far."

The stones are loose underfoot, and their make-do shoes get powdered white. Soon, there are bigger rocks on the track, jutting out like monuments or scattered in a mess. The view is clear across the sunlit plains all the way to Vicenza: bare vineyards and fields, ditches, little rivers, terracotta rooftops, church towers—some bombed and broken, some intact—columns of Nazi vehicles moving on the roads.

Primo could be in one of those trucks. If Primo is in one of those trucks, not even a Blackshirt cousin can help now.

Maria looks around, touches the surfaces, checks for moisture. There are no ferns here, just dry lichen and strings of ivy. "Stand by me, keep the bag open and ready."

She eases her pocketknife into the rock where it's cracked and breakable. She levers it off. Nothing. She finds another cleft, and works at it gently until the surface piece comes away. Nothing. She tries another opening. And another. And another. And then she finds it. A coil of lizards hibernating, one wrapped over the other.

"Quick," she says to Amelia. "The sack." She tips them in. Six of them. Almost one each for everyone, a meager dish. Her mouth waters. Immediately she finds another nest. She flicks the lizards in. "We need more."

Amelia is horrified. "Not for me."

"Flesh makes flesh."

"Primo wouldn't—"

"You need the meat," says Maria. For a moment she remembers poor Delfina. "Or God won't give you any children."

"We've got the guinea pigs."

"For now—"

"And anyway, God *will* give me children."

"Let's hope they're grateful and eat what's on their plates."

Then there is a sound that they both recognize and don't want to hear ever again. At first it's droning, distant. Fireworks that are not fireworks. The sounds of Christmas Day, and Palm Sunday, and that sunny Sunday in May, and all the bombs in between.

Maria keeps chipping away at the rock. She's working fast, but her hands are shaking. She cuts her finger. She slips. She cuts a lizard. She grips the shaking knife. When her harvest of lizards is up to two dozen, she stops. She is out of breath. The noises are louder now, unmistakable. The planes are going back and forth. Her belly is clenched.

"That's enough!" she says to Amelia, or to the Allies, to both. "Tie the bag. Make it secure."

There are spots of blood seeping through the sackcloth. Wasted nourishment.

There is blood on her hand, lizard blood, her own blood. She licks it clean.

She goes to the path's edge beyond the rock.

Amelia stands by her side.

There in the distance, where the city is, in the luminous pale blue sky: a giant, filthy, spreading cloud. This is another big bombardment. How many times can it happen? Planes fly back and forth, back and forth, a constant sickening rumbling drone. *Thank God it's not us—but where is Primo right now?* Her son is being captured by Nazis on the ground. He's being crushed by bombs from above.

"It's the Americans again," says Amelia.

"And the British. They're liberating us," Maria says, trying to sound brave for her daughter.

"Why are they bombing the city? Why are they bombing us? Why aren't they bombing the Nazis—"

"Let's get home," Maria says, even though it's safer here in the hills.

The children have no school to go to since the Christmas bombing. And the people of Fosso have lost their church. Its jagged walls are buttressed by poles and piles of rubble. The old mural of Fortuna's Wheel—the man climbing to the top, the man sitting smug on his throne, the man at the bottom falling into a devil's mouth—lies in a broken heap.

"We've got to take all this home while we can." Maria is determined that her son has returned and is standing in the kitchen, unharmed, alive. She can't wait to get back to him.

~

IN FOSSO THE SIREN is howling. Shops and shutters are closed. There are only military men and their vehicles in the streets. It's like curfew, even though the sun is shining.

When they reach home, Maria throws a stone up at the first-floor windows.

Arsenio opens the shop door.

Maria would rather see another son. "Is Primo back?"

"No."

"Any word from him?"

"Nothing," Arsenio says. "They're bombing everything. He could be dead."

"Don't be stupid." Maria hands over the net and the heavy bags. "Here, help Amelia with all this. I'm going to the *osteria* to get news."

"But the siren—"

"I can hear the siren."

Arsenio looks inside one of the bags. He grins. "Their tails have come off." He always grins when he's not sure what to say or do.

"So they've woken up, then," Maria says. "Don't let anything escape. Now help Amelia. I'll be back in no time."

She doesn't want her daughter at the *osteria*. Amelia is too pretty. The place is like a Nazi boardinghouse. At first they had respect. Now they'd violate her and throw her out again, ruin her for life. Maybe the convent would have her back before Spring, when the silkworm eggs need tending. She was safer there. God knows what's happened to Beppe's wife and daughter. No wonder the poor man's a drunk.

The planes sound closer, rumbling in her bones. The siren howls.

The *osteria* is empty. It seems the military men are being kept busy elsewhere.

Qui non si parla di politica o di alta strategia. Here nobody talks of politics. Despite the poster above the bar, Beppe babbles. "Oh, Maria! The alarms came too late. The bombs came before they knew it. They didn't expect them after last night. They bombed the place last night. It's the end of Vicenza. They're not just going for the Germans, they're going for anyone, anything that moves. Three hundred planes! They called it a terrorist bombing—"

"Who did?"

"The Nazis. The Fascists."

There's a new poster on Beppe's wall calling youth to join the Company of Death. For Honor and Victory—*Vittoria*. Her own name again. Under a black-eyed skull with a dagger in its teeth.

"The Allies are using a new type of bomb, it's an experiment, they explode at the very last minute. They're the worst for humans, like thousands of little bombs exploding everywhere, it's to cause the most damage, not for buildings but for humans—"

"Have you seen Primo—"

"Who thinks of these things? And those bombs like a toy, in funny colors, appalling. It's the end. And big incendiary bombs, and those pencils that blow up in your face, like the ones in the fields, and the ones that look like chocolate to trick hungry children who just want a bit of sugar. They pick them up. A bit of sugar. And they're gone. Little children. Who thinks of these things?—Why are you out? You should be at the refuge."

"Have you seen Primo?" Maria asks again. "Don Goffredo saw him in Vicenza, but maybe he was mistaken." She wants to hide like a lizard inside a mountain. She's trying to keep herself steady. Could Primo have made his way through all those bombs? She thinks of his beautiful face.

Bombers fly overhead, louder than any air-raid siren. She can't hear anything else. Bombers roaring. More bombers. On their way to Vicenza. Or from. Or back again. Everything is shuddering.

Beppe shakes his head. His eyes are red and swimming now. He strokes the bar like a comfort blanket. "You know I haven't seen Teresa for—I haven't seen my girl either. I can't—" He pours himself three fingers of wine. He downs it in one gulp. "It's curfew. You should be at the refuge. Or at home. If you're going to die, you should be with your kin."

Maria wants to feed her son. She wants to make polenta with birds, but first she has to catch the birds. That is her mission. She will feed her son. Planes or no planes. "Beppe, do you have any oil, even rancid? We have to make some *ves-cio*."

Beppe wipes his nose on his sleeve. He wipes his eyes. His shirt is a disgrace. He needs a woman. He's a drunkard. He wipes his nose again. "What have you got to barter?"

Lizards and snails

MARIA IS DETERMINED TO IGNORE THE SOUND OF AIR-craft, on and off, close overhead and in the distance. "Amelia, stoke the fire and start preparing the lizards."

Amelia grimaces. "How?"

"Like frogs," Maria replies.

"I'm not hungry," Bruna whispers to her sister.

"Of course you are," Maria replies. The girl is pale. She needs meat. "And I'll put you in charge of the snails. They're a delicacy."

Bruna smiles at the praise.

"Shouldn't we go to the refuge?" Cecilio says.

"I'll send you to the refuge on your own," Maria snaps. "What if Primo comes home?" She knows it's not a proper answer. Primo could go to the refuge too.

Amelia kneels on the floor and takes deadwood out of one sack, making a neat pile near the stove.

Squatting by the other sack, Cecilio pokes at it now and then, cautiously touching the places where it's spotted with blood. Nothing seems to move inside.

"Go and tell your father we've got mistletoe," Maria says to him.

Amelia feeds kindling into the stove.

Bruna coughs at the smoke.

"And extra wood," Maria says as Cecilio heads for the door. "And oil. Find Arsenio. You boys can build a fire outside to make the *vescio*. The bombers have done their worst for today."

Silently, she tries to pray for Primo's safe return, but the sounds of the morning's bombs are still thundering in her head.

~

IT'S THE MIDDLE OF the night when Maria awakens. She's been having nightmares. It could be the strange meat. No, she thinks, the portions were too small, and nightmares come to her anyway.

With polenta, the lizards were palatable enough, fried in salvaged oil and herbs. They would have tasted better if she'd used nice butter, salt and pepper. She has butter buried under the squash patch. She doesn't know how long she should keep it—nobody can say when the war will end.

Achille and the boys caught no birds. Perhaps there are no birds when there are planes. He will try again tomorrow.

Bruna wouldn't eat the lizard meat until she was told she had to. Amelia cried.

The snails will need garlic, herbs and a dash of wine. They'll be good with polenta. But first, they must be starved in grit for a few days, five days at least, before the remaining live ones can be rinsed of their slime, rinsed and rinsed again, then gutted. Their black spiral innards are tiny and awkward. Bruna can do that work with her deft little fingers. Cecilio can help her—he has no school to go to.

Amelia, lying beside her, is breathing the deep breaths of sleep.

Where is Bruna? Lately, she's taken to creeping into bed with them both, but now she's not here.

Maria hears her coughing in the kitchen.

Bruna is always coughing. She has sensitivities, not like her big sister who has a tough constitution. The stove will be cold. What is Bruna doing in the kitchen?

Maria edges slowly out of bed, so as not to wake Amelia. She wraps herself in an overcoat. She slips another pair of socks on her feet. Shuddering at the cold, she feels her way through the darkness and into the kitchen. She wants to switch on the electric light, but it's blackout. She makes do with a candle.

Bruna is by the guinea pigs' cage under the table. She has lifted off their cloth cover. She looks mournful. She's shivering.

"What are you doing?" Maria asks.

"I'm hot," Bruna says. She sounds breathless.

Maria kneels down and touches her daughter's clammy forehead. *"Dio mio,"* she says. "You've got a fever."

"I'm sorry," Bruna says.

Maria feels guilt stabbing her inside. "There's no need to be sorry, little one."

Bruna starts coughing again.

As Maria cleans the bloody phlegm from her daughter's hand, she tries to keep herself calm, but her nerves are wild. She remembers Duilio's coughing, his balled-up handkerchiefs and bloodstained bed linen.

"Come, *carissima*," she says, and takes her girl into her arms, envelops her in the overcoat. She can feel Bruna's heart beating, faster than her own frightened heart. Smaller. It feels as if both their hearts will break.

"Will you have some broth?" Maria asks quietly. She doesn't know what she can give her. A drop of wine, perhaps. "Fruit in syrup?"

Bruna's breaths are noisy. "I'm not hungry."

Maria heard those words earlier in the day, and wonders now that she didn't notice them. Bruna should have been hungry. Everyone is hungry. She thought her girl was being fussy about the unfamiliar meat. Now that she's holding her, she can feel her bones. Her baby bird is cold and shivering. She's not hungry. She's coughing blood.

What can doctors do about tuberculosis? Put her in a sanatorium, like Duilio. He's been there two years now. Severo's wife died of consumption. Doctors cost money. Sanatoriums cost money. Primo has nearly all the money. And Primo has the bicycle. Maria tries to calculate how much money she kept. But her head is a mess of numbers. Maybe they can sell some land. But nobody is buying or selling land. Perhaps they can borrow money from the priest. Or someone. Achille can run for the doctor now. No, it's curfew. He'll be caught by Germans and sent to a labor camp. Arsenio can run for the doctor. If he gets caught, they'll let him go, he's too young for them, too young to fight Allies or build Gothic Lines. But even if he makes it as far as the doctor's house, and even if he persuades the doctor to come at this hour, there's not much a doctor can do now that can't be done in the morning. It must be three on the clock, or four.

Bruna is wheezing, but she's not gasping or panicking.

Perhaps it's just bronchitis.

Bruna coughs. Her pale face looks almost blue in the candle-light.

Maria closes her eyes and rocks her daughter, keeping her warm, holding Bruna's head against her. She doesn't want to let go of her, ever. She thinks of Tito and Ignazio, her two dead infants gone to Heaven. She remembers the photograph she saw of Duilio's baby, laid out in the coffin, tiny hands arranged in prayer and looped with rosary beads.

But Bruna is four years old. She's not a baby.

Maria must wait until morning. And when curfew ends, she will send Arsenio to fetch the doctor. She will tell him to run all the way to Campolongo. Achille can slaughter one of the guinea pigs. Amelia can get the jar of fruit from its hiding place. The syrup will soothe Bruna's throat. The doctor will come straightaway on his bicycle. He will do his tests and decide that Bruna just has a fever, as children do, war or no war, there's medicine for that. Or bronchitis, which passes—he'll say to keep her from smoke and cold. Or pneumonia, which is dangerous, but can simply go away.

Bruna has fallen asleep in Maria's arms, wheezing with every breath. Her mouth is open. Her eyelids are fluttering.

It's a long dark night of waiting until morning.

Maria strokes her daughter's damp hair. Little children succumb to tuberculosis, worse than adults. The thought makes her feel faint.

~

IN THE DARKNESS BEFORE DAWN, still holding Bruna tight in her arms, Maria stands and stares blindly at the Madonna of the Mountains. She hopes for guidance. Intercession.

Oh, Maria, your baby bird wasn't hungry, and you didn't notice. She was coughing, and you took it in your stride. You don't even know how long she has been coughing.

If the poor girl has consumption, she can't tell you when she caught it.

Look into your soul, Maria, look into your heart. Look into your bed.

Did you give it to her?

You still don't know if you're contaminated. You don't dare to think it. You breathed in his tubercular breath, his sweat, his spit, his spore-filled pillow. The disease lies low for weeks, for months—for years if it wants to—before it shows its ugly face.

It lurks, Maria, like the worst sly poison.

Your other infants here in Heaven are eager for their sister, Maria. They long for her. But I cannot describe for you the sorrow in their eyes. They are weeping at your guilt.

I do not pity you, Maria.

You don't want pity.

You must pray.

Holy oil

ARSENIO HAS BEEN GONE FOR HOURS. HE'S OUT OF BREATH. "There's no doctor. All those bombs in Vicenza. He went there to help."

"When is he back?" Maria knows it's a stupid question as she says it.

Arsenio shrugs.

If the doctor is in Vicenza with bomb victims, he is not in Fosso for sick children. He might return today, tomorrow, next week or never. "Did you ask people?"

Arsenio nods. "Where's Bruna?"

Maria glances toward the bedroom door. "Amelia's with her."

"I ran and ran. I used the field paths. I steered clear of all the Germans." He grins. "Like a spy."

"Good boy," Maria says, despite her nerves. "What about the money I gave you?"

"I didn't lose any." He fishes in his pockets.

"Take it to the herbalist. You know where he lives?"

Arsenio nods.

"If he's not at home, go to the church at Campolongo. He might be at Mass. Ask him to cycle here. Tell him the symptoms. If he's not there, ask the priest. Don Goffredo knows everything."

~

THERE IS NO HERBALIST. His bicycle is gone. His wife hasn't seen him for days. The Nazis may have apprehended him for something. Or he may have gone off with the Partisans.

Arsenio returns in the evening, with the priest.

"Forgive me," Don Goffredo says at the back door. "Your good boy here told me about your girl."

Maria lets him in. The air is icy and she is impatient to shut out the night.

Achille has slaughtered a guinea pig and grilled it whole. Amelia has made polenta. Cecilio has dug up the jar of butter from underneath the hard ground of the squash patch. Maria has tried to feed Bruna.

The girl won't eat anything without coaxing. She struggles to breathe, and coughs, and sleeps.

"I said to myself, I'll come here to see how she is." Don Goffredo smiles.

"Do you know where the herbalist is?"

The priest shakes his head. "I'm sorry, Maria. Everything is up in the air."

"Will you say a prayer for her?" She clutches at the rosary beads in her pocket.

The priest nods.

Maria leads him through to the bedroom where Bruna lies asleep underneath a pile of coats and blankets. There's a spattering of blood on the pillow.

Amelia is sitting at the bedside.

"I've visited many sick children this past year," Don Goffredo says. He gazes at Bruna for a long time before speaking again. "She hasn't reached the age of reason—"

"She's four years old," Maria says, her heart drumming.

"In the absence of medical men . . ." The priest frowns and ponders, scratches his neck, sighs a long, slow sigh. "Let me bless this dear, sweet soul. The Sacrament can do good for the health of the body, not just the soul, I've seen it with my own eyes."

Maria knows what his words mean. He's talking about the Last Rites. She wants to die. She wants to die instead of Bruna.

"Let us gather the whole family," the priest says. "Our prayers are stronger when we are together. We must be at one with Christ in this vale of tears that is our earthly pilgrimage."

"Go fetch the others," Maria says to Amelia.

"Peace to this house," Don Goffredo says. And then he speaks in Latin. He has a bag, like a doctor's bag.

Maria wonders that she didn't notice it before.

He opens the bag and takes out a crucifix, a linen cloth, a bottle of water, a bottle of oil, an olive sprig and two shallow bowls.

The family is here now, kneeling around the bed in candle-light.

Maria cannot bring herself to look at anyone but Bruna.

The priest touches the crucifix to Bruna's lips. He pours holy water into one bowl, dips the olive sprig in it, and sprinkles the room. He goes close to Bruna and whispers Latin words into her ear. He turns his head and seems to listen. He nods as if he's hear-ing Bruna speak. He asks everyone to pray for her.

Maria bows her head. *Dear God*, she says the words as quietly as she can, *God the Father, God the Son, God the Holy Spirit, dear Mother of God in Heaven, dear saints, dear angels and archangels . . .*

When everyone has prayed for a time—Maria has no idea how long, her head is rushing, everything feels slow—Don Goffredo anoints her little girl.

He touches Bruna's eyelids with the blessed oil, murmuring words in Latin, then he wipes the oil off with his linen cloth, then he anoints her ears, left and right, her nostrils, left and right, murmuring Latin all the while, her innocent lips, her hands, her feet. He wipes his hands clean with the cloth and sets it down.

There are more words, Latin words that Maria recognizes from Mass, and then other words, more words than she can bear to hear, in Latin, more Latin, on and on, before his hands make the signs of blessing and the Sacrament is over.

Risi e bici

"MAMA, MAMA, MAMA, MAMA!" CECILIO CALLS FROM downstairs. "It's Primo! Primo is back! Primo!"

Maria runs out of the kitchen, stumbles down the outside steps and into the backyard, into the blinding afternoon sunlight, along the path, past the empty coops and cages, past the straggle of onions and beets, and throws her arms around her darling smiling boy. He is alive. And he has all his limbs.

When she lets go, Primo puts his suitcases down. He unfastens the bag from his back and drops it to the ground. He looks like a refugee with his baggage. He's lost weight. It's been five days. He still has his glasses.

"We ate lizard. It's like fishy chicken," says Cecilio.

Primo ruffles his little brother's hair. "Lizard?"

"On Friday we're going to have snails," Cecilio says.

"Mama . . . ?"

"After the Germans, the Partisans came. They cleared us out. Even the chickens," says Maria. "It's meat."

"So you're here," says Achille, striding along the path to his returned son. "Were you successful? Where's the bike?"

Maria gulps. She didn't notice. It must be on the street.

"I traded it," Primo says. "No choice. Anyway, it was falling apart. We can get another one—"

"Who gave you permission?" says Achille.

"You've been eating pests. I come back with food. I got through shelling and slaughter and mines, dead people everywhere. I'm alive. And all you care about is the bike?"

Achille's fists are flexing. He's ready to hit his son.

Arsenio is here now. Good. A distraction.

"Boys, pick up the bags," Maria says. "Your brother has come a long way." She doesn't tell him that Bruna is lying in a fever on her deathbed.

Upstairs in the kitchen, Primo sits at the top of the table. He's taking charge. Like the head of the family.

Achille shoves at the back of his chair and gestures for him to move.

Primo takes his time getting up.

Achille sits. Everyone is at the table now, except the girls.

Primo remains standing, as if he's making a speech. "The Allies are coming up from the south. The Germans are retreating—but they won't tell you that—and they're destroying everything. Railways. Crossroads. Bridges. They've got labor camps north of here, northeast of here, and a death camp near Trieste. And the Black Brigades are set up in convents, against the army, against the *carabinieri*, but they're really after Partisans. I saw a big long train heading south, flatcar after flatcar loaded with German tanks. They're forcing people to go out and fill craters with a shovel, even when the air raids start again, so you know what happens: everyone gets massacred. There's no difference between day and night."

Maria gazes at her son. He's here. Standing. Unhurt, just a few cuts and grazes.

"In Vicenza people ran outside—because of the May bombings— they didn't want to be buried under rubble. They were running out of the city and throwing themselves into ditches. But these bombs are different. I saw carts piled this high with bodies. All the straw was red with blood. And the road, red everywhere. And wailing, you've never heard such wailing. It was like Hell. They're taking the anti-Fascist medical people out of prison and putting them to work. They're using the seminary as a hospital but they don't have the drugs and they need blood. I gave them blood." Primo rolls up his sleeve to show the bruise.

"You need to eat meat," Maria says. She can't help herself.

"What did you buy?" Achille stares at the table. He doesn't even look at his son.

"I went from farm to farm, on dusty back roads—not the main roads, they're barricaded. And the main bridges are mined."

"What did you buy?"

"Everyone said no, or they wanted crazy prices. Inflation's gone mad. Those marks were worth nothing. I made it to Altavilla—"

"Edda!" Maria gasps. "How is Edda?"

"I couldn't get near the place. There were Nazis everywhere. It's some kind of headquarters. I saw officers' cars. I didn't see her, but I saw Rodolfo, almost by chance."

Achille curses under his breath.

"He put me in touch with some Americans. They were in hiding, working with the Resistance—"

"How is my sister?" Maria asks.

"Rodolfo said her nerves are shot. They've got enough to eat but he couldn't give me anything. The place where we met—" Primo stops and turns to face Achille. "You should save your curses for the Occupiers and the Communists."

Maria stiffens. She's braced for the two men to fight.

"And you should know your place."

"Achille—"

"Rodolfo's a crook," Achille says quietly. "He gave your precious son nothing. Am I surprised? He's made a fool of him. And of me. I curse him. I curse your sister's husband, and I curse your sister for marrying him."

Maria has her hands deep in her apron pocket. Her fingers roll a scrap of paper, over and over. She realizes with a shock that it is

Duilio's note. *When I summon you, when I am well, you must come.* She shivers. When did she put it here? She coughs.

"And I curse your cousin." Achille stares at her. "Who coughs."

Maria coughs again, she can't suppress it. "You are cursing my family—"

"I am cursing your cousin. And the bed your cousin infects—"

"Boys, help your brother get the bags on the table." Maria gestures to Cecilio and Arsenio.

It works. Everyone is distracted.

Maria offers her seat to Primo.

He smiles his big, proud smile, with his white, perfect teeth, and his beautiful dark eyes. "Look at this," he says. And he opens up one suitcase as if it's full of treasure.

It's full of rice.

"There's enough here to keep us going for a while. Still, this is the prize . . ." Primo opens the other suitcase. He lifts the lid off a brown box and takes out one small tin after another. He adjusts his glasses and studies the labels. "Dried eggs. Tobacco. Some kind of fish, sardine or herring. Jam. Something meat. Tinned cheese. Real cocoa! How long since we've had cocoa? I think this is a pudding. Here's margarine—it's not butter, but almost. Sugar—a tin of sugar! Mixed vegetables. Fruit in syrup. Biscuits. Preserved milk, better than cream, and sweet . . ."

Cecilio's mouth hangs open, and a spray of saliva shoots out like a tiny fountain.

Arsenio touches the tins. "It's like a dream."

"Yes! And the girls will love this: a bar of soap. Where's Amelia? Real soap that smells nice and doesn't look like camouflage."

Maria is waiting for more. But there is no more. All those Reichsmarks, and the money she stole from Duilio's, and the bicycle. The family bicycle. All that, and dear Primo has come back with only this. She is speechless. Voiceless. She swallows hard. She coughs. She tries to calculate how long she can make the flashy foreign tins last. How far she can eke out the corn in the granary.

If they can make it through Winter, if it's not a harsh Winter, and hope for good Spring vegetables, and wait as long as possible for the vegetables to grow bigger ... They still have some guinea pigs, she reminds herself. The miserable remains of her buried provisions, if they haven't been eaten by vermin. Achille can make more *vischio*, but he hasn't caught any birds. In her head, she divides up the tins, each one into seven parts. A portion will be smaller than a lizard. She wonders how they will survive the Winter. Especially Bruna.

"Where's Amelia?" Primo asks again.

Maria's insides are all tight and twisting. "I was thinking of sending her back to the convent so she can learn more—that's if they're still working silk ... So she can be safe."

"But the Black Brigades are in the convents, I told you—" He claps. "And this—I nearly forgot!" Primo opens his cloth bag and takes out a white ceramic jar with a cork lid. "Heavy as a rock. Meat extract."

There is silence in the room.

Achille speaks at last. "Is that all you've got?"

"Yes, that's all. For now." Primo's voice is hard and resentful.

Achille shakes his head. Slowly. Left, right, left, right. His face is white. Then red all over. There is saliva at the corner of his mouth.

The children look at their hands, the floor, the tins.

Achille thumps the table with his fist. All the food shakes and jumps. Rice leaps out of the suitcase.

Primo slams it shut.

"Enough!" Maria cries out. "It's food. We need food." Her voice is good and tough, but in her head she wants to lie down, and close her eyes, and go to sleep, and stay asleep, and have no nightmares, no dying children, no dead children, no children, no food, no men, no girls, no war, no disgrace, no hunger, no pain, no noise, no fear, no thoughts. "Bruna has consumption," she says at last to Primo, without looking at him. "The priest has given her the Last Rites."

Achille thumps the table again and roars.

A tin rolls off the edge. Loose rice scatters, falls to the floor, scatters some more.

Maria is on her knees, never mind her stockings, gathering grains of rice into her apron, with the children at her side, picking and gleaning, Primo too.

She hears the scrape of Achille's chair and the sound of his boots and the slam of the door.

~

MARIA PLACES THE SIDEWAYS-GLANCING Cossack doll on the bed. Bruna will be comforted to see it when she wakes up.

The Madonna of the Mountains is watching everything with serene, unblinking, immortal eyes.

Maria stands before her shrine.

She was born with the war, the Madonna says. *She always had her sensitivities. But it's your fault she's lying deathly white in a bed. You neglected your girl just as you fussed and fretted about your boy. Will you never learn, Maria?*

You pray by her bedside, you bring her food you've made with your best ingredients, your remaining this and hidden that, I don't care what recipe or dish—your fledgling can hardly eat. She is as still as a stone in a lake, paler than a saint. She's almost here with me in Heaven. The immortal soul doesn't eat the food of your world, no matter that your food is love.

Yes, Maria, food is love.

But before you get lazy, before you rest on your haunches, don't trick yourself into believing—not for a moment—that food replaces love.

One last guinea pig

BRUNA CLINGS FEEBLY TO LIFE, BUT SHE SLEEPS AND SLEEPS. The doctor, when he visits at last, is gloomy.

In just one month, one bitter cold Winter month, the miraculous American food box is finished. Maria keeps the tins. They might be useful. She throws nothing out. But they are shining rude reminders of the bicycle Primo bartered away, and the last of the currency.

The suitcase of rice is nearly empty—she has sold some, cooked some. The hidden provisions are all but finished. The pot of meat extract is scraped clean. She's saving the last guinea pig for dinner at Christmas. Christ's birth was a miracle, and the three magus-kings, the shepherds who found their way, they were all miracles . . . Perhaps a miracle will happen before the Epiphany.

Head bowed before her Madonna shrine—without fresh flowers, just old, dried, faded blooms—Maria prays.

The worst of Winter is still to come, the Madonna says. *Your fledgling breathes, she lives, Maria, but every rasping breath is not a sign. It is just a breath. One breath now, and then another. No promise that there will be more. Her body yearns to be dust again.*

And there are warnings in Nature that this will be a Winter worse

than most. You have no firewood, you village idiot. A miserable lot of coals
for the bed warmer. Too little food for the table. Polenta is not enough.
You're failing, Maria, lizard-catcher that you are—you wanted money
and respect, but you're worse than that witch Delfina.

Your little girl is on the brink, your husband is broken, your perfect son
has given away the family treasure, and your contaminated cousin waits
for you until his coughing stops—and then what, Maria?

Will he summon you as he wrote? You know he will.

Will you return to his bed of sin? You know you must.

You should have burnt your cousin's note, my dear—his words of love
and his threats. Perhaps you wanted to keep it, after all. You've kept it a
long time, and it wasn't always in your apron pocket. You must have put
it there. You're getting careless.

~

BEFORE CHRISTMAS, TWO MEN appear. There are military men
everywhere, and local men who can't fight, and men who pass
through Fosso like water through a colander, avoiding capture. But
these strangers come into the shop as civilian customers, and they
don't turn away when they see there's nothing to take or buy. They
linger.

One is lean and white-skinned. The other is a Blackamoor with
a face straight off a coffee tin. Both wear long grubby coats, like
locals, and beige pants, too short, gray gloves, black boots, black
berets. They speak Italian.

Maria knows there's no such thing as a black-skinned Italian,
unless the lost colonies in faraway Africa can be counted as Italian.
She should have cooked and eaten the last guinea pig. But perhaps
it is her boy they want, to fight and die for them, whatever they're
fighting for. There are so many causes now, so many sides. Or
maybe it's a woman's body they want. She's forty-six, she's old, but
she's not too old. She's heard the stories of violation, and nice
girls—even old women—turned into whores for their hunger. She
looks at the men's faces. She can't tell if they will hurt her.

"We were given your address," the pale one says. His gestures are alarming. He jerks his hand and points.

Maria looks toward the shop door, terrified of who might come in next. *Consorting with an enemy is prohibited.* She thinks of those bodies hanging in Bassano.

"We come from Altavilla," the Blackamoor says. He almost sounds Italian, but there's no getting past his face.

I don't believe you, Maria thinks. But she knows not to say it or show it. "You can see, our shop is empty," she says. "I have nothing to sell. Nothing to give." *And nothing for you to take,* she wants to add.

"Please don't be frightened," the Blackamoor says. "We need accommodation."

"Just for a night or two before we move on." The pale one glances at the door. He smiles and his teeth are big like those on a horse, and very white.

"We were told to look for the sign on the shop front. *Generi Alimentari.* We know it's a big risk for you—"

"Aiding and abetting . . ." She stops. His accent. She remembers the Americans who came to the *contrà* after the First War. They brought goods and animals for a new start after the Austrian devastation. "Who told you?" she asks.

"We can't say," the Blackamoor answers. "Someone in Altavilla."

Altavilla again. Do they mean Rodolfo and Edda? Primo when he was there? Harboring stray Italians is a crime, not reporting them to the military police is a crime, just passing the time of day with them is a crime, punishable by death. Italians on the run are deserters or traitors or Partisans or escaped prisoners of war. They are all enemies of the Repubblica Sociale Italiana. Foreigners are even worse than Italians. Much, much worse. She is committing a crime just talking to them.

"You've seen the posters," she says. "I have to report you. Or the Nazis will execute us. Even the children. They'll hang us off the trees like meat."

The white one glances toward the back door.

"Who are you?" Achille is here at last. Holding an ax. He could knock them both to the floor with one blow.

Maria talks to him in dialect. "They want to stay here a night or two—"

"We do business, not politics. We don't take sides," Achille says to the men. "We'd be killed for it. Or tortured. You've heard of the Banda Carità and—"

"We've got nothing to feed you," Maria says.

But the Americans pull out cash. They lay it on the counter. Dollars. Reichsmarks. Lira notes. Enough to buy overpriced black-market chicken, and pork, and grain, and olive oil . . .

Her mouth waters.

"Money's no use in prison." Achille mutters at her in dialect. "And no use in the grave."

"It could buy us food—"

"If I could do the deals, not Primo. He's worse than a girl. All that cash for a couple of fancy tins—"

"*Before* the grave," Maria says.

"We don't even have a bike—"

"We can get you a bike." The Blackamoor hears well. He even understands dialect.

Maria's hands are in her apron pocket, fretting at a scrap of paper, over and over. It is not Duilio's note. She destroyed that in the fire. Her cousin is getting stronger, keeping warm, being fed, but she cannot look to him for protection.

Achille stares at her.

She coughs. And now she's thinking, with these men, and their money, with mortal risk, with a new bicycle, and with Winter, the coldest bitterest worst Winter, and with skinny Bruna white-faced and coughing, and Death's shadow darkening each new day, and with Duilio waiting to destroy her marriage . . . *To whom is victory?* Maria thinks. *To whom is Vittoria?*

"We owe the Americans," she says out loud. It feels like jumping off a mountain edge.

Before his prison days, Achille might have taken his hand to her for speaking over him like this in front of others. But now he is a lizard without a tail.

"Perhaps we can help our liberators?" She says it to Achille as if she's asking for his permission.

He straightens like a soldier. He is still holding the ax.

"It's just a few days." She lowers her voice. "We need the money. Or else we *will* be in the grave before this Winter's out." She whispers, "Bruna first." And the thought of her baby girl dying pinches at her throat.

"Very well," he says. As if it is up to him.

Pipo and Baldassare

Everything is piece by piece, Maria thinks. God's creation of this world, day by day. War. Hunger. A sick child's convalescence. Mountain water on granite, drop by drop. A woman's reputation. Stitch by stitch. The advancement of the seasons. Tough skins on onions. Thick tight husks on corn. Wet leaves falling heavily, after clinging long and withering on the bough. It's one leaf here, one there, but slowly a heap forms. Webs are strung in midair. One here, one there. Then, at first invisible, spiders appear everywhere, spinning bigger and wider, disregarding war but sure of a harsh Winter to come.

In the first days when she could wake and leave her bed, little Bruna was terrified of the Americans hidden in the cellar.

Why did they not go away? Perhaps it was the persistent snow, filling and blocking and walling in everything.

They stayed.

They are staying.

And gradually, as if each day could matter to Fortuna, as if each investment of a day makes a heap of lucky days, like snow, flake by flake, accumulating—each day that the Nazis and the Fascists have not stormed into the house and arrested everybody, each day that the money grows, and the supplies grow, the Americans seem less dangerous, more welcome.

If this time is like a warm deceiving November before a bitter Winter, Maria doesn't care. It feels like luxury. It feels like hibernation inside a rock. It feels like biding her time because this war will never end, and she might as well be fed and warm and standing when the bombs fall on their heads.

Bruna sleeps and rests and coughs. Sometimes, carefully, gently, she takes the Americans their meals, and water in bowls so that they can wash. Sometimes, she brings up their waste, and their cash, which she hands over to Maria. And sooner or later—Maria is not sure when—the men have names. Bruna calls the white one Pipo, like the blackout plane, or the American plane, any plane that can't be identified. He says he is a pilot, saved by Partisans when he crashed. Maria wonders if those Partisans ate her chickens. And the black man is a pilot too. Bruna calls him Baldassare, like the third wise magus-king. She is nothing if not fanciful. He teaches her words in English. *Bless iu, meri Crismas.* The men pay Primo to carry secret messages—on foot, and soon by bicycle, the promised bicycle bought with their money, messages hidden inside handlebars and frame, to villages and to cities. Through checkpoints. The world is all black market, gray market, inflation, poverty. And Primo, taking risks, oblivious to Fortuna, returns with messages and parcels and the cash that is now plentiful.

If I'm meant to die, I die, he says. *You only die once.* He has become a hero.

One day they have salted beef. And chocolate. *Don't forget that in the month of January, he lives well who has grain in the granary.*

Maria stops coughing. But Bruna does not.

In this harshest Winter people have ever known, the basin at the village pump is frozen in, no use to all those women who can't do their washing at home. The lake at Merlo is solid ice, meters deep; the Germans drive trucks across it just for fun. In the mountains, people are going mad with snowblindness.

On the eve of the Epiphany, Scopeton walks into the shop. The sausage-fingered militiaman has a new uniform, but he looks haggard, gray before his time. His side is not doing so well now. *To whom is victory?*

Even so, the man who arrested Achille has the power to arrest Maria. And all her kin. The Americans are downstairs in the cellar. All he has to do is look.

He acknowledges her with a Roman salute.

"Greetings," she says.

"We're looking for your cousin."

"Which cousin?"

"You know who I mean. Your *aiutante* cousin."

"Duilio's in the hospital," Maria says.

"Apparently not."

"In Monastero—"

"Apparently not."

"Is he well now? Did they let him out?"

"We thought you might know where he went. I know you were close." His face is set hard, his mouth is mean, but his fretful eyes are those of an animal that knows the hunt is on. The Allies are advancing from the south. They've taken Rome. They have Rimini. "He's gone missing just when we need our brothers most, with the threat of the Communists and the terrorist Allies. If you're hiding him—"

"How could he get here? He's sick. And the mountains are locked in by snow. We all are." She keeps her eyes distant, her voice neutral, but inside she feels the fear in her nerves. Duilio is on the loose. And Scopeton could demand to search the cellar.

"If he's up to no good," he says, "if he's being a bad Fascist, you know there will be retribution."

She can't imagine Duilio being anything but a devoted Fascist. He must have lost his mind. He must be on his way to Fosso. Seeking her out. "Have you come here to tell me that?"

"If you hide him, even for a day, there will be retribution. That's what I've come to tell you."

Scopeton looks around the shop, and then toward the storeroom, where the trapdoor to the cellar is, where the Americans are. "Incidentally, how long has it been since this place was searched?"

There's a big stone in her gut, but she knows to keep her face pure and hard, like the Madonna of the Mountains. *Pura e dura.* "You can search this place right now," she says. "We're used to it. We've got nothing to hide. You can see we've got nothing much at all."

Scopeton looks toward the back door. "If he shows up, you know it's your duty to report him immediately."

"I've seen the posters," Maria says, her pulse settling, because she knows that this stupid sausage-fingered man has lost this deal. *Chi ga 'na bona boca ga 'na bona borsa.* The one who has a good mouth has a good purse. "I know my duty," she adds. It sounds respectful.

Scopeton salutes and turns to leave the way he came.

Maria stares at the floor where he walked, gazes at the traces of water where snow crystals melted off his fancy Fascist boots.

Duilio is nowhere, missing, somewhere, on his way. He promised he would come to claim her. All he has to do is tell people, tell Achille everything, in front of the family, and Amelia would remember the messages to and fro—*look nice*—and Duilio would be free to take Maria away like some mistress-whore, destroy her family, tear her from her children. He still has the power of the State on his side. Unless she turns him in for desertion. They're after him. No, he would take revenge on her, on her family.

She sets about cleaning, just to calm herself down. Then she is weighing rice, weighing cornmeal, calculating the worth of the supplies that can be on show without raising suspicion. She is dusting shelves, scrubbing them, polishing them. Counting coupons. Adding up the books, both rationed goods and not.

The water from Scopeton's boots has disappeared into air.

Duilio could turn up, today, tomorrow, and find the Americans in the cellar. He could denounce her and make a triumph of betraying his flesh and blood—it must have been Duilio who denounced Achille. She has not dared to think it before, not properly, not clearly—she suspected Nevoso, and Attilio the baker, others, even Benedetta the station-master's wife—but now she feels sure that the cousin who got her husband out of prison is the devil who had him jailed.

~

SLOWLY, THE SNOW MELTS here, turns to grubby slush under Nazi tires there—falls off in clumps, revealing broken walls and cracks. There is some food on the shop shelves, though the gaps are greater than the stock.

Maria serves officers and police of every class and kind. Not one of them asks to inspect the cellar. Everything is falling apart. The Gothic Line. The phony republic. She shows her Party card to men in uniform, she reminds them of her sister Edda whose big house is the home of German Army Command. Still, her gut clenches every time the shop door opens, or a long black car slows on the street outside.

Then one day, as natural as the birds migrating, the Americans go. To Switzerland, or to the Alps, Partisan country. Maria says a rosary in thanks. And Bruna, who was scared in the beginning, sheds tears, because she's feeling better, little by little, and because they made her feel important. *Meri Crismas.* And Primo sheds a tear, because he knows he was important. And Achille softens and relaxes, because the danger has gone, and the threat of execution has gone, and they have a bicycle again, and God knows how much cash.

Maria knows how much cash. She counts it when she can, just to feel the reassurance of the numbers. She hides it in places nobody knows, not even Achille. If they arrest him, he will have no secrets to give away.

~

THE SNOW MELTS, and the filth under Nazi tires runs off into drains, and rain washes at the gathered grime, and cold sometimes freezes it into treacherous ice, and the Nazis are blowing up every-thing, sabotaging or destroying what they can to make everything worse for the Allies, but worst of all for the Italians, and night is like day for the lightnings of war, and Vicenza is bombed in Febru-ary, and the Germans fight back, and again on the day of Christ's Passion, unleashing phosphorous fires from the sky, and the winds of Spring scatter the fires like seeds to start new fires, and the Ger-mans fight back. A panicking Nazi officer in Forasacco sells a stock-pile of shoes, thousands of shoes, at a bargain, to desperate locals who need shoes. The Partisans free Bologna, and there are more bombs, the Allies are bombing the guts out of the Veneto, and blind Fortuna is blasted to dust along with the Fosso church walls, and the CLN Partisans show their faces and wave their flags for all of Northern Italy. On a Spring day of light sifting rain, there is news that the Allies have crossed the Po River and poured into the plains, and that cities have been taken by Partisans with locals rising up against the Germans. And American tanks are entering the cities, and cigarettes are being handed out—blond tobacco that makes blue smoke—and American food: flour whiter than any flour ever seen, and powdered milk, freeze-dried soup in big bins, salted but-ter and dark yellow cheese. The city people are jubilant, but in the countryside around Fosso, the war lingers. Retreating Nazis shoot locals and children hiding in the rocks where Maria and Amelia caught lizards, and small-time Fascists are killed in Fascist-hunts, as sudden as wildfire, dozens in a day. That militiaman Fratasso is dragged into the piazza at Campolongo and shot in the head, in front of his wife and children, and the notary Nevoso and his wife are shot in their home. Scopeton is nowhere, and Duilio is still missing, and the big-time Fascists have already slipped away like water into cracks. But not Mussolini. He is captured, disguised as a German, with his lady-friend, and their bodies are hung by the feet, bloated and mauled, in a piazza in Milan, for all to see. And Hitler has killed himself, and his wife. And Tito occupies Trieste. Maria burns her Party card, Bruna has roses in her cheeks and the bells that are not broken ring.

1948

Fireflies

I T'S THE END OF THE *SAGRA*. THE AIR IS FULL OF CIGARETTE smoke and bottled scent and sugary fritter oil. The dancing has stopped. Everyone is saying goodbye. A kiss on the left cheek, the right, the left. All the girls and boys.

"Where's Amelia?" Maria says.

"She was with that friend of hers, Agata." Primo frowns.

Amelia appears from behind the chapel where the ancient yews are. She's by herself.

"Where have you been?" Primo asks, grabbing her arm.

"I needed to . . ." She has a sly look on her face. "You know." Her lipstick is smudged.

"Couldn't you wait?"

"Jesus, Mary and Joseph," says Amelia, "it's a long walk home."

A group is gathering, mostly Primo's friends. He flirts with a pretty girl as she walks past.

"You shouldn't be wearing lipstick," Maria says in Amelia's ear.

Primo turns to Arsenio. "And you," he says. "What's taken you so long?"

Arsenio shrugs. At seventeen, he's the youngest in the crowd.

He does whatever Primo tells him to do. *Don't go there, do this, follow me.*

"Here's Agata." Amelia loops arms with her friend.

Agata has been dancing with the same fellow all night. He looks skinny and weak, but the girl has a crossed eye and she's older than the others—her family would be happy to see her married to anyone.

"Come on," says Maria. She wonders if Bruna, with her sensitivities and her frailty, will be hard to marry off.

The night is warm and damp after a day of soft rain. The air is sweet with the scents of Spring: almond blossom, fruit blossom, lilac. There's plenty of wheat this year, rows of it growing in thin green walls, tidier than armies—but there are still dark scarred patches of earth, rubble and rubbish, blackened fields, ruined bridges.

People have been working hard for the Reconstruction. Long days of labor, even Sundays and holy days. Repairing railways and rebuilding houses. Everything will be new.

They have survived, her entire family, even little Bruna with her mortal illness. The shop is full of goods; the shelves are loaded with food. Primo is dressed in the finest linen and cotton and a silk scarf, all new. There's money in silk.

Maria tries not to worry about money. Since before the war, everyone has worried about money, and the prices went up times twenty, doubling in one year. Everywhere is devastated. But everything will be new, everything is possible.

The girls walk ahead and Maria follows with the boys. She can walk forever. Her legs are as strong as her daughter's—even if she feels a rheumatic ache or two, and a pain in her hip. Her stride is as long and as straight as Amelia's.

The broken roads are wet with rain, shining with starlight and moonlight. Frogs leap across her path from one ditch to another, catching the moon on their backs. They have survived the war too.

It's another three kilometers to Fosso. The road changes from thin mud to paving and back to mud again. Her shoes will not resist the wet—their cork soles are already crumbling. But it doesn't matter. There are bats in the air, darting black against the lilac sky—not bombs, not leaflets, not falling parachutists, not crashing planes.

As she walks, Maria listens to the chatter.

"The world is getting better now," Amelia says.

Agata laughs. "Yes, it is."

"We can just walk like this. In the quiet. Without a thousand trucks and tanks."

"Without barricades."

"No curfew. I love being out after dark."

"No crazy crowds of men."

"Jesus, Mary and Joseph, no more crazy men!"

Refugees, evacuees, returnees from the slave camps, escaped prisoners of war, Partisans . . . they were everywhere, lurking, appearing suddenly, sometimes in a straggle, sometimes in crazy swarms. Everyone was in the wrong place. And the men who were in their usual, proper places went crazy too, with riots and strikes.

"My little sister got better."

"Thank God."

"Zia Edda got her house back from the Nazis, and she got to keep their grand piano—"

"That nobody knows how to play." Agata laughs again.

"It'll be worth plenty when she sells it, you watch. And Papà got his fields back. And I can feed the silkworms. And Beppe at the *osteria* got his wife back from Germany."

"But he's still a drunk."

"But she can still cook. He'll be happy again. And we have food. Meat in tins! Who ever imagined food like that? And the whitest flour I've ever seen. Mama says it's like a fantasy." She calls back to Maria. "Don't you, Mama?"

Maria nods in the darkness.

"It *is* a fantasy," Agata says.

"It's American," says Amelia.

"I don't mind the Rhodesians, and the South Americans almost speak Veneto, but I'm scared of the well-mannered British ones, and the smiling Americans—"

"Even if two of them lived in our cellar—"

"Even if their generals are giving money to all of Europe."

"They've got so much money," says Amelia.

"They've got everything."

"No wonder everyone's emigrating."

Primo and Arsenio are talking loudly now about a beauty contest, the measurements of a perfect woman. They're not thinking like tailors or coffin-makers. They're talking as men do.

Arsenio can do arithmetic fast, even though he stopped going to school when it was bombed. The teacher started classes in her house thirty kilometers away, so he lost interest and worked in the shop instead. *You've got to study so people don't cheat you*, Edda always said.

Amelia looks back again, moonlight catching her smooth young face. "And my brothers missed every roundup."

There were so many armies, so many arrests, so many vendettas, so many boys in hiding, in granaries, in convents, in cellars, and so many who got caught—and other ones still missing—but Primo and Arsenio weren't reported, or press-ganged, or sent away to a camp. They were lucky. At the crossing by the station-master's house, Maria saw those trains with bars on the windows packed with frightened faces, heading north to Germany. Boys just like her sons and, she'd heard, *carabinieri*, Jews, ex-Fascists. Duilio saved her family from the worst.

He has not summoned her.

Maria silently thanks God and crosses herself.

Those trains are no more.

Achille doesn't beat her anymore. He hasn't taken his hand to her since he came back from prison.

And he isn't in disgrace anymore. His fortunes have turned with the war. It was good to have those Allies in the cellar.

She crosses herself again.

Now the Liberators are all over the place and girls are giddy with their attentions. Some of them have married and emigrated. It sounds like a dream, everything brand-new and beautiful. No rations. No politics. Maria imagines losing her daughter to an American. Would Amelia leave her family? It will be silk season soon. Do they have silk in America? Amelia knows how to rear silkworms, thanks to the silk women and the nuns. She's the first in the family to have a real trade. *A trade is as good as a dowry.* Silk work is better than a dowry. Her daughter's not stupid, she wouldn't throw all that away, but she is young, so she has romantic, foolish notions. She should not be wearing lipstick. It's the easy girls who wear lipstick, the cheap girls who give themselves to American soldiers for food or chocolate or soft toys. It's the easy girls who go to a *sagra* unchaperoned, leaving the door wide open for temptation and trouble.

There's almost one *sagra* for every calendar moon. Celebrations of the harvest, the local saint, the local cheese, the *porcino*. Sometimes they're in small towns like Ventana or Dueponti, or Santa Croce, where all the thieves are. Sometimes they're further afield, across the ruins of the province, in bigger towns, the mountains, the seaside. The *sagre* used to be Fascist Saturdays, all uniforms and anthems, but now they're full of dancing and sticky nougat and secret proposals and girls getting light-headed and becoming fallen women.

"What do you think of Bartolomeo?" Agata asks Amelia.

Maria strains to hear every word.

Primo and the others are still talking loudly, about cars and racing, about cycling, their heroes, the forthcoming Giro d'Italia.

Amelia squeezes her friend's arm. "I think he likes you."

"Do you really think so?" Agata says.

"I know so. I saw how you two danced. The way he looks at you. He's nice."

Maria keeps listening, but the two girls walk on in silence.

Between silk seasons, Amelia works hard in the shop and the *orto*, she looks after the little ones, she honors her mother and father as the Commandments say, and yet she has her ways of getting around Achille, even Primo. She looks in mirrors when she thinks Maria doesn't notice. She won't be tied down. But what can Maria do? Even Mussolini couldn't control his own daughter. Women will be voting next month and it will be democracy. Ever since before Amelia was born there have only been dictators.

"Look: fireflies!" Agata points into the darkness.

Their dancing, disappearing shapes are magical. Maria remembers night skies bleached white with fighting, brighter than day. There was fire, but no fireflies.

"Let's make a wish," says Amelia.

"No. An American plane crashed here. It feels unlucky," Agata says. "Remember when they machine-gunned the women and children in Cagliari?"

"Who?"

"The Americans. And in Grosseto, at Easter, they gunned down everyone, even children on a merry-go-round, even children herding geese—"

"I heard they came back and shot the priest," Amelia says.

"He was trying to give Absolution to all the dying people. There were other places too, other stories, not just propaganda, before they got to the north."

"Jesus, Mary and Joseph, they destroyed everything."

"People ran out and stripped that pilot, you know, they took his boots, his watch, everything."

"Only because they were desperate, and he was dead. If he'd been alive, they would have saved him. Like the ones we had in the cellar." Amelia tickles her friend's neck. "Aren't we lucky Bartolomeo got through safe and sound?"

Agata pinches her. "And someone else?"

Amelia glances back behind her.

The boys are not listening.

Maria pretends not to hear.

Amelia says something to her friend. Her voice is quiet.

"Promise," Agata replies. "But the walls have ears, and the world has eyes, you know."

"Jesus, Mary and Joseph, you sound like there's still a war on!"

The two girls burst out laughing, and they almost skip instead of walking, and Maria feels a pang of envy, which is a sin, but just for a moment. She decides, as she's walking, to tether her girl like a pony, if she can.

She's nothing if she's not a mother, and her daughter who survived the war with unscarred lungs must have an unblemished reputation, so that one day she can have a proper wedding, an eleven-o'clock Mass in the bright sight of day, around Easter like a well-off girl, at the reconstructed church, which will be nice and new, to a man who's high in the world, and straight-boned, and strong. And her own father will be proud, if he's still alive then, God willing.

But time can wait.

Lent

MARIA SITS AT THE KITCHEN TABLE AND SLITS OPEN THE envelope. She has made fresh coffee. Real coffee. She pours herself a little cup and tips in two heaped spoonfuls of sugar. She stirs. Spring sunlight streams in through paper-free windows. She unfolds the letter from Egidia. Papà's name is printed at the top.

SAINT JOSEPH'S DAY, 1948

Dearest Maria Vittoria, my darling sister,

How long since we have spoken or written. I miss you and cherish you. I must tell you that our cousin Duilio was found after all this time. He has been living wild three years, worse than that madwoman Delfina, stealing food, foraging, wild as an animal. I don't know where he was living. Someone said in one of the tunnels from the war of '15, where they used to store ammunition on the way to fighting the Austrians, etc. It must have been unbearable cold. And he had TB! God knows how he survived. Poor dear Claudia says it was his fear that kept him alive. But she goes from bad to worse. She should have mar-

ried. Well, his suffering is over. You know the reprisals still go
on here and there. Some Fascist-hunters found him and exe-
cuted him.

Maria gulps her coffee and coughs. She replaces the cup on its
saucer but it tips over on its side. She stills the clatter with her
hand. Her fingers are sticky. She reads the words again.

and executed him

Duilio dead?
She reads the line again.

Some Fascist-hunters found him and executed him. I think they
made him talk. He confessed to many bad things, he said all
sorts of things. You must know before you hear them from
someone else. They say he cleansed people, I don't know how
many, including that madwoman Delfina. He must have exe-
cuted her some time after she made that wild public scene in
Monastero when you came up for Onora's funeral. Or was it
Valeria's? God rest their souls. I don't know what else he said
before he entrusted his soul to God but it is appalling shame to
us all that our cousin is a Murderer. That madwoman was
good for nothing but she was harmless and deficient. And
wicked gossips are saying that thing again about her being
some kind of kin. Our uncle may be aged and failing in mind
but he would certainly deny it. The shame is too dreadful. It
makes me want to run away, for example, emigrate. But we are
as poor as church mice compared to you. And I wouldn't leave
our mother now. Some people are saying you were very close to
him but I know you hated him, as we all do, even though he is
our blood. I could hate him even more now, but he is in God's
hands so the time for hate has passed. I wrote as soon as I
heard to let you know. Before you hear it from others. The
shame!

Kind regards to Achille and the children.
Your devoted sister, much love always,
Maria Egidia and family

"Mama, what's the matter?" Amelia is here in the kitchen.

Maria folds the letter over. She wants to hide it.

"Is it bad news?"

Maria shakes her head. No, it is not bad news. "They found Duilio. And he's dead." Her voice is tight. Duilio is dead. And his accusations have died with him. She feels relief, but it's cold like mountain water, and it washes away his threats, and yet she must not feel good about any man's death, especially not her cousin's. Even if he was a murderer.

She wants to know what he said to the people who caught him.

Amelia sets the coffee cup upright on its saucer. She sits down. She's very still and quiet. "I hated him."

Maria is shocked.

"Good riddance." Amelia is gazing at Maria, looking into her eyes without blinking.

"Wash your mouth out with soap and water," Maria says, trying to sound firm.

"Didn't you hate him too?"

"He's family."

"But don't you hate him?"

What does Amelia know about her visits to Duilio? She was the one who brought back his message that very first time. *Look nice.* Her girl's not stupid. But she knows nothing.

"God hears everything you say."

"I hate his guts. Your Blackshirt cousin." Amelia is provoking her.

"He helped us," Maria says, feeling weak. "We survived the war."

"I'm glad he's dead."

"Me too," says Maria at last. And it's true.

Holy Monday

YESTERDAY WAS PALM SUNDAY, WHEN JESUS RODE INTO Jerusalem on a donkey and the people put palms down to welcome Him. Today Jesus cursed the fig tree and made it wither, to show that people can make anything come true if they pray for it hard enough. Although rationing is still enforced—even now there are coupons for meat, and bread, this much milk, that much butter, extra for railway workers and gondoliers and veterans—Maria has eggs from the new chickens, and flour from the Americans, and clean sweet water from the bore pump. Not a soul can argue with that.

She walks back from Attilio the baker's with the family's bread allowance in the crook of her arm. The sun is white and mild. She passes the shop and continues to the piazza, where Achille is working with the men to rebuild the church and campanile.

Next to the others—the foreman, and Beppe from the *osteria*, red-faced and limping, Calvinetto with his paunch, the skinny tailor and his son, and Don Goffredo fussing like a woman—Achille is tall and handsome, still strong despite his middle age. His muscles are like armor.

He hasn't noticed her.

The campanile is nearly finished. She gazes up the scaffolding to its top, and the sun makes her squint. She sneezes.

When she looks back, Achille has gone.

She continues watching for a while, as the men carry stones and bricks, or hammer frames, or wheel cement. Some sing. Men are happy building. Everything will be new. She wonders how long it will be before they can all go to Mass again here. Men don't like going to Mass. Men are happy fighting. Men are happy eating.

Achille reappears, advancing very slowly with a great weight on his back. It's not bricks or sand, but a bronze church bell.

She doesn't know if it's one of the old bells repaired, or a new one.

He's the only man powerful enough to carry such a thing. He moves heavily. She remembers the day he came to win her, the huge *gavegnà* basket loaded on his head. He carried a donkey in the First War, or a man, or a cannon—she doesn't remember the details, and it doesn't matter. He was strong then; he's strong again now. She watches him with admiration.

When he sees her, he comes toward her, staggering beneath the weight of the bell. He is breathing deeply. The ropes dig into his shoulders. He has that angry look she recognizes in his face.

Maria knows to be scared, even though she is the one who can run.

"Your daughter," he gasps when he is close. "They told me. No-good fellow. Name of Verdon. Firmino. On the war pension. Scurvy. Pneumonia. Communist—"

"Who told you—"

"Think of your father. All he did for you. All we've done for her. She can't throw it away. Our honor." He stops talking to take a breath. He is bent under his load, but he tries to straighten a little. "You didn't keep your eye on her. Set an example. Or maybe you did. Do something."

He glares at her, then turns, carefully, and makes his way toward the campanile, step by slow step. A church bell with legs and boots.

Now she's remembering the walk back from the *sagra*, Amelia's talk with Agata. Her smudged lipstick. Could Amelia be courting with a sickly veteran or a Communist? This must be malicious gossip. Men like gossiping, even if they pretend they don't. When she gets home, she will clear things up with her daughter.

Set an example. Or maybe you did.

She still doesn't know what her husband believes. She denied everything. It was her word against Duilio's. And now Duilio has been silenced.

Achille's words are hinting and accusing. He doesn't dare say more, or worse, in case he makes it true.

When he gets home he will hit her, she feels it in her bones. He will hear the news about Duilio, and that will make him even angrier. Unless Primo is there too, to protect her.

~

MARIA CLIMBS THE STEPS. She pauses at the back door.

Amelia is in the kitchen making pasta with the new machine. She's singing to herself, the field-daisy rhyme Maria used to sing, one petal after another, losing count.

El me ama	He loves me
El me abrama	He covets me
El me abracia	He hugs me
El me vol ben	He cares for me
El me mantien	He supports me
El me ama	He loves me
El me abrama	He covets me
Nol me vole	He doesn't want me
El me dise su.	He tells me off.

Maria pushes the door open. "They say you've been dancing with some fellow and he's courting you."

Amelia turns the pasta-machine handle hard.

The machine is silver and smart. There is nothing else so fancy here, just the ancient meat mincer and the old Neapolitan *caffettiera*.

Sheets of pasta are draped like calico cloths over the backs of chairs. The place looks like a laundry.

Amelia brushes a lock of hair from her eyes with the back of her floury hand. "I dance with boys, but I don't let them take advantage," she says. "Who's been telling you things? Who was in the shop just now?"

"Never mind who told me what."

"You want me to get married, don't you, before I'm too . . ." She doesn't say *too old*. "You were already old when you had Bruna— you could have died."

"Look at me," Maria says. "Look me in the face. And stop that noise."

Amelia keeps turning the handle of the machine until the dough finishes feeding through the rollers. She drapes the pasta sheet over the last free chair. She's taking her time. There are still two more slabs of dough to press. She covers them with a damp cloth. She wipes her hands on her apron, brushes hair away from her eyes again. She faces Maria with the gaze of an innocent.

Maria grabs her shoulders. "Tell me you're not seeing this fellow Firmino."

"I've heard of him," Amelia says. "I've seen him at Mass."

Maria shakes her.

"I've met a boy called Firmino," Amelia says. "He's nice enough. He has good manners. And I've met Bartolomeo—"

"That's the name of Agata's fellow."

"And Giorgio. And Fiorenzo. Giorgio was on a British prisoner-boat that had a German flag as a decoy—but it got sunk by the British. Then he was caught in fishing nets with a whole lot of fish and fifteen men—all dead, except him. Then he was sent to a British concentration camp in India, and they machine-gunned everyone when they closed the camps. All except his camp. He came back weighing thirty-six kilos, but he was alive—"

"You've been dancing with Firmino Verdon."

"Maybe I did. I don't remember."

"So it's true."

There are tears now, gathering in the edges of Amelia's eyes. "I don't know. I don't remember."

"If you're lying to me, if you've been dancing with him . . . You *have* been dancing with him—"

"I don't lie to you, Mama." Amelia is blushing with shame, lying to her own mother. "Why don't you want me to dance with him?"

"They don't give out war pensions for nothing."

"He fought for Italy."

"He's weak. He's had scurvy. And pneumonia."

"Papà had malaria."

"But your father is strong."

"You have to be strong to walk here all the way from Russia."

Maria has heard the stories. Italian soldiers stuck for months in Godforsaken trenches, eating like beggars, the long freezing nights. Then walking back to Italy without directions or supplies. Thousands of kilometers in snow and mud and danger. On foot. In stupid Summer uniforms. Everyone dying everywhere.

"He fought for his country," Amelia says. "Our country."

"You deserve the best," Maria says. "We're not gypsies or paupers. We've worked so hard. We're . . ." She doesn't say the words, but she's thinking of money, and respect, and Papà with his printed notepaper, and Primo, and property, and the well-stocked shop, and not starving like Delfina, and appearances. *Bela figura.*

"He'll die," she says. "It's like animals: you don't put a runt with the best one."

"Mama, he's a good man. And he's kind."

"But he's got no money!"

"He's not a pauper."

"He's a Communist!"

"They care about the poor, don't they? Like Jesus did."

"Have we taught you nothing? He won't be able to support you. When I was young—"

"It's not the same now, Mama—"

"Shut up, shut up!" Maria thumps the table. The flour and the dough jump into the air. "You need a man to look after you."

There's fear in Amelia's eyes. Then boldness. "The way Papà looks after you?"

Maria slaps her face. Her hand hurts. "Don't talk to me like that."

Amelia stares at the floor. There are red finger-marks on her cheek.

Maria doesn't know what to do.

No se rifiuta nessun, gnanca se l'è gobo e storto. Refuse nobody, even if he's hunchbacked and crooked. Papà called them stupid sayings. He knew to reject a bad deal. Amelia is her beautiful, straight-boned, sweet-natured girl who went to school and has learned the skill of silkworms, which is as good as a dowry. She doesn't need a dowry. She has survived the war with her honor intact. And she's healthy, unlike frail Bruna. She can pick and choose.

Amelia speaks at last. Quietly. "Why can Primo do whatever he likes? He courts girls. Why can't I choose the husband I want?"

"Your father will kill you," Maria says, almost in a whisper.

"What have you told Papà?"

"What should I tell him? It's Papà who told me. What do you have to say for yourself?"

"I don't love Firmino. I just know him." She looks guilty now. "There's nothing to worry about."

"If you have anything to do with him again—ever—we'll send you to a house of correction. You think you know what curfew means? I'll lock you up. Worse than the Germans. Get down on your knees."

Amelia obeys and kneels. She clasps her floured hands in prayer.

Maria holds her by the wrists. "Promise me." Her grip is hard.

"I promise."

"Promise me you'll never go near him again. Not for any reason. Promise me on my mother's life. And mine."

"I promise."

Maria stares at her, looking for lies. *Don't trust anybody. Not even your own daughter. Girls are trouble.*

She lets go, walks out and back to the shop downstairs.

Holy Week

EVER SINCE THE BOMBING OF THEIR CHURCH, THE PEOPLE of Fosso go to Mass in Campolongo. Just before Holy Week, someone painted a hammer and sickle on the piazza wall. Primo is fretting because Yugoslavia on their doorstep should be a warning to everybody. Maria wonders if the priests or the Americans will repaint the wall, and then she wonders if anyone will paint a new mural of Fortuna and her wheel inside the Fosso church.

All men—Achille, Duilio, Nevoso, Fratasso, the politicians—all men can tumble off a throne into a monster's mouth. In Schio, more than fifty locals were killed because they were Fascists, while other locals returned from a death camp in Austria, miraculously alive. Some Partisans are big heroes now, but others are still locked up in prison. This mortal world is more fickle than Spring. It feeds a man, or it spits in his face, or both. Fortuna is veiled and blind.

People attend Mass from all around, not just from Campolongo. The hatted women sit on the left of the church, packed together tighter than at Fosso; the bare-headed old men and boys sit on the right, a sparse gathering as usual. The Fascists have disappeared, or they're wearing different clothes. It's safe to hate Germans again.

On Holy Thursday, the day of the Savior's Last Supper, all crucifixes and images are shrouded in purple cloth, full of mystery and anticipation. Maria is proud and pleased: little Bruna, nearly eight years old, is one of the fasting girls who kisses and scatters rose petals from ribbon-covered baskets—but the girl's hunger and excitement make her sensitivities worse, and she wheezes.

On Good Friday, the crucifixes are unveiled. Maria and her daughters make the Stations of the Cross, praying for each stage of Christ's journey to death, but lingering longest when His mortal body collapses under the weight of the Cross. *Jesus falls the first time. Jesus falls the second time. Jesus falls the third time.*

The tabernacle doors are wide open. There's no need to genuflect because God is not inside. The air is cold. Maria thinks of Golgotha and Mauthausen, all skulls and rock and humiliation, and she shivers.

Don Goffredo flings himself on the flower-covered altar with more passion than usual.

Does he mind that he's just the helper at Campolongo, not the main priest? she wonders. No, priests must have no pride. They exist to serve and be humble, even if they are always given the best chickens and the best eggs.

Easter Sunday arrives at last. It's a Mass like no other: there is more wax, more incense, more sprinkling of holy water, the paintings and statues have been unveiled, and all of Maria's family is here, even Achille.

Cross-eyed Agata is here too, with her family. Amelia and Agata give each other holy cards. And Firmino is here among the men, his red hair bright as a beacon. He exchanges greetings and cards with Agata, but he knows to stay away from Amelia. He knows that he is banned. Still, he can't be banned from church. At least he goes to Mass—lots of men don't bother. He coughs. Maria remembers that he had pneumonia. He's a weakling. Perhaps he still has pneumonia. Bruna will always have consumption deep inside her. Firmino coughs like Duilio coughed with his TB. He's a Communist. And he has red hair.

But Amelia has made a promise to Maria.

Lent is ended, Don Silvano says from the pulpit.

Everyone can eat what they want after forty days of sacrifices. Maria and her family have refrained from meat, even prosciutto. They've had no sweet things. No wine. Secretly, sinfully, she thinks everyone fasted enough during the war to count for forty years' worth of Lent. She crosses herself.

Today she has prepared thick duck and bean soup with bigoli. And polenta with birds—all those birds caught by Achille with good *vischio* on the nets. She can't wait to suck the tasty meat off their tiny bones.

Are we sure we didn't deserve that punishment? Don Silvano is sermonizing about the German occupation.

Did we deserve the famine, the devastation? Don Silvano asks the congregation. He's not expecting an answer. *The scourge of Salò?* He's talking about the war's last years, the Italian Social Republic, Hell on Earth.

Maria looks up at the church ceiling where the Holy Family floats in pink and blue clouds. Their faces are childlike and tender. On behalf of Amelia, she prays to Jesus, Mary and Joseph, each one separately, and then all together. She clasps her hands tight.

Achille is on the lookout for eligible men. He will find his daughter a suitable husband. A choice of suitors, if there's a choice to be had. This war, like the other one, has taken so many men.

Maria looks at her daughter sitting near her. Her dear girl is as pretty as a church painting. She was conceived in the moon's dying phase, the right time for planting, which is why she's strong and healthy and she'll give birth to lots of children, no doubt about it—when the right man is found, who's just as strong and healthy as she is. He must be well-off too.

~

THE ELEMENT OF MAN is the earth; the element of birds is the air; that of fish is water, but for women it is honor.

Oh, Maria, Maria Vittoria, remember your dowry account. Vaca, scrofa, cagna, troia! *You lowly thing, you were worth less than groceries. Your father had to pay a man to take you away, even when you were untouched by men.*

You knew nothing about desire.

Your daughter dances at the precipice of desire.

You know the dangers, the inebriation of being admired, the seductive music that leads to the altar of the self, the abyss that opens beneath frolicking feet . . .

All this you chose to forget, because in your heart of hearts you are envious of her—you never had so much freedom. And you are guilty too. Look nice, *your cousin said, but it was your daughter who brought his words to you. Remember what Achille said when he bore that great bell of God on his back. Your daughter's honor is your honor.*

Now she's the one who's dancing, flirting, courting. She's sweet and trusting. Independent. Ripe for ruinous sin. But the guilty mother cannot preach virtue to her young. Watch that she doesn't slip from your care and run away like a lowly gypsy.

Don't trust anybody. Not even your own daughter.

Clearing the granary

A<small>T HOME, AMELIA STARTS THE CAREFUL WORK OF PREPAR-</small>ing the attic. She is in charge here. She is confident. Maria is her helper.

They clear away the last remaining corncobs, hard as wood, clattering in a sack, downstairs. Good for feeding the animals.

They brush the racks, one by one, wooden frames and wire mesh, posts and supports.

Maria sweeps the floor, runs the broom along the rough roofbeams, stoops to clean the little windows and low walls. It's dusty work. She's not young anymore. Her joints and bones ache, but she doesn't show it.

Amelia looks for traces of mice, signs of eating, signs of excreting. She paces slowly from one end of the space to the other, checking for drafts. It's warm up here from the kitchen below. She leans against the chimney bricks, unbuttons her blouse, and fans her face with a newspaper.

Maria sees her blush.

I grow old in your absence, Amelia murmured one night in bed, in her sleep. But in the light of the next day, Maria wondered if she'd dreamed it.

Her daughter's days are full of work, though not the usual duties of the *orto*, or the livestock, or helping in the kitchen, or taking care of the little ones when they're home from school. Besides, Cecilio is fourteen now, so he doesn't need looking after. It's eight-year-old Bruna who needs attention. Her breath still catches when she's tired. She will always be delicate. Maria was too old when she had her. War-worried and going gray. Amelia was right.

Two weeks before the feast day of Saint Mark, one week before the national election, Maria and Amelia fill two tin drums with water and carry them upstairs, above the shop (where customers talk at Achille about politics and chickens and funerals) and up more stairs to the granary. They're careful not to spill or slip. Maria is reminded of her days carrying water pails to and from the well. Her daughter's arms are strong, even stronger than her own.

Amelia has youth in her favor.

She mixes quicklime into the water. She mops the walls, the roof and the floor. The granary is ghostly and moist, clean and dripping.

On the day of the national election, there's a line of men and women all the way down to the tailor's house. Maria and Achille go together, and Primo too, terrified that Italy will turn into Yugoslavia, a Communist Soviet state. Amelia's still too young to vote. All her life there was only Mussolini and war. She has no interest in politics at all.

Maria helps her set out a line of sulfur-beeswax candles in tins to fumigate the space. They light the wicks and watch the unholy glow dance across the roof-beams. It's a greater stink than Hell; the Devil himself would be odorless here. The fumes creep into every unstopped paper-thin crack, every flight-hole, every wood-knot.

With veils on their faces, mother and daughter keep watch until their eyes and nostrils begin to sting.

Maria's throat tightens. She coughs.

Amelia takes her hand to lead her out of the attic.

The candles are safe in their tins. They'll eventually burn out, and then the job will be done. Every spore, every pest, will be dead.

Tomorrow they will stuff any conspicuous cracks and holes with newspaper—old news of important men in chambers and important men on balconies. There will be no drafts for Amelia's silkworms.

~

IT'S LATE APRIL NOW, and all over Italy officials are counting ballots, votes for Communists and votes for Christian Democrats. It's a two-horse race, and all the men are fretting, smoking cigarettes, grumbling in huddles at the bar and in the piazza, while Amelia completes the final silkworm preparations.

She rubs the racks with wormwood leaves, silvery gray and aromatic. This is the last protective measure against parasites and pests. She lays out yellow sheets of clean sugar-paper on the wire mesh, tier by tier.

Apart from the cast-iron stove that Achille will haul up the stairs on his back, the *camaròn* is ready.

In the world outside, in Achille's fields, the mulberry trees burst into leaf.

Precious eggs

AMELIA IS CALLED TO THE PRESBYTERY TO COLLECT HER silkworm eggs on the feast day of Saint Mark, not a day earlier, not a day later. It's an auspicious sign.

Once tiny as poppy seeds, precious as black pearls, the eggs have started to hatch. They have been watched and cared for, all day, every day, all night, every night. The silk women work in shifts. The priests and altar boys stay out of their way. The worms have waited so long: Summer, Autumn, Winter and Spring. They have waited blindly for today, Liberation Day, exactly three years since the Germans knew they had to pack up and run away.

At Mass, the sermon is about freedom and democracy, and getting Saint Mark's body back from Egypt disguised as pork meat. Achille likes this story—it shows how clever Venetian merchants are. The priests are happy, and Primo is happy, and so Maria is happy, because the Christian Democrats have won the national elections. The Americans don't like Communists, but they have plenty of money for Christians. The new church at Fosso will get finished in no time.

The family gathers for a special lunch: rice and peas, rabbit roasted with herbs, piles of fresh greens, and crostoli pastries sprinkled with lots of sugar. Maria looks proudly at her family, eating her food, plenty of it, second helpings, third helpings, plates wiped clean. Bruna and Cecilio get sugar in their hair and everyone laughs. Maria can't remember another time when they were all together and laughing.

After lunch, the family disperses: Primo to the *osteria*, Achille and the boys downstairs to renovate shelving and paintwork in the shop while it's closed for the holiday, Bruna to help in the *orto*. Bearing a platter of crostoli for the silk women, Amelia walks back to Campolongo.

She returns with her silkworm babies in a stack of cardboard boxes. The chickens fuss and scatter at her side. Maria is picking pests out of the radicchio. Bruna is with her.

"The *bacolini!*" Bruna says.

"How are they?" Maria asks, looking up from her work.

"All good," Amelia says. "Hungry."

"Do you need the boys to help with the leaf-picking?"

Amelia frowns for a moment, then smiles her best smile. "No, no need. This will do for now, and I can pick enough for tonight and tomorrow."

"Good," Achille says, standing at the back door now. "We'll get more work done in the shop."

"I'll help you unpack," Maria says to Amelia.

"Can I come too?" Bruna says.

"We've got to finish up here first. Then you can play with the chickens." Maria feels guilty about little Bruna for a moment. "Or with your doll."

She follows Amelia upstairs to the granary.

They leave their clogs on the stairs.

Amelia opens the first box. The eggs are white specks; they used to be dark. The little gray caterpillars are out in the warmth and wriggling, tinier than eyelashes. They have been lifted onto sheets of cardboard, and some of them have already climbed through holes in the paper to the layer of green above. They eat to live, they live to eat. They're in a cozy tangle with bedding of the youngest tender mulberry leaves, cut finer than spaghettini, as finely as capelli d'angelo.

"Do we need the stove?" Maria asks.

"The air's already warm and dry, the way they like it."

Amelia lays out her baby silkworms and their greenery on the paper sheets. She moves with sacred precision, like Don Goffredo with the Eucharist, the chalice, the cloth.

Maria has nothing to do. She stands and watches. She feels useless. "I'll leave you to it," she says, and returns to the garden.

Bruna's Russian doll is strapped to her back now, like a baby. She is extracting slugs and tiny snails from between the radicchio leaves. Her knees are dirty from kneeling on the earth.

"I'm sure there are more pests this year," Maria says. "The Winter wasn't cold enough."

"The chickens will be happy," says Bruna.

They move on to the next row.

The sun is weak in the sky when Amelia comes out into the yard holding Achille's old *gavegnà* basket. It's big and unwieldy to carry by hand.

Bruna stops work to watch her.

Maria looks up. "Your father had that on his head the first time we met."

"I know the story." Amelia grins. "Papà was strong as an ox and walked up the steepest mountain without puffing or perspiring, carrying a ton of tobacco leaves—and that was in the days before he had his own fields. And his neck wasn't bent, and his back was straight, and anyone else would have stooped under the weight. That's when he came to marry you."

Maria feels happy. She remembers putting on her mother's violet oil to meet her betrothed. She can almost smell it now.

Amelia ties the *gavegnà* to the bicycle and sets off down the path to the road.

"I'll be back around dusk, maybe after," she calls out, without looking back, and she rings her bell. It's like a little laugh.

As Maria watches her go, she feels a stab inside. It's the mother's sorrow at seeing her grown-up daughter fly away.

Amelia

AMELIA ADORES CYCLING. THE ROADS ARE FLAT, APART from the broken stretches and the lumpy places where mines used to be. There's never enough slope to work up a sweat. Mama complains and misses the mountains, but the plains are easy. Amelia can see for miles. Today, everything looks brighter, sharper. Wildflowers line the road in pink, yellow, white, blue, red and purple sprinkles. The earth is mild and moist. All of Nature is green and alive. Bell towers and cypresses spike up beyond wheatfields and vineyards. The hills are bluer than the Madonna's veil against the horizon.

A very old *contadino* rides toward her, gasping, brown and sinewy, whipping his bicycle like a donkey. She can see he has no teeth. Seeds and leaves fly out of his broken straw hat. He slows down, salutes her, and points ahead with his sickle, wordless, before whipping his machine-beast into action again. Almost no one had bicycles until after the war.

Amelia grins and says a prayer of thanks to Saint Mark for this blessed day.

Papà's mulberry trees border fields and irrigation ditches. Their crowns are packed with new growth and not a hint of blight. Tomorrow all the leaf-pickers will be here, maybe Papà and the boys too. Each cartload will go to the silk factory past Campolongo. It's money, but the really good money will come later, with the silky cocoons.

Today Amelia has the place to herself. She leans her bicycle against the mulberry house. It's nothing more than one room with cement walls, a wooden door, tiny barred windows and a tiled roof. Unbroken by the war, it stands on the edge of Papà's last field. Inside, Spring sunlight beams through the little windows like the presence of God in paintings. The space is small, but it's cozy. It's the perfect place, the only place, to meet her beloved.

She unhooks the best pair of mulberry-leaf cutters.

Bells ring out from the church at Fraoleto. Amelia thinks today for the first time that the sound is a little crazy, tumbling and eddying, like something out of control. She has less than an hour to harvest before dusk. She must work steadily. She knows what she's doing. The time is right.

Mulberry trees are easy. They have no thorns or poisons. The leaves are tender and transparent, some bigger than her hand, big soft hearts with serrated edges. Their stalks are easy to cut.

She goes from tree to tree. Handful by handful, she fills the *gavegnà*. The leaves are as fine as organdy. She will have to cut them up when she gets home. At last the basket is full and heavy. She ties it firmly to the bicycle. The ditch is full of insects, the busyness of wings. The church bells sound. Her timing is perfect. This is an auspicious day.

She returns to the nearest tree, cutting extra leaves, to make a carpet for the mulberry house floor. It's patient work, to and fro. She enjoys it. She can think about anything and everything— except Firmino, who will be here soon. She mustn't think about him, or she'll lose time. She has waited months! Soon the dirt floor is green, and soft as skin.

She thinks about the bright blue egg that appeared last week on the roof. How did it get there? Did its mother lay it in flight? Was it abandoned? Would it ever hatch? It was so blue on the terracotta, so alone. It looked as if it would roll off and shatter with nothing more than a breeze. It disappeared as mysteriously as it had arrived, no trace of its shell in the dust or the grass.

Inside the mulberry house it smells good, of fresh-cut green. She wonders if it's the scent that stirs the appetite of the *bacolini*, and draws them out to hatch. She wonders if their mouths water. She wonders if other beasts—rabbits, or pigs, or chickens—salivate when they smell food. She thinks about the soft heavy breathing of pigs, about Saint Mark smuggled back to Venice as pork meat. She wonders about the color of his flesh. Pork meat is pale and pink; the pork-shy Egyptians must not have looked properly. Maybe that's the point of the story. Today men in Venice give their sweethearts, or their mothers, a *bocolo*—such red, red rosebuds grew at the saint's grave. Oh Jesus, Mary and Joseph, she will die of ecstasy if Firmino gives her a *bocolo*.

They held hands once, only once, after a *sagra*, while they were walking. His hand was cold, hers was not. She thought, *We're made of different meat.* Sometimes he coughs and catches his breath, but she is strong enough for both of them.

Her fingernails are green with sap that doesn't turn dark or stain, but her hands are feeling a little sticky. She hears the bells from Fraoleto again, and she knows that Firmino, if he's constant, will soon be here. She sits on the green mulberry-leaf floor and waits.

~

THE LIGHT THROUGH THE barred windows dims to half light, half shadow, now more than half, nearer dark. She hears him before she sees him. The sound of his bicycle. The squeal of brakes. But how does she know it is him? What if it's Primo or Achille, here to punish her? She grabs at the cutters and holds them tight. She's ready to defend herself. Someone is at the door. The world is quiet outside, but the air is concentrated with insects, birds and bats. The handle turns. She squats, ready to pounce.

The door opens.

"Amelia?" whispers the voice.

She leaps at him. She throws her arms around him and holds him tight.

He laughs.

She drops the cutters.

He drops the *bocolo*.

The bocolo!

"It's been so long," he says. "I grow old in your absence."

Auspicious words—her own words, sent through the air like the Holy Spirit. They are destined to marry. No matter what.

"Let me look at you," he says, drawing away from her but still holding her, as naturally as if he has held her this way before.

He gazes at her, his eyes unblinking and admiring, his mouth not quite smiling but pursed and pleased. He's trying to hold himself back, she can see that in the gloom. His copper hair catches the shaft of evening light and he is the sun, he is the sunset.

"Even lovelier than I remember." He grins. "I am so lucky!"

"I missed you at Mass this morning."

"I couldn't bear it."

"Have you missed me?" she asks.

"I can't think of anything else," he says. And he caresses her waist, the small of her back, lightly. His hands are cool through the cotton of her dress. She feels exquisite shivers inside her body, in every vein.

"You smell of violets," he says.

It's true. She has dabbed her neck and wrists with Mama's precious violet oil, made in the mountains by Nonna. It's the scent of romance, she doesn't know why—her mother only wears it for Mass and special occasions.

"And you smell of roses," she says.

"That reminds me." He lets go of her and drops to his knees to pick up the rose. "This is for you," he says, still kneeling. "For my secret angel."

"Do you still want to marry me?" she asks, looking down at his upturned face.

"I'm the one who's kneeling," he says, laughing. And then he coughs.

Will he always cough? Will he die, as Mama said? No, Amelia will take care of him and feed him and make him strong.

"Will you marry me, Maria Amelia Montanari?"

She takes the *bocolo* and grips its stalk. She feels thorns against the flesh of her fingers, on the palm of her hand. The sensation is exciting and intense, like the Holy Spirit concentrated in points of fire. If the thorns draw blood, it will be a sign. She looks. The drops of red look black in the gloom.

"Yes," she says. "I haven't changed my mind." She sinks to her knees and faces him. The bed of mulberry leaves is soft and cool. She could pray to him like this. He could pray to her. But the words would be their own words, not the prayer-words they know by rote.

Kneeling, they lean toward each other, and they kiss, chastely.

They kiss and kiss until the mulberry house is dark and only starlight seeps in through the barred windows. They are lying down now. Their hands explore and stroke and press. She can smell him, taste him, feel him. She catches fleeting glimpses of him, an edge, a wisp. His lips tickle her neck, his fingers reach under her dress; he caresses her thighs, she's wet and she aches for him to touch her wetness but he pulls back.

Her heart is drumming. Desire and fear and excitement drumming.

He speaks at last. His voice is a whisper. "We've got to wait. I have to ask your father—"

"They'll never say yes. And Primo will kill you first, or me." She can feel tears welling in her eyes, though not enough to spill. She can end this now, get up off the floor and go home, frustrated, marry a man her parents want, and go to church, and everyone will be happy.

Except her. Except Firmino.

If she gives him her virginity, there'll be no argument, no choice. Her heart is loud in her head, and she imagines it beating loud in the fields of Fraoleto, throughout the entire Veneto, the whole world. This is her decision. The only way.

"Our only time is here and now." She begins to undo his shirt, she unbuttons his pants, slips her hand inside.

He sighs.

He pulls up her dress and peels off her undergarments until she is exposed like Eve, and his hands are warm, and he strips to nakedness like Adam, and he makes love to her bared breasts. She fills his mouth with her body, and she feels a kind of ecstasy all over, thrilling in waves, cascading like church bells, and he pushes into her, pressing farther until her resistance gives, and he is deep inside her, and their bodies press together in a slippery tangle, and he groans like a wounded man and she knows that he is hers, and she is his, and if Jesus, Mary and Joseph will have it, this is the moment that their firstborn child begins its life miracle, here and now.

They lie together, side by side, him inside her, her wrapped around him, until gently, finally, they disentangle.

"I've got to go now, or they'll start to notice." She picks herself up from the floor, and brushes off the soft leaf that clings to her arm, another from her thigh, her calf. "You're my beloved, and we'll get married now, even if we have to elope."

"I'll find a priest," Firmino says. "I'll go to a city. Vicenza or Padua."

"And if my parents don't say yes, after we're married by a priest, we can go anywhere. Start a new life. In Australia or Argentina."

"I love you, Amelia, more than life. We can go anywhere."

She wipes her face on her undergarments—there must be lipstick all over, but she can't see properly in the darkness. She smooths her dress, tidies her hair.

"I have nothing to give you," his voice says. "No proof, no ring."

"I can't go home with the rose, but I can keep it in my heart," she says.

"Here." His hand reaches hers. He gives her something. "I've kept it with me ever since Russia."

"What is it?"

"A cloth badge. It says DON. The river where we nearly died."

"You didn't die," she says tenderly.

"It was made in Dachau. For Cossack SS officers to wear—Russians were killing Russians. I couldn't stop thinking, *Someone made this.*"

Amelia wonders how he came by it, but she says nothing. She strokes the smooth weave with her fingertips.

"I'm sure a man sewed it. I held on to it all the way home. I thought, *If I keep this safe, I can keep the man alive.* I think it's lucky."

Amelia tucks the lucky charm into her dress. "It's safe with me."

"You're safe with me."

They embrace. For the last time. Until when? She can't bear any more waiting. They must be married soon. But Jesus, Mary and Joseph, she has no idea who will be where when she gets home. She'll have to avoid being seen, or questioned. They mustn't smell her. She will have to go straight up to the attic, to feed her hungry silkworms.

She jumps on the bicycle and feels a spill of liquid from deep inside her. She is a mess. If anyone sees her, they'll see she's a mess. It's late, too long after dusk. She rides by dim moonlight and starlight. There are bats in the air, insects, birds of prey, the heady scent of lilacs, church bells sounding the hour, some near, some far, some so faint they feel like a memory. Amelia has a harvest of sweet, young mulberry leaves, and a heart full of love.

~

THE SHOP IS DARK when she returns. Papà and the boys are no longer working. The lights are on upstairs. It's dinnertime. They will all be there. How can she slip past them unobserved in this state? She can't. She rides to the village pump. No one is about. The place is dark. The water is gushing, noisy as a stream in the mountains. She remembers the snow-melt at the back of her zia's house in the *contrà*, and the madwoman who sat in a piazza fountain, washing herself shamelessly in public.

Amelia lifts her skirts, cups the cold water and tries to wash the blood off her legs, misses, wets her clothes. She checks the streets. Still nobody in sight. She douses herself in the freezing cold water. She drinks. She washes the violet oil off her neck and wrists. She washes the smell of Firmino off her body, although she'd rather keep it. She kicks at the water, embraces it until she is thoroughly drenched, clean and carefree as a frog.

She gets back onto the bicycle, shivering.

She is not carefree at all. As she shakes down her skirt, she thinks of that madwoman in wet petticoats, and how Mama was upset.

Amelia rides home the back way, walks the bicycle up the garden path and rests it against the wall.

She unties the *gavegnà* and carries it upstairs. It feels like a shield.

Saint Mark's feast

W HEN AMELIA WALKS IN THE DOOR, MARIA IS AT THE STOVE, taking an iron ring away from the pot-hole to lower the cooking heat. She's holding the hook with the ring at the end of it—she can't put it down. Her daughter is dripping into a puddle on the kitchen floor.

The younger ones stare, openmouthed. Achille and Primo stare too. Arsenio grins. Cecilio copies him and laughs out loud.

Amelia grips the *gavegnà* with both hands.

"What's happened to you?" Maria says.

"I fell in a ditch." Her face says it's a lie. "I was covered in algae. I rode home and washed it all off at the pump."

"Don't catch a cold," Bruna says.

Amelia blushes. "I have to go upstairs and cut these leaves. I'm not hungry." She puts the basket down and goes straight into the bedroom next door.

Maria looks at Achille. He's not happy. And Primo is scowling. Maria is in a panic. She stands still, not knowing what to do. She puts the iron ring back in its place on the stove. The beans can wait.

Amelia appears again, wearing clogs and a different dress.

They are all watching her.

She picks up the *gavegnà* without looking at anyone. She seems unconcerned. Carefree. She goes upstairs to her work.

The room is too quiet for so many bodies.

"What's your daughter been up to?" Achille asks.

"I'll take care of this," says Maria, wiping her hands on her apron.

In the bedroom, there's a trail of water droplets on the floor. The wet dress is on a hanger, dripping. The coverlet is rumpled and damp.

Maria lifts the pillows. She lifts the sheet and blanket. She lifts the mattress corner on Amelia's side and there's something. She grabs it and turns it over in her hand. It's a cloth badge, in the shape of a pointed shield, the kind of thing military people wear sewn on a pocket or sleeve, but it reads DON. On the front, it has stripes. It's soaking wet.

What can she say to Achille? To Primo?

Nothing else in the room looks different. She checks inside the wardrobe. Under the bed, where Amelia's wet shoes are. The cold and empty bed warmer. The credenza.

The Madonna of the Mountains gazes blankly into the distance. She looks serene, as ever, but there's the hint of a frown on her forehead. The little children under her cloak are eager for answers.

There's no time to pray. Maria sits on the bed and thinks. She turns the cloth badge over and over in her hands. DON. She doesn't know what it could mean.

Amelia went to Achille's fields to pick mulberry leaves for her silkworms. How long does it take to ride all the way to Fraoleto, past Fraoleto, to fill the big basket, and come back again? She took too long. Maria tries to work out the hours, but her head's in a muddle.

Upstairs, her daughter is starting the slow, patient work of mincing the mulberry leaves with her special knife. Finer than spaghettini, finer than capelli d'angelo, just as the silk women of Campolongo taught her.

DON. The stripes on the front are red and blue and gold. The shape is a shield. Machine-stitched. The backing cloth is black. It's wet. Amelia was soaking wet when she walked in.

Maria stands and goes over to the hanging dress. She sniffs it. She detects a trace of violet oil. Since when has Amelia been stealing her perfume? For a moment, she remembers going to visit Duilio, and she feels the heat of shame.

Achille will be furious.

She walks out of the bedroom and into the kitchen. "Children, time for bed." She looks pointedly at each one.

Bruna and Cecilio kiss her good night before they go.

Arsenio wants to stay, like a grown-up, and dawdles. Maria dismisses him with a nod.

Achille is sitting at the head of the table, saying nothing.

Primo says quietly, "Why was she so late? She's been up to something."

Maria sits down next to him. Her thoughts are scattered. She's not thinking at all.

Achille speaks at last. "What are you holding?"

Her hand is a fist on her lap, holding the cloth shield. She should have hidden it. She should have put it in her apron pocket. There's no choice but to put the evidence on the table. She's in trouble now too.

"It's from the Russian front," says Primo. "The river Don."

"Where did she get it?" Achille asks.

"Or when?" Maria prays that her daughter did not take possession of this thing today. "She might have been keeping it for months."

Silence fills the room like something solid pressing against her ears.

"Amelia!" she calls out.

Nothing.

"Amelia! Come down here at once!"

Silence.

Primo jumps to his feet and is up the stairs in no time.

He almost tumbles back into the kitchen with his sister behind him. He has her by the hair. She loses a clog. She falls onto the kitchen floor.

"What have you been up to?" He jerks her head back.

"The silkworms," Amelia whimpers. She clears her throat. "You know what I've been doing. The thermometer was low. I lit the *parigina* to get the heat up. I've been chopping the leaves really fine. They need ten feeds a day—"

"You never miss dinner," Maria says.

"Why were you so late?" Primo says, still gripping her by the hair. "And why were you soaked, like a street urchin?"

"What's this?" Maria says, holding out the Russian shield, shaking it.

"It's a present," Amelia whispers. She starts crying.

"Who from?" Primo says into her face. "And why is it wet?"

"Give it back. It's not yours to take!" Amelia tries to stand, but Primo holds her down.

"It's that Firmino, isn't it?" Maria says quietly. "I said to stay away from him. I told you what we'd do."

"You're not leaving this house," Primo says.

"I wouldn't leave the silkworms anyway," Amelia says.

"We'll find you another man," Achille says. "A suitable husband. You can choose—"

"But I love . . ."

Maria stands up now and shoves the chair against the table. She throws the Russian thing onto the floor. "*Bruta bestia. Bruta bestia.* How can you do this to me?" She strides over, pushes Primo out of the way, and shakes Amelia's shoulders. "You swore on my mother's life. You promised me."

Then she stops still. She runs her hand along Amelia's shoulder. Along her hip and thigh. She leans in close and whispers, "Where's your underwear?"

The house, the children, the silkworms, the priests, the whole of Fosso is leaning in and listening.

"I have to marry Firmino," Amelia says firmly, softly.

The kitchen is silent, but Maria's blood is booming in her head. She is too fainthearted to ask the question.

Achille, suddenly here beside her, slaps Amelia hard in the face, again and again. His hand is big. He doesn't speak, he just curses, the same words over and over. *Bruta canaja*. Ugly lowlife.

Amelia closes her eyes and tries to protect her face, but he pulls her hands away and keeps hitting her. Her lip is swollen and bleeding. She ducks and gets away. Primo grabs her and wrestles her to the ground. She wriggles free and stumbles upstairs to the granary and bolts the door.

Silence.

Violet oil. Herself. Her daughter.

They go after Amelia, both men filling the wooden stairs, bellowing, thumping at the door with heavy fists, and bellowing more, both of them together, shouting for her to come out. Maria wants them to stop, she should stand in their way and protect her daughter—but then she thinks, she hopes, she knows that they won't break the door because the door is worth something—good wood and hard work. And they wouldn't do anything to harm the silkworms because they're worth a fortune.

Between two saints

THE NEXT MORNING MARIA SENDS LITTLE BRUNA UPSTAIRS
with polenta and milk.

"Don't say a word to your sister."

At noon Bruna takes up lunch on a plate, asparagus and eggs.
Sparasi e ovi.

At night, when the family gathers, Maria sends Bruna to Amelia
with leftover rabbit and greens.

"Not a word."

Arsenio takes up the first sacks of fresh mulberry sprigs. He,
too, is forbidden from talking to his sister.

This is a shunning silence. Achille hasn't talked to Rodolfo for
years, so Primo shuns Rodolfo too. And there are others, other people to avoid or disregard. The notary's family. The fellow who sold
them the chickens that died. People who have crossed them.

Amelia has crossed them.

Maria goes up to the attic whenever she can, to keep watch, but
she never says a word. Her daughter is a prisoner, hidden like a
Partisan or a Jew.

As each day passes, the *bacolini* become *bachi*, they get paler, and
they get hungrier. They need constant attention, nights, days.

Maria sits and darns.

Amelia pierces paper and places it delicately on top of the *baco-lini*. She spreads the finely minced leaves across the paper in an even layer, combing with her fingers. This is their bedding and their dinner. They will climb up through the holes, leaving their dirt and old leaves behind them, ready to be collected and composted. In the next weeks they'll get bigger and bigger. They'll start to leave behind their molted skins too. They'll need more and more attention, feeding, warming, mucking out. They'll expand from a few racks, to all the racks, like an overcrowded city, filling the attic with their chewing and climbing, their noise and then their silence.

It's early Summer. The corn has been planted. When the temperatures in the *camaròn* rise too high, Amelia opens the windows and lets in cooling air. Sometimes, if the wind is right, Maria can smell roses. And oleander, the smell of innocence—but just one of its flowers can kill an ox.

The weeks are filled edge to edge with wordless checking, feeding, transferring, cleaning. After the third molting, the silkworms are happy with their mulberry leaves rough-cut or whole. After the fourth molting, they get to eat the stalks too. They need feeding four times a day. They are as fat as fingers, and just as long. The racks are filled with writhing, the constant whisper of leaves and chewing jaws.

Maria realizes that she looks forward to this quietness, this time away from the world of people. She watches Amelia work to the rhythms of the silkworms. Her days are beautifully calm and strange. The piercing and laying out of paper. The chopping of leaves. The spreading of fresh greenery. The transfer to new racks. The relocation, one by one, of silkworms that have been left behind. The clearing of the *scarti*. Checking the thermometer. Stoking the stove. Emptying the ashes. Piercing more paper, with larger holes, as the silkworms molt and expand. Chopping more and more leaves, rougher, bigger pieces for bigger, greedier jaws. Redistributing the pale fat bodies, giving them extra space to grow.

The supply of leaves grows bigger too. Sacks and more sacks are deposited at the top of the stairs. Arsenio delivers them one day, Cecilio the next, puffing with the effort.

Amelia knows what she is doing. She is devoted. And independent. She has a livelihood all her own. But Maria knows she will not run away.

In the outside world, Achille and Primo are making inquiries about suitable men for her. They've also found a house of correction for wayward girls and, near Verona, a convent for postulants. But there has never been a nun in the family—nuns don't have children, or money, or the influence that priests do. They don't want a nun in the family. Everyone is agreed on that. The attic is enough to confine her for now.

In mid-May, Arsenio and Cecilio start to deliver the supply of twigs for the *bosco*. The boys know what to do. It's the same as last year.

Amelia checks the twigs. "These are good," she says out loud. "Pliable and dry."

She shows Maria the patient work of tying them together into bunches. "Here, like this." And her soft, young hand touches Maria's hand.

Amelia sits and ties Spring heather and vine-stalks tight with twine at one end, and splayed like little trees, with countless places for the *bachi* to attach and start spinning their cocoons. She sits and ties, sits and ties, one *fascio* after another, and slowly a huge heap accumulates around her.

Maria helps her. She works more slowly. The pile she makes is smaller.

Amelia has missed Mass, twice now, and it's a sin, but Maria says—to Bruna, to Cecilio, to customers in the shop: *Amelia is too unwell to go to Mass*. It's not a lie, because her daughter's infatuation is a kind of sickness. But she will get well. And then she will be free to go to Mass again.

To make up for Amelia's missed Masses, Maria says the rosary on her knees in the attic every day. But her mind wanders. How do black worms become white? How do chewed leaves become spun silk? These are miracles. God's dreams. She does not dare to ask what happened to Amelia's underwear that day.

It's late May now. Amelia starts to plant her twig-trees, sticking them through the mulberry-leaf bedding and into the wire mesh below. Rack by rack, she makes a forest for her silkworms to climb. This is what they want. They spend their lives climbing.

They don't all go up at once. Some are faster than others, some more mature, some braver, bolder. Others will follow, or lag behind. Some will need to be helped up. *Just like people*, Maria thinks. It's Amelia's job to keep an eye on all of them, like God watching from Heaven. She waits for the first one to climb. And there it is.

How do they know when they've had enough of the eating phase? How do they know what day it is, and what size they should be? How do they know where to stop and spin, which twig, which height, which perch to make home? They are full of their own destiny, each generation as certain as the last. They know when. They just know.

Each climber stops, settles, drools a continuous trail of silk, spinning, spinning, wrapping itself in a fuzzy oval of lemon yellow or purest white. The color is God's work—or chance.

Amelia is so patient, and patience is one of the virtues—Maria is glad to see it.

The silkworms need days to make their cocoons, and then more time to keep growing and making silk inside the cocoons, until the beginning of June. This year they won't live to the feast day of Saint Peter. Some years they do. It's a matter of luck: Saint Mark at the start, or Saint Peter at the end. Saint Peter died upside down on a tree; Saint Mark was dragged through streets on a rope.

The silkworms are blightless, determined, precious, demanding, climbing, spinning, doing what they know to do, dreaming of their escape to the world of wings.

~

MARIA WANTS TO GET rid of the Russian shield. She doesn't have any use for military decorations, but she can't throw away anything good. She can't even throw away bad things, rotten things, broken things. They all have their uses, just as troublesome girls do.

She opens her sewing box: here are cloth patches for appliqué work, felt flowers, spools and bobbins, thimbles, a pin cushion, packets of new needles, rolls of ribbon, trimming, bits of lace and bias tape.

The DON badge can go underneath.

Her fingertips trace its edges. She turns it over and over. She sniffs at it. Nothing. The machine-made stitching is precise. She touches the lettering, the smooth polished thread, the fine ridges between the stripes. Gold, blue, crimson. She strokes the colors. She doesn't know what the stupid thing means. She doesn't want to know.

She hides it and closes the box.

~

ONE MORNING MARIA ENTERS the *camaròn* just as her daughter flicks something into the stove. "What are you doing?" she says, breaking the shunning silence.

Amelia shrugs as if it's obvious. Now she's the one who's not speaking. It's almost disrespectful.

Maria looks about for clues or signs. She glances at the thermometer, the bed of mulberry leaves on the floor, the table, marked and stained with a thousand green knife-cuts, a hundred thousand. The open windows. The breakfast tray delivered by Bruna, as usual, the coffee.

"You haven't eaten your breakfast."

Amelia says nothing. She's making a point.

Maria walks over to the racks and surveys the *bosco*. It's studded with cocoons. They look as if they've sprouted there, like big fuzzy buds in a forest of twigs, waiting to break into flower one day—which they must not do. There's no movement, apart from one or two solitary silkworms, the very last to find a perch.

The attic is silent now.

Amelia's work is entering its final phase. In two weeks, maybe sooner, she will begin the delicate task of detaching the cocoons, one by one, starting with the ripe ones. She has the eye.

"After we've sorted the cocoons ..." Maria doesn't finish her sentence. She feels sad, distracted. She doesn't know what will happen after this work comes to an end. She can't bear the thought of Amelia going away—to a house of correction, or to a husband. Still, there is time. Her daughter must stay on to mind the silkworms throughout their cocoon days, their detaching and sorting days, their selling and boiling days, the salvaging of twig-silk days, the dismantling of the *bosco* days ... Perhaps a suitable husband will be found by then.

Maria turns and goes downstairs.

Ripe cocoons

I T'S THE FIRST DAY OF JUNE, ALMOST FOUR WEEKS UNTIL THE feast day of Saint Peter.

Maria has hoed the topsoil to catch weeds and let in water. She has gathered salad leaves, bitter chicory, arugula and radicchio studded with tiny brown snails, their crushable shells skin-thin. Achille and Arsenio work in the shop, slicing, weighing, wrapping, selling, telling stories, making customers feel welcome and happy. Cecilio and Bruna are at school. Primo is out driving his new car. He's a businessman, doing deals, talking about the Giro d'Italia, and bicycles, and heroes—everyone is talking about the Giro d'Italia. Still nobody is talking to Amelia.

The cocoons are ripe. The creatures inside are fat and brown. Maria can't see them but Amelia knows. She has the eye. It's time to detach them, before they spoil the silk with the red acid of their escape, or turn magically into moths—a cloud of moths is an empty purse.

In the linen cupboard, Maria finds her wedding sheet, with its border of dainty white birds and flowers. *He loves me, he tells me off.* She always had a fine sewing hand, but now her fingers are aching and swollen, and mostly she uses a machine. What those sheets have seen! Her virginity, blood, sex, birth, afterbirth . . .

The silkworms don't need embroidery, just plain clean cotton.

She takes an old darned double bedsheet upstairs and lays it out on the floor of the *camaròn.*

Amelia walks over to her silent *bosco,* where she says a prayer of Grace.

"Jesus, Mary and Joseph," she whispers, "may the harvest be good."

Maria kneels and begins a rosary as Amelia starts to detach the cocoons, like fruits. Her touch is soft and light, but full of intent, as delicate as picking mulberries. She starts with the ripest ones, the ones she knows are finished. She gathers them carefully, one by one on folded paper, and tips them onto the bedsheet. They tear softly away from their twigs, leaving drifts of silky stuff behind—she will gather this too, for socks and coarse yarn, once the cocoons have been dealt with. She gathers and she picks, she picks and she gathers, until a huge heap of cocoons, some yellow, most white, fills the sheet.

The time comes to sort the *falope* from the *galete,* the unfinished ones to keep at home and work for yarn, and the finished cocoons which will yield a single silk thread hundreds of meters long, sometimes almost a kilometer. Maria imagines a silk thread trailing all the way to the campanile at Fosso, past it, to the cemetery where her dead babies rest.

Little Bruna arrives to help with the sorting. Her eyes are bright.

"So you're here?" Amelia smiles. "I wondered."

No reply.

Maria glances at Bruna approvingly.

"Remember what I taught you last year?" Amelia says. "The *galete* are solid and heavy. The *falope* feel light, you can see through them. They go in the baskets. Did you see Agata at church?"

Bruna nods.

"Did she give you a holy card?"

Bruna nods.

"Dear Agata. You know she used to work in a factory, between here and Venice, making bobbins for spinning? When the war came, they changed her job and she made fuses for bombs. I think it was work like this, precise work, and patient."

Maria, Amelia and Bruna sit and hold each cocoon up to the light, one after the other. They sort and they sort, all day, until there are two heaps. The good ones by far outnumber the bad ones. They'll sell for a great deal of money. Achille will be able to buy a nice plot of cleared land. Perhaps everything will be forgiven and forgotten then.

Amelia smiles again. "Agata always wanted to marry a gondolier or a dockworker—they earn really good money. But imagine what it's like when all the roads are made of water. What a bother. And it's cold in Winter. Damp cold is the worst. And I would miss her madly if she went to Venice. Where would I be without Agata? Where would I be without you, my little lamb?"

Bruna straightens up and smiles.

It touches Maria's heart that Amelia is babying her little sister and being so cheerful.

"After we take this lot off to the works, you'll help me pick the short silk from the *bosco*, won't you?" Amelia says. "But how will we get to the silk-works? Mama, have you got a cart ready? We need a cart—"

"We've got a car! Primo—" Bruna clamps her hand on her mouth.

"A car? What kind of car?"

"It's outside, on the road," says Maria, surprised at the sound of her own voice after all this time.

With one hand still covering her mouth, Bruna points to the low window in the corner of the attic.

Amelia picks her way around the cocoon heaps, and stoops to see Primo's fancy automobile parked outside. It's as glossy and beautiful as the piano the Nazis left behind at Edda's.

"The big black car?" Amelia asks.

There are no other cars.

Bruna nods.

"I'll have to dress up then."

The silk-works

THE JOURNEY TO THE SILK-WORKS IS GRAND, LIKE A WEDDING or a funeral. The warm June sun is out. Primo has taken the car roof off. The radiator grille is made of wire mesh finer than the racks in the *camaròn;* the black enamel panels shine as brightly as polished mirrors, and the upholstery is of finest, smoothest leather.

Amelia sits in the middle of the front seat, wearing her best dress: pink crepe rayon with a black velvet belt and floral lace appliqué.

Primo drives. He has tan gloves like a racing driver's.

Maria sits next to Amelia, hemming her in. She has dressed up too. Shoulder pads and a flowing skirt. A dab of violet oil behind each ear.

Inside the boot, and in the back seating area, their precious cargo is wrapped in bedsheets, huge white bundles resting on racks: all the good cocoons, ready to be sold and boiled. Every now and then a breeze catches the cloth and makes it ripple with life. But the lives inside are still. The silkworms are sleeping.

The car is a Nazi car, though there's not a swastika in sight, and Primo got her for a song. Despite his weakness for extravagant things, he's getting better at business every day. It makes Achille both proud and jealous.

"She's a war trophy—the Germans lost!" Primo says to anyone who shows an interest, even a curious glance. He drives very slowly, so that friends and strangers can stop and stare. He warms to the admiring glances of young women. "Every Italian who drives a Mercedes is a jab in the eye for Fritz. We did our bit, we hid Americans in the cellar, and you know what kind of risk that was—look what happened in all the reprisals. It's only right that we should drive an enemy officer's car. It appeals to my sense of humor."

The shunning silence still holds for Amelia.

"It's style," he says. He's showing off.

Duilio would have been impressed, Maria thinks.

"Feel the leather," Primo says. "Softer than a baby's armpit. My little brother spent all night on the backseat, he just wanted to sleep there."

It's true. But poor Cecilio had nightmares about Nazis.

Once they clear Fosso and Campolongo, Primo stops the car to pull the folded roof back up. It's a complicated business.

Maria and Amelia sit and wait without saying any of the words that they have been holding back.

They drive along the raised roads edged by ditches or canals, sometimes with lines of plane trees, their trunks like camouflage patterns, young crops in the fields beyond, below. American army trucks rumbling.

Primo speaks to Amelia for the first time in over a month. His voice is loud. "So have you learned your lesson?"

Amelia nods.

He looks at her sideways. "Say it."

She raises her voice above the noise of the engine. "I've learned my lesson."

"Explain," says Primo. "Tell me what you've learned. And don't forget: God is listening."

I am listening, Maria thinks.

"I've had all that time with the silkworms," Amelia says at last. "Looking after them like a parent. I've been watching them grow up. And protecting them." She glances at Maria, then back to Primo. "Like Mama has always done for us—"

"And Papà," Primo says. "*And* he looked after the Americans in the cellar."

It was for the money, Maria thinks, *the Americans paid lots of money. We had nothing to eat.* But she doesn't say it.

"And how ungrateful I'd be if . . ." Amelia bites her lip. "Well, I don't want to throw that back in anyone's face. It'd be worse than a jab in the eye. And, Mama, you don't deserve it, after all your hard work. And the risks you took. And Papà. For us."

Primo seems to think this is a good answer. He takes one hand off the steering wheel. He looks casual, as if he's always had a car. The road is straight and open; there are no trees now. Wildflowers and butterflies drift at the edges. The sky is big and blue.

Maria feels excited about everything at once: the wide world of the province beyond Fosso, the admiration of strangers, the luxury of the automobile, the speed, the squinting sun, her daughter's contrition, the approaching sale.

"And what about this Verdon fellow?" Primo turns to look at Amelia again. He glares, and Maria knows he's looking for signs of cheating or lying.

"Firmino? I haven't heard from him since . . . since . . ." Amelia doesn't complete her statement.

Of course not. He's been banned. Even Agata has been told to stay away.

Primo can't hide his satisfaction. "He hasn't tried to write or visit—and what does that say about him, then?"

"I don't know."

"I'll tell you what it says about him. It says that he's a coward and a liar—not to mention his political views—it says that he's a man like any other man, a common man and we—you—deserve better. Take it from me: I know how men think. I know how men talk. They say what you want to hear, so you'll give them what they want. And you think that's love, but it isn't. It's animal. And then they don't respect you. They treat you like rubbish. Worse than a conquered country, a slave race. Do you understand what I'm saying to you?"

He sounds like a politician, or a priest. He's like a father. Maria feels so proud of him.

"Yes," Amelia says.

"So you've given up on him?"

"Yes."

"Say it again, properly: you've given up on him?"

"Yes, I've given up on him."

"I knew you'd see sense. You're young. You need guidance. That's why we—"

"Could Verdon buy you a car like this?" Maria can't stay silent any longer.

Amelia pauses. "No, he couldn't."

"You see?" Primo slaps the steering wheel. "Fellows like that will take us all back to the dark ages. Like those poor mountain cretins with limps and stammers and crossed eyes—"

"Like my friend Agata?"

"Poor girl, yes, with her looks she's lucky to be engaged."

"Engaged?"

"Didn't you know?" Primo smiles. He's still punishing his sister, letting her know what she's been missing. "Your friend Agata is getting married."

"Suspiciously soon, if you ask me," Maria adds.

"When?"

"I don't remember," says Primo. "Soon. It's a Tuesday."

"Odd day for a wedding," Maria says, "but maybe she's in a hurry."

Amelia strokes the velvet belt on her dress. She smooths the bows, flattens them. "You will let me go to her wedding, won't you?"

"We'll discuss it—me, Mama and Papà. Hush now." Primo drives more slowly as he concentrates on signs and turnings. They're not far from the silk-works.

"Please, Primo," Amelia pleads. "She's my dearest friend."

"I said we'll discuss it."

Primo pulls into the piazza before the tall white buildings of the Aziende Agrarie. The façades are painted in big capital letters: here is a flour mill, a shop, a furnace, the silk-works.

There's a sparse gathering of people. Carts. Donkeys. Small trucks. But nobody has a luxury car. The crowd parts like the Red Sea and Primo parks right in front of the main door.

He gestures toward the back. "Let's see how much we can get for this lot."

Amelia crosses herself and prays in a whisper. "Dear Jesus, Mary and Joseph . . ."

"Let me handle the negotiations. You say nothing, unless they ask you about the feeding or whatever. Mama, you can guard the car."

Bearing witness

"PRIMO GOT US A GOOD DEAL ON THE SILK," ACHILLE SAYS. "SO I'll be buying another field, if I play my cards right." He looks pleased.

Maria knows it was Amelia's work that made the money to buy land, but Primo is the man of business. Achille respects him in his way, even though he doesn't like to show it. Ever since that fight, perhaps. Or since the Americans in the cellar—Primo was their man of business.

The family is at the table for Sunday lunch, all of them together. The shunning silence is over. Arsenio is uncomfortable. He looks to Primo for clues. He doesn't know how to be with Amelia now that she's out of the granary. Cecilio—with the beginnings of a first mustache, though not enough to shave—is quiet and cautious. Little Bruna sits close to her sister, every now and then touching her as though she's a holy relic.

Maria has decided to behave as if nothing has changed, as if her daughter has spent the last eight weeks in amongst the family as usual.

The silence may be over but there's not a lot of talk as they mop up *fegato alla veneziana*. It's Amelia's favorite dish. But Maria didn't make it specially for her.

Since the sale, Amelia has not left home. She has extracted rough silk from the unfinished cocoons, and worked the short silk from tufts and drifts in the *bosco*. At the time when her silkworms might have stumbled into the world as moths, she was dismantling their empty perches, stacking all those twig bundles with the firewood, emptying the discarded leaves and skins and droppings into the compost barrel, and adding rainwater, to make rich manure for the fields. The leftover bedding paper is here in the kitchen, ready to use for lighting fire in the stove.

Paper is gold, Maria thinks, remembering the old posters. *La carta è oro.*

Now the granary is clean again, ready to store new corn. It's empty of life. And yet there are ghosts up there, the spirits of Amelia's silk moths, and all the prayers and secret thoughts pressed against the bare wooden rafters like clouds.

"I have more good news." Achille clears his throat. He sits up straight and tall, as if he's on a throne. He removes an envelope from his pocket.

Everyone stops eating and waits.

"It's in American, but there's a translation here. *To whomever it may concern*," he reads. "*RE: Mr. Achille Montanari, Merchant, War Veteran and Resident of Fosso (Veneto Region).*"

Primo looks at Maria as if to ask what she knows about this.

Maria shakes her head slowly. Achille has been keeping it a secret.

The letter is typewritten, and on top is an emblem with an American eagle. Maria knows the Austrian-Hungarian eagles and the Fascist eagles and the Nazi eagles and the American eagles. They all love eagles.

"*This gentleman and his family merit unreserved welcome in any country recognized by the Government of the United States of America. Mr. Montanari's services, at risk of life and freedom, contributed to the Allied liberation of Italy's northeast during the time of enemy occupation.*"

"Who wrote it?" Maria asks.

"An American general," Achille answers.

"Let me see." Primo takes the paper from Achille's hand. He fidgets with his glasses. He reads out the name of the letter-writer. Not an easy name like Pipo or Baldassare. It sounds famous.

"Did he come here?" Maria asks. "To Fosso? Did you meet him?"

"I've never seen him," Achille replies.

"Me neither," Primo says.

"But he bears witness to what we did," Achille says. "The sacrifices we made."

The general is a man in a uniform in a military office far away, Maria thinks. Perhaps he is sitting in the recaptured palazzo where the Nazi Colonel Wolf sat during the war. Or perhaps he's actually in la Mèrica, in New York, where the Statue of Liberty is, signing letters like this for every Italian who hid a spy in the cellar.

Primo holds the paper as if it's Veronica's Veil. "Do you know what this means, Mama? We can get away from all these peasants and gossips. We can hold our heads high. We can build the world we want, wherever we want. Our Destiny is great, we can live like princes."

"It's addressed to me." Achille holds out his big empty hand until Primo gives the letter back. "Besides . . ." Achille folds it, returns it to the envelope and pockets it. He rolls a cigarette, lights up, inhales and blows a ring of smoke that rises, rippling, to the ceiling while everyone watches. "I'm the head of this household. I'll decide what my letter means."

Maria turns to Amelia. "Make your father his coffee. And Primo."

Amelia goes to the stove.

"What dress do you wear when you're a witness?" Bruna calls across the kitchen to her.

Amelia puts the *caffettiera* on the heat. "Witness?"

"Shut up or God won't give you any children," Maria says to Bruna.

Arsenio and Cecilio smirk.

Bruna blinks. She's about to reply.

"Go out and play with the chickens." Maria feels a pang of guilt as soon as she's said it.

"Chickens don't play," Bruna says matter-of-factly. "They're stupid. They panic." She stays where she is, seated at the table.

"It's like punishment," says Arsenio.

"What did Bruna mean?" Amelia says. "About the witness?"

Primo looks at Maria, then at Achille, then back to Maria again. He heaves a sigh. "Your friend Agata has asked us if you can be a witness at her wedding."

Amelia prepares the coffee tray.

"It's not a first-light Mass," Maria says.

"So we can presume she hasn't strayed," says Primo. "Mind you, anyone can pay the priest for the eleven o'clock. Does her fellow have money?"

"It's whether she wears white or not," Maria says. "In my time we couldn't afford white, not for a day's use. Only the veil."

"I paid for the veil," Achille says.

"Bruna, come and help me." Maria takes her time getting up. At the sink, she starts washing the dishes, making a clatter. "If the bride wears white, and it's dishonest, it's a mockery of the Virgin."

Bruna is at Maria's side now, polishing the cutlery dry with a cloth.

"It is strange they chose a Tuesday, and so soon," says Primo.

"Saint Peter's Day," Maria says.

"The groom is a watchmaker," says Amelia quietly.

"That explains it," Maria says. "He's the patron saint of locksmiths too."

Amelia takes the coffee tray over to her father and brother. The cups and saucers rattle. "The bride is my dearest friend," she says.

The men tip sugar in. They stir. They drink. Achille slurps his coffee from the saucer.

"Very well," says Primo at last. He taps the table as if he's counting. "But there are conditions."

~

IN THE EVENING, BEFORE DUSK, Maria gathers pretty summer blooms to make a posy for the Madonna: cornflowers and dianthus—cream and pink and striped—with a halo of feathery fennel.

Alone before the shrine, she says her rosary.

She waits.

Eventually, the Madonna speaks to her.

You have a pretty daughter who works silk for the family, who stayed inside like a prisoner without one single lock or key. She has learned gratitude and contrition.

But perhaps she still wants to fly away.

You don't dare ask her.

In case she lies.

In case she tells you the truth.

She is not like you, she's young, and her hands don't ache or swell, and she doesn't give a fig or a bean about a man's prospects.

She is not like Achille either, who abandoned the one he wanted, the first Amelia. He obeyed his parents. He waited for a girl like you, Maria. You were never the one.

He's keen to line up suitors—not that there's much choice. He's picky and he's choosy, and so he should be. Your daughter is a flower. She has never had a fever or a cough.

I've heard you cough, Maria. You still don't know if you have consumption. It can lurk for years. Your life has been spared thus far, but there are conditions. There are always conditions.

You must pray and pray, Maria, pray to me, keep up the rosaries, pray and pray to hold Amelia, tie her like a loose twig with twine, fix her to the family tree, feed her—food is love, Maria—work her with patience.

And hope.

Vendetta

For: Montanari, Generi Alimentari, Fosso

Maria rips open the un-stamped envelope and pulls out the note. It is handwritten—scrawled—but signed by nobody.

> WHEN A FILTHY FASCIST DIES HE WAILS—
> HE SQUEALS ABOUT A SHOP THAT IS FULL OF
> FOOD—IT IS TOO WELL STOCKED—AND A SON
> OF MILITARY AGE WHO AVOIDS HIS DUTY—
> THE FILTHY FASCIST KNEW—SILENCE HAS A
> PRICE—WHEN WE VISIT WE WILL HAVE
> A FIERCE APPETITE

She looks around as if the person who wrote the note might be here, just now. But it's early morning and the shop is not yet open. There is no one about.

Duilio's death was like a shadow leaving her soul. She prayed guiltily because she felt better when he died than when he lived, and not because his soul was going to Heaven.

It is the time of Reconstruction, and the seasons are easy, and the shop really is well-stocked with food, all kinds, even imports and luxuries, and Duilio is dead, but here he is again, come back to haunt her. Did Egidia say he was tortured?

Maria looks for her sister's letter, and finds it upstairs in the credenza.

> *You know the reprisals still go on here and there. Some Fascist-hunters found him and executed him. I think they made him talk. He confessed to many bad things, he said all sorts of things.*

The Fascist-hunters could be anybody.

> *I don't know what else he said before he entrusted his soul to God but it is appalling shame to us all that our cousin is a Murderer.*

~

WHEN THE VIGILANTES ARMED with weapons and accusations come to raid the shop, Primo defies them.

"Read this, from the highest American general: my father's a hero."

The strangers stare. They can read. They don't want to read. They have pistols and knives.

"You wrote that yourselves," says the one with the rifle.

It's hard to tell where he's from. He speaks Italian, not dialect, and he has a cloth across his face. They all do. They are here because of politics, or greed, or bad luck.

"The Allies are our friends and protectors," Maria says as calmly as she can. If only she could know what Duilio confessed before he died. These men might expose her shame, or Achille's shame. Or they might know nothing.

One of them mutters something.

"We're as good as Partisans." Primo still holds the letter, at a safe distance. "I'll get the Americans onto you if you hurt us."

"They're local now," says Maria. She glances at the shop door as if an American is about to walk in. "They're here all the time."

One of the men pulls at the hem of the rifleman's jacket.

Primo shakes the letter at them. "We didn't kill anybody. We didn't rob anybody. So you can go to Hell. Or you can leave in peace right now—but I never want to see your faces again."

We can't see their cowardly faces anyway, Maria thinks.

As suddenly as they appeared, they disappear.

She is terrified, braced for their return. Relieved. Exhausted. Grateful to Primo for defending her, for defending the family.

He comes to her and holds her tight.

She hears the crackle of paper in his breast pocket. She loves the general's letter. It wards off new and unpredictable dangers. She loves that her bold and beautiful son has taken it away from his father.

"I'm beginning to hate this place," Primo says.

Maria has a fantasy now of moving to a Promised Land where there are no vigilantes, no Fascists, no Partisans. No vendettas, no bombs, no rations, no shame. No past. Where they can all begin a new life, fresh and pale as Spring blossoms. Innocent as a soft baby.

Saint Peter's feast

"IS AMELIA HERE?" PRIMO SLAMS THE DOOR BEHIND HIM. "DON'T tell me. I know she isn't. You don't have to tell me—"

"What's going on?" says Achille.

"You'll wake the little ones," Maria says. She's been worrying all day. Amelia went with Primo to Agata's wedding. It's late.

"I don't care." Primo throws his jacket on the floor. "They can't sleep. Not now. Never again." He paces up to the kitchen table and lands his fist on it. Twice. Three times. As if he's crushing a cockroach.

"Where is she? What's happened?" Maria's voice is almost a shriek. Last night she had dreams about a baby. Always a bad sign.

Primo kicks the firewood box against the wall. Twigs from the silkworm *bosco* scatter on the floor. "She tricked me." He picks up a chair and holds it high. He smashes it down onto the floor, but the chair stays whole.

"Where?" Maria's voice is tiny.

"She's run off with that Communist." Primo's eyes are full of anger and shame.

"Stupid boy, it was your job to keep an eye on her!" Achille says. "After everything we've done for her. What were you doing—

showing off your car? Flirting with girls? You've been tricked by a girl." Then he turns to Maria. "This is all your fault—"

"I wasn't there," says Maria. Her heart is being stabbed by swords. *Survived the war but lost the daughter.* How could Amelia do this to her? "Oh, Amelia."

"She can't hear you." Achille hits the table.

Primo is squatting on the floor with his fists on his forehead.

"Was *he* there?" Maria asks him. They made sure the Verdon fellow would not be there. It was one of the conditions.

"Her damned hero from the damned Russian front. No. He wasn't there."

Maria thinks of the DON badge, that stupid stitched thing she found under the mattress, soaked, the day her daughter was missing her underwear. That was two months ago.

Maria gets up and goes to her sewing box in the next room. She brings it back into the light of the kitchen. She should have found out what happened to the underwear. She should have gone to the wedding.

She opens the lid. She tips all the contents onto the table. Skeins, bobbins, braid, ribbons, needles, pins, patches, everything—and Duilio's two steel wedding rings. She piles everything back into the box as quickly as possible. Her hands are shaking.

"What are you doing, you madwoman?" Achille mutters.

"It's not here," she says. "*Bruta bestia.* The Russian thing is not here."

Amelia

AMELIA'S LAST GLIMPSE OF HER BEST FRIEND'S WEDDING is through strands of her own hair, blown by the wind. It is a moment she decides to memorize in her mind like a photograph: forty people seated at tables in the evening air, enjoying their second feast in one day, white napkins tucked into collars to protect best shirts, colorful dresses, elbows on white cloth-covered tables, the legs of wooden chairs like little ladders lined up in rows. Primo off guard now, and sitting away from the women, arguing about politics. Agata and Bartolomeo at the head table. An old house with red geraniums in its windows. A huddle of cypresses. A field of half-grown corn on one side. A leafy vineyard on the other side. Swallows and sparrows in the air. Clouds of cigarette smoke. Song—everyone singing. Quail bones. Crumbs.

Amelia is riding the bicycle as fast as Fiorenzo Magni. He was winning the Giro d'Italia while she was sitting in the attic working the short silk. She is faster. Despite Agata's heavy bike. Despite her high heels. Despite her best dress, the pink crepe skirts hitched up to her thighs. If she doesn't get to Santa Croce in time, if she doesn't make it to Firmino in time, she will be caught and stranded and punished worse than she can imagine. She thinks of bodies hanging

off trees, people dragged out of their houses, force-feedings, beat-
ings, shootings—all the things she has heard and seen—one time a
Partisan, another time a Fascist, other times someone, anyone,
caught up in someone's else's vengeful rage. She doesn't want to
think of these things on her wedding day, but the thoughts are like
shadows on the road as she races her bicycle into the violet gloom.
It's as if she is riding through ghosts from her adolescent years:
dead here, bombed there, burnt here, dark vendettas everywhere.
She has been shunned like a gypsy, like a delinquent, like that wandering madwoman in Mama's *contrà*. She has been shunned by her
own family, despite her years of silk-working, despite the money
she makes for them to buy more land, despite her work in the *orto*
in every season, despite looking after the little ones, cooking and
serving, doing the laundry, going to Mass, honoring the saints, despite her wanting to marry a good and decent man for love. What
can be so wrong about love?

What if Firmino is not there?

Amelia rides and rides, faster than Fiorenzo Magni. Past orchards and coppices, wheatfields and cornfields, past lines of vegetables, lines of nut trees, lines of vines, past ricks and stacks and
heaps and coops and stalls and stables and porticoes and lofts. She
rides on raised roads along ditches, past army trucks and harvest
carts, across rebuilt bridges and temporary bridges, along train
tracks and *contadino* tracks, swifter than Gino Bartali, swifter than
Fausto Coppi.

What if Firmino is not there?

Tonight, Agata and Bartolomeo will place a carafe in the middle
of the field. All will be well if the egg white in the water looks like
the sailboat of Saint Peter. Their luck depends on the stars and the
dew. Amelia prays to Jesus, Mary and Joseph that the stars and the
dew behave and all will be well. *Dear Agata dressed in white and married.*

She wishes Agata could be her witness.

What if Firmino is not there?

When at last Amelia approaches the little town of Santa Croce, she heads for the campanile. It leans crookedly toward the baptistery. The two buildings almost touch—she's never seen them from this angle, it's as if they're kissing. Amelia can read the clock, and the hour is late, but it's the light that matters. His secret message on the holy card said *when the light fades.*

She stops and leans her bicycle against the church wall. There is not a person in sight. Not a cat, not a dog. All the robbers of Santa Croce are still sleeping, but she supposes they'll be up soon for their nightly work. The church bells strike nine, deep and beautiful, into the darkening sky. Her pretty pink dress is crumpled and damp with perspiration. Even though she went to Confession this morning, she is in no state to be married. She takes her handkerchief out of her purse and dabs her face, applies fresh lipstick, smooths her hair. She snaps the purse shut, composes herself and walks to the church door, holding the lucky DON badge which she found in Mama's sewing box. She has no flowers, no veil. Her knees are weak. She pushes the door open.

He is there. Kneeling.

Far away, near the altar, four figures are kneeling.

Firmino's hair like copper catches the light.

One of the men is a priest.

And two others—police?

She walks down the aisle alone, and the church echoes her footsteps. The seats are empty. She's never been here before. In the glimmering chapels on either side, she glimpses a young widow praying, an old man kneeling, another woman sitting, head bowed. They are oblivious to her.

The four men are standing now.

Firmino is grinning like a boy. His hands are clasped in prayer but she can see, even from here, that he is holding a *bocolo*. Maria Amelia Montanari has never seen a rose so red.

And now, here she is, at the end of the aisle, cold and damp, her heart as light as a jittery moth, her knees like string, and the priest is introducing himself, it's his job to help people in need, he says, he's decided that dusk is as good as dawn, and Firmino can't stop smiling, he's in a proper suit, his shirt is white, his skinny friend Giorgio here is his witness, fresh out of the hospital—they grew up next door to each other, he's the one who fought in Africa, the one with nine lives—and this kind old fellow here was on a bicycle, he had nothing particular to do.

The very old, very brown *contadino* wears a uniform with the braids and epaulets cut away and patched, and the army fabric dyed to deep plum. Amelia recognizes him, but she can't think why. She hands the DON badge to Firmino, and he gives her the *bocolo*. Then he gives her a veil. It's a magic trick. She can't think where he was hiding it. It was his mother's, God rest her soul, he says.

And the priest says Mass and all the prayers and benedictions just like a proper eleven o'clock wedding, just like Agata's wedding, still so vivid in her mind, and it makes her want to cry that Agata can't be here, but she is here somehow, because it was Agata who planned this wedding secretly with Firmino—they are sharing a wedding day—and now Firmino is putting a gold ring on her finger, and her palms are still striped by the bicycle handlebars—she rode so hard—and Giorgio gives her a gold ring to put on her husband's finger, and Firmino has beautiful hands, and there is no rice to throw, or mother to embrace, but Amelia is so exhausted, and relieved, and happy, she thinks she might just die and go to Heaven. Instead they sign the great big book of weddings, Amelia, and Firmino, and Giorgio. The old man can't sign because he can't write, so the priest gives him an ink pad and he marks the page with his thumbprint.

As they walk out of the church of Santa Croce with no wedding bells, no ecstatic Liberation bells, just the steady tolling of the hour, Amelia remembers where she has seen the old man before. He was whipping his bicycle and saluting with his sickle that day she rode to the mulberry house and gave her virginity to Firmino.

It's dark outside. The streets of Santa Croce are still deserted. Amelia and Firmino are married, and they will have a drink, and they will have lots of children far away from here, in Lumignano, where the peas are the sweetest in the world.

The best peas

27 AUGUST 1948

Dear Mama,

I had to do this. Jesus, Mary and Joseph, I pray for you to understand. I love Firmino with all my heart and hope you will look kindly on me one day. We are in Lumignano. The peas here are the sweetest and the best in all the world. You could visit me without telling Papà or Primo, or write to me. But I know that I am dead to you. I will tell my children, I'm going to have lots of children, how good your gnocchi are. They will ask me when will they try your gnocchi. I will tell them patience. Like working silk. I pray to Jesus, Mary and Joseph, and Saint Monica too because the priest recommends her. I know you won't write back. There are tears in my eyes.
Love and best wishes from my heart for your good health and happiness and for all the family.

> *Your loving daughter,*
> *Amelia*

It was a proper wedding, except that you were not there.

Maria opens the door to the kitchen stove and feeds the letter inside. She doesn't want to read these words again. She doesn't want anyone else to read them either. And now, as she watches the paper curl and blacken and glow, she remembers the day she walked into the attic and Amelia was putting something into the fire of the *parigina*, even though the temperature was warm and the windows were open . . . Why in God's name didn't she question her daughter properly then?

She knows now that the sly, cross-eyed friend passed notes from Firmino to Amelia, using Bruna as their messenger. The little one didn't understand the words. They wrote in code, like spies in the war, and joined up writing on the back of holy cards.

Holy cards! This must be some kind of sacrilege.

Not just sacrilege. Amelia has committed sins far worse. She has eloped. She has disobeyed the Commandment that says she must honor her father and her mother. She has lied. Pretended to repent. Missed Mass. Broken promises. Hoodwinked her brother in public. Humiliated him. Humiliated them all.

Set an example. Or maybe you did. Achille's words pierce her again now.

Her girl and that boy found some crooked priest in Santa Croce, where they're all thieves. Even the priest must be a thief if he can take a respectable girl with prospects and skills and beauty and her reputation intact—was her reputation intact?—and give her away to the first Communist that darkens his crooked door. The priest is probably a Communist too. Did he hear Amelia's Confession before her wedding?

Maria can't bear to think what her family will say, her sisters, her scornful brothers. And Achille's family. Don Goffredo, the gossiping priest. The neighbors, the tailor, the station master, the people at the *comune*. It's all Maria's fault. She is the mother. How will she face her customers? She can't face them.

Achille used to talk about emigrating. The war is over. They have that letter from the general—it's like a passport. They can go to a place where nobody knows them. Those vigilantes could come back any day. Achille is always on guard in case they do. There must be a place where nobody knows about Duilio. Or Achille. Or Amelia. They can make a fresh start.

Maria keeps watching the fire inside the stove, the place where her daughter's letter was. She sticks the iron rod in and hits it about. Ashes and sparks dance and fly. There is nothing left. Amelia's letter does not exist. Amelia does not exist.

1950

Late Wintertime

THEY WILL EMIGRATE. MARIA HAS BEEN TO THE *COMUNE*. She walks all the way home without opening the parcel again, waiting until she's indoors.

She sits at the table.

Here are the new passports, the itemized bill which she's paid, their own documents returned and the typed letter from the Australian Legation in Rome.

> I, therefore, confirm that all is in order for you to leave for Australia with these documents which cover all members of your family with the exception of Amelia.

That girl should have been named Delfina. What is worse: eloping—and lying with a man outside of marriage—or hoodwinking Primo? He is as furious today as if it happened yesterday.

Telegraphic address "AUSMIGRANT"

Maria imagines telegraph poles in a line the length of Italy: felled by war, springing up again in the Reconstruction. War is so much pointless work of great consequence, done, undone, redone. Her work is useful, done, undone, but of no consequence at all. She can't even keep a daughter on the straight Christian path.

Certificates to the effect that no pulmonary
disease is present—

Maria thanks God in Heaven that Bruna has passed the medical tests. Her lungs are not scarred or shadowed. Maria has passed the tests too. It is a blessing. Would that accursed Firmino pass? No, his lungs are sure to be wrecked. He'll be lucky to last as long as Duilio did. He couldn't go to Australia if he wanted to. *Don't trust anybody. Not even your own daughter.* Especially not your own daughter.

Amelia has had a daughter—it serves her right, she doesn't deserve a son—and Maria tore up the baby girl's photograph when it arrived, and the letter, and tossed the scraps into the stove. And that very day the polenta had lumps in it like gristle, and Achille got mad, and the boys sniggered, and she threw the lot at the stupid chickens, who couldn't believe their luck, even when it landed in their eyes.

She has never had a passport before, not even an Italian one. She's had a primary school certificate, ration cards and coupons, a Fascist Party membership card, a permit to allow passage between Nazi-occupied Verona, Vicenza and Padua, a permit to run a business, but never a passport. Its cover is black and textured like linen. She strokes the surface. It gives her comfort.

In the middle there's a strange crest, embossed in gold. She has seen all kinds of insignia. On men's uniforms and vehicles and occupied buildings. But the government emblem here is not threatening at all. It's strange, almost silly. Two animals standing by a shield. One is some sort of ostrich. The other looks like a giant mouse, or a deer, with huge round haunches. But it's a kind of dog, a *guro* dog.

Canguro, Achille said. *That's what they have in Australia.*

And there is her name inside. Written in blue fountain pen. *Mrs. Maria Vittoria Montanari.* Nobody remembers the Vittoria part of her name anymore. Everyone calls her Maria, just Maria, the invisible part of any girl's name, the most commonplace name of all. It's always been this way. Except with her cousin. *A chi la Vittoria?*

And here is her profession in English: *Housewife.* That must be shopkeeper or grocer. And here is her place and date of birth—but who knows really whether she was born before midnight or after?

Her passport portrait was made by a professional photographer in Vicenza. She sat and posed in his studio, just meters across the street from a bombed Palladian palazzo, weeds and sky showing through the wreckage. The city is still half rubble but there's no sign of those shouting Nazi posters anymore . . . Was that colonel really called Wolf or was it a name invented to frighten people?

She stares at her photograph. Her black fur collar, big and luxurious. Pearl earrings. Dark hair swept back like a woman of means. The gray doesn't show in the picture. Her face is without lines. Her lips are full. The lipstick was a good idea, even in black and white. She thinks of all the photographs—that family portrait from the First War, her wedding picture with Achille, her own family in the Second War—and she realizes that this is the first time she has been photographed alone.

Staring at herself like this is just as wrong as looking in mirrors, it is the Devil's work, but Maria cannot have enough of her special document. She could eat it with her eyes. It's a work of magic that means escape from these plains choked with the ruin and rubbish of war.

No matter what people say about the Reconstruction and the Marshall Plan, this place is where shame lurks around every corner as far as Lumignano—beyond Lumignano and as far as the mountains. Oh, Amelia, how could her own daughter do such a thing? The humiliation. In Australia, nobody will know about the runaway girl. Amelia does not exist over there.

Australia is the other side of the world, far away from everything, further even than America, unspoiled, full of space, peace, whatever a person can imagine. Everyone has seen Calvinetto's beautiful poster. There are mountains and flowering green slopes, with pink-blossoming trees and wheatsheaves, healthy sheep and horses, work for men and tractors, white washing hanging on the line. It almost looks like home, the years of her girlhood. But it's not poor. And everything is new. A person can start all over again, like a soul wiped clean by Absolution.

Lent

LAST WEEK SHE COLLECTED THEIR TICKET OF PASSAGE. ALL the names are there except Amelia's. Today the new wooden trunks arrive. The kitchen and the bedroom are full of suitcases and boxes and piles of things taken out of drawers and cupboards.

Emigration used to be Achille's idea. When he first arrived at the *contrà* with that huge load of tobacco leaves on his head, his neck straight and strong, it wasn't long before he started talking about the New World.

Now it is Primo's idea. And Maria is nothing without her first best son.

She has aches in her back, her hands are swollen and creased, sometimes she feels dizzy—but at fifty-two she's not too old to start a new life.

She hears Achille and the cabinetmaker on the steps outside. They're bringing up the trunks.

She lets the men in.

The first trunk looks like a treasure chest. It's painted brown and fitted with metal bands, braces and handles.

The cabinetmaker is out of breath. "Good day."

"Greetings," Maria replies.

"Over here," says Achille, edging backward.

"Are all of them the same?" she asks.

They lower the trunk to the floor. The cabinetmaker pats it. "Yes, each one the same. Built to survive a shipwreck."

Maria crosses herself.

"Let's get the next one," Achille says, and they go.

She starts packing at once. A leg of the best homemade mountain prosciutto, a wheel of Asiago cheese, a wheel of grana, homemade wine, her favorite vegetable seeds—everything wrapped in waxed paper and cloth. She fills the gaps with bags of unshelled nuts, kilos of almonds, walnuts and hazelnuts. She packs tablecloths, coffee cups in a set, white plates, utensils, the mincer, her pasta machine, fire-blackened pots and pans. All protected with paper.

She prepares coffee for the men.

They return. They disappear. They return.

There are six trunks altogether, to go into the ship's hold.

While the men sit, and smoke American tobacco, and drink coffee laced with grappa, Maria continues with the packing.

"I don't blame you for leaving," the cabinetmaker says. "Get away from all these spies with nothing better to do than gossip . . ."

Is he talking about Amelia?

"Sometimes I wish I could just pack up and go," he says. "But I've got too much keeping me here."

"The New World's good for business. We've always wanted the adventure," says Achille. "But the war got in the way."

"Ah yes, and you did your time in prison." The cabinetmaker shakes his head. "Damned Fascists."

"Even after the war," Achille continues as if he hasn't heard. "We've had vigilantes in the shop. Common thieves. Just when we're all trying to rebuild the country—"

"Wasn't your cousin a Blackshirt?"

"*Her* cousin," Achille grunts. "Black *sheep*. Dead."

Maria burns with shame, but she says nothing. She packs her best dowry handiwork wrapped specially in pillowcases, a stack of good bed linen. She goes to and fro with the clothes and shoes and hats they won't need now or on the journey, meters of fabric, her sewing machine, her sewing box, folded curtains, doilies, bedspreads, rosary beads, underwear.

She hesitates now, holding the coat that Duilio gave her. She glances at Achille, but he's not looking at her. He's paying the bill. She packs the coat—the nice fur trim can be reused. She piles blankets on top.

"That confirms it," says Achille, when the cabinetmaker is gone. "We're doing the right thing. People are jealous. Even this fellow."

"Jealous?"

"It's our success. That's why they gossip."

She shakes her head. She thinks of Amelia. "People come to the shop, and they buy things, they need us, and we prosper. But there's contempt in their eyes." She pauses. "Or else it's pity."

"We've got our health," Achille says. "We sold the shop for a fortune. And anyway, our customers aren't ours anymore. I'm going down to finish the accounts."

She listens to his footfalls on the steps outside. She returns to the job of preparing for a new life. Soon—at last—they are emigrating to la Mèrica. And she will be a new person.

~

OH, MARIA, YOU KNOW those tests don't tell the whole story. You might be spared from consumption—this is within God's power—but blind Fortuna cannot show such mercy, just as she shows no favor.

You must count your blessings and count your sins.

Income and outgoings.

Make an inventory.

Can you feel the flames of Hell licking, crackling, at your feet? A boat can take you to the end of the Earth, to the moon, to the end of the universe, but no place is too far for the all-seeing eye of Heaven. I am the Star of the Sea. I know your sins and secrets. I know what the gossips say.

You and your first cousin.

Achille and the ammasso.
Amelia and her good-for-nothing.
I know your trinity of shame.
Oh, Maria, you must confess properly.
I'm still waiting.

The stocktaking

MARIA IS AT THE *CONTRÀ*, BACK WHERE SHE CAME FROM, here to say her farewells, with her man and her brood. Goodbye to blood, the blood that is hers, but flows in other bodies. Dressed in her finest, showing them that she's a woman of means, a lady with property and fur collars, and a ticket to Australia.

When she reaches the top of the slope—the place where she stood breathless, yearning for the first sight of a husband—when she reaches the track that leads to the well, the walnut tree, the animal stalls—she looks around, expecting a crowd, expecting the extended family to gather about, admiring, wanting to be near her, wanting to inhale the sophisticated whiff of her. But the place feels empty. And the campanile bells ring from farther down the valley, and the sound grips her heart.

Then a door opens. It's the door to her old home, empty now of mother and father, filled with wifeless brothers and their progeny, and their progeny's progeny, and Claudia, who opens the door— her younger, prettier sister who never married and never will. She's not so young or pretty now. She looks a little mad, Maria can't help herself from thinking.

Claudia is not dressed properly for the glare of day. Her clothes

are stained and disheveled. Her streaky hair is as untamed as a forest shrub grown up and out to find the light. She rushes at Maria,
embraces her. She weeps. She clutches Maria's shoulder blades,
strokes her fur collar, grips the meat of her and says she'll never let
her go. Claudia is like a servant for her brothers. She shows Maria
her old overworked hands, her bitten nails. Her teeth are brown.
She smells of sour milk. Maria thanks God and the Madonna that
she's staying the week with Egidia.

The nieces and nephews and brothers spill out of the same door,
and other doors, the faces and bodies that look like Maria, like re-
flections of everyone she ever knew: her grandfather's shape, her
father's forehead, her mother's down-turned mouth, her cousin's
gesturing hands, her aunt's walk—this way, then that. Maria sees
Duilio in eyes that share no secrets with her. She sees Duilio in a
young man's sexless haunches.

She greets them all, kisses their faces, shows them her heirs, her
pride in order, as ever, the boys first and best: Primo, Arsenio,
Cecilio, then Bruna. There's no Amelia, because Amelia does not
exist, and everyone knows it. Nobody says her name. But Maria is
thinking her name all the time, and the name of Amelia's girl-baby,
Grazia, named to spite the Virgin, Ave Maria full of grace, and the
picture she tore up is inside her head, and she wonders if she'll ever
see her grandchild in this life. Still she says nothing.

She goes inside. She eats sopressa, drinks homemade wine and
mineral water. She knows the plates, the floor, the rough, raw ceiling beams. Little has changed since her childhood, but she notices
the white enamel stove, an electric light, a new paper calendar on
the wall with a picture of the Sacred Heart.

Maria leaves Achille and the boys with her brothers, to smoke,
to talk business, as men do. They discuss modernizing. Profits.
Costs. The scourge of taxes, the curse of unions. Sports.

She goes with Claudia to the cemetery. It's a citadel of stacked
and sleeping bodies. She prays to her resting mother and resting
father, united in death last year, retired in Purgatory or Heaven—
she can only hope and pray that they're in Heaven. Papà died an old

man's death, despite the wars that tried to claim him young. And Mama died three months after him, had a dream about her dead sister Luigia come to take her for a walk in the mountains, to gather violets as they used to, and the cuckoo was calling even though it was the deep of Winter, and they picked ripe figs and sweet grapes in the thick of snow, and the very next day when she woke, her eye socket was black as charcoal because her brain had bled, and she remembered her dream, and fell asleep forever.

At the cemetery, poor Claudia weeps some more. Together they brush their parents' vault-stone clean of pine needles caught in whitest webs. They remove bird droppings stuck like paint. They have to chip and chisel with knives. They'll wake up the dead. Maria crosses herself. She prays.

Then she cleans the stone of the murderer Duilio, dead two years, tortured and consumptive and mountain-wild like the witch Delfina, entombed with his infant and his proper wife, who in the afterlife must know everything now, everything that happened since he first tried to steal a kiss long ago. It panics her to imagine what he might have said under torture, and what those vigilantes might know. Can a murderer go to Heaven?

Maria visits Duilio's father, a withered, twisted vine of a man, still clinging to life without wife or son, alone in the world if it weren't for the cousins who prop him up, like posts.

He hardly recognizes her. He gazes into space and grumbles and curses.

On the credenza there's a picture of poor Zia Luigia, looking just like Mama. And there's a photograph of Duilio, taken when he was young and his dark-shadowed eyes were sensitive and sad, and there was no such thing in the world as a Blackshirt or a Black Brigade, and he was going to be a priest.

"Here," Maria says to the old man. She opens her purse. "These belonged to Duilio." She hands over the two worthless steel wedding rings. *ORO ALLA PATRIA.* She won't take any part of her cousin to Australia—unless she's carrying his TB. She hasn't coughed up bloody spit; she hasn't lost her voice. But it can still happen. They can still turn her away at Genoa. Those pricey migration X-rays don't tell the whole story. Nothing, and nobody, tells the whole story—Maria knows that.

Her uncle paws at the rings in confusion.

She studies the old brute's face, looking for secrets, looking for shame. *There is no shame because he has no conscience*, she realizes. She wonders if he ever had a conscience. When did his pizzle wilt and die? Did he father more than one bastard baby? Did the madwoman look like him? Maria tries to picture the apparition that haunted her childhood, the ragged creature that ranted from a piazza fountain. It doesn't matter whether Delfina looked like him or not.

Duilio killed his own sister. The thought has never been so clear before. It feels like an avalanche inside, choking her.

Her uncle mops a leaking eye. Not tears, but an ailment.

Maria looks at him with pity, without compassion.

When they say goodbye, she knows she will never see him again. His grave is hungry.

Everything has changed, and yet nothing has. She feels sick. She notices that hideous black round thing with Mussolini's profile. Her uncle uses it as a doorstop. She wants to kick it, but it would hurt her foot.

And later, Egidia serves the best veal, even though she is as poor as a church-mouse. She whispers into Maria's ear that she wants to emigrate with her, God knows she will follow as soon as she can, with her husband and her children. Maria gives her useful things from her life in Fosso. She is shocked at her sister's broken house.

And the brothers, one envious, one attentive, give Maria more to take on the voyage, even though the trunks are already packed. She can't forget that they sent her firewood in the darkest cold of war. She is forever grateful. She'd clean their house if she had time. She'd wash their clothes and feet.

These wifeless men give her a giant bottle of grappa with sprigs of asperula floating inside, and precious rosary beads of pearls and gold, one set for each of the children—except Amelia—and a brooch of gold for herself. She weighs it in her hand. It's solid.

I'm worth something, she thinks. *Papà with his printed notepaper would be proud of me.* She's got la Mèrica in her sights at last, a whole new world. It's not just talk. She's got a handsome son with brains and dreams, and the shop sold for a fortune—if only Papà could see all the goods she counted up for the sale.

Maria knows exactly how many goods. She's done the stocktaking. It took days and days. She has counted every ham, every cheese, every slab of baccalà, every bag of beans and grain, every tin of fish, every box of biscuits, every *etto* of salt—precious salt: she remembers a time when salt was like money, when she scraped out the scopeton barrel for salt, when everyone had headaches for lack of salt, when the Nazi-Fascists tortured traitors with gutfuls of salt. It wasn't so long ago. Five years. That's all. Fortuna's Wheel turns fast and Maria doesn't forget that, not for a minute.

In the afternoon, almost evening, she walks alone along the path she used to tread with the pole bearing water pails weighing on her young shoulders. She looks down into the well. She sees nothing.

I am your face in the water, mad Delfina said a long time ago. *If you marry you'll die.*

Duilio's wife died in childbirth. Severo's wife died, and Vito's wife died. Maria's entire life was given away to Achille. So the witch in her way was right. Amelia has been dead to Maria since the day she eloped. But poor unmarried Delfina died too. There's just no proper grave to mark it. Maria remembers wondering if the woman had a soul, and this memory is shameful to her now.

She heads for the wooded slopes beyond the *contrà*, where she knows she will find flowers. She gathers sprigs of scented pink daphne and violet-blue liverwort. She picks other wildflowers without names. Delfina must have been christened, she was looked after by a priest, but who chose her name?

Maria makes her way back to the path where the woman once sprang up before her like an apparition.

She pulls a wire clip out of her hair to bind the flower stems together. She places the posy on a big rock. It's pale gray limestone, almost white, and it sparkles here and there like sugar. Maria knows this rock, all the rocks. She bows her head and prays for Delfina's soul in Heaven.

At night, in the *contrà*, in Egidia's humble house, Maria dreams of slaughtering the *guro* dog for meat, and a mutilated man wants to marry her, and Delfina tears down the *cesso* walls with her filthy bare hands, and Maria is polishing the stove with pumice powder but it never comes clean—she scrubs and scrubs, her fingers aching and swollen. She wakes with the cockerel crowing, loud through the shutters, first at the hour of night, which is three on the clock, and then at four to say it's morning, and she stirs again at the squawking hour of the day, when the hand strokes five on the clock, and she feels as fretful as Saint Peter who denied the Lord Jesus three times in one long night. She wakes up full of sweat and ghosts, her nightdress twisted in a bundle.

And the campanile bells ring from the valley and she could die for the sound, but she knows she can't die now, not with her blotted inventory of unconfessed sins. She will never hear her bells again.

~

AT THE END OF the main path, they gather. A cuckoo sounds from beyond the *contrà*. A tiny fly lands on Maria's nose. It's the time of cyclamens and streams, new piglets, the big wash. The air smells clean. Achille is glad to get going, and Primo has had enough of backwardness and brown teeth, even though there's a sentimental look in his eye.

Dear magnificent Primo! Maria would not go to the ends of the Earth without him.

Despite the solemnity of the occasion, Bruna is playing games with her cousins. The children won't have cousins in Australia. Bruna is nearly ten years old, but she seems to have been a child forever, a dreamer, and always delicate, even before her tuberculosis. It's no wonder: she was born with the war. Perhaps the sea air will be good for her sensitivities. Maria wonders for a moment if her youngest will survive the journey. She's the only daughter she's got.

The huddle of embracing bodies is familiar and foreign all at once. Maria holds herself back from crying. Her heart is beating faster than the heart of a fallen fledgling, but she's not about to show it.

"Who will do the work in Italy now?" her brother Severo jokes. "Maria always does the work!" He yearns for la Mèrica, but he doesn't have the guts. His wife died young. His sons look like gypsies next to Primo.

"Write, Maria, send us letters, won't you?" Vito says. He makes no mention of his dead madhouse wife. His children all look sane. "We want every bit of news."

"Lucky you went to school, so no excuse," Severo says. "Though it's Edda who has the fine handwriting."

Egidia whispers in Maria's ear. "Dearest, I'll follow you, we'll follow you, before next year, before I'm forty-one, God willing." She holds Maria tight.

The breeze is suddenly warm, as warm as Summer, and it wraps around Maria's neck like a veil.

"Feel that air," Egidia says. "The *föhn* wind, it's the last time you'll feel it, falling from the peaks."

"A taste of Australia, maybe," Vito says. "They say the weather's always hot."

"We're going to Autumn now," says Achille.

"Ah yes, our Spring, your Autumn, everything's the opposite."

"Come on, then," Primo says. "Mama, you've got two more sisters to see in two more valleys."

"Give them our regards," says Vito.

"Sometimes I forget I'm not the eldest," says Severo. "Our best regards."

"Cecilio! Bruna!" Achille calls out and claps, one, two.

"And then we go to Sassone. The in-laws will be offended if they get less time than you." Maria does not look forward to being with Achille's family even for an afternoon.

"And the shop can't stay closed forever," Achille says. "Or the customers will go somewhere else, and the buyers will pull out, and then where would we be?"

"Australia, just the same." Primo is impatient now for the New World.

"You've sold all those fields," Severo says. "You'll live like millionaires in the desert."

Everyone has hugged and kissed everyone, three generations, more than once. No, not everyone.

"But where's Claudia?" Maria asks.

Severo rolls his eyes.

Achille checks his shiny new watch and frowns.

Maria runs back to the house.

Inside, Claudia is sitting at the kitchen table, looking at a little book and turning its pages fast, one by one, without reading. Pressed flowers—alpine stars and faded blue gentians—fall out.

"I found it, I found this," she says, looking up at Maria. "It's your book. That you read before you went away." Then she flicks at the golden edges of the pages with her thumb, like a man playing cards. Flick, again and again.

Maria recognizes the long-lost book in an instant. It's *The Christian Bride*. She remembers the words, the way it spoke to her: *for my dear young girl.*

"Here." Claudia holds the book out to Maria, but she doesn't leave her seat. "Before you go away. Again."

Caffè-caffè

THERE'S ONE WEEK LEFT BEFORE THE BIG TRIP.

Maria rides her bike to Altavilla. Edda can only meet her at the perimeter gates. Rodolfo says he was cheated when he bought the black Mercedes from Achille. And he knows about Achille's curse on him. Everyone from Altavilla to Fosso knows about the curse. Maria is banned from his property because she is the wife. And Achille's blood flows in her children's veins, fifty percent. So they are banned too. No matter that Edda is her own sister, born and bred in the same house.

"I will miss you," Edda says. She doesn't open the gate. She stands behind the wrought-iron bars and holds on to them, like a countess keeping her distance. Her face is a mirror to Maria's own, but always younger, nine years younger, nine years prettier, and smarter too.

"I will miss you too, dear sister," Maria says. "I'll send you wool." *Real wool, not baggy Lanital.* She's feeling thirsty. She leans on her bike.

"No need, no need, we have everything we want," says Edda. She doesn't know what to do with herself. She toes the ground. Her shoes are new. She shakes her head. "God, haven't we seen some times!"

Behind her is the driveway, white gravel, white dust, edged with lavender and oleander, leading to the farmhouse, grand and decayed. *In the Palladian style.* That's what Edda used to say. Maria knows it isn't true. Palladio was a famous architect of palazzi: the wrecked villa in Vicenza, the bombed basilica. Weeds grow tall in such a short time. How long before the weeds take over? Edda is no countess. And her husband is no count.

Doves swoop and land on the pantiled roof. The green shutters on all the windows are closed. Rodolfo's new car is parked in front, black against white, the overpriced-underpriced Mercedes. It was a Nazi car, Maria thinks, so it was always going to be unlucky. The main door of the house is open, tall, revealing nothing but darkness inside. Rodolfo is home. In fact, he's probably watching.

"But this is crazy," Edda says. "I can't let you go without offering you a coffee at least."

"*Caffè-caffè?*" Maria teases.

"*Caffè-caffè.*" Edda nods and smiles. She opens the gate, and it clangs in the sunshine. Doves take flight. A lizard darts across the dust.

The two sisters walk the length of the driveway, each with a hand on the bike between them, leading it like a well-behaved goat by its horns.

Blood and water

THE CEMETERY AT FOSSO IS DAZZLING WHITE IN THE SPRING sunshine. Maria follows her usual path. It's a straight line to the vault. Here, behind the wall of carved marble names, lie stillborn Ignazio and baby Tito, both taken by God before their time. There are blank stones above and below them, ready for the names of parents and siblings. Achille, Maria Vittoria, Primo, Arsenio, Cecilio, Maria Bruna. Will those bodies die here or in Australia? Only God in His Heaven knows the answer. And Amelia, will her name be engraved here?

Maria remembers all seven births, struggling, night, day, long labor, ripping, breeched, little water, flooding water, crumpled, dead, early, easy—but now she's mixing them up in her mind. Primo was the first and the best. He wrenched her agony out of her in shocking screams. He slipped out swimming in blood and water, opened his perfect pink mouth and bawled, fed on her spilling breasts like a lion cub, hungry and certain. Even though Primo was small and lightweight, Achille was proud of the handsome baby boy with all his fingers and toes, and a Montanari grip.

Maria cleans the rain-spattered dust off the vault stone. She replaces her faded felt and wire flowers with nice new plastic ones.

She says a whole rosary, standing all the time, passing the beads through her fingers.

"Farewell," she says to her little ones behind the blind white marble. "I will pray for you at every Mass, even in la Mèrica."

And then she goes, thinking that Australia might as well be Italy, because it's another place on this lowly Earth and her babies are on the other side of the sky.

Grace

You and I know about Hell, Maria, yes we do. I've seen it through the chain-mail screen of Heaven. I've heard the screams, and at night you dream of it sometimes, the flames devouring your swollen feet and racing up the spill of your graying hair, reeking like a pilot roasted alive in his cockpit, worse than a firebombed field of manure, stinking like a burnt-out bunker, while devils stab at you, forever and ever.

There's a narrow path to Heaven, Maria, if you purge your soul of sin before you die.

Australia.

Australia is Purgatory. A place of penance and purification.

~

"MAMA," AMELIA WHISPERS. SHE is standing at the end of the pew. There's excitement in her voice.

Nearly two years have passed since Maria has seen her, and it shows, even in the gloom of the Campolongo church. Her face is fatter. Her shape has changed. Childbirth has a shape. She looks well. She's holding the baby in her arms.

"Maria Grazia, meet your nonna," Amelia says as she sits down. "She's asleep, shall I wake her?"

Maria fixes her gaze on the altar, at the pollen-stained lilies in the floral display. "You didn't deserve a boy, after what you did. Serves you right." God's flame burns and flickers. "Don't tell me she's got red hair."

"She's chestnut, like you," Amelia says. "Look."

Maria doesn't turn to look. "I'm not here for that. I'm not here at all. If Primo knew—"

"If Primo knew."

Maria doesn't know what to say. "If Achille knew—"

"Him too. If he knew. I don't care what they know. Do they know that I'm happy, even without them?"

"Listen to you, speaking like a madwoman in church. God is listening. Have you been to Confession? Are you going to Mass?"

"Yes, of course, Mama. I do the flowers at the church in Lumignano. We have a beautiful Madonna, you should see her. And the best peas in the world."

"I'm not coming to Lumignano."

"Firmino sends his kindest regards."

"I don't accept them. Take them back."

"He's a devoted father—"

"I heard he's a Communist."

"He's a very good husband."

"He ruined our family."

"He takes good care of me."

"Until he keels over. Then you'll come begging."

"But you'll be in Australia," Amelia says quietly.

"So we won't get in each other's way, then," Maria says, even though her heart is leaping.

"Mama, I pray for you every day."

"Don't waste your prayers. If you really cared for me, you wouldn't have . . . And Primo—"

"What Primo thinks: is that all you care about?"

Maria doesn't know what to say. The answer is probably yes. No, the answer is no, she cares about all her children, even her dead babies, even Amelia, hopeless, willful, disgraceful, shameful, darling Amelia sitting right here next to her for the first time in almost two years, and never again.

"Mama, I'm here to see you, to wish you well, to say farewell and I'm going to miss you. I do miss you. Your granddaughter misses you."

Maria's heart is still leaping but she keeps her eyes on the altar. Everything here is in order: faultlessly ironed, positioned, straight-edged, polished. And God's red flame keeps burning, constant. This church escaped the war without a crack. The piazza, the campanile, everything was spared—even the presbytery where Amelia collected her *bacolini*. There's no more silk-working to be done. Achille has sold the mulberry-edged fields, the *parigina* stove, the racks, the lot. He sold the equipment from the shop too: the scales, the slicing machine, the grinder, the cutter. Always better to sell to a stranger. Rodolfo is complaining to everyone about the damned car.

"Look, Mama, she's looking at you, she wants you to hold her," Amelia says.

The baby's dark eyes are open now, round as buttons. Her fat arms are clutching at the air. She has woken without crying.

Amelia passes her over, and Maria has no choice but to take her granddaughter into her arms.

"Dearest baby Jesus," she says before she can help herself. It's been so long since she held a baby.

Amelia's eyes well up with tears. She wipes her nose. She wipes her cheeks.

Grazia's skin is softer than rose petals. Her tiny fingers clutch Maria's creased thumb. Her grip is fierce. It's a Montanari grip, strong as a boy's.

Maria kisses her cheek and breathes in her scent. Innocent. Sweet. Familiar. "You'd better grow up to be a better daughter—" she says. "I'll pray for you, tiny one, even in la Mèrica."

She doesn't want to let go, but she hands the baby back to Amelia. "I'm not here. You haven't seen me today. Only the priests know about this meeting. I have to go."

Amelia is blubbering now, worse than Bruna ever did.

"It's not a funeral." Maria wants to say more, but she can't.

She wants to say that she has read Amelia's letters, every letter every month, more than once, again and again, always in secret. She has never written back, but she has kept the letters safe, apart from the first ones which she burnt in anger. And now she has packed them in her special bag, the bag that she will keep with her in the cabin on the ship, not in the hold. How will Amelia write to her in Australia? There is no address to write to. Can she bear to lose her daughter forever?

No, she doesn't want to say more. She doesn't know what to say. What can she say?

She embraces Amelia, not too close or tight, with the baby in between. "I'll pray for you too."

And she gets up, moves out of the pew, genuflects, crosses herself, then walks slowly down the side of the church, past the chapel of Mary stabbed by her seven swords of sorrow, and the chapel of Saint Sebastian with his body pierced by arrows, past the votive offerings, the mess of candles, the charity box, the holy water font, to the small wooden door set into the huge wooden door, and out into the piazza where the bright sunlight makes her squint and sneeze. She half expects to see Primo, but there is no one about. Just pigeons on the steps. Not a priest, not a gossip, not a soul. She is ready for the journey to Genoa and the big ship that is waiting there.

The vernal equinox

ItIS THE FIRST DAY OF SPRING, HALFWAY THROUGH LENT. MARIA stands with her family in a circle around their bags, all together, on the dock. They stare at the huge ship. People press in on all sides— uniformed workers calling out, sailors, photographers, vendors, smokers, beggars, crooks, tourists. There are sobbing embraces here, rolling trolleys and cages there. She knew the ship would be huge, even if she is from the country and has never been near a ship before. She knew it would have to be big to carry nine hundred people. That's as many bodies as Fosso has. But she has never imagined how big a ship could be.

It is taller and wider and longer than any one thing she has ever seen. It's not bigger than a whole city like Vicenza, or this mad-house port-city hundreds of kilometers from home—but Genoa is not one thing. The ship seems bigger than Fosso, but Fosso is also not one thing—there is a church, shops, a piazza, streets behind the main street. The ship is one thing and it is also a town. Maria is troubled by its name: *Filadelfia*. The word reminds her of some-thing.

She and her family make a tighter circle around their luggage. They are dressed in their Sunday best: suits and ties, starched shirts, new skirts, fur, hats, heels. All their suitcases are new, some cardboard tied with string, some leatherette. They will carry on board just what they need for the next month. There will always be clean things to wear because Bruna will help her do the laundry for everyone. Along with her clothes and underclothes, Maria has packed her Madonna statue and Amelia's letters.

She has surrendered the wooden trunks, loaded with their life-possessions, to be stowed in the ship's hold. She doesn't know what the food will be like in Australia, or how scarce dressmaking cloth will be. If they get stranded on land or sea, she can feed her entire family on ham and cheese. She's determined that they'll never go hungry again.

Music comes from a gramophone nearby. More music comes from a button accordion. The tunes clash for a while, and then the button accordion settles into the gramophone's song.

"Filadelfia, Filadelfia, Filadelfia." Bruna makes up silly words to the tune. "My favorite thing in all the world is Filadelfia, Filadelfia, Filadelfia—"

Arsenio kicks her and tells her to be quiet. He's a young man now, and he's trying to be like Primo.

Cecilio sniggers.

"We're pioneers," Primo says to everyone and no one.

"Since when?" Achille asks.

"The ship's been doing this for no time at all, not even a year."

"Doing what?"

"Carrying people. Sailing to Australia."

"Who told you?"

"I heard."

"I heard she used to be a cargo ship," Achille says.

"There's not one tiny bit of luxury," Primo says. "Mama, those fancy posters we saw were for the new ships they're building, with tourist class."

"Next time," says Maria.

Achille frowns. "Next time?"

"I heard it was a warship bombed by the Germans and dragged

up from the seabed," says Arsenio. "They had to hack off a ton of coral. They had to build our cabins in the hold—they used to have cannons and guns in there. Now it comes back to Italy loaded with wool and things, never people."

Cecilio is gloomy. "Everyone goes to Australia, but nobody comes back."

"That's rubbish," says Primo.

Cecilio looks sheepish. He's still a boy, not yet sixteen, still under his brother's thumb.

Primo stands on Arsenio's suitcase to make himself taller. He clears his throat to give a speech. "I have in my pocket our family's key to the best life in Australia," he begins. He places his hand on his chest. His new gold-framed eyeglasses catch the Spring sunshine. He keeps the general's letter close to his heart, in a soft leather wallet. There are tears in his eyes as he gazes toward the horizon. "And I promise not to waste one drop of this almighty opportunity."

Bruna starts singing again. "Pipo, Baldassare, generale . . . Pipo, Baldassare, generale . . ." She was the one who gave names to the Americans in the cellar, Pipo after the spy plane, Baldassare like the third wise king. Maria didn't think to give them names. They were the men in the cellar who did not exist: high risk, high income. The black one was an officer, a pilot, and the white one, who said he was a pilot, turned out to be an important spy, the reason for the general's letter.

"Before leaving Fosso forever, I counted the money we've made as a family," Primo says, ignoring Bruna.

She stops singing and listens.

Arsenio grins.

Cecilio starts to clap, then stops as Primo continues.

"Everything has been sold: our land, our home, our shop, the stock, the car, all the equipment, even the *gavegnà* that my father here wore on his humble head when he first caught sight of my beautiful mother . . ."

Maria feels herself blush.

Achille nods and stubs out his cigarette with his shoe.

"Everything has been sold and, my dear family, we know that everything has a price. Don't let anyone tell you otherwise, especially not the Communists. But the American general's letter has a value that is priceless, uncountable. In our beloved Italy, the past weighs too much. It oppresses us. In Australia, our destiny is what we make of it. The future is in our hands. We must work together. The doors are open for us. Australia is the land of tomorrow."

Nobody claps or sings or says anything. Nobody smiles. They just stand there, silent in the noise and press of the crowd, feeling the weight of Italy's past: Maria's secrets, Achille's shame, Amelia's disgrace.

Maria looks away for a moment and sees a man with his arm in the air, posing for a photograph, hand clenched into a fist. Through the crowd of heads and bodies, she glimpses his bearded face. His stout belly. He's wearing a CLN Partisan badge. A blue scarf.

Suddenly he looks at her.

Their eyes meet in a flicker of familiarity, as each one recognizes the other. Scopeton. The Blackshirt who arrested Achille. Who escaped the reprisals. Who disappeared.

He turns to face the photographer and smiles without showing his teeth.

Has Achille seen him? Maria checks. No. Would Achille recognize him? No, her husband had been blindfolded. Yes, he would recognize him from the shop. Maybe. Maybe not. No, the fellow is bearded and fat, like a disguise. Primo? No. It was only Maria who saw Scopeton again and again, with those messages from Duilio, and those threats.

When she looks again, Scopeton has vanished, like a marsh-spirit.

Is he going to be on the ship? They have the rest of the day and night on board before setting sail. She can find out. They can disembark. What will he do to them? Will he denounce her? No. He's acting the Partisan now. He's not going to say, or do, anything. He has more to hide than they do, than anyone does.

"Let's go!" says Primo, waving his arms like a bandleader. "Everyone, gather up your things."

"Are we sailing away now?" asks Bruna.

Primo laughs. He's happy. "No, no, we have to settle in and sleep on the ship tonight. We sail tomorrow."

Maria and her family climb the ship's gangway. Their clothes look so smart and new. *Bela figura.*

"We cut a fine figure," she says to Primo.

But they are third-class, like most people, and they are nothing compared with the fancy few who are going cabin-class. Those passengers have porters and jewels and expensive coats.

Primo squeezes her hand. "Mama, we will never be third-class again."

And now Maria realizes that the ship is not bigger than any one thing she has ever seen—she has seen mountains. She glances down at the water far below, slopping slowly this way, then that, like a giant breathing thing. If they fall, they will all drown the same, first-class or third-class. None of them can swim. Achille could drown in a ditch. Primo is fearful of water. And yet he is their leader; he has taken the place of Achille. Now he strides forth like the man who owns the ship. He means business. Her dear, handsome, clever son is the future.

Stowaway

Hᴇʀ ᴄᴀʙɪɴ sʟᴇᴇᴘs ꜰᴏᴜʀ. Fᴇᴍᴀʟᴇs ᴏɴʟʏ. Aᴄʜɪʟʟᴇ ɪs ᴏɴ ᴀ lower deck with the three boys in a twelve-bed dormitory. Men are not allowed in the women's quarters, not even husbands. Men and women can only meet in public places on the upper decks. Maria quite likes this enforced separation, even though it's unnatural, and a woman should always have her men nearby to protect her. She and Achille have slept in separate beds for years, ever since he came back from prison—but not in separate bedrooms. She wonders what she will do in this new strange season, this Springtime that is already Oceantime, with boats for traffic instead of cars and carts, with water below, not earth, and a confused moon to sow or bleed by. There are cooks to do the cooking, and cleaners to do the cleaning. There are no animals here to tend or slaughter, no garden to maintain, no preserves to make, no shop to manage. No shop! What work will Maria do? What will she do with herself all day?

There are bunk beds fixed to the walls. Bruna stares at them, excited but not breathless—perhaps the sea air is good for her.

Maria tests the bedding with her hand. The mattresses are plain and narrow but they're not filled with anything rough. There are white rails on the sides, like hospital beds. The floor is solid but it sways—so those rails have a purpose. There is no window, not even a little round one, but there is a fan. A single electric lamp hangs from the low ceiling. Maria is glad she has brought a flashlight with her. Everything is clean and white. Over a low washbasin there's a mirror and a fold-down tabletop that hooks back to the wall. She and Bruna must share these things with two strangers.

"Please, Mama, let me sleep on the top bed," Bruna asks.

It suits Maria to take the lower one. Sometimes she gets dizzy.

There's a suitcase underneath the bunk on the other side of the cabin. The buckles are open. Its owner has left it unlocked, easy for any thief. *Don't trust anybody.* But Maria is not a thief, and perhaps the owner has nothing to steal.

The door opens and a woman enters. She's short and handsome, about Amelia's age, but well-dressed, like a city woman, in a white blouse and smart gray pencil skirt. No sign of children.

"How do you do, I'm Rachele." She shakes Maria's hand and smiles, a beautiful big smile, but her eyes are sad.

"My name is Maria Vittoria. The little one is Maria Bruna. Is there someone else with you?"

Rachele shakes her head. "I'm on my own. I'm from Venice. You?" She speaks with a Venetian accent.

"A town called Campolongo. Not far from Venice. So we're *paesani*, almost kin."

"Are you Jewish?" Rachele asks.

What a peculiar question. There were Jews on the Nazi trains, but Maria has never known a Jew. Jesus Christ was King of the Jews, and He was killed by Jews.

"No," says Maria.

Is this what it's like to make conversation with a stranger who's not a customer, not a neighbor, not a relative or family friend? Maria doesn't know how to behave in such a situation. She sits down on her bed and suddenly her whole body feels tired.

Bruna cuddles up next to her.

They watch Rachele open her suitcase.

Maria has never seen so many books. She can't imagine how

people have time to sit around and read books, but she supposes somebody has to.

Rachele takes out a silver object, like a long thin brooch. "I'm not exactly living here..." she says, almost to herself, attaching the brooch carefully to the rail of the bed. "But it'll protect me while I sleep."

"Mama," Bruna whispers. "Can we have one too?"

"No."

"It's called a mezuzah. It normally goes on the main doorway," Rachele says, still trying to make it stay put. "If you're Jewish."

It's not straight, Maria thinks. She remembers the *fascio* on Duilio's front door, telling the world who lived inside and what he believed, giving himself away—which had to be bad luck, like putting a plague-cross on the house. He was lucky to live as long as he did. How did this woman survive the war if she had a sign on her front door? The Germans took away all the Jews they could find. The trains from Venice went through Fosso and sometimes they stopped at the crossing. She wonders now if Bruna's doll belonged to a Jewish girl who got away in time, before the Germans came.

"What happened to your doll?" Maria asks Bruna.

Bruna takes it out of her suitcase and hugs it. The red hair is tousled. The felt face is worn and darkened where Bruna has stroked it. The doll still has two boots.

Rachele smiles. "The Pope warned there'd be Cossacks in Piazza San Pietro, but he didn't say anything about Filadelfia."

Maria doesn't know what the woman is talking about.

Bruna kisses the doll's face. "Firmino," she says. "Firmino."

"You think of another name right now or I'll throw that thing into the sea."

Bruna looks ready to cry.

"Here, help me unpack the Madonna, like a good girl. She'll keep us safe. Like that brooch." Maria leans over and opens her suitcase, careful not to let Amelia's letters be seen.

The Madonna of the Mountains is wrapped in soft undergarments. Maria checks it for damage. The glass bell jar is intact.

Nothing inside has moved, apart from the necklaces, which can be jiggled into place.

"Bruna, why don't you set her up somewhere we can both see her and pray to her."

Bruna puts down her doll and tries to find a spot.

Rachele watches.

The Madonna looks enormous and out of place here. She will not fit on the basin edge. Inside bed rails, she will topple onto the floor when the ship moves. Besides, she doesn't leave enough space for a body to sleep. On the floor, she's in the way of everything. The cabin is small enough as it is. And there's another person to come.

"She'll just have to stay inside my suitcase, under my bed," says Maria. "Even if she can't see out, we know she's there."

"Like a stowaway," Rachele says with a smile.

No chickens

At night in bed, before sleep, Maria lies on her back, even though it aches. Bruna is lying on the bed above her. Rachele the Jew is lying in her bed on the other side of the cabin. Is she a Communist? The fourth bunk is still empty.

They have all been registered and checked and cleared. No sign of consumption. Even Bruna passed her tests without a mention of her TB. There are no obstacles to emigration now. It's a feeling lighter than wine or dancing.

They have eaten dinner in the refectory with hundreds of men seated in rows, in every direction, and some lonely-looking women in a huddle. She saw no sign of Scopeton. The tables, covered in white paper, made long lines that joined in the distance like a road. There were no windows, no sight of the sky, and no sight of the sea. There was plenty of food, platters and platters, like at a wedding. The cooks wore tall white hats. The boys were happy. Achille ate with great appetite, plate after plate. *It's not as good as my cooking, is it?* Maria asked him. He shook his head. *Nobody makes gnocchi like you do.* His mouth was stuffed full of meat and vegetables.

"You have a lot of books," Bruna says into the darkness of the cabin. She should be saying good night. "Are they for school?"

Rachele replies. She is just a voice. "I had to leave school in 1938 when I was ten—how old are you now?"

"She's ten." Maria wonders if Bruna can work out this woman's age—she's twenty-two, like Amelia.

"Do you go to school?"

"Not on the ship," Bruna answers. "I'm emigrating."

"But you'll go to school when you get to Australia, won't you?"

"I'll go to a convent school with nuns, and I'll have girls to play with, my own age, instead of chickens." Bruna seems to have lost her shyness. "When Mama's angry, she sends me off to play with the chickens, but chickens are stupid and don't know how to play. And, anyway, there are no chickens on the ship—"

"Stop your babbling or God won't give you any children." Maria kicks the bunk above her.

"School is very important," Rachele says.

"You've got to study so people don't cheat you," Maria says. Sometimes she wishes she'd had more schooling. But she can write and do arithmetic. People don't cheat her. What more could school have taught her?

"I was taught by Jewish academics who were thrown out of the universities. Our school was . . . spontaneous. My parents and the other adults had to improvise. With the Racial Laws, that's all they could do. They protected me. I didn't know to worry. I was a child like you."

Maria can't remember when she was ten. All she can remember is work, the same at any age: the well, the river, the washing, the wood-fires, the carrying, the animals, the harvesting, the prayers, the seasons. *Se lavora par magnare e se magna par lavorar.* One works in order to eat and eats in order to work.

"But then the deportations started in 1943, in the Winter just after Armistice. They got the Jews who had no money, the unwise ones, the very old ones who couldn't get away, and newborn babies. Have you been to Venice?"

"The streets are made of water," Bruna says.

"The addresses are complicated and difficult to work out. Sometimes the locals, if they were Fascists, helped the Germans find people. But others helped us instead."

Maria thinks of checkpoints, and spy planes, and Nazis on every road, in every requisitioned room. She thinks of Edda's house, like a Nazi hotel. The Nazis hated Italians. Would Duilio have helped the Nazis? She hates the Nazis. "Not all the Fascists helped the Germans . . ."

"Are you a Fascist?"

"No, of course not," Maria says quickly. She remembers burning her PNF card. "We supported nobody. We had no politics. We had a shop to run."

"Everything is political." Rachele's disgust is plain, even in the darkness. "So-called neutrality destroyed my family."

Maria imagines losing her family. She can't think of anything worse in the world. This young woman has lost everyone. Poor, poor, poor girl. She's spirited, like Amelia. Maria swallows hard. She tries to hold back guilty tears, but they run out of the corners of her eyes and onto the pillow. Amelia has lost all of her family. Emigration is making an orphan of her.

"I'm sorry," she says to Rachele, to Amelia. She has never apologized to anyone like this. Without details or excuses. Without Absolution. She has never apologized at all. It feels like a huge stone lifting from her soul. Like liberation. "I'm so sorry."

The cabin is quiet. Just the noises of the ship.

"Rachele . . ." Bruna says at last. "How did you get away?"

"We paid the Partisans. A lot of cash. Some of us escaped to Switzerland."

"Mama says you always need money. No matter what's going on. Peace or war."

"And the moment you leave your front door, you need even more money than if you stay at home," Rachele replies.

"We didn't stay at home," says Bruna. "We're emigrating."

"My mother sewed money in my coat lining, and in all of our coats," Rachele says. "We hid money in the heels of our shoes. It's hard to believe it's not even seven years ago. I was fifteen. I grew up fast."

She is exactly the same age as Amelia. The fourth bunk is empty. Amelia should be in it. Amelia is the missing one.

"I heard they rang bells all over Italy," Rachele says.

On Liberation Day, for one stupid innocent day, the bells that weren't wrecked rang without pause like a thousand weddings. The family was living on secret food then—with cash from the men in the cellar. Everyone was exhausted by the slow, vicious years of Salò, and the settling of accounts afterward.

"When we came back," Rachele says, her voice soft, "our little house was occupied by refugees, as many as twenty of them. Our friends and neighbors were missing. We didn't know who was dead or who would return. Every day was a surprise. Nothing was certain. It took us years to get our home back."

"If you got your home back, why are you leaving it?" Bruna asks.

Rachele is quiet.

Maria opens her eyes, but the cabin is as black as a moonless night. Not even the silver brooch can be seen. She touches the flashlight next to her pillow. She closes her eyes again, and more tears spill out.

Rachele seems to have fallen asleep. But then her voice is sudden: "Bruna, would you like me to teach you something—say, mathematics?"

"And your books?" Bruna says.

"And my books," Rachele answers. The way she says it sounds like *good night*.

La Madona de le Montagne

IN HER NARROW BUNK BED, WITH BRUNA SLEEPING ABOVE, THE Madonna resting below, and Rachele the Jew taking deep breaths, almost snoring, Maria tries to remember Amelia's letters. There are words and lines from one letter, and another, all floating and jumbled in her memory.

Quietly, carefully, so as not to wake the other two, she pulls her suitcase from under the bed and opens it. Her hands find the letters in a bundle, tied with ribbon.

Under her sheet and blanket, with the flashlight on and facing the wall, she reads.

Cara Mama, each letter starts, knowing that there would be no reply. That girl was strong and stubborn from the very beginning. *Dear Mama*.

She opens one envelope after another. They are all mixed up.

This is letter number 13.

This is letter number 19.

This is letter number 5 . . .

I did a test and planted seeds when the moon was waxing, on purpose, and the plants were all barren, just as you would expect, but I wanted to do the test.

Little Grazia smiles whenever she sees a face, it can be a cartoon, or one day it was a politician's poster. She knows to smile for a real person. So everyone falls in love with her.

This was during the festival of the pea, you know the peas here are the sweetest and the best in all the world.

My figure has gone completely but Firmino says he loves me whatever shape I am.

They still sleep with their animals in the winter, just to keep warm, they still get their water from a pump. Zia Egidia talked about moving to Australia, but you must know that because she is coming to be near you.

Last night Firmino had a fever. Today I ruined the polenta. I've never done that before.

Firmino's friend Giorgio died. All these years after but it was the war that killed him. I did the flowers for his funeral. I do the flowers at the church now every week. His name will live on when we have a son. I'm going to have lots of children.

I know you won't respond. There are tears in my eyes.

Jesus, Mary and Joseph, the weather has been bad here, the worst fog I have ever seen. They say it is pollution. I never see fireflies anymore.

Dried pressed flowers fall out of the envelopes. Wild columbine.

Firmino is kind and good with children.

*Jesus, Mary and Joseph, I don't know how you managed
to bring us up with the war and the shop and everything
going on.*

~

THE MADONNA OF THE MOUNTAINS is resting, swaddled, in the
suitcase under the bed. *Stowaway*, Rachele called her.

Maria sleeps, but the Madonna of the Mountains does not sleep.

Australia is Purgatory. A place of penance and purification.

*Behold this endless space, and mineral deserts, tin towns, virgin land
ripe for clearing and cultivation—your mortal father would have an extra
beat in his heart if he could see it—never mind the Blackamoors roaming
about half-naked, and everywhere poisonous serpents. Behold the* canguri
*which are not dogs at all, but game animals that ravage crops with their
bounding, and make tough steak. It's a land of misfits.*

Behold the faraway State of Vittoria.

*The roads are not paved with gold. Many roads are not paved at all,
and the railways are few—there's been no Mussolini. But the roads are
not broken either—there's been no war. There's still gold if you look for it.
You cannot eat gold, Maria, it would break your aging teeth, but you can
always sell it.*

*The rivers don't flow with milk and honey—you knew that, you're not
stupid. But the rivers don't flow with blood either, not like the torrents
where you come from. They are brown and slow, because the land itself is
old, it's wearing down, stooping, crumbling with age. Even the mountains
are low, Maria, not like the mountains of your youth.*

Put down roots in Australia. Start a new orto, *plant trees that will
yield their plenty before you're too old to chew. Let your magnificent son
see you with perspiration on your brow, as once you impressed Achille. You
can grow old with grace and honey—but only if you pray to me every day.
Attend the first Mass. Honor the Mystery. And you will celebrate your
white-haired anniversaries with gold and more gold.*

But first you must confess your sins—no matter that you confess in Italian to a priest who speaks only Australian. Your repentance will fly to Heaven. Because repent you do, Maria, I know this in the fiber of my mantle, in the weight of my golden crown.

Confess. Write to Amelia. Ask her for forgiveness.

Wake up, Maria!

The Madonna of the Mountains is standing at the end of the bunk. She's the size of a human, stocky and short, weighed down by her enormous crown and heavy cloak. The shape she makes altogether is like a gold and blue mountain. She fills the cabin. "What do you want, Maria?"

"You know what I want," Maria says, but the sounds come out strangely, as if she's speaking someone else's language.

The Madonna is astonished. "You're talking back to me."

Maria makes an effort to nod. "I tried to keep everything the way it should be—"

The Madonna puts her jeweled finger to her smiling lips, as if to say *silence.* "Everything has changed. Everything does. You remember Fortuna on the church wall, I know you do. You've done well, my shrewd one, considering . . . The boys were favored in every way—they even had the best food. And of the girls, you weren't the oldest, or the youngest, or the prettiest. You weren't even the smartest. You were on the shelf, with not a decent taker in sight. Remember that First Big War, it was a harrowing of manhood, it turned upright men into tunneling trench-worms. But, Maria, that was all a game of *briscola* when you think about what came after . . ." The Madonna shakes her head slowly, muttering, "Filthy, dirty work, war. Men make the mess, then women have to clean it up. So much cleaning up to do. We clean up the mess with tears—the water washes, the salt disinfects. How many tears are needed!"

Maria tries to speak. Her mouth is locked and unyielding. "I was scared."

"But you came through. It's almost a miracle. You survived. And the children too. Think of all those mothers who lost their sons— I, for one, know how that feels. Think of all those girls who were raped and ruined. You avoided the work camps and the concentration camps, the press-gangs, and the vendettas—"

"We were hungry. My little girl nearly died."

"Through the worst of winters, you ran the shop, you put food on the plate, you were the man—no wonder you have arms like a man."

Maria can lift a man's weight of washing. Maria can do the work.

"Heaven is full of women, Maria. It takes a special kind of man to get here. Men have all the money, and money is dirty—eggs are so much cleaner." The Madonna strokes her bib of jewels.

Maria tries to reach out and touch the sparkles. She can't move her hand at all.

The Madonna opens her celestial-blue cloak. The rasping fabric looks stiff and heavy, like a shop awning. The lining is the richest red. And there, strung between her hands, are three glowing baubles on invisible thread, each one painted with a scene. The first is a bundle of *fascio* sticks in a *gavegnà* basket. In the second picture, a sprig of mountain herbs floats inside a grappa bottle. The third one shows a bunch of twigs for silkworms to climb.

"I see them," Maria says. She is weeping now, but she can't feel the tears. She is weeping and weeping. This is her trinity of shame.

The Madonna's gaze is stern. She says nothing. Then she closes her hands together and the baubles vanish. "Have you seen the stars in the night sky, Maria? They are pinpricks in Heaven's pavement, which is pierced like a chestnut pan. They are tiny glimpses of the divine light." She leans in and her crown tickles the underside of Bruna's bunk. "There's a girl crying out to you. She's been betrayed. She's you. You can't trust anybody, but you can trust me."

"Please . . ." Maria tries to say.

"What do you want now, Maria? Everything is possible."

"You know what I want."

"Go on: name it."

"Heaven." Maria tries to say. "Forgiveness."

"But first, my furrowed chestnut . . ." The Madonna looms. She shines. "Forgive yourself."

~

MARIA WAKES IN SOFT LIGHT. There's a deep rumbling beneath her bed. She's in the mountains, at Egidia's, she's in Altavilla, and a big thresher is threshing, she's in Sassone, with Achille's family snoring loudly next door. Where is Achille? She is in Duilio's bed. She is alone. The snoring is louder than a monster. She can feel its vibrations in her belly. She is on the ship. In her cabin. Bruna is above her. Amelia is in the bunk bed opposite. No, it's the Venetian woman with the silver bed-brooch, lying there, reading one of her books by flashlight. It must be day.

Rachele looks across at Maria and then looks back to her book. It must be early. Too early to talk.

Maria checks her watch. It is when a cock should be crowing the third time to announce the hour of the day—what hour is five o'clock in the middle of seawater? The ship's great engines are throbbing, but it's not yet time for the *Filadelfia* to sail. There are hours to go, Mass and breakfast, before setting out to sea.

The Madonna is nowhere to be seen.

Maria gathers up Amelia's letters from the bedsheets, makes a bundle, and re-ties the ribbon. They are all crumpled and out of order. No matter. Before hiding them, she checks Amelia's address again. She knows what to do. She will get a pen and some paper from the priest, or from the captain, from someone, and some stamps—no, she will get a postcard, and she will write to her daughter, and post the card before the ship sets sail. But what can she say after all this time? She's not used to writing, unlike her sister Edda, the clever one. She must prepare the words.

Cara figlia, she will write. *Dear daughter. I have missed you. I read your letters. Grazia is the spitting image of you. Your father and your brothers have no idea I am writing to you. They would be very angry with me if they knew. I am glad you go to church and you are doing the flowers for the church. I never forget you in my prayers. Our Lady knows. Please forgive me.*

Maria Vittoria (Mama)

Quietly, she opens the suitcase and packs Amelia's letters away. She touches the Madonna's glass-domed jar, wrapped in soft undergarments. She stares at the Madonna's moon-round face in the gloom.

The Madonna stares silently back.

Last night, Maria realizes now, she had a dream. Every other night of her life when she's woken up, she's been in the middle of a nightmare, in a panic, fleeing or falling. She didn't know what a good dream was. She feels calm now. Almost happy.

Tiny wild cyclamens

ACHILLE IS WAITING FOR MARIA AT THE ENTRANCE TO THE ship's picture-theater.

The sight of him delights her. She asked him last night, before bed, before segregation, if he would join her at Mass in the morning, and he promised nothing. She can't remember the last time he came to Mass. But here he is with the boys, dressed in their best.

"Papà!" says Bruna.

Maria smiles. "I'm glad we're here, all together." The only one missing is Amelia.

Achille nods. He looks tired. "They were too stirred up to sleep."

"Everyone in our dormitory snores," says Primo.

"You too," Arsenio says.

Primo gives him a shove.

"Everyone's scared of drowning," Cecilio mumbles.

"All the more reason to pray," Maria says. "Let's go in."

She has never been inside a picture-theater before. It's not like a church, except for the rows and rows of seats, and the aisle in the middle. The paneled ceiling is low. The walls are plain. There are no statues, no windows, no Stations of the Cross. Instead of a canopied altar and tabernacle, there's a curtained wall with a table in front of it. A vase of flowers sits on a white tablecloth.

The hour is early, but already a crowd has gathered, and the seats are filling with men and women and children, mixed together on both sides of the aisle.

Maria sits next to Achille—Bruna on her left, the boys beside him. Her heart is full of gratitude. They are all attending Mass. She must say Grace.

Achille strokes the polished wood trim on the arm of the seat. He's admiring the finish.

Maria looks at his hand—creased skin, raised veins, his worn wedding ring—and she puts her hand on his.

Achille looks at her, and she holds his gaze.

In his eyes she sees memory. Years, decades, work, pain, war, fortitude—so much memory.

"La Mèrica," she says. And her heart leaps.

"Australia," he says. He grips her hand. "Vittoria."

Everyone stands for the priest.

His vestments are ordinary but he has a scallop shell hanging from his neck, like Saint James the pilgrim.

"Let us pray," the priest says.

Maria joins her hands in prayer. She bows her head, closes her eyes and listens.

"Lord, Father in Heaven, bless these your humble pilgrims, bless the journey which soon they undertake, that it may profit the health of both soul and body. Lord, Father, look mercifully upon Your servant Pius, whom You have chosen as the chief shepherd to guide Your Church through the hardships of war and in this time of peaceful renewal. Amen."

~

WHEN MASS IS FINISHED, Achille and the boys head for the mess deck, while Maria remains to say extra prayers with Bruna.

Outside the picture-theater, she makes small talk with some

women, because that's what people do, she is learning this now. It's like chatting to customers in the shop, but without selling things to them.

Two of the women are from Dalmatia, a part of Italy utterly lost to Yugoslavia. They spent three years without a nationality, moving from one refugee camp to another. Another woman is a proxy bride. She was married in her village church—a proper eleven-o'clock wedding, not a shameful dawn ceremony—to an absent bridegroom in faraway Australia. His best friend stood in for him, said the words and even put the ring on her finger. The Holy Sacrament of Marriage is what will protect her from the lonely men on the ship who might take advantage. The other woman, a desperately poor *contadina*, has missing teeth, and legs misshapen by rickets. She's never eaten so well as on the ship. She hopes her son in Sydney eats this well—he sent the money for her ticket—it is the land of plenty, after all. Everyone has seen the newspaper advertisements about the Utopia of the South.

Maria's *Christian Bride* book warns against chatter and murmuring. It's idle and wasteful, even if it passes the time. She has never before had to pass the time. There was never quite enough time. But now she has time as vast as oceans, and nothing to do with it.

"Come, Bruna, let's explore."

They see a children's room, a ladies' lounge, a smoking room. Everything looks solid and new. They climb stairs to the upper deck.

Bruna holds Maria's hand.

They gaze at the endless water, deep glass-blue—and Maria remembers home. The mountains, not the plains. Her real home, with her mother and father, and tiny wild cyclamens, and her sisters when they were young, and the cuckoo's call, and the pig's pink skin beneath its sparse hair, and the rushing rinsing river, and polenta soaking in hot milk. With a stab of remorse, she thinks of dead Delfina and says a silent prayer for her.

"Mama, it's time for breakfast," says Bruna.

The gong is sounding.

They will join with the men again.

"Mama, can we watch a cine-film at the picture-house?"

It must be decent if it's where they hold Mass. "Yes," Maria says.

A chorus of voices rises from a hum all around them on the ship, growing louder and louder.

There are poisonous fish that look just like rocks.

There are beavers with beaks, that lay eggs and suckle.

There's still gold if you look for it. But America or Argentina would have been better.

Tobacco, fruit, sugarcane, logging, roads, any job they've got.

The locals don't drink wine.

More than six men to every girl, you've got to stand out, they can just take their pick.

Don't believe everything you hear—they've got strikes and marches and slums and TB.

Five years, no more. Then I'm coming back rich.

Maria gives her postcard to a uniformed man (no eagle emblems, just anchors on his hat and buttons). She wants Amelia to read it right now, but she knows she must wait. By the time Amelia receives it, Maria will be far away, on the other side of the world. There is too much water, impossibly deep.

Time to sew

IT IS ALMOST A SIN TO GAZE AT MIRRORS, BUT THE MIRROR IN THE cabin is impossible to avoid. The space is small. Maria sees her reflection the moment she walks in through the door. It's as if she's seeing herself for the first time. Without her fur-collared coat on, she looks old, and old-fashioned.

She takes the shoulder pads out of her blouse and drops them onto the bed.

Her skirt is not long enough, or short enough. And it's shapeless.

"Bruna, help me with some sewing."

Within minutes, Bruna is sitting on the floor and pinning the skirt's hem, taking it up, making sure that it's even all the way around. Her fingers are precise and quick.

The new hemline is just below the knees. Maria can sew it fast.

She might even taper the skirt a little. Her sewing machine is in the ship's hold, but she can do the seams by hand.

The skirt will need ironing. She knows where the laundry is.

Oceantime

MARIA LEANS AGAINST THE RAILINGS WITH HER FAMILY, on a high deck, breathing in salt air that stinks of diesel. Achille, Primo, Arsenio, Cecilio, Bruna—they are all silent.

People move, but mountains stay put.

Maria feels the swaying swell of the seawater below. The world is a bowl, and it makes the same slow swaying motion inside her, like fear, like excitement. She wants to wave a white handkerchief at someone, because everyone is waving, and everyone is tearing an invisible ribbon tied to someone, but there is nobody in the crowd that she knows, not a brother from the *contrà*, not even Edda from the plains. Not even her silk-working, letter-writing, darling daughter Amelia. Genoa is a place full to the edges with strangers.

Maria holds Bruna's hand tenderly, tightly. And the feeling inside her is like hope.

The ship pulls away without a ripple of water. It's almost nothing, but all the bodies roar.

CODA

Food, family, history

Se lavora par magnare e se magna par lavorar.

We work so we can eat, and eat so we can work.

Maria's gnocchi

The potatoes should be white inside, yellowish outside, not too wet. You must look inside to see. Boil the potatoes in salted water with their skins on. Take off the skins with your hands while the potatoes are hot. Mash the potatoes well in a big bowl. Add an egg. Mix in some flour, enough to make dough, about a handful. Salt if needed. Mix quickly. On a floured surface, use your hands to roll the dough into lengths like thick rope. Cut the dough into dumpling-sized pieces. You can make a nice shape if you thumb each one on the back of a fork. Lay the gnocchi out separately on a floured cloth. In a large pot of water on a hot fire, boil the gnocchi, a few at a time so they don't stick together. When they are floating, they are ready. Remove with a skimmer and place in a serving dish. Douse with rich meat sauce. Keep working in small batches until they are all done.

Delfina's gnocchi

Dighe de sì, dighe de no,
Copa le vecie, le giovani no!
A le giovani on piato de gnochi,
A le vecie minestra sui oci!

Say yes, say no,
Kill the old women, not the young!
To the young ones a plate of
   gnocchi,
To the old women, soup on
   their eyes!

For keeping—sopressa sausage

SOPRESA

You need half a pig or more, at least nine months old, raised on a diet of whey, cooked cornmeal, potatoes and roasted chestnuts. Cut the pork meat into sections and cool for a day or so. Still working in the cool, separate the bones, skin and nerves. Use the best parts: thighs, nape, shoulder, stomach, throat-fat and loin. Clean the meat thoroughly before grinding it. Season with salt and black pepper. Mix thoroughly and press into natural intestine sleeves with a diameter of at least eight centimeters, or as wide as two hands making a circle. Dip into hot water and massage the shape to get it smooth and right. Bind with hemp string all the way down, first lengthways, then horizontally in lots of tight rings. This helps to get any air out. Hang the sopressa to drip for half a day in the kitchen or similar warm place. Keep drying and aging in a cool place (not too cold) for four to ten months, depending on the size. The skin eventually becomes white, then gray-brown with mold. The meat inside should be pink or faded red, and the flavor will now be delicate and slightly sweet.

Wintertime—stockfish baccalà Vicenza style

BACALÀ A LA VISENTINA

Pound the stockfish (dried cod) with a wooden rod or mallet. Soak to soften it for three days, changing the water every four hours. Pat the fish dry, skin it and cut open lengthwise to remove all the bones. Cut or rip it into small pieces. Finely chop onions and fry them gently in olive oil without browning. Add rinsed, boned and chopped anchovies. Next, add the stockfish pieces, minced parsley, milk, olive oil, salt and pepper. Cover and stew very slowly over embers for four or so hours. Eat warm, an hour after cooking, or after letting it settle for a day. Serve with polenta.

Springtime—"wild asparagus" or wild hop shoot omelet

FRITAIA COI BRUSCANDOLI

At the time of year when the chickens are laying plenty of eggs, and the *orto* is yet to yield its best, gather *bruscandoli*, which grow spontaneously in uncultivated fields and along watercourses. Wash well and tamp dry with a cloth. Separate the tender top parts from the tough bases that are not worth eating. Cut the tops into pieces. Mince some onion. Heat some lard in a pan, or olive oil with a pat of butter. Fry the onion on a gentle fire without browning, then add the *bruscandoli.* Tip in a little water to braise rather than fry the mixture. In a bowl, break the eggs, add milk and a little salt and pepper, and beat with a fork. Mix in a little grated grana cheese if you have some. Pour this egg mixture into the pan with the *bruscandoli* and cook over a low fire. Let it settle and cook, then use the lid of the pan or a plate to turn the omelet over and cook the other side. This recipe can also be made with foraged *pissacan* dandelion, nettle, mallow or poppy leaves.

Summertime—fruit conserved in syrup or in grappa

FRUTI SIROPAI O SOTO GRASPA

Use cherries, apricots, peaches or plums, not too mature. Thoroughly wash and dry the fruit with a clean cloth.

To conserve with syrup:

Scald the fruit in boiling water. Halve and stone. Set aside. In a pot, bring water to boil. Stir in sugar and lemon juice. Keep simmering until the liquid becomes a syrup (reduced to about half), then take it off the fire. Place the fruit in boiled jars. Pour the syrup over the fruit. Seal and boil the filled jars.

To conserve with alcohol:

Place fresh fruit inside clean glass jars. Sprinkle with sugar and add some orange or lemon peel. Cover with strong white grappa. Put lids on and let rest for a few days. Then add more grappa, close to the top. Seal airtight and keep in the cellar, storeroom or similar cool, dark place.

This fruit will last forever.

Autumn—bigoli pasta with duck sauce

BIGOLI CO L'ARNA

A *bigolaro* machine is used to make pasta like rough spaghetti, thick as knitting needles, good for catching fatty sauces. To make the sauce, pluck the bird, then clean it thoroughly. Clean the gizzard inside and out. Set the liver and heart aside. Put a big pot filled with plenty of water on the stove and add carrot, an onion studded with cloves, celery, parsley, bay leaf and salt. Add the duck with gizzard and bring to the boil. Simmer for an hour or two, skimming occasionally, then take the meat out. Finely chop the raw liver and heart. Gently cook these in a pan with butter, minced garlic, salt, pepper and sage leaves. Add the boiled gizzard, finely chopped. Cook the pasta al dente in the strained duck broth. Drain the pasta, toss with the sauce and sprinkle with grated grana cheese. Eat the boiled duck later as a main course with green sauce. Ideal for the feast day of Our Lady of the Rosary or Madonna della Vittoria.

Recipes for torture—castor oil or salt

OJO DE RIZENO O SALE

These recipes are to feed an Italian who is anti-national—one who insults Mussolini, violates Autarchy, laments the invasion of Abyssinia, blames the regime for unemployment, criticizes the alliance with Nazi Germany—or is an outspoken Socialist, Communist, drunkard or habitual criminal.

Castor oil drink:

With or without using a cudgel, pour good castor oil (about a liter) in a continuous flow down the gullet, while firmly holding back the head and pinching the nose. Variation: follow with a live frog or toad down the throat. Feeding should be timed so that acute diarrhea occurs in public.

Kitchen salt:

If salt is not too scarce or precious, feed it generously and repeatedly to the spy or traitor in order to create acute stomach pains and fear of death.

Recipes for Autarchy—oil, meat and coffee

OJO, CARNE E CAFÈ IN AUTARCHIA

Oil:

Add powdered firewood ash to rancid olive oil in a bottle (weight proportions of 1:3). Give the bottle a good shake and let it settle for a day, away from strong light and heat. Shake it again. Wait for two or three days. Using soft cotton cloth as a filter, carefully strain the salvaged oil into a new bottle, ready to use for cooking.

Meat:

Fill a tub with powdered wood ash collected from the stove. Take meat that's gone off, wrap it in muslin and bury it in the ash. Leave in a cool place. After two hours or so, the ash will have done its work. Heat a pot of water and mix in some vinegar to wash the meat. Use clean paper to tamp the meat dry. Cook as soon as possible.

Coffee:

Collect seven days' worth of spent coffee grounds and add them to a saucepan of water with a pinch of roasted ground chicory root. Boil and cool seven times. Let the sediment settle. Pour the coffee liquid through a fine cloth into a clean jug. Use as a base for caffe latte.

Recipe to last longer—polenta with salted pilchard

POLENTA E SCOPETON

Hang one salted pilchard (or a sardine) from the ceiling. Make sure everyone at the table has a slice of hot grilled polenta in their hands. All at once, let everyone reach up and out to the scopeton, to wipe their polenta against it. Reuse the fish at other mealtimes, reviving it with olive oil and a little heat. Eventually it will disappear.

Amelia's rice and peas

RISI E BISI

For this traditional Saint Mark's Day dish, you need freshly harvested baby peas. The best peas in the world come from Lumignano. Make a broth with their shells and set it aside. Finely chop an onion and fry it with minced pancetta. When the onion is golden, add short-grain raw rice (one handful for each person) and continue cooking over a moderate fire, stirring constantly, without bruising or crushing the rice, until it is translucent. Add the pea broth, one ladle at a time, cooking in between each ladleful. When the rice is half done, add the peas with a handful of minced parsley. Continue cooking until the rice is al dente, but keep it wet. Take it off the fire and stir in a pat of butter, some grated grana cheese and a dash of pepper. Let it settle.

Importing foodstuffs

Store precious foods (e.g., Maria's best homemade mountain prosciutto, uncut wheels of cheese, specially selected Italian vegetable and fruit seeds) wrapped in generous layers of waxed paper and cloth, packed tightly in vermin-proof trunks, in the ship's hold or similar cool place. Unpack foods for inspection. Australian customs officials do not know Autarchy. They do not know the meaning of war or money. It is their job to burn food. Their fires are pure as bushfires, pure as Hell.

Polenta

Boil plenty of salted water in a cauldron on a hot fire. Sprinkle coarsely ground cornmeal like slow rain into the boiling water until you get the right density, constantly stirring with a big wooden spoon to avoid lumping, crusting or burning. Keep stirring vigorously over a low fire until the polenta starts detaching from the sides of the pot, usually in forty minutes to an hour. Don't stop stirring. If the polenta starts to get too hard, add hot water. Lift the cauldron off the fire and pour the polenta with an energetic shove onto a big wooden board. Let the polenta settle into a nice soft round form, ready to cut. The smell is nostalgia, so it is the past, but it is also hunger, so it is the future.

Acknowledgments

SPECIAL THANKS TO SEVEN BRILLIANT DIVINING WOMEN: ALMA Valmorbida, Annemarie Neary, Gillian Stern, Clare Alexander, Kathy Robbins, Louisa Joyner, Celina Spiegel.

Thanks to the ZenAzzurrian writers for years of support, insight and challenge: Anne Aylor, Annemarie Neary, Gavin Eyers, Jude Cook, Nick Barlay, Oana Aristide, Richard Simmons, Roger Levy, Sally Ratcliffe.

Thanks for encouragement, soundings, research snippets, a favor or a wise gift: Adriano Romagnolo, Balzo/Bob/Hattie/Ian, Ben Coffman, Cristina Scapin, Davide Ferrauto, Eleanor Rees, Erminia Fortunato, Francesco Checchi, Gillian Simpson (ANMM), the Italian Historical Society, Jeanne Johnson, Madeline Hopkins, Mariano Valmorbida, Mark Gordon, Mary Tenace Bauer, Nadia Valmorbida, Naved Nasir, Nicolò Capus, Sophia Dunn, Speranza Dorigo, Tara Wynne.

Thanks to all those at Spiegel & Grau who have turned my heap of paper into a beautiful book.

ABOUT THE AUTHOR

ELISE VALMORBIDA grew up Italian in Australia, but fell in love with London. She's a designer, writer and teacher of creative writing. In recent years, she produced an independent feature film. Her fiction includes *Matilde Waltzing*, *The TV President* and *The Winding Stick*. Her nonfiction includes *SAXON: The Making of a Guerrilla Film* and *The Book of Happy Endings*.

elisevalmorbida.com

ABOUT THE TYPE

This book was set in a Monotype face called Bell. The Englishman John Bell (1745–1831) was responsible for the original cutting of this design. The vocations of Bell were many—bookseller, printer, publisher, typefounder, and journalist, among others. His types were considerably influenced by the delicacy and beauty of the French copperplate engravers. Monotype Bell might also be classified as a delicate and refined rendering of Scotch Roman.